Tender Mercies

HISTORICAL CHRISTIAN ROMANCE

VIVIAN BELLE

STERLING RIDGE PRESS LLC

Dedication

For the ones who survived what they were certain would consume them.
And for the God who was never uncertain at all.
Vivian Belle

It is of the Lord's mercies that we are not consumed, because his compassions fail not. They are new every morning: great is thy faithfulness.
— Lamentations 3:22–23

About Vivian

Vivian Belle is a talented author known for her sweeping **Historical Christian Romance** novels set against the untamed beauty of the American frontier. With a deep love for history and storytelling, she brings to life **resilient heroines, steadfast heroes, and faith-filled journeys** in the vast, rugged landscapes of the past.

Nestled in the **majestic mountains of northern West Virginia,** Vivian finds endless inspiration in the rolling hills, winding rivers, and boundless sky that mirror the spirit of her stories. When she's not writing, she enjoys **kayaking on tranquil waters, hiking through breathtaking mountain trails, and, of course, getting lost in a good book.**

Vivian's novels capture the heart of **faith, love, and perseverance**—where strong women and honorable men overcome life's trials to find hope, home, and happily-ever-after. Whether she's exploring the great outdoors or crafting her next frontier romance,

Vivian's passion for adventure and storytelling shines through in every word she writes.

Visit Vivian on the web: www.vivianbelle.com

Also By Vivian Belle

Stand Alone Novels

Where the Heart Finds Home

Faith on the Frontier

Love in Hopewell Creek

Abigail's Promise

Beneath Montana Skies

Rocky Mountain Promise

Hearts Unbroken

Beneath the Oregon Pines

Journeys of the Heart

Providence Ridge Series

A Bride Worth Keeping

Stronger Than the River

Contents

Chapter 1

The star wagon crested a long rise, and the valley opened below them, so wide and walled in by mountains that Eliza Miller stopped thinking about the dust on her collar and the ache in her back and simply stared. She had studied maps of Montana Territory in her father's parlor, traced mountain ranges with her fingertip, and read every description she could find in the territorial guides borrowed from the Philadelphia Free Library. She had imagined herself prepared. She had not imagined this.

To the east, the Absaroka Mountain Range rose steep and dark from the valley floor, climbing in thick timber to a ragged line of bare rock summits. To the west, the Gallatin Mountain Range formed a long, forested wall that closed the opposite horizon, less jagged but no less immense. Between them, the valley stretched in green bottomland, the July sun pouring down over all of it with a brightness that had no ceiling and no edge, and at its center, a scatter of wood-frame buildings lined a wide dirt road.

The driver shifted and pointed with the handle of his whip toward the valley floor. "That's Providence Ridge."

Eliza leaned forward on the bench seat. The town looked impossibly small against the mountains, as though someone had set a child's model village at the foot of a cathedral. She counted buildings and ran out before she reached a dozen.

"Is that the whole of it?" she asked.

"That's it. Good town, though. Folks keep it clean and mind their business, mostly. You've got the mercantile, the boarding-house, the livery, the marshal's office, a blacksmith, and a lumber mill south of town. Everything a town needs."

The road descended, the wagon wheels cutting into ruts baked hard by the July sun. Eliza held her valise steady on her lap and kept her free hand on the seat rail as the wagon jolted over stones. Her carpetbag was wedged between her feet, and behind her, her trunk slid against the mail sacks with every rut and drop. The trunk was her mother's, a large dome-top Saratoga with brass fittings and floral paper lining. It had looked perfectly reasonable on the train platform in Philadelphia. Out here, against the wilderness and dust and open sky, it looked like it belonged to someone who had packed for the wrong life.

Previously, when she had envisioned Providence Ridge or the Montana Territory as a whole, she had not imagined the absence of everything she had known for twenty-two years. There were no street vendors, no carriage wheels on cobblestones, and no church bells marking the hour. Here there was wind in the grass and trees, the steady rhythm of hooves on packed earth, and above it all a sky so wide and brilliant blue it made her feel like a thumbtack pressed into the edge of a gigantic map.

The bridge over the Yellowstone River was new timber; the planks were still unseasoned and pale. The wagon rattled across it with a hollow drumming that startled a pair of ducks from the shallows downstream. Eliza looked over the rail at the river running fast beneath them, clear enough to see the stones on the bottom in some spots, and wider than she had expected.

"This bridge was just finished last month," the driver said. "Before that, there was a ferry."

Beyond the bridge, the road curved south, and the town drew closer. A half mile of open ground stretched between the river and the first buildings, and during that half mile Eliza saw the town take shape: wood-frame structures with false fronts, a few painted, most showing bare timber that had dried to a silver-gray in the mountain air. Wooden boardwalks connected the main buildings, raised above the dirt road on timber frames. Horses stood tied at hitching rails in patches of shade. Two wagons sat along the road, one stacked with fresh-cut lumber. A dog slept in a doorway with its nose between its paws.

She noticed that the boardwalks had been swept. She noticed flowers in a window box on the mercantile, bright red geraniums in a tin planter. She noticed that the buildings, though modest, stood straight and sound. For a place this small, this far from anywhere, the town was well kept.

The wagon pulled to a stop in front of the boardinghouse, a sturdy two-story building with a wide porch running its full length. Two long benches flanked the front door, and the porch caught the afternoon sun. Across the road, a two-story mercantile stood solid and prosperous; a sign above the door read Pemberton's Mercantile.

Eliza stepped down from the wagon seat and stood for a moment with her valise in one hand and her carpetbag in the other. She looked up at the building her aunt had kept running through widowhood and four years of solitary work. It was one of the two largest buildings on the street, timber-framed and square-shouldered, with the solid look of something built to last.

The driver hauled her trunk from the wagon bed, carried it up the porch steps with a grunt, and set it just inside the front door. He straightened and touched the brim of his hat. "There you are, miss. Good day to you, and welcome to Providence Ridge."

"Thank you," Eliza said. "For the trunk, and for the good company on the road."

He gave a quick nod, and then he was down the porch and up on the seat, clicking the horses forward before she could say another word. She watched the wagon continue south along the road, the mail sacks shifting in the back of the wagon, and the horses plodding as if they had done this route a hundred times.

She straightened her traveling dress. It was a well-made Philadelphia day dress in dark blue cotton, respectable and practical by any Eastern standard. Out here, it was absurd. The fabric was too fine, the buttons too neat, and the sleeves fitted and fastened at the wrist in a town where she had already seen two women with their sleeves shoved past the elbow. She looked exactly like what she was: a city woman who had packed for the life she understood and arrived in one she didn't.

She stepped onto the porch of the boardinghouse and went inside.

The entrance was warm and carried the mingled smell of bread, coffee, and something savory. To the left, a dining room held a long table set for the evening meal, with plain crockery and flatware laid at eight places. To the right, a parlor with a settee and two chairs faced the front windows. A desk near the staircase along the back wall served as the welcome station, and beside it, in a straight-backed chair with a book open on her lap, sat a small, slight woman with silver hair pinned in a careful twist.

The woman looked up, and her face softened into a smile that was unhurried and warm.

"You must be Eliza," she said as she closed her book with her thumb holding the page. "Your aunt has been asking every person who walks through her bedroom door whether they've seen a young woman arriving from Livingston. She's had me check the mail wagon schedule three times last week alone."

"I'm afraid she didn't know the exact day I would arrive," Eliza said. "The connections from Livingston were uncertain."

"That has not stopped her fretting. She had Winnie press the sheets in the spare bedroom three days ago, just to be ready, and yesterday she had me sweep her sitting room twice to make sure it was fit for company." The woman rose from her chair with careful, deliberate movements. "I'm Edith Aldridge. I've been helping your aunt since her fall, and she has told me enough about you that I feel I could write your biography."

"All favorable, I hope."

"Every word." Edith set her book on the desk and gestured toward the back of the building. "Come. She'll be glad to see you."

Eliza followed Edith past the desk and through a short hallway that ran behind the kitchen. She could hear the rhythmic sound of a knife on a cutting board through the kitchen doorway as they passed. The hallway led to Leora's private quarters at the back of the building.

The sitting room was small and tidy, with a braided rug on the plank floor and two windows that let in the afternoon light. A sewing basket sat beside one of the chairs, and a stack of books occupied the small table between them.

Through the doorway to the left, Eliza could see her aunt propped up in bed against a bank of pillows, a quilt pulled over her lap, and a half-finished piece of mending set aside on the coverlet.

Leora Hanscombe looked up, and six years collapsed. "Oh, Eliza. Come here and let me look at you."

Eliza set her bags in the doorway and crossed the room. Leora reached for her with both arms, and Eliza bent and let herself be gathered in. Her aunt's embrace was stronger than she remembered, and she smelled of lavender soap and clean cotton and the faint sharpness of liniment. Eliza pressed her face against her aunt's shoulder and held on.

"Let me look at you properly," Leora said, pulling back but keeping both of Eliza's hands in hers. "You're all grown up. You look so much like your mother it took my breath away for a moment."

"Thank you. Many people have told me I favor my mother, and that pleases me." Eliza squeezed her aunt's hands gently. "You look well, Aunt Leora."

"I look like a woman who has been held hostage by a mattress for three weeks and is strongly considering setting it on fire." Leora's voice was dry and fond at once, and the combination was so entirely her that Eliza felt the knot of travel-weariness between her shoulders begin to ease. "Sit. Tell me everything. Was the journey terrible? Have you eaten today? You look thin."

"The journey was long, and I ate this morning. I'm fine, Aunt Leora." Eliza pulled a chair close to the bed and sat. "Let's talk about you. How is your leg?"

"Improving. Slowly. More slowly than I have any patience for."

"May I look?"

Leora gave a short nod, and Eliza folded the quilt back carefully. The splint was well made, solid pine slats bound with clean linen strips, and the wrappings were fresh. She ran her fingers along the binding, checking the tension against the skin, then pressed gently along the shin above and below the break.

"Does this hurt?" She asked, pressing just above the splint.

"It hurts when someone presses on it, yes."

"And here?" Eliza moved her hand lower, to where the ankle met the foot. The skin was taut and warm beneath her fingers. Leora's ankle and lower calf were puffy and discolored, carrying more fluid than a three-week-old fracture with proper rest should hold. She pressed her thumb gently against the swollen skin and watched the impression linger before it slowly filled back in.

"That," Leora said quietly, "is tender."

Eliza drew the quilt back over her aunt's legs and sat up straight. "You've been getting up."

"I have been trying to get up because the boardinghouse doesn't run itself, and the good people helping me in my absence, bless every one of them, cannot be expected to manage everything to the standard this place requires."

"Your ankle is swollen, and the tissue is holding fluid. That means you've been bearing weight on this leg, and more than once." Eliza kept her voice gentle but didn't soften the words. She had nursed enough patients to know the difference between firmness that helped and firmness that only provoked, and her aunt's expression told her she was walking the edge. "The bone cannot heal properly if you keep loading it before it's ready. Complete rest, Aunt Leora. Not most of the time. All the time."

"And who is going to manage the boardinghouse?"

"I am."

"Oh... Eliza. I am so tired of lying in this bed doing nothing. I simply want to move around a little and get my blood flowing again. Furthermore, I am miserable."

"In due time. For now, you must rest. I'm going to prop your leg up on a few pillows as well to help with the swelling."

Leora studied her for a long moment, her gaze sharp and assessing, and Eliza held still and let herself be measured. Whatever her aunt found in her face must have been sufficient, because the set of her jaw softened and something closer to relief moved through her expression.

"Your mother would be proud of you," Leora said. "She would also tell me to stop arguing and listen."

"She would. And she would be right."

Edith, who had remained standing in the sitting room doorway throughout, spoke up. "I have said the same thing every day for three weeks, but she doesn't listen to me."

"I listen to you, Edith."

"Hearing and listening are two different activities, Leora, and you know the difference as well as I do."

Eliza pressed her lips together to keep the smile from reaching her face. Leora caught it anyway and waved a hand in mild surrender.

"Very well. I will stay in this bed and rest. I'll allow my niece to take charge of the boardinghouse, and I promise not to set foot on the floor unless the building catches fire." She paused. "And even then, I will weigh my options."

"Good," Eliza said. "Now tell me what I've walked into. Is the boarding house running okay? Any emergencies I need to tend to first?"

Leora laid it out with the precision of a woman who had been running the numbers from her pillow for three weeks. The boardinghouse had eight boarders at present. Meals ran three times daily: breakfast at six, lunch at noon, and supper at six in the evening. In the first days after the fall, women from town had rotated through the kitchen to keep meals going, but most had their own families, and the help had thinned within the week. Edith had been coming each morning to sit at the welcome desk, greet arriving travelers, and check on Leora, but she had her own home and obligations and couldn't manage full days.

"A little over a week ago I hired Winnie Callahan," Leora said. "She cooks and cleans and is such a joy to have here helping me. She's capable, and the boarders are satisfied with her meals, which is more than I could say for everyone who volunteered in those first days, God love them."

"But she's one person," Eliza said.

"She is one very hardworking person doing a job that keeps her on her toes. I so badly want to get up and help her. I feel useless just lying here."

Eliza stood. "I'm going to meet Winnie. Then I will take stock of the kitchen, the stores, and the linens, and by supper tonight I'll have a plan."

She left her aunt resting and followed the sound of the knife on the cutting board back to the kitchen. It was a large room built for the work of feeding people. A massive cast-iron cookstove dominated the far wall, throwing heat into the already warm day. A long worktable ran down the center, its surface scarred from years of blades and dough and daily use. Shelves of crockery and supplies lined two walls, and pots and ladles hung from iron hooks overhead. A window over the washbasin looked out onto the side yard, where neat rows of herbs and a few vegetable patches caught the afternoon sun.

A young woman stood at the worktable, slicing onions with quick, efficient strokes. She wore a work apron that had already earned its keep for the day, and she looked up when Eliza appeared in the doorway with an expression of immediate and certain recognition.

"You're Eliza," she said, setting the knife down and wiping her hands on her apron. "Your aunt has talked about nothing else for days. I'm Winnie Callahan."

"Nice to meet you, Winnie. I'm Eliza Miller." She stepped into the kitchen and extended her hand. "Aunt Leora says you've been keeping this place fed and running well."

"Fed is fair. Running well might be generous." Winnie's smile was warm and easy. "There's coffee on the stove if you want it. You look like you've earned a cup."

"I've been on a wagon trail for a day and a half, so I shall agree with you. Coffee is much needed." Eliza accepted the cup Winnie poured and took a sip of the strong, hot liquid. "How many are we feeding tonight?"

"Eight boarders. Edith has been taking supper with Leora to keep her company. And now you, so eleven." Winnie returned to her onions. "Stew and biscuits tonight. I was going to make a dried-apple compote if there are enough apples in the cellar, but I haven't had an opportunity to check."

"I'll look. What about linens?"

"We're down to the last clean set of towels for the guest rooms, and I haven't been able to get to the mending."

"It sounds like I need to see to the laundry right away. I'm certain I need to inventory the pantry as well." Eliza took another sip and let her gaze move over the kitchen with the assessing eye of a woman who had managed a household since she was sixteen. The stove was clean but needed blacking. The supply shelves were organized but thin in several places. The worktable could use a good scrubbing with coarse salt. The floor had been swept but needed a proper mopping. Everything was functional, but the edges were fraying.

"I'll take over the house management," Eliza continued. "You keep the kitchen running smoothly. Between the two of us and Edith, and perhaps whoever else may be willing to lend a hand, we can get this place back to where my aunt wants it."

"Your aunt wants perfection."

"My aunt wants competence, and she has a right to expect it." Eliza finished her coffee and set the cup in the washbasin. "I'm going to unpack and settle in."

"The spare bedroom in your aunt's quarters is ready for you," Winnie said.

Eliza carried her valise and carpetbag through the hallway to the small bedroom off Leora's sitting room. It was plain and clean: a narrow bed with a patchwork quilt and a washstand with a basin and pitcher. There was a hook on the wall for clothing, a small pine dresser, and a window that looked out onto the wide-open grasslands, sloping up toward the timbered foothills to the west.

She hung her hat on the hook, poured water into the basin, and washed the trail dust from her face and hands. She unpinned her hair, twisted it tighter, and pinned it again. Then she went back to the kitchen.

"Winnie, could you help me with something, if you wouldn't mind? My trunk is still sitting in the entry, and I cannot manage it alone."

Winnie set down her knife and wiped her hands. "Of course."

They walked together to the front entrance, where the Saratoga trunk sat just inside the door, its brass fittings catching the light from the parlor windows. Winnie studied it for a moment, then bent and took one of the leather handles.

"On three," she said.

They lifted it together and carried it down the hallway in short, careful steps, the trunk swaying between them. They set it at the foot of the narrow bed with a shared exhale, and Winnie straightened and pressed a hand to the small of her back.

"What did you pack in there?" she asked. "Half of Philadelphia?"

"Most of my wardrobe, some medical supplies, and every book I couldn't bear to leave behind."

"You brought books all the way from Philadelphia?"

"My father is a printer. Leaving books behind would be like leaving family."

Winnie laughed at that, a quick, genuine sound that warmed the small room. "Well, you and Edith are going to get along just fine. That woman would trade her supper for a good book and consider it a fair bargain."

"Wonderful. I look forward to getting to know Edith better. I have a feeling we will enjoy sharing the books we love." Eliza straightened and brushed her hands together. "For now, I want to write a letter to my father letting him know I've arrived safely, and then I will come and help you in the kitchen."

"Please, Eliza, do not feel as if you have to help me. I've got the kitchen under control. Go write your letter and take a few minutes to rest from your travels."

"I appreciate that, Winnie, but I will help you. It will give me a chance to learn my way around the kitchen."

"Well, I won't argue with an extra pair of hands." Winnie paused in the doorway. "It's lovely outside this afternoon. You ought to sit on the porch and write your letter there. After a day and a half in a wagon, you deserve some fresh air that isn't full of road dust."

Eliza smiled. "That sounds like fine advice."

Winnie nodded and left the room.

Eliza knelt before her trunk. She unlatched the brass clasps and lifted the curved lid. Her dresses were packed on top, layered in tissue paper, and beneath them a coat, her second pair of boots, and her mother's Bible wrapped in a cotton handkerchief. She found her stationery box tucked along the side, a small wooden case that held writing paper, envelopes, a steel-nib pen, and a stoppered bottle of ink. She took the case out, then reached deeper into the trunk and pulled free a clothbound copy of Longfellow's poems, thick enough and firm enough to serve as a writing surface.

Eliza left her room and followed the hallway to the front of the boardinghouse. In the dining room, a gentleman sat at the long table with a cup of coffee and a folded newspaper. He glanced up as she passed, and she offered a polite nod, which he returned with a quiet "Good afternoon, miss," before going back to his reading. She stepped through the front door and onto the porch.

The sun had moved well past its peak but still hung above the Gallatins, and the light lay warm and full across the boardwalk and the packed-earth road. The air was dry and clean, carrying the faint scent of earth that had been holding the sun's heat all day. From somewhere toward the south, the distant whine of the saw blade at the lumber mill rose and fell in a rhythm that seemed to belong to the town the way church bells belonged to Philadelphia.

Eliza settled onto the bench to the left of the front door. She set the book flat across her knees, laid a sheet of writing paper on top of it, opened her ink bottle and set it carefully on the bench beside her, dipped the steel nib, and began.

Dear Father,

I have arrived safely in Providence Ridge after a journey that was long but without serious difficulty. The star mail wagon made steady time over the pass road from Livingston, and I was grateful for clear weather the whole of the way. Montana Territory is everything the guidebooks described and a great deal they saw fit to leave out. The mountains are beyond anything I could have imagined from a map. There are two ranges, one to the east and one to the west, and the valley between them is wider and greener than I had any reason to expect. The town sits right at the center of it in a beautiful valley, and though it is small, it is tidy and well kept, and the people I have met have been kind.

The boardinghouse is sturdy and well built, two stories with a wide front porch where I sit writing this. Aunt Leora is in fair spirits, though her leg is healing more slowly than she would prefer. I have examined it and believe she has been doing too much too soon, which will not surprise you. I have made my position clear on the matter, and I believe she will listen now that someone is here to manage the house properly in her place.

I have met Mrs. Edith Aldridge, who has been helping Aunt Leora since her fall, and Miss Winnie Callahan, who has been cooking and keeping the boardinghouse running. They are both good, capable women, and between the three of us, I am confident we can see things right until Aunt Leora is on her feet again.

The country here is stunning, Father. Far wilder than I expected, and far bigger than any map could show. I confess I was not fully prepared for how large everything is or how quiet. But the air is clear, and the sky seems to go on without end, and there is a kind of steadiness to this place that I find comforting.

Please do not worry about me. I am well, and I am where I am meant to be for now. I will write again when I have had time to settle properly.

With love, Eliza

She read the letter through twice. She hadn't mentioned that her dresses were conspicuously wrong for this place, or that the town had fewer buildings than a single block in their neighborhood at home, or that the nearest telegraph was in Livingston. The nearest anything else was a full day's ride over a mountain road. She had not mentioned that her aunt looked thinner than the last time they had been together or that the boardinghouse needed more attention than one woman and a hired cook could reasonably provide. She hadn't mentioned the Absaroka Range filling the eastern sky above the rooftops across the road, its highest ridges still holding the day's last warmth while the valley floor settled into the blue-gray cool of late afternoon. Looking at those mountains made her feel both very small and, for a reason she had not yet sorted out, reluctant to look away.

She had told the truth. She had simply chosen which parts to send.

From the porch she could see the full stretch of Main Street running north toward the bridge and south past the remaining buildings. Across the road, she could see there were a few shoppers moving inside the mercantile, and the door stood open to the warm air. A horse whinnied at one of the hitching rails down the street. Somewhere a door closed, and then the quiet settled back in, wide and unhurried, broken only by the creek's low murmur and the occasional call of a bird.

Eliza folded the letter, slid it into an envelope, and wrote her father's address in her careful hand. She stoppered the ink, wiped the pen nib clean, and tucked everything back into the stationery box.

She gathered her things, stood, and went inside to find her coin purse. She had a letter to mail and an aunt to check on again, and thereafter, eight boarders to help feed and a kitchen to learn. The list in her head had grown since she arrived, and the day was not finished with her yet.

Chapter 2

The tea had steeped too long and gone bitter, but Eliza drank it anyway, settling into the chair beside her aunt's bed with the cup balanced on her knee and the last of the evening's noise fading around them. In the kitchen, Winnie was banking the cookstove for the night, and the faint scrape and clang of the iron damper carried through the hallway.

Leora had propped herself higher against her pillows and was watching Eliza with a hint of amusement in her eyes. "Tell me about supper," she said. "And leave nothing out, because I will ask Winnie tomorrow and she will tell me the truth."

Eliza smiled. "Supper went well. The stew was excellent, and I mean that honestly. Winnie has a sure hand with seasoning. The biscuits were good, the coffee was hot, and every plate came back clean. I served and cleared while Winnie managed the kitchen, and between us we had the dining room set, fed, and scrubbed down in good order."

"And the boarders?"

"All eight were at the table. Mr. Drumond asked me to tell you he hopes you are feeling better and that the stew was the best he's had since he arrived. Mr. Linden said much the same, though with fewer words. The two mill workers were polite and hungry — they looked as though the day had taken everything out of them and the stew was putting it back. Mrs. Crenshaw told me she has been praying for your recovery every morning and that she intends to keep doing so until you are back on your feet."

"Winona Crenshaw has been praying for me since the day I opened this boardinghouse. She stays here every other month when she comes to visit her children who live here. I believe she considers me a permanent project."

"She also asked whether you were eating enough and said she had a recipe for bone broth that would mend a fence post."

Leora let out a sound that was half laugh and half sigh. "That woman could feed an army on faith and root vegetables."

"Everyone of them asked after you," Eliza said. "They miss you."

Leora received that quietly. Her hand rested on the quilt, and her thumb traced the seam of one of the patchwork squares in a slow, absent rhythm, the way a person touches something familiar when the thing they are feeling does not yet have words. "They are good people. Most of the visitors I have are. I have been fortunate in that."

A light knock came at the sitting room door, and Winnie appeared with a second teapot on a tray, steam curling from the spout. She set it on the small table between the chairs.

"Fresh pot," she said. "This one hasn't sat long enough to strip the finish off a table."

Eliza looked down at her cup. "Was it that obvious?"

"You were drinking it earlier with the expression of someone taking medicine." Winnie turned to Leora. "Do you need anything else tonight, Mrs. Hanscombe?"

"I need a new leg, but barring that, no. Thank you, Winnie. Go rest."

"Good night, then." Winnie paused and looked at Eliza. "And you should rest too, when you can. You've been going since you stepped off that wagon."

"I will," Eliza said.

Winnie gave her a look that suggested she had heard that particular promise before — the kind of look women who work on their feet learn to give women who don't know how to stop — and then she was gone, her footsteps fading down the hallway toward the front of the building.

Eliza poured fresh tea for them both. The cup warmed her hands, and she held it a moment longer than necessary, letting the heat settle into her palms. The day had been long enough to feel like two, and her body was only now beginning to register the full weight of it.

"I like Winnie very much," Eliza said. "She is a lovely person."

"She is a gift from God above, and I mean that without exaggeration."

"We discovered this evening that we're only a year and a half apart in age. She will be twenty-one in November." Eliza took a sip and let the heat settle. "She handles that kitchen with more confidence than women twice her age, and she has a way about her that puts people at ease. The boarders trust her. I could see it at supper — she remembered how Mr. Drumond takes his coffee and she had an extra biscuit set aside for Mr. Linden to take to his room for his midnight snack. Those are not things a person does because she was told to. Those are things a person does because she pays attention."

"She pays attention for certain. It's a rarer quality than people think." Leora shifted against her pillows and turned the teacup in her hands. "Now. You have told me about the stew and the boarders and how capable Winnie is. I am grateful for all of it. But I didn't ask you to travel fourteen hundred miles just to give me a supper report." She let that sit for a moment, the way she let most important things sit — not for drama, but because she believed words deserved the space to land before more words covered them over. "How are you, Eliza?"

"I'm well. Tired from the journey, but glad to be here."

"That is all fine and dandy, but I am asking after you, Eliza. Not specifics from your travels. How are you in general?"

Eliza took a sip of tea and considered her aunt over the rim of the cup. Leora had always possessed the ability to ask a simple question and make it feel like a door being opened into a room Eliza had not planned to enter. She had inherited it from her sister Caroline, or perhaps Caroline had inherited it from her — it was impossible to tell with the Hanscombe women which way the current ran.

"I am well," she said again. "Truly. This past year has been good to me. I finished my work with the Benevolent Society's fever hospital auxiliary in March. It was hard work, but I am glad I did it. I learned more in those wards than I thought possible. Wounds, fevers, infection, the proper way to keep a sickroom clean and a patient comfortable." She paused. "I think I found my calling in that work. I didn't expect it, but it felt right. It felt like the thing I was meant to do."

Leora studied her. "Your mother could walk into a room where someone was suffering, and the room got quieter. Not because she told anyone to hush, but because something about her presence made the noise seem less necessary. She simply brought peace wherever she stepped. I suspect you have the same quality."

The mention of her mother landed the way Leora always placed Caroline's name — with tenderness and without apology, the way a person sets down something precious on a sturdy table. Eliza felt the familiar tug of it, the pull toward a place she kept carefully tended but rarely visited in company.

"I think about her often when I am caring for someone," Eliza said. "She taught me more than she knew. How to keep a cool cloth on a fever without waking a patient who has only just fallen asleep. How to read a person's face when they say they are comfortable but they are not. How to sit with someone in pain without needing to fill every silence with words." She turned the teacup in her hands. "I miss her. I miss her every day. But the missing has changed. It is not the way it was in the first year, when it felt like the floor had been pulled from under everything and every room in the house still expected her to walk through it. It is quieter now. Steadier. More like carrying something than being carried away by it."

"Grief does that," Leora said. "It doesn't leave. It just learns to sit down."

They were quiet together for a moment. Through the raised window, the river murmured its low, constant sound — the sound Eliza was already beginning to recognize as the voice of this valley, the way the bells of Christ Church had been the voice of her Philadelphia mornings.

"She would have loved knowing you went to the fever hospital," Leora said. "She would have worried herself sick over it, and then she would have told everyone at church that her daughter was the bravest woman in Philadelphia."

"She would have sent me with twice as many supplies as I needed and a note pinned inside my apron."

Leora laughed at that, a real laugh, brief and warm, and the sound of it in the lamplight room carried the particular comfort of family — of being known by someone who had known the person you missed most. "She would have. She absolutely would have."

Eliza set her teacup down and turned the conversation. "Tell me more about this place, Aunt Leora. Not the daily operations. Tell me how it came to be."

Leora looked at her for a beat longer than the question required, and Eliza could feel her aunt measuring the turn of the conversation—noticing how neatly she had stepped from one room into another, closing the door on talk about her mother without a sound. But Leora didn't press. She took the offered subject the way a woman who has survived widowhood learns to accept a change of weather: without complaint, because she understood the cost of standing in the open too long.

"Your uncle Harold and I came out to this territory eight years ago," Leora said. "We had been talking about it for two years before we actually made the move, and Harold would have talked about it for two more if I hadn't finally told him we were either going or we were going to stop pretending we might. He laughed at that. He always laughed when I backed him into a corner, because he knew I was right and he knew I knew he knew." She took a sip of tea. "We came out and settled in the valley. Harold took work wherever he could find it, and I kept house and learned how to live in a place where winter meant something different than it did back East. Those first years were lean, but we had each other, and we had the Lord, and we had enough to eat, and that was sufficient."

"What made you decide to build the boardinghouse?"

"The town was growing. The lumber mill was just getting started, and there were men coming through looking for work. Travelers on their way to or from the Yellowstone country needed a place to stop and eat and sleep in a proper bed. Harold saw the need before I did. He said, 'Leora, this town needs a place where a hard working person can sit down to a decent meal and sleep in a clean room, and there is no one in this valley better suited to run such a place than you.' He was right about the need, and I suspect he was flattering me about the rest, but it worked."

"It wasn't flattery if it was true."

"It was both. Harold was very good at that," Leora's voice carried no weight of performance, no invitation for sympathy. She was telling the story of a man she had loved the way she would tell the story of how the boardinghouse was built — because both were facts of the same life, and the facts were laced with the kind of affection that only years of waking up beside someone could produce. "We built this place with our own hands and the help of four men Harold hired. He did the framing. I did the planning. We argued about the size of the kitchen for a week straight, and I won because I was right and because Harold had the good sense to know when a fight wasn't worth the trouble."

"And the porch — was there an argument about it?"

"There was no argument about the porch. We both wanted it and refused to live somewhere without a porch to relax on after a long day's work," Leora looked toward the window. "We opened the doors and had six months of what we had built. Six months of watching people come in tired and hungry and leave fed and rested. Six months of Harold finishing the trim work and fixing hinges and telling every boarder who walked through the door that his wife ran the finest establishment between Livingston and the Yellowstone." She paused. "And then one morning he didn't come to breakfast. I found him in his chair in the sitting room. He had been reading his Bible. His heart simply stopped."

Eliza reached across the quilt and covered her aunt's hand with her own. Leora's fingers were warm and rough and steady beneath hers.

"The doctor said it was likely his heart had been troubled for some time," Leora said. "Harold never mentioned any pain, but Harold wouldn't have mentioned pain if you set him on fire. He was that kind of man." She turned her hand over beneath Eliza's and squeezed once, firmly—the grip of a woman who had learned long ago that grief and strength are not opposites but neighbors, sharing a fence line. "So I kept the boardinghouse. Because it was what we built, and because closing it would have felt like losing him twice. And because people still came through Providence Ridge needing meals and clean rooms. The world didn't stop when my Harold went on to heaven, though at the time I wished it had."

"Four years," Eliza said. "You have run this place alone for four years."

"I have run this place with the help of good neighbors and the mercy of God for four years. I am not foolish enough to pretend I did it alone." Leora released her hand and reached for her tea. "But I will admit that the foolish part was believing I could keep working forever and nothing would hold me down. Then I broke this leg and needed more help than I ever imagined."

"You have help now."

"I do. And she packed a trunk the size of a horse trough, so I've heard, and brought books from Philadelphia."

Eliza allowed herself a small laugh. "The books are essential."

"You are your father's daughter," Leora's expression changed — not softening, exactly, but settling into something deeper, the way a creek bed reveals its true shape only when the current slows. "He wrote to me, you know. Probably the same day you received the letter I sent you. He said you had made up your mind within an hour of reading my letter, and that nothing he said could have changed it, and that he was proud of you and terrified in equal measure."

"That sounds like Father."

"He loves you, Eliza. He worries."

"I know. I wrote to him this afternoon. I told him I was well, and that you were in fair spirits and that the town was tidy and the people kind."

"And was any of that the whole truth?"

Eliza picked up her teacup. "It was enough of it." She took a sip that was more punctuation than thirst. "Now, tell me what you need me to do for the boardinghouse. What are the gaps I need to fill first?"

"The biggest need is hands. Winnie is doing the work of two people, and I'm afraid she will drop down from exhaustion at some point. I managed it when I was on my feet because I have been doing it for years and I know every shortcut this place allows. But she is still new to all of this, as are you. Running the kitchen, keeping track of inventory, being at the beck and call of boarders, and learning how to run this place efficiently will run you both ragged."

"I was thinking the same. Is there anyone in town I could hire? Even for a few hours a day, to help with laundry and heavy cleaning?"

"There are several women who might be willing. Margaret Pemberton at the mercantile knows everyone's situation. She would know who is available and who could use the work. Hattie Pemberton, her daughter, does fine sewing and has offered to help with mending before, though she has her boy Timothy to look after."

"I will do my best to go to the mercantile tomorrow and ask."

"Good. Beyond the help, you need to take a full inventory of the pantry and the root cellar. I was behind on ordering before I fell, and Winnie has been making do with what we have and purchasing what is already on the shelves at the mercantile. She has also been kind enough to bring in some vegetables from her own garden. I just know there are staples we are low on, and I haven't placed a freight order with Pemberton's in nearly a month. That needs doing right away before we find ourselves short."

"I will inventory everything tomorrow. I will go through the pantry, the cellar, the linen stores, and the cleaning supplies. Then I will sit down with Winnie and work out a weekly schedule that accounts for meals, laundry, room cleaning, and whatever mending has piled up." Eliza set her teacup on the tray and folded her hands in her lap. "I also want to set a regular time each day to come in and check on you, look at your leg, and make sure you are comfortable. Perhaps we could make a daily habit of having lunch together, since the dining room is quieter at midday."

"I don't need to be checked on like a child, but lunch with you would be nice."

"You need to be checked on like a patient with a broken leg who was caught trying to get out of bed because you wanted to go into the sitting room, according to what Edith told me."

Leora opened her mouth, closed it, and took a sip of tea instead.

"I will also write out a daily schedule for myself," Eliza continued, "so that Winnie and I are not tripping over each other's tasks. She keeps the kitchen, and she does it very well. I will manage the house, the boarders, and the supplies, and stay out of her way unless she needs an extra pair of hands for serving. We share the heavy work as needed. Edith comes in the mornings to sit at the desk and keeps you company as well. Between the three of us, and whatever additional help I can find, we should be able to keep this place running to your standards until you are back on your feet."

"My standards are high."

"Your standards are earned. And I intend to meet them."

Leora set her cup on the tray and looked at her niece with an expression that held something she didn't put into words — pride, certainly, but also the particular ache of a woman who had loved a sister and lost her, and was sitting in a lamplight room watching that sister's daughter become the kind of woman Caroline would have recognized and claimed. "You really are your mother's daughter."

"I take that as the highest compliment you could give me."

"It is."

The lamp on the bedside table had burned low, its flame barely taller than a thumb, and the room had taken on the close, warm quality of a space where people had been talking long enough to forget the hour. The sounds from the rest of the boardinghouse had gone completely quiet — no footsteps overhead, no voices carrying through the walls, no kitchen clatter. Just the two of them and the low lamp and the fading warmth of the tea between them.

"Before I retire to my room for the evening," Eliza said, "I want to look at your leg again."

"You looked at it this afternoon."

"I did. And now it's evening. I am here to help you with the boardinghouse, Aunt Leora, but I am also your nurse while I am here. The two jobs share a roof."

Leora didn't argue, which told Eliza more than any complaint would have. She folded the quilt back carefully and examined the splinted leg by the low lamplight. The splint bindings were still firm and clean. She ran her fingers gently along the shin above the upper edge of the splint, pressing lightly against the skin. Then she moved to the ankle and lower calf, where the swelling had been visible that afternoon.

The puffiness was the same — possibly a shade worse. She pressed her thumb against the skin near the ankle bone and watched the impression hold, the tissue slow to return, reluctant in a way that made her take a second look. When she laid the back of her hand against the skin along the shin above the splint wrappings, she felt a warmth that had not been there this afternoon. Slight, but present. The kind of warmth that meant something was beginning rather than ending.

"How do you feel?" she asked, keeping her voice easy.

"Tired. Sore. My leg feels the same as it did this afternoon."

"Any sharper pain? Anything that feels different from yesterday?"

Leora considered. "Perhaps a bit more tender than usual. But I have been in this bed all day, which I am told is what I am supposed to be doing, so I imagine some soreness is to be expected."

"It is," Eliza said. She smoothed the quilt back into place and tucked the edge beneath the mattress with careful hands. "Keep it elevated tonight. The extra pillow beneath your leg is important."

"The extra pillow is annoying."

"Keep it in place, Aunt Leora. I will check again in the morning."

Leora studied her for a long moment, and Eliza could feel the weight of her aunt's attention testing the edges of what she had said against what she had not said. Eliza held the look and kept her face calm, pleasant, and firm. After a moment, Leora exhaled and settled deeper into her pillows.

"Good night, Aunt Leora."

"Good night, sweetheart. I am very glad you are here."

"So am I."

Eliza carried the tea tray down the hallway to the kitchen and set it on the worktable. The cookstove ticked as it cooled, and the kitchen held the layered smell of the day's work — stew, biscuit flour, the faint vinegar tang of Winnie's cleaning. She washed the cups and the pot in the basin, dried them, and set them in their places on the shelf. Then she stood for a moment with her hands on the edge of the worktable, the wood cool and scarred beneath her fingers, and let the quiet of the building settle around her.

The warmth she had felt along Leora's shin felt a touch warmer than it had this afternoon. She was certain of it. It could be because her room was warm from the heat of the day and the quilt her aunt insisted on keeping across her legs certainly wasn't helping.

It could be nothing. Legs confined in splints ran warm. Swelling fluctuated. A body fighting a fracture sometimes rallied its defenses toward the injury in ways that looked alarming and meant nothing. She had seen it before.

But she had also seen the other thing — the thing where warmth along a fracture site meant infection creeping in, or through tissue stressed beyond its tolerance by a bone that had not been permitted to rest. She had seen that in the fever hospital, and the women who had taught her there had spoken plainly about what happened when it was missed.

Eliza dried her hands on the kitchen cloth, hung it on its hook beside the basin, and turned down the lamp until the flame guttered and went out. She walked through the dark hallway to her small room off Leora's quarters, undressed by the thin light coming through the window, laid her dress over the back of the chair, and climbed into the narrow bed. The patchwork quilt was lighter than the one she slept under in Philadelphia, and the mattress was firmer, and the sounds outside the window were entirely wrong — no carriage wheels, no distant voices, no clock tower marking the quarter hour. Instead, there was the sound of the river, running its low and constant conversation with the stones, and the wind moving through grass she had not yet walked through, and beyond both of those a silence so deep it seemed to have weight.

She closed her eyes and said her prayers — for her father, for Leora, for the strength to do well by both of them — and sleep came before she reached the amen.

Chapter 3

The last of the breakfast dishes were stacked and drying on the rack beside the washbasin. Eliza stood at the pantry shelves with a pencil and a scrap of paper, counting jars. Fourteen quarts of canned tomatoes. Eight green beans. Three peaches, which would not last the week if the boarders kept requesting compote. She wrote the numbers in a neat column and moved to the next shelf, where the flour bin sat lower than it should have and the sugar was down to a quarter of its tin.

Behind her, Winnie was scrubbing the cookstove surface with a stiff brush and a rag dampened with vinegar water. The sharp tang of it carried through the kitchen, mixing with the lingering warmth of the morning's biscuits and the deeper, steadier smell of coffee that was sitting on the back burner. The dining room had emptied over the last half hour, and the kitchen had settled into the quieter rhythm of cleanup and preparation that followed every meal service.

"The pantry is looking mighty thin, wouldn't you agree?" Winnie asked without turning from the stove.

"Agreed," Eliza said. She crouched to check the lower shelves, where the lard tin sat beside a half-empty bag of dried beans and a small crock of molasses. "We are low on flour, sugar, lard, and salt. The coffee is adequate for another week, perhaps ten days if we are careful. The canned goods will carry us, but not by much. I plan to place an order at the mercantile today if I have time, tomorrow at the latest."

"Mrs. Pemberton will know what is available on her shelves for us to replenish our stock quickly and what needs to be freight-ordered. Anything that comes by freight takes over a week at best, longer if the roads wash out." Winnie set the brush in the basin and wiped down the stovetop with a clean cloth, running her hand along the surface to check for any grit she had missed.

"Good to know. I intend to speak with Mrs. Pemberton about hiring additional help for us as well. Aunt Leora suggested she might know of someone in the community seeking employment." Eliza straightened and added another item to her list. The pantry was organized well—everything in its place, nothing wasted—but the shelves had the look of a larder being drawn down steadily without being replenished, and the gaps between the jars told their own story.

Winnie had finished with the stove and was standing at the worktable, sorting through a basket of eggs she had brought from home that morning. She held each one up to the light, checking for cracks.

"Winnie, I noticed there is no church here in town. Is there one outside of town, perhaps?" Eliza asked.

"We have no church building. Not yet, anyway. Mrs. Pemberton has been talking about getting a schoolhouse built that would serve as a church too, but it is still in the planning and they haven't broken ground." Winnie set the last egg into the bowl and wiped her hands on her apron. "Church services are held right here in the boardinghouse dining room. Reverend Hale comes through on his circuit every other Sunday and leads worship. He is a lay preacher, not ordained, but he is as good a man as you will find in this territory, and his sermons are honest and short, which the congregation appreciates."

"And on the Sundays when he is not here?"

"Sometimes Reverend Hollis comes, but his visits are sporadic as he is a circuit preacher that covers much of the territory. Most often, someone from the community leads. Usually Mr. Pemberton or Mr. Gallagher will read a few passages from the Bible and open up a discussion or share their thoughts, and then we sing. Lots of singing on those Sundays. Half the town crowds in here." Winnie smiled, and the smile had the quality of a memory being visited while it was still warm. "Those are good days. There is something about all of us gathered around these tables, singing hymns we all know by heart, that makes this place feel like a real congregation even without a church building."

"I look forward to it," Eliza said. She meant it more than the words carried. The idea of worship held in the very room where meals were served and boarders sat down to supper each evening touched something in her that the grand sanctuaries of Philadelphia never had—not because those churches lacked beauty, but because this room lacked pretense. She thought of the dining room table she had helped clear moments ago, its scarred wood and plain crockery, and pictured it dressed for Sunday worship—the same table, the same room, the same people, made holy not by architecture but by the willingness to gather. The image fit this town in a way that told her something true and honest about it.

"Speaking of gatherings," Winnie said, "this Friday is the Fourth of July."

Eliza looked up from her list. She had been keeping track of the days since leaving Philadelphia, but the holiday had slipped past her in the rush of arrival and settling in. "I had forgotten. What does Providence Ridge do for the Fourth?"

"Everyone comes together Friday evening down by the creek. The whole town, near about. Families bring food and blankets, and we spread out along the flat stretch south of the bridge that crosses the Yellowstone. Reverend Hale will be here for it this year, so there will be a short sermon and a prayer before we eat. After that, it's just fellowship. Children run wild; the men sit around and talk, and the women feed everyone who wanders within reach of a basket. Mr. Hart from the blacksmith shop usually brings his fiddle. A few other community members may bring instruments as well."

"That sounds lovely."

"It is. You will meet nearly the whole town in one evening." Winnie carried the bowl of eggs to the shelf near the stove and set it in its place. "My Luke's family is coming in from the ranch for it. The Dixons. You will like them."

The mention of Luke changed something in Winnie's face—not dramatically, but unmistakably, the way the first light of morning changes a window from dark glass to something you can see through. Eliza noticed it and felt a quiet warmth at the glimpse, this unguarded tenderness in a young woman who carried herself with such capable composure the rest of the time.

"I look forward to meeting them. I sense Luke is rather special to you," Eliza said as she folded the inventory list.

Winnie's smile deepened, but she didn't elaborate, and Eliza liked her the more for it—for the way she held the feeling close instead of putting it on display, the way a person cups a candle flame in the wind not because they are hiding the light but because they want to keep it burning.

"I'm going to check on my aunt before I inventory the cellar; she was asleep when I looked in on her this morning," Eliza said, "and then I will clean the rooms upstairs."

"She was awake when I brought her tea at half-past six. She drank half of it and told me the biscuits yesterday were slightly too salty, which I took as a sign she is feeling like herself."

Eliza smiled at that. Leora's standards, even from a sickbed, remained precise enough to detect a pinch of salt. It was, in its way, reassuring.

She left the kitchen and walked down the hallway, her mind already sorting through the list of things she intended to accomplish before midday. Cleaning the rooms upstairs. The mercantile order. The cellar inventory. A conversation with Margaret Pemberton about hiring help. The mending basket she had noticed growing beside the parlor settee. The morning stretched ahead of her, full of tasks, and the fullness of it felt familiar and steadying—the same current that had carried her through her father's household, keeping everything in order and running smoothly, through the Benevolent Society, and through the fever hospital auxiliary. There was always something next, and the something-next kept the rest of it at a manageable distance.

Leora's bedroom door was open. Eliza stepped inside, and she sensed something was wrong before her aunt said a word.

The window was raised, and the morning air moved through the room, carrying the faint earthy smell of the grass beyond the building. Yet, the room felt close, held-in, and still. Leora had pushed her quilt down to her knees and was lying against the pillows with her eyes closed. Her face carried a flush that had not been there last night—not the warmth of sleep, but something brighter and less even, sitting high on her cheekbones and along the line of her throat. A fine sheen of perspiration stood along her hairline and across her collarbone.

"Aunt Leora?"

Leora opened her eyes. The effort of it seemed to cost her more than it should have. "Good morning, sweetheart."

"How are you feeling?"

"A bit under the weather." The words came slowly, measured in the way of someone choosing them with care, as though the choosing itself required energy she was rationing. "I believe the heat of summer is getting to me."

Eliza set her inventory list on the bedside table and pulled the chair close. She laid the back of her hand against Leora's forehead, and the skin beneath her touch confirmed what her eyes had already told her—warmer than yesterday, warmer than last night, warmer than bed rest and a July morning could account for. She moved her hand to her aunt's cheek, then to the side of her neck below the jaw, feeling for the swollen tenderness that would tell her the body's deeper systems were responding.

"When did you begin feeling unwell?"

"I woke with a headache. And my stomach is not settled. I couldn't finish the tea Winnie brought." Leora gestured toward the cup on the bedside table, still half full, the surface gone cold and flat. "It is likely nothing. The weather has been warm, and I have been lying in this bed so long that my body has forgotten how to regulate itself."

"Are you nauseous?"

"Mildly. It comes and goes."

"Any dizziness? Weakness?"

"Eliza, I am a fifty-two-year-old woman confined to a bed with a broken leg. Weakness is my natural condition at present."

"Aunt Leora, I need you to answer me plainly."

Leora held her niece's gaze for a moment, and whatever she saw in Eliza's face dissolved the resistance. "Yes. I feel weak. More so than yesterday. And the nausea is worse when I try to sit fully upright. It came on rather suddenly when I first tried to sit up this morning."

"I need to look at your leg."

She pushed the quilt aside to the foot of the bed. The swelling she had noted the previous evening had worsened visibly overnight. The ankle and lower calf were puffy, the skin stretched and taut, holding fluid that a night of elevation should have drawn away but hadn't. When she moved her attention up toward the shin, where the fracture sat beneath the splint, she could see redness spreading above the upper edge of the linen wrappings—an angry, uneven flush that had not been present twelve hours ago.

She pressed the back of her hand against the skin above the splint bindings. The warmth she had felt last night was no longer slight, no longer questionable, no longer the kind of thing that could be explained by July heat and bedclothes. It radiated from the tissue with the steady insistence of something that had been building through the night while both of them slept.

"I'm going to unwrap the bindings," Eliza said. "I need to see your full leg."

Leora closed her eyes and nodded.

Eliza worked the linen strips carefully, unwinding them with steady, unhurried hands. She kept her movements slow and smooth because the leg was tender and any jarring would cause pain, and because she could see in the set of Leora's jaw that the pain was already considerable. The outer wrappings came away cleanly. The inner layer—the one that sat closest to the skin along the shin—resisted, and when she eased it free, she saw why.

A split in the skin ran along the front of the shin, roughly two inches in length, positioned over the ridge of the bone where the tissue was thinnest and the blood supply poorest. The wound edges were swollen and raised; the surrounding skin inflamed in a ring of red that darkened to a deep, angry color at the margins. A thin line of cloudy fluid had seeped from the split and dried along the lower edge of the bandage she had just removed. The tissue surrounding the wound was hard to the touch and hot beneath her fingertips — the kind of heat that announced itself immediately, that did not require a second check.

"Aunt Leora," Eliza kept her voice level. "When did this happen?"

Leora opened her eyes. She looked at the leg, at the exposed wound, and then at Eliza's face. The resistance that had been holding her expression in place gave way to something quieter—the plain resignation of a woman who had known this conversation was coming and had run out of hallway to avoid it.

"Two days before you arrived," she said. "Sunday evening. I had sat up in bed, then shifted to sit upright. I simply wanted to be in a different position and get my blood flowing. My backside was hurting me something fierce. I just wanted to move around a bit. When I shifted my legs off the bed, the splint struck the bedframe. The skin split. It bled some, and it hurt a good deal. I couldn't believe it... it just happened so fast. I didn't think I had hit the bedframe that hard."

"And you didn't send for a doctor."

"Edith was here at the time, and I called for her to come help me. We cleaned it with warm water and soap. We wrapped it in clean cloth. It is just a surface wound, Eliza. I have had worse and tended to them myself."

"A surface wound on a broken leg, over the bone, in tissue that is already strained from a fracture three weeks old." Eliza heard the edge in her own voice and pulled it back. She pressed two fingers alongside the wound and felt the tissue resist—firm where it should have been soft, swollen where it should have been flat. The infection had moved past the wound and settled into the deeper layers beneath the skin. "How long has it looked like this?"

"I haven't looked at it since Edith and I wrapped it. It's been sore since then, and yesterday I noticed it would sting if I moved too quickly."

"Why didn't you tell me last night when I examined you?"

Leora was quiet for a moment, and when she spoke, the words carried the plain honesty of a woman too tired and too sore to manage anything else. "Because you had just arrived. You had enough to worry about with the boardinghouse and the supplies and the hundred other things I asked you to come here and help with. I didn't want to add to your burden. And because I thought it was healing."

"It is not healing. It's infected."

"I can see that now, Eliza."

She sat back in the chair and looked at the wound. She made herself look at it the way she had been trained to look — not as a niece frightened for someone she loved, but as a nurse assessing what she could see against what she knew. The redness extended in an uneven pattern roughly two inches beyond the wound margins in every direction, which told her the infection was advancing through the tissue rather than holding at the site. The cloudy fluid on the bandage meant the body was fighting, spending what it had to clear what it could not heal on its own. The warmth. The fever. The nausea. The weakness that had arrived overnight.

This was no longer a wound. It was a system responding, her aunt's body recruiting every resource it had to fight something that was gaining ground.

"Aunt Leora, is there a doctor in the area?"

"There is. Dr. Porter. He arrived here in Providence Ridge last month. He's the one who set my leg and made the splint."

"Where is his office?"

"Across the street, next to the land office." Leora's voice had grown quieter, the fight leaking out of it the way air leaks from a room when a window is opened. "He is a good man, Eliza. Young, but capable. This town is fortunate to have him."

Eliza rose from the chair. "I am going to send for him right now."

She covered Leora's leg with a clean sheet from the dresser, arranging it carefully so that nothing pressed against the wound, and then left the bedroom. She could hear Winnie in the kitchen—the sound of a spoon against the edge of a pot, steady and ordinary.

"Winnie."

Winnie turned from the stove, and whatever she saw in Eliza's face made her set down the spoon and give her full attention.

"My aunt's leg is infected," Eliza said. "There is a skin split on her shin that has been there since Sunday, and an infection has set in. She has a mild fever; she is nauseous; and the tissue around the wound is hot and inflamed. I need the doctor."

Winnie was already untying her apron. "I will fetch him."

"Tell him it is an infected wound with spreading redness and signs of systemic illness. Use those words. He will know what they mean, and he will know to come quickly."

Winnie hung the apron on its hook and was moving toward the front door before Eliza had finished speaking.

"Winnie." The younger woman paused with her hand on the doorknob. "Thank you."

Winnie nodded once and was gone. Eliza heard her boots on the porch, quick and sure, and then the sound thinned and disappeared as she crossed the road.

Eliza stood alone in the kitchen. The cookstove ticked. The pot Winnie had been stirring sent a thin curl of steam toward the ceiling. Through the window over the washbasin, the morning sat bright and indifferent on the herb garden and the grassland beyond. The sky was the same enormous blue it had been yesterday and the day before, unchanged by what was happening in a bedroom at the back of this building.

She took several deep breaths and then walked back through the hallway, past her aunt's door, and into her own small bedroom.

The canvas medical kit sat on the dresser where she had placed it the night before. She untied the cord and unrolled it across the narrow bed. Clean linen strips. Carbolic salve. Tincture of arnica. Comfrey root. Witch hazel. Surgical scissors. Muslin. Camphor liniment. Willow bark. Each item in its pocket, each pocket in its order—the order she had learned at the fever hospital auxiliary, the order her hands remembered even when her thoughts were running ahead.

She needed clean water, a basin, and clean cloths. She needed the carbolic salve and the witch hazel. She would make a comfrey poultice if the doctor agreed, and she would brew willow bark tea for the fever and the pain.

Eliza rolled the kit closed, gathered it against her chest, and carried it back through the hallway to her aunt's room.

Leora was lying with her eyes closed again, her breathing steady. Eliza set the medical kit on the bedside table and unrolled it beside the cold cup of tea Leora hadn't finished. She moved the water pitcher from the washstand to the small table, found a clean cloth folded in the linen stack on the dresser shelf, and wet it with cool water. She wrung it out and laid it across Leora's forehead, gently, the way her mother had taught her—not pressed flat, but draped, so the coolness reached her temples.

Leora opened her eyes at the touch.

"The doctor is coming," Eliza said.

"You are frightened."

"I am concerned. There is a difference." Eliza pulled the chair closer and sat. "The infection needs proper treatment, and it needs it now. But do not worry… I have seen worse than this, Aunt Leora. In the fever hospital, I tended wounds that were far more advanced, and many of those patients recovered well. This was caught in time, and you are fortunate."

Leora reached for her hand, and Eliza took it. Her aunt's fingers were warm, and her grip was weaker, as though the fever had already begun its work of drawing strength from the places that needed it least to send it to the places that needed it most.

"You are a good nurse, Eliza."

"I'm your niece, and I'm not going to let this leg get any worse." She held Leora's hand and kept her voice steady, though the steadiness required the same deliberate effort as keeping a lamp flame burning in a draft—not difficult, exactly, but requiring attention that could not be spent elsewhere. "And you, my dear aunt, must not hide things from me. This could have become far worse in a matter of hours."

She sent up a prayer as quiet and instinctive as breathing. *Lord, guide the doctor's hands and mine. Let this mercy have come in time.*

She released her aunt's hand, rose from the chair, and began preparing the wound site for the doctor's examination. There would be time later for the fear she was not allowing herself to feel. Right now there was work, and the work was a mercy, and her hands knew exactly what to do.

Chapter 4

The splinter had driven itself a full inch beneath the calloused skin of Hank Tillman's palm. Samuel Porter held the man's hand flat against the examination table, lamplight angled close, and worked the fragment free with a pair of fine-tipped forceps.

Tillman was a broad, sun-darkened man who hauled timber six days a week and had hands like saddle leather. He sat in the chair beside the table, talking about the new circular saw blade the mill had freighted in from Butte, as if Samuel were not currently pulling a piece of Douglas fir out of his flesh.

"It cuts cleaner than the old one, I'll say that much. But the teeth are set wider, and the sawdust comes off in chunks instead of powder. Gets into everything, including my boots and under my collar." Tillman winced as Samuel drew the forceps back, bringing with them a sliver of wood as long as a sewing needle and nearly as thin at the tip but ragged and thick at the base where it had broken off. "The boys are still getting used to the feed rate. Jensen caught a kickback yesterday that threw the whole log sideways."

"Anyone hurt?" Samuel set the splinter on a clean cloth and examined the wound. The entry point was red but not deeply inflamed. No sign of remaining fragments. He reached for the bottle of carbolic solution on the shelf beside the table.

"Bruised Jensen's pride more than anything. He won't stand on that side of the carriage again, though."

"I expect not." Samuel cleaned the wound with a square of cloth dampened in carbolic, working thoroughly around the puncture site. "Keep this clean. Wash it thoroughly with soap and warm water at least twice a day, morning and evening. If the redness spreads past the edges of the puncture, or if you see any discharge, come see me. Don't wait."

"It's a splinter, Doc."

"It's a puncture wound in a hand that handles rough timber and dirty rope ten hours a day. An infection in your palm could cost you the use of your fingers or even your entire hand. Soap and water. Twice a day." Samuel wrapped a clean strip of linen around the hand, snug but not tight, and tucked the end in. "And if Jensen's bruised pride is giving him any trouble sitting, tell him I have liniment."

Tillman laughed at that, a short bark that seemed to surprise him. He flexed his wrapped hand experimentally, nodded his approval, and stood. "What do I owe you?"

"Two bits."

Tillman dug a quarter from his trouser pocket and set it on the edge of the table. "Much obliged." He collected his hat from the hook by the door and was gone, his boots heavy on the boardwalk planks outside.

Samuel cleaned the forceps with carbolic, dried them, and returned them to the instrument case. He wiped down the examination table, folded the cloth with the splinter inside it, and dropped it into the waste pail. He recorded the visit in his ledger at the desk by the window: *Tillman, H.—splinter removal, right palm. Deep puncture, no fragmentation. Carbolic wash, clean dressing. Instructed on wound care.* He noted the date and the payment and closed the ledger.

Through the window he could see a stretch of Main Street. A freight wagon sat along the road with its tailgate down, and a dog had settled beneath it in the strip of shade the wagon bed threw across the ground. July had settled over the valley like a thick wool blanket no one had asked for, and even this early in the day, anything that cast shade didn't go unused. The mountains filled the western sky beyond the rooftops, their upper ridges already catching the full morning sun.

He turned from the window and glanced at the slate board hanging beside the cabinet where he chalked each day's appointments. Three patients scheduled for the afternoon. A rancher's wife with a persistent cough he wanted to listen to again. A miner from the south camp who had been complaining of joint stiffness that Samuel suspected was the early stages of rheumatism. And old Mrs. Creighton, who came every two weeks with a new complaint that was never quite the complaint she actually wanted to talk about, and who left feeling better after thirty minutes of conversation and a peppermint from the jar he kept on the shelf for that purpose. He had learned in his first week here that Mrs. Creighton's ailments were real enough to her, and that what she needed was a man who would sit and listen without checking the clock on the wall. He could do that. There were worse ways to spend a quarter hour than making an elderly woman feel heard.

He crossed the room to the supply cabinet against the back wall and opened it. The carbolic bottle on the instrument shelf was low, and he pulled the larger jug from the cabinet's lower shelf and unscrewed the cap. He was pouring carefully, tilting the jug with one hand and steadying the bottle with the other, when the front door opened.

"Dr. Porter." Winnie said, slightly winded, her cheeks flushed. "Mrs. Hanscombe's niece sent me to fetch you. Her leg has taken a bad turn. There's an infected wound on the shin with spreading redness, and her niece says she has signs of systemic illness."

Samuel set the carbolic jug down and recapped it. "A wound? When did she hurt herself?"

"I believe this past Sunday. Eliza said, The skin is split on her shin."

He pulled his medical bag from beneath the examination table, opened it, and checked the contents with the quick, cataloguing attention that had become second nature in years of frontier practice. Scalpel. Forceps. Probe. Carbolic solution. Iodoform powder. Clean linen. Suturing kit. Laudanum. Everything in its compartment, everything ready. "Tell her I am coming."

"Her niece is tending the wound right now."

That stopped him for half a second. "Her niece is tending the wound."

"Yes, sir. She sent me with specific instructions to tell you it's an infected wound with spreading redness and signs of systemic illness. Those were her words."

Samuel closed the bag and fastened the clasp. Leora had mentioned that her niece was coming from Philadelphia to help with the boardinghouse, and he had pictured what he supposed anyone would picture: a young woman from the city arriving to cook meals and clean while her aunt recovered. Not someone who would use the phrase signs of systemic illness and mean for a doctor to hear it the way a doctor would hear it.

"Thank you, Winnie. Go on back. I'm right behind you."

Winnie nodded and was out the door before he had finished speaking. Samuel took his hat from the peg, picked up his bag, and followed her. He crossed Main Street at a walk that was just short of a run, his boots raising small clouds of dust from the dry road. The boardinghouse sat directly across and slightly north; its wide porch caught the full force of the morning sun. He took the porch steps two at a time and went through the front door without stopping.

The boardinghouse was dim after the brightness outside, and he moved through it with the familiarity of a man who had been in this building a half dozen times in the past few weeks. He passed the dining room on his left, and the desk by the stairs, and continued down the hallway toward Leora's private quarters.

He paused in Leora's doorway.

A young woman was kneeling beside the bed. She had removed the bandages from Leora's shin entirely, and the linen strips were folded neatly on the bedside table. He noticed an unrolled canvas kit that held small jars, tincture bottles, and clean cloths. She was bent over the leg with a square of dampened muslin, cleaning the wound with careful, deliberate strokes that moved outward from the wound margins—the correct direction, away from the wound rather than toward it, which meant she had been taught to do this and had learned the lesson well enough for it to become automatic. Her sleeves were rolled up past her elbows. Her hair was auburn, pinned up but beginning to come loose at the nape of her neck.

He cleared his throat. "Ma'am, step away from Miss Leora's leg, please."

She looked up, and her eyes were blue, clear, and steady, and held a composure that didn't match what he expected to find in a room where a loved one lay feverish with an infected wound.

"And you are Dr. Porter," she said.

"I am. And you are cleaning an infected wound without my knowledge or instruction."

"I am cleaning an infected wound because it needed cleaning." Her voice was calm and precise, the diction of a woman from the East, and there was nothing apologetic in it. "I have been using a solution of warm water and Castile soap. I have not applied anything else. The wound has been exposed for about fifteen minutes, and I have kept my hands and all materials clean."

"Samuel, this is my niece, Eliza Miller. Eliza, this is Dr. Samuel Porter," Leora said, her voice tired but carrying the particular firmness of a woman who was about to put an end to something before it became something else entirely. "Now that we are all introduced, could you both please remember that there is a patient in this bed?"

Samuel carried his bag to the bedside and set it on the floor beside the chair. The young woman—Miss Miller—shifted to give him room, but she didn't leave. She moved to the opposite side of the bed and stood with the cloth folded in her hands, watching him. He was aware of her attention the way a man is aware of a lamp in the corner of a room: it didn't interfere with his work, but he knew precisely where it was.

He looked at Leora's leg, and what he saw tightened the muscles across his shoulders. The split was roughly two inches long over the tibial ridge, the wound margins swollen and inflamed. The surrounding skin was an angry red that radiated outward in an uneven pattern, widening toward the ankle where gravity and poor circulation had given the infection the most room to advance. The tissue was hard when he touched it, and the warmth coming off the shin was substantial.

"Mrs. Hanscombe, when did this happen?"

"Sunday evening. I already told Eliza the full account. I moved my legs off the bed and my splint struck the bedframe. My skin split. It quite shocked me when it happened."

"And you didn't think to send for me."

"Edith and I cleaned and wrapped it. There was no need for you to come when this was simply something we could take care of. Besides, it was Sunday, a day of rest, I might remind you, Dr. Porter."

Samuel turned his attention from the wound to his patient. He laid the back of his hand against Leora's forehead, then moved it to the side of her neck. Warm. Not dangerously so, but enough to confirm what Winnie had reported.

"How are you feeling? Any nausea?"

"Some. It comes and goes."

"Dizziness?"

"A little."

"When did that start?"

"This morning. Yesterday I started feeling a tingling in my leg. Today it's a bit more sore."

Samuel nodded. The progression told him the infection was no longer confined to the wound site—it had moved into the surrounding tissue and was beginning to declare itself through the body's general defenses. Fever, nausea, weakness. The signs of a system being asked to fight on a front it had not chosen. He examined the wound edges, then the tissue above and below the skin split. He pressed gently alongside the wound and felt the resistance of inflamed tissue that had thickened beneath the skin.

"The redness extends approximately two inches beyond the wound in every direction," Eliza said from the other side of the bed.

He looked at her. She was standing with her hands folded, and her expression was attentive without being anxious—the expression of a woman who was waiting to be useful, not waiting to be told what to think. She was reporting what she had observed, not asking for his opinion of it, and the clinical accuracy of the statement caught him off guard for the second time in as many minutes.

"I noticed," he said.

"I also noted cloudy discharge on the inner bandage when I removed it. And the tissue surrounding the wound is indurated."

She had used the word indurated. Hardened. The correct medical term for tissue that has thickened and firmed due to inflammation and fluid accumulation beneath the skin. That was not a word a helpful niece picked up from a home remedy book. That was a word learned in a ward, at a bedside, from a physician or a supervising nurse who expected precision.

"Where did you train?" he asked.

"I nursed my mother through a two-year illness when I was young. After she passed, I completed the nursing training course at the fever hospital auxiliary in Philadelphia. Eighteen months of supervised instruction in wound care, fever management, and bedside assessment. I also worked with the Ladies' Benevolent Society, visiting the sick in their homes and assisting with convalescent nursing."

"The fever hospital auxiliary, you say." He studied her for a moment. Philadelphia's fever hospitals handled typhoid, scarlet fever, diphtheria—the diseases that moved through tenement wards and overflowed charity beds. The auxiliary nurses worked under physicians, but they worked hard. They saw wounds, fevers, delirium, and death. They learned by necessity what many medical students learned by lecture. "I'm aware of it."

"Yes. I learned quite a lot from my time there."

Samuel looked at the supplies she had laid out on the bedside table. Clean linen strips, neatly rolled. A jar of carbolic salve. Witch hazel. A small bottle he recognized as tincture of arnica. Comfrey root. Willow bark. Everything arranged in the order a person would use them, from cleaning to dressing to pain management. He had seen surgeons with less organized instrument trays.

He turned back to the wound. He needed to irrigate it thoroughly with carbolic solution, assess whether the deeper tissue required drainage, apply an antiseptic dressing, and get Leora started on a regimen that would fight the infection before it advanced further. This was treatable. But it required daily attention, and it required someone capable of providing that attention consistently over the coming days. He had been that someone for three weeks, checking in between his other patients and trusting Leora to follow his instructions. That trust had not been well placed.

"Mrs. Hanscombe," he said, "this infection is serious, though not life-threatening yet. I believe we caught it in time. The redness spreading beyond the wound tells me the infection is moving into the surrounding tissue, and your fever and nausea tell me your body is fighting to contain it. I need to clean this wound thoroughly, apply a carbolic dressing, and I will have to check it every day until the redness recedes, and the discharge clears."

"How long?" Leora asked.

"If we are diligent, a week. Possibly longer. I will not promise what I cannot guarantee. But this was caught before the infection reached bone, and that matters a great deal." He held her gaze. "You must never tend to something like this yourself again, Leora Hanscombe. I will not tolerate it. I am right across the street, and regardless of what day of the week it is, I am always available to you or anyone else in this community."

Leora clamped her mouth shut and nodded. Her face was pale against the pillow, the flush of fever visible on her cheeks and along the line of her throat.

Samuel opened his medical bag and began setting out his supplies on the bedside table.

"Miss Miller, I will need fresh water. Warm, not hot. And a clean basin."

She set the cloth down and left the room without hesitation. He listened to her footsteps move down the hallway toward the kitchen, quick and purposeful.

While she was gone, Samuel spoke to Leora plainly. "You should have sent for me on Sunday."

"Nonsense, Samuel Porter."

"A skin wound over a fracture is not something to brush aside, Leora. The bone is close beneath that tissue, and infection has a shorter distance to travel than you think. If this had gone another two days without treatment, we would be having a very different conversation."

"I know that now," Leora said. "My niece already lectured me, and she was no gentler about it than you are."

"Good. I'm glad your niece lectured you."

"She is a capable young woman, Samuel. I asked her to come help me run this boardinghouse and never dreamed she'd be nursing me as well." Leora gave him a look that carried equal parts affection and reproach. "You shouldn't have scolded me in her presence. Not a good first impression on your part, I might add."

"I didn't scold you. I told you the truth."

"You most certainly did scold me, young man."

Samuel didn't argue further because arguing with Leora Hanscombe when she was right was a poor use of anyone's time. He had learned this in his first week of treating her. The woman would accept bad news, accept pain, and accept instructions she would rather not follow, but she would not accept being told she was wrong when she knew she wasn't.

Eliza returned with a basin of warm water and a clean cloth draped over her arm. She set the basin on the bedside table, moving the cold tea and the canvas kit to the top of the dresser to make room.

Samuel irrigated the wound with a diluted carbolic solution, working carefully along the wound margins and into the split itself. Leora's hand gripped the edge of the mattress, and her jaw was set, but she made no sound. Eliza had moved to the head of the bed and held Leora's hand.

"There is no deep abscess," Samuel said. "The infection is in the soft tissue surrounding the wound, which is what I expected given the pattern of redness. I am going to apply iodoform powder directly to the wound. It will help fight the infection at the site. Then a dressing of clean linen soaked in carbolic, and a fresh linen wrapping over that."

"Will the iodoform sting?" Leora asked.

"No more than the carbolic did."

"That is not a comfort, Samuel."

"It was not intended to be one." He dusted the wound with iodoform powder, working it into the wound margins with a light hand. Then he laid the carbolic-soaked lint over the site, covered it with a layer of clean, dry lint, and began wrapping the linen strips around the shin. His hands were large against the linen, but his touch was careful, each wrap laid with even tension so that the dressing held without pressing on the swollen tissue.

Eliza watched the dressing procedure, and Samuel could feel the quality of her attention—it wasn't the worried attention of a family member watching a loved one being treated. It was the focused, evaluating attention of someone who was learning what she could from how he worked and measuring it against what she already knew.

When the dressing was secured, he sat back and looked at Leora. "I want the dressing changed twice daily. Morning and evening. The wound must be cleaned with carbolic solution at each dressing change, and fresh iodoform applied before the new dressing goes on. I will check in daily, but between my visits, the dressing changes need to be done by someone who knows what they are looking at."

"Eliza can do it," Leora said.

Samuel looked at Eliza, and she met his gaze with the same steady composure she had shown since he walked through the door. Nothing in her posture asked for his approval.

"Are you comfortable changing a carbolic dressing on an infected wound?"

"Yes."

"And I'm sure you know what to look for. Changes in redness, changes in discharge, increased warmth, and any signs that the infection is advancing rather than receding."

"I do."

"If you see any of those things, you send for me immediately. You do not hesitate, nor attempt to treat an advancing infection on your own."

"I understand, Dr. Porter." Her tone was polite but firm.

"When did you arrive, Miss Miller?"

"I arrived yesterday."

"Yesterday." He looked at the canvas medical kit on the dresser, at the row of tinctures and salves, and at the neatly rolled linen. A woman who had arrived yesterday from hundreds of miles away and had her medical kit unpacked and organized on a dresser the way he kept his instrument case ready beneath the examination table. "You brought your own supplies."

"I always travel with basic medical provisions, Dr. Porter. It is a habit from my work with the Benevolent Society. We often visited homes where supplies were scarce, and it was easier to carry what I might need than to arrive unprepared."

Samuel nodded. He began packing his own instruments back into his bag, placing each item in its designated compartment. "The willow bark I saw in your kit. Were you planning to brew tea for the fever?"

"If you approved. I wasn't going to administer anything without your knowledge."

"I approve. Willow bark tea for the fever and the pain, brewed strong. Three times a day. It will help more than laudanum at this stage, and it won't dull her senses the way laudanum does. I want her awake and able to tell us if something changes."

"I agree."

He fastened the clasp on his bag and stood. Leora had closed her eyes; the effort of the treatment and the conversation were written in the lines of her face. The cool cloth Eliza had placed on her forehead earlier had been refreshed at some point during the dressing change—Samuel couldn't say exactly when, couldn't point to the moment it had happened—and the fact that it had been done without announcement or interruption told him more about the woman standing nearby than any credential she had offered.

"Mrs. Hanscombe," he said, and Leora opened her eyes. "You are going to stay in this bed. You are going to let your niece tend to this wound. You are not going to shift your legs off this mattress or attempt to manage your boardinghouse from this room. The fracture needs stillness to heal, and the infection needs your body's full strength to fight it. Every bit of energy you spend worrying about biscuits and boarders is energy your body cannot spend on recovery."

"You are telling me to lie here and do nothing."

"I am telling you to lie here and heal. There is a difference."

She glanced at Eliza. "He is not always like this. Please excuse his bluntness."

Eliza smiled at that, a brief warmth that changed her face entirely and made her look younger than the composed young woman who had met him at the bedside with clinical vocabulary and steady hands. "No worries, Aunt Leora. I've been exposed to worse bedside manner."

Samuel picked up his bag and looked at Eliza. "Miss Miller, I will return tomorrow to check the wound. Again... if anything concerns you before then, my office is across the street. I am there most of the day, and my living quarters are upstairs. Knock at any hour."

"Thank you, Dr. Porter."

He turned toward the door, then stopped. "Miss Miller."

"Yes?"

"What you did this morning was sound. The cleaning, the preparation, the way you handled the wound. It was good work."

She held the compliment without flinching from it or brushing it aside, and the steadiness of her acceptance told him as much about her as the medical vocabulary had. She did not deflect it into modesty. She didn't diminish it with a qualification. She received it the way a person receives something they have earned—simply and without apology.

"Thank you," she said. "And it was a pleasure meeting you."

"It was a pleasure meeting you as well."

He walked down the hallway toward the front of the boarding-house, his bag in his hand, and the dim hallway gave way to the brighter light of the entry. He stepped out onto the porch and stood for a moment in the full heat of the morning, settling his hat on his head and letting his eyes adjust to the brightness after the close quarters of Leora's room.

Main Street lay before him, dry and rutted and ordinary—the freight wagon still sitting with its tailgate down, a man loading sacks of something onto its bed, and the dog still claiming its patch of shade beneath the undercarriage. The mercantile across the way had its door open to the heat, and he could see the red geraniums in their tin planter bright against the porch railing.

He stepped off the porch and crossed the street toward his office. Halfway across, he stopped.

He stood for a moment with his bag in one hand and his hat brim shading his eyes, looking back at the boardinghouse. The wide porch. The two benches flanking the door. The building, solid and square-shouldered, stood against the backdrop of the Gallatins rising to the west.

Somewhere inside that building, a woman he had met twenty minutes ago was preparing a willow bark tea for a patient, using supplies she had packed in Philadelphia and carried with her over a fourteen hundred mile journey. She had used the word indurated. She had cleaned the wound in the correct direction. She had refreshed a cool cloth on her aunt's forehead during a procedure without once interrupting the procedure to do it.

He had been the only medical practitioner in Providence Ridge for a month. He hadn't minded the solitude of it—he was accustomed to working alone, had built his career on the self-reliance that came from being the only doctor within a day's ride, and had made his peace with the weight of it the way a man makes peace with the weight of his own boots after enough miles. But standing in the middle of Main Street on a Wednesday morning in July, looking back at a boardinghouse he had walked out of many times without pausing, he felt something shift—not dramatically, not with any word he could have named if pressed, but with the unmistakable sensation of a question arriving that he had not known to ask.

He turned and walked the rest of the way to his office, mounted the boardwalk, and went inside. He set his bag beneath the examination table, hung his hat on the peg, and crossed to the desk by the window. He opened his ledger, uncapped the ink, and recorded the visit in his careful hand: *Hanscombe, L.—infected skin wound, left tibial ridge. Spreading cellulitis, mild systemic response. Carbolic irrigation, iodoform dressing. Willow bark tea initiated. Wound care delegated to niece, E. Miller—trained, fever hospital auxiliary, Philadelphia. Daily follow-up scheduled.*

He set the pen down and looked at what he had written. In six years of frontier practice, he had never noted a family member's training in a patient's record. He had never had a reason to.

Chapter 5

"We need more flour than that," Leora said, her reading spectacles low on her nose as she studied the supply list Eliza held between them. "Double it. And add another twenty pounds of sugar. We go through sugar faster than any single commodity in this building, and I will not run short in the middle of July with Winnie baking pies for our travelers staying with us on their way to Yellowstone."

Eliza penciled the correction on the list balanced on her knee. She was sitting in the straight-backed chair beside Leora's bed, the remains of their lunch on the small table near the door—two bowls of the potato soup Winnie had made, both nearly empty, and a plate with the last quarter of a biscuit that neither of them had claimed. The windows were open to the afternoon, and through them came the steady sound of a wagon being loaded somewhere along the street and the distant ring of hammer on iron from the blacksmith's shop, each strike arriving a half second after the one before it with a regularity that made it part of the town's breathing rather than a disruption of it.

"I had meant to go to the mercantile yesterday," Eliza said. "I spent yesterday afternoon scrubbing the upstairs rooms, and by the time I finished the last one, it was nearly suppertime. The mercantile order went entirely out of my head."

"That is why you pin the list to the kitchen wall, where you will see it every time you walk past."

"I did pin it to the kitchen wall. And then I walked past it multiple times without reading it."

Leora gave her a look over her spectacles. "You are your mother's child. Caroline could organize an entire church supper and forget to eat at it."

Eliza smiled at that because it was true. Her mother had been the kind of woman who sent food to every sick neighbor in the parish and then stood in her kitchen at nine o'clock at night realizing she hadn't eaten since morning. Eliza had inherited the habit the way she had inherited her mother's auburn hair and her father's handwriting.

She added cornmeal and baking soda to the list and tapped the pencil against the paper. "What about soap? We have four bars left in the storeroom."

"Order a full case. And add laundry bluing. And see if Mr. Pemberton has any decent lamp oil in stock. The last batch smoked terribly. I received two complaints from boarders about their wicks."

Eliza wrote it all down, the list growing longer with each item Leora remembered. Her aunt's memory for inventory was precise even from a sickbed, and every addition came with the certainty of a woman who had managed this boardinghouse alone for four years. Eliza had seen ledger-keepers in Philadelphia with less command of their figures than Leora Hanscombe had of her pantry shelves, and the thought pleased her.

"Always keep extra on hand," Leora said. "You will never regret having too much flour. You will regret having too little on the morning ten men sit down expecting flapjacks."

A knock came at the open door, and Eliza looked up to find Dr. Porter standing in the hallway. He had his medical bag in one hand and his hat in the other. He was leaning slightly into the room, the way a man does when he's arrived at a conversation already in progress and is waiting for a reasonable place to enter it.

"Good afternoon," he said.

"Dr. Porter." Leora set her spectacles on the quilt and folded her hands. "Come in. We were just solving the great flour shortage of 1884."

"I wasn't aware there was one."

"There isn't. My niece is going to the mercantile today to ensure it stays that way."

Samuel stepped into the room and set his bag on the floor beside the bed. He looked at Eliza. "How is the wound today?"

"Improved," Eliza said as she set the supply list on the small table. She had been composing this report in her mind since seven o'clock that morning, arranging her observations the way she had been trained to deliver them—specific, ordered, and without editorializing. "I changed the dressing at seven. The redness has receded approximately half an inch from where it was yesterday. The tissue along the wound margins is less swollen, and the discharge has thinned and cleared considerably. Still present, but no longer cloudy."

Samuel pulled the chair from the corner of the room and positioned it near the bed. He sat and opened his bag, removing the carbolic bottle and a square of clean lint. "Any fever this morning?"

"I checked at seven and again at noon. Cool both times. No nausea since yesterday evening."

"And the pain?"

"Better," Leora said. "It aches, but it's a dull ache, not the sharp kind. I slept well last night."

"Good." Samuel moved the quilt aside from Leora's leg and began unwinding the linen dressing with careful hands. Eliza stood and came around to the foot of the bed, where she could see the wound as he worked. She watched him peel back the carbolic-soaked lint, his fingers steady and sure against the tender skin, lifting the dressing away from the wound bed without pulling—patience in the motion that she recognized as the mark of a man who had learned that the last half inch of a dressing removal was where careless hands undid the healing the dressing had been protecting.

The wound looked better. Even from where she stood, she could see the difference from yesterday. The angry red that had spread in an uneven pattern outward from the split had drawn back noticeably, and the wound margins, though still swollen, had lost the tight, shining quality that signaled deep inflammation. The tissue around the split was pink rather than red, and the skin had softened.

"You are right," Samuel said, looking at the wound. "The redness has receded. The iodoform is doing its work." He pressed gently alongside the wound with two fingers and watched Leora's face. "Tell me what you feel."

"Sore. But nothing sharp, and nothing that travels up my leg the way it did yesterday."

He nodded and continued his examination, probing the tissue above and below the wound site, checking the skin temperature with the back of his hand.

"The induration is resolving," he said. "The tissue is softening. That is what I wanted to see," he looked at Eliza. "Your dressing change this morning. Walk me through what you used."

"Carbolic solution diluted to the same strength you mixed yesterday. I irrigated the wound, applied iodoform powder to the margins, laid carbolic-soaked lint over the site, covered it with dry lint, and wrapped it with clean linen. I also brewed the willow bark tea, and she drank a full cup at half past seven."

"Did you note any odor when you removed the morning dressing?"

"None. The discharge had a faintly sour quality yesterday, but this morning it was clean."

"If you two are quite finished discussing my leg as though it were a specimen in a jar," Leora said from the pillow, "I would like to remind you both that the rest of me is still here, and this particular conversation is putting me very nearly to sleep."

Eliza pressed her lips together to keep from laughing. Samuel looked at Leora with an expression that suggested he was deciding whether to apologize or continue, and the brief hesitation before he chose was the most uncertain she had seen him—a man who spoke plainly about infections and dressings caught momentarily without a clinical vocabulary for a patient's impatience.

"My apologies, Mrs. Hanscombe. We will try to make your wound care more entertaining."

"I am not asking for entertainment, Dr. Porter. I am asking for mercy. You are both speaking a language I do not understand, and I have been lying in this bed for three and a half weeks with nothing to listen to but my own thoughts when I'm alone. At least give me a conversation I can follow."

"That is fair," Samuel said. He applied the fresh iodoform powder, laid the carbolic lint, and began wrapping the clean linen. His hands were large against the bandaging, but his touch was precise, each wrap laid with even tension. "I will attempt to speak more plainly. Your leg is healing. The infection is retreating. Your niece's dressing work this morning was exactly right, and I am satisfied with everything I see today."

"Thank you. Was that so difficult?"

"Not at all."

"Then perhaps you might speak plainly more often when visiting your patients, Dr. Porter. Not everyone has a trained nurse in the family to translate."

Eliza handed him the small scissors from his bag when he reached the end of the linen, and he cut the strip and tucked the tail neatly against the wrap. She noticed that his hands, large as they were, worked with a fineness that surprised her. She had seen surgeons in Philadelphia whose hands moved with less care.

She stepped back and returned to her chair.

"I want to continue the same regimen," Samuel said, repacking his bag. "Dressing changes twice a day, carbolic irrigation each time, iodoform to the wound. Willow bark tea three times daily for at least three more days. I will come again tomorrow to check."

"Very well," Eliza said.

Samuel closed his bag and looked at Leora. "Do your best to get some fresh air on your leg. Staying under a quilt all day holds in heat. It is July, and the temperature outside is warm, but I understand it is easy to catch a chill when one stays in bed day after day."

"I will do my best, young man."

He turned toward Eliza. "How are you finding Providence Ridge, Miss Miller? You have come a long way from Philadelphia."

The question caught her off guard.

"I have yet to explore much beyond the boardinghouse, but what I have seen is beautiful," Eliza said, and she meant it. The mountains visible from the boardinghouse porch filled the sky in every direction, and the light here was different from anything she had known in Pennsylvania. It changed through the hours in ways that kept catching her attention—the way it fell sharp and clean across the rooftops in the morning and then softened through the afternoon until the whole valley seemed to hold its breath before evening. "The air and scenery alone were worth the journey. I didn't expect that. In Philadelphia, the air is heavy, especially in summer. Here it feels as though you can breathe all the way to the bottom of your lungs."

"It takes some adjusting," Samuel said. "The elevation is higher than you are accustomed to. You may find yourself winded on hills for the first week or two."

"I noticed that yesterday, climbing the stairs with an armload of linens. I thought I was simply tired from traveling, but now I suspect the altitude played a part."

"It did. Give yourself time. Your body will adjust."

"Have you adjusted?" she asked. "You are new to Providence Ridge as well, correct?"

"Yes, I have been here since the first week of June. A little over a month now." He turned his hat in his hands, a slow rotation that seemed more habit than intention—the absent motion of a man whose hands were rarely still. "I have been in small towns and railroad camps for most of my career. Colorado, Wyoming. This is the first place I've been where I have an actual office with a door and a window."

Leora was watching them from the pillow with her hands folded on the quilt and an expression that was attentive and quiet—the expression of a woman who was taking careful note of something and choosing, for the time being, not to say a word about it.

"I hope to get out and explore a bit more," Eliza said. "I haven't been beyond the porch yet, and I would very much like to see the rest of the town and the creek and the valley."

"There is a good deal to see," Samuel said. "The valley is wider than it appears from town, and the creek is worth walking to. You must take time to wander alongside the Yellowstone River as well; it's a peaceful, enjoyable walk beside such a strong body of water. And another tip... the Absaroka Mountains are better appreciated from the benchlands above town than from the street."

"I will have to find the time. For now, the boardinghouse is keeping me well occupied."

"And my leg is keeping her further occupied," Leora added. "Though I expect that once Dr. Porter declares me sufficiently healed, my niece will have half the valley explored."

"Your niece will explore the valley when she has your kitchen pantry fully stocked and has found a helper to assist with cleaning and upkeep around here," Eliza said.

Samuel stood and picked up his bag. "I have a patient coming in shortly, so I should get back across the street."

"Would you mind if I walked with you?" Eliza picked up the supply list from the table and folded it in half. "I need to get this order to the mercantile, and I want to see what Mr. Pemberton has on his shelves that I can bring back today rather than waiting for a freight order."

She turned to Leora. "I will be back within the hour. Do you need anything before I go?"

"I need you to take your time while you are out. Stop and enjoy the beauty around you. There is no reason to rush back here and hover over me. And bring me back a peppermint stick if Mr. Pemberton has them."

"I will see what I can do."

Eliza walked with Samuel down the hallway toward the front of the boardinghouse. Their footsteps fell into an easy rhythm on the wooden floor. The hallway was cool compared to Leora's room, where the afternoon had been collecting heat through the open window, and she could smell the scent of yeast dough being prepared for dinner.

They stepped out onto the porch, and the full breadth of Main Street opened before them. The packed earth of the road was dry and rutted from wagon traffic, and across the way the mercantile stood solid with its wide boardwalk and the red geraniums bright in their tin planters. A man on horseback passed at a trot, heading north toward the bridge, and two women stood nearby speaking with baskets over their arms.

Samuel walked beside her down the porch steps and across the street. His stride was unhurried. At the mercantile steps, he stopped.

"Miss Miller, if you have a spare moment, you are welcome to come see my office. It isn't much, but I would enjoy hearing your opinion on a better arrangement, since you have experience working within a medical setting in the city."

"I would enjoy that, Dr. Porter. Perhaps tomorrow, if the afternoon allows it."

"Tomorrow would be fine. I am there most of the day."

"Then I will see what I can manage." She looked up at him. The afternoon light was on his face, catching the deep blue of his eyes and the fine lines around them—lines that came from squinting into sun and wind, not from age, and that gave his face a specificity it would not have had without them. He was a handsome man in a rugged, outdoorsy way.

"Good day, Dr. Porter."

He put his hat on and touched the brim. "Good afternoon, Miss Miller."

He turned and crossed the boardwalk toward his office, his bag in his hand and his stride unhurried. Eliza watched him go for a moment—the tall, broad-shouldered shape of him moving through the shade of the boardwalk overhang and back into the sun—and then she turned to the mercantile door, unfolded her list, and went inside.

Chapter 6

The bell above the mercantile door gave a single bright note as Eliza pushed it open, and she stopped two paces inside to let her eyes adjust.

The mercantile was larger than she had assumed it would be. The ceiling rose high enough to accommodate tall shelving along both walls, and every inch of that shelving was occupied. Bolts of calico and muslin stood upright beside coils of hemp rope. Tin pails hung from hooks above a row of canned goods, their labels turned outward in a careful, deliberate hand. Kegs of nails sat beneath a display of hand tools, and above them, a shelf of patent medicines in brown glass bottles caught what light came through the front windows. A glass-fronted case near the register held smaller goods: buttons, sewing needles, packets of pins, and a row of penny candy in glass jars whose colors looked almost defiant against the plain dark wood.

A counter ran the length of the back wall, and behind it a set of shelves held what appeared to be special-order items and mail.

A small postal window was cut into the wall to the left, with a wooden mail rack beside it, the letter slots arranged alphabetically and most of them holding something.

A woman came through a doorway behind the counter, carrying a bolt of dark blue fabric balanced against her hip. She was sturdy and of modest height, with black hair streaked through with silver and pulled into a tight bun at the back of her head.

"Good afternoon," the woman said. "May I help you find something?"

"Good afternoon. I have a supply order from the boarding-house. I'm looking for Mr. or Mrs. Pemberton."

The woman set the bolt of fabric on the counter and turned fully toward Eliza. Her expression changed, and Eliza watched the recognition arrive in quick succession, like someone assembling a face they'd been hearing described for weeks.

"You're Eliza," the woman said. "Leora's niece."

"I am."

"Oh, my dear girl." Margaret Pemberton came around the end of the counter and crossed the space between them with a quickness that belied her frame. She took both of Eliza's hands in hers, and her grip was warm and firm and entirely without ceremony. "I have been waiting for you to walk through that door. I'm Margaret Pemberton, and you have no idea how glad I am to finally lay eyes on you."

"Mrs. Pemberton, it's a pleasure to meet you. Aunt Leora speaks of you so often I feel as though I already know you."

"She's said the same of you, and more besides." Margaret squeezed her hands once more before releasing them. "I've been checking on her every day I can manage. I'm so pleased you came.

Leora needed family, and she needed someone who could take hold of that boardinghouse and keep it to her standards."

"I'm doing my best. I'm mostly trying not to disrupt what's already working."

"Wonderful. If you need me to help with anything, don't hesitate to ask. Now. You said you have a supply order?"

"I do." Eliza unfolded the list and handed it over. "Aunt Leora supervised every line of it, so I can promise you it's thorough."

Margaret glanced at the page and gave a quick, full laugh. "Forty pounds of flour, twenty pounds of sugar, a full case of soap. Yes, this has Leora written all over it." She turned toward the back of the store. "Amos! Come out here, please. Leora's niece is here with an order that's going to keep you occupied for the next hour."

A door at the rear of the store opened, and a man came through carrying a wooden crate balanced against his hip. He wore an apron, and his shirtsleeves were rolled past his forearms. He set the crate down on the counter with a thud and looked at Eliza.

"Miss Miller," he said. "Welcome to Providence Ridge. Your aunt has been telling us about you for weeks now."

"Mr. Pemberton. Thank you. I hope she hasn't set expectations too high."

"She's set them precisely where she always sets them, which is high enough to keep the rest of us working hard to be better people." He said as he reached for the supply list Margaret was holding out and settled a pair of wire-rimmed spectacles on his nose.

"I have most of this," he said after a moment. "Flour, sugar, salt, lard, coffee, cornmeal, baking soda, and soap. Lamp oil I have, a different supply from what Mrs. Hanscombe said smoked too much. It's the Fremont brand, out of Helena. Burns cleaner, in my experience."

"She mentioned the last batch smoked badly."

"It did. Several customers told me the same. I switched suppliers two weeks ago." He folded the list and tucked it into his apron pocket. "The laundry bluing I'll need to freight in. I sold my last box on Monday. The extra flour beyond what I have on hand, I can add to the next freight order. The wagon's due in nine days, weather permitting."

"That would be fine. The immediate need is what you have available today."

"I'll start pulling it now. Most of what's on this list I can have boxed up and delivered to the boardinghouse within the hour." He looked at her over the wire-rims. "Unless you're wanting to carry forty pounds of flour across the street yourself."

"I'll leave the heavy lifting to you, Mr. Pemberton."

"A wise decision." He tucked his spectacles back into his apron pocket and moved toward the shelving along the right wall where the bulk dry goods were stacked. He hefted a flour sack from one of the shelves and set it beside the crate with ease.

Margaret touched Eliza's arm lightly. "Come sit with me while he works. I've got a hundred questions for you, and Amos will holler if he needs anything."

She led Eliza toward the front of the store, where two wooden chairs sat near the window with a small table between them. A tin coffeepot rested on a trivet, and Margaret poured two cups without asking. The coffee was good, noticeably better than what the boardinghouse had been producing from Leora's remaining stock, and Eliza told her so.

"That's the advantage of running a mercantile. I get to test new brands of coffee, and I believe this one is a keeper. Amos placed an order for more of it, and we'll be stocking it on our shelves soon. Now. Tell me honestly, because Leora won't. How is she?"

"Healing, but it's been slower than any of us would like. There was a complication with her leg that Dr. Porter has been treating, and it's responding well now. He examined her this afternoon and was pleased with the progress."

"A complication?" Margaret's cup paused halfway to her mouth. "What kind of complication?"

"A wound on her shin that became infected. She didn't mention it to anyone. Dr. Porter has been treating it with carbolic dressings, and the infection is receding, but it's added time to her recovery."

Margaret set her cup down carefully. "An infection. Lord have mercy. I was over there Saturday afternoon, and she seemed to be mending fine. When did this happen?"

"Sunday evening, she bumped her splint against the bedframe, and the skin split. She and Edith cleaned it and wrapped it themselves."

"And she didn't send for the doctor."

"She didn't. I sent for Dr. Porter when I realized she had an infection."

Margaret shook her head slowly. "That woman... she's tough as nails and believes she can do everything on her own. Thank the Lord you got here when you did. And you brought real training with you, from what Leora tells me. A hospital in Philadelphia?"

"A fever hospital auxiliary. Not a hospital in the full sense, but the training was thorough."

"Thorough enough for Dr. Porter to trust you with her wound care, and that man doesn't hand over trust on medical matters to just anybody." Margaret took a sip of her coffee. "He's a good doctor. We were in a bad state for a doctor before he came. We had a fellow pass through who called himself a physician, but he only lasted three months and left owing Amos twelve dollars in supplies. Samuel Porter is a Godsend."

From the back of the store, Amos's voice carried over the shelving. "Miss Miller, does Mrs. Hanscombe prefer the yellow cornmeal or the white? I've got both."

"Yellow," Eliza called back. "That's what Winnie's been using."

"Much obliged."

Margaret smiled. "He knows every customer's preferences better than they know them themselves, but he always confirms. It's his way of making certain nothing's changed since the last order."

The front door opened, and the bell rang again. A woman entered carrying a market basket over one arm. She was perhaps in her mid-thirties, lean and sun-browned, with capable hands and the kind of posture that suggested she rarely sat still.

"Ruthann!" Margaret rose from her chair. "Come here, child... have you met Miss Miller? She's Leora Hanscombe's niece, just arrived from Philadelphia to help run the boardinghouse."

The woman shifted her basket and offered her free hand. "Ruthann Brennan. My husband, Frank, and I have a homestead up the valley, north end. Pleased to meet you, Miss Miller." Her handshake was quick; the grip firm and unhesitating. "Mrs. Hanscombe has been talking about you something fierce. I don't think there's a soul in this valley who didn't know your name before the wagon brought you in."

"I'm beginning to understand that," Eliza said.

"Will you be at the Fourth of July gathering tomorrow evening?" Ruthann asked.

"I intend to be there."

"Good. Bring whatever you can manage. I'm bringing two crocks of baked beans and a dried-apple cake, and it still won't be enough. Never is." She turned to Margaret. "I need a quarter-pound of baking soda and a spool of white thread if you have it. And has any mail come for us?"

"Thread is on the second shelf, left side. Baking soda, I'll weigh out for you, and I'll check to see if you have any mail." Margaret said as she moved toward the counter.

Ruthann collected her thread; Margaret weighed and wrapped the baking soda in brown paper, and then retrieved her mail.

"Give my best to Frank," Margaret said. "And tell him Amos placed the order for the wire he wanted for his fencing. It should be here by the beginning of next week."

"I'll tell him. Good day, ladies."

Ruthann left with a brief wave as Margaret returned to her chair. "Ruthann is such a joy to us all. She and Frank have been homesteading north of town for six years now. Good people, hardworking as the day is long, and she puts up preserves that would win a blue ribbon in any county in the territory."

Eliza sat back down and turned her cup in her hands. "Speaking of hardworking. Aunt Leora mentioned you might know of someone in the community who'd be available for part-time work at the boardinghouse. Laundry, heavy cleaning, that sort of thing."

"I can think of two women who might be willing. Let me speak with them first. I would rather not put forward anyone's name without knowing their situation hasn't changed since I last heard."

"Of course. I'd be grateful."

"I'll have an answer for you by the end of the week." Margaret set her cup down on the small table. "Now. Tomorrow evening. I want you to come and put everything else out of your mind for a few hours. This is the one evening all year when the whole town sets down its work and just gathers. Families bring what they have, if they have it to share. Please don't feel as if you need to bring anything; just having you there will be enough. We spread blankets along the creek bank south of the bridge, and there's more food than any reasonable number of people should be able to eat, which is precisely how it ought to be."

"Winnie told me about it. It sounds like a wonderful tradition."

"It's the best evening of the year, and I'm not exaggerating. We've been holding it since Amos and I first settled in this valley, and every year more families come. There's something about all of us spreading out along that creek with good food and no worries of the work that we set aside that'll be waiting on us later anyhow. It's just a good, relaxing evening of fellowship."

She paused and looked toward the window. "We don't have a church building yet. We don't have a proper schoolhouse. But we have this one special time of year, and for now it's enough." She turned back to Eliza. "Though I intend to change the church and schoolhouse situation before I'm too old to swing a hammer."

"Winnie mentioned you have plans for a schoolhouse."

"Plans, pledges of labor, a list of families willing to contribute timber, and a husband who tells me I'm getting ahead of myself."

Margaret glanced toward the back of the store, where the sound of Amos stacking crates was steady and purposeful. "I'm not getting ahead of myself. I'm getting ahead of the need, which is altogether different. Every child in this town deserves a proper schoolroom, and every family deserves a place of worship that isn't someone's dining table, much as I love Leora's dining room for the purpose."

"It's a worthy goal."

"It's the only goal that matters, in my estimation. Commerce keeps a town alive, but a church and a school are what make it worth living in. Amos will come around. He always does when I'm right, which is most of the time."

Amos appeared from behind the shelving with a crate balanced against his chest. "I heard my name."

"I was telling Miss Miller that you're a reasonable man who occasionally needs a little time to arrive at the correct conclusion."

"I am a man who is currently carrying thirty pounds of sugar, and I'm grateful to God for the strength he's given me." He set the crate beside the others he'd assembled on the counter. Three were lined up now, packed tight and labeled in his careful hand. "Miss Miller, I have everything on your list that I've got in stock. Flour, sugar, salt, lard, cornmeal, coffee, baking soda, soap, the Fremont lamp oil. The laundry bluing and the additional forty pounds of flour will come on the next freight wagon. I'll deliver what I have to the boardinghouse within the hour."

"Thank you, Mr. Pemberton. I appreciate it."

"Happy to do it." He paused and reached beneath the counter. His hand came back with a glass jar filled with red-and-white-striped peppermint sticks, and he drew three from the jar, wrapped them in a twist of brown paper, and set them on the counter. "No charge. Tell your aunt those are from Margaret and me, and tell her we hope she feels better soon."

"I will relay the message, and again, thank you, Mr. Pemberton," Eliza said as she walked toward the counter. She took the peppermint sticks and tucked them into her apron pocket. She turned and offered her hand to Margaret.

"It was a pleasure, Mrs. Pemberton."

"Margaret. Please. And the pleasure is mine, truly. I'll see you tomorrow evening down at the creek."

Chapter 7

Owen Gallagher had a voice built for argument, the way some men had hands built for plowing, and he was putting it to full use under the cottonwood tree near the creek. Samuel was trying to decide whether the potato salad or the fried chicken was the better thing on his plate.

"I'm telling you, Paul, I've seen freight wagons come through in the past two weeks loaded with nothing but timber bracing and drill steel. That's not speculation. That's tonnage. A man doesn't haul drill steel on a pass road for the pleasure of the scenery."

Paul Higgins stood with his plate balanced in one hand and a chicken leg in the other, chewing with the unhurried patience of a man who'd heard Owen make a case before and knew that interrupting only extended the performance. He swallowed, wiped his mouth with the back of his wrist, and said, "Owen, I stable the horses that pull those wagons. I know what's coming through. I'm not arguing the freight."

"Then what are you arguing?"

"I'm arguing whether it means anything yet. A mine's not a mine until somebody pulls something out of the ground that's worth more than what it cost to dig the hole. Right now, all I see is equipment going south and money going with it."

"That money is wages, Paul. Wages for men who'll spend those wages here in this town. At your livery, at Pemberton's mercantile, and at the boardinghouse."

"And if the assay comes back short, those men pack up and those wages go with them, and all we've got is a road torn up by heavy freight."

Samuel listened and ate. The potato salad was better. Somebody had put fresh dill in it and a measure of vinegar that cut the richness. He didn't know whose it was, but he intended to find out.

Owen turned to him. "Doc, you've been quiet. What's your position on the mining?"

"My position is that this potato salad is exceptional, and I'd like to know who made it. I'm a doctor, Owen. My opinion on mining is worth about as much as your opinion on suturing."

"Fair enough," Owen said, and his irritation broke into something closer to amusement. "But you mark my words. Six months from now this town's going to double in size, and you're gonna be busier than you've ever been. Miners get hurt, Doc. They get hurt regularly, and they get hurt badly."

"I'm aware." He'd set enough broken fingers and cleaned enough rock dust from lacerations in other territories to know exactly what Owen meant.

The gathering spread along the flat ground south of the new bridge, where Providence Creek bent wide and the cottonwoods grew tall enough to throw a good deal of shade. Blankets and quilts covered the grass in a patchwork of faded colors. A food-laden pair of sawhorses laid with planks served as a common table that held baskets, crocks, and covered dishes. Samuel had noticed several cakes, two crocks of beans, multiple vegetable dishes, a ham somebody had smoked until its glaze crackled dark as molasses, and more pies than he'd ever seen in one place.

East of the creek, the Absarokas rose in a wall of timber and bare volcanic rock, their prominent ridges still holding light. The valley floor had already cooled, and the air had that particular stillness that came when the day's wind dropped and the mountains held the valley like a cupped hand. A bullfrog called from the creek bank, low and steady. Somewhere downstream a child shrieked, and another child laughed, and the two sounds braided into the murmur of voices and the occasional knock of a tin plate against a serving spoon.

He'd been here in Providence Ridge for a month now. Long enough to know most people by name and some by habit. Long enough to have treated Owen's youngest for an earache, delivered a bottle of tonic to Ruthann Brennan for her headaches, and pulled a fishhook out of Mica Hart's thumb while the blacksmith sat perfectly still and said nothing, which Samuel respected more than he'd said. He'd treated patients and had gotten to know his neighbors, and the two categories overlapped in ways they never would've in a city or a larger community.

But being trusted wasn't the same as belonging. When the gathering arranged itself into clusters of old friendships and shared loss and winters survived, Samuel was aware that his history here could be measured in weeks. These people had built this town. They'd buried children in its soil, rebuilt after floods, and kept each other fed through bad years. His presence was welcomed. His place was still taking shape, the way a new fence post needs a season of weather before it sits firm.

Paul made the shaping easier. Paul Higgins accepted a man exactly where he stood without asking how he'd gotten there. Their friendship had taken hold the second week of June when Samuel brought a lame horse into the livery and Paul diagnosed the problem before Samuel had finished describing it. Then they'd spent an hour talking about the particular insanity of travel on some of the nearby mountain roads. Paul was easy company, and he genuinely enjoyed talking to him.

Owen excused himself to rejoin his family, his seven children scattered across two blankets in varying states of restlessness. His wife, Nora, waved from the far blanket as Owen crossed the grass toward her with his plate.

"Seven children," Paul said, watching him go. "I can't keep track of my own hat."

"You can't keep track of many things, my friend."

"That's the truth. But at least I don't have seven small people adding to the problem." Paul took another bite of chicken and looked out across the gathering. "Who's that with Winnie Callahan? The woman in the blue dress."

Samuel didn't need to look. He'd noticed her ten minutes ago, when she'd come down the path from Main Street with Winnie beside her. He'd been listening to Owen and eating his supper when Eliza Miller had walked into the gathering, and he'd lost four sentences of Owen's argument entirely, which was fortunate.

She wore a blue dress, fitted at her waist, with lace at her collar and cuffs. The fabric was finer than what most women would wear to a creek-side picnic on a Friday evening, and her auburn hair was pinned in a style that belonged in a parlor in Rittenhouse Square, not a clearing beside a Montana creek. She walked with the posture of a woman who'd been taught to carry herself with elegance and poise.

"That's Miss Miller," Samuel said. "Leora Hanscombe's niece. She came from Philadelphia this week to help run the boarding-house."

"The one Amos mentioned has been looking after Mrs. Hanscombe's leg?"

"She's been assisting with her aunt's care, yes. She trained in Philadelphia as a nurse and seems quite competent."

Paul looked at him.

"Competent," Paul said.

"That's what I said."

"You said it the way a man reads a label off a medicine bottle. Is she competent like a good farrier is competent, or competent the way you say the word when you don't want to say the word you actually mean?"

"She's a trained nurse providing capable care to a patient with a complicated fracture. That's what "competent" means."

"Mm-hm." Paul drank from his cup and let the conversation sit, which was worse than pressing, because the silence gave Samuel room to hear himself. He sounded like a man trying to describe a sunrise using the word adequate.

Across the gathering, Margaret Pemberton had intercepted Eliza and Winnie near the common table. Margaret was speaking with both hands, the way she did when something delighted her, and Eliza was listening with her head tilted slightly to one side. She listened to Margaret the way Samuel had seen her listen to Leora, with a stillness that gave the speaker her full attention. Margaret said something, and Eliza laughed, quick and unguarded. Her whole face opened with it, the careful composure giving way to something less measured, and Samuel looked down at his plate because he'd been watching long enough.

The creek ran clear over its stones behind him. A group of children were wading in the shallows downstream, their trouser legs rolled to the knee, and their voices carried in the cooling air. Mica Hart had brought his fiddle and was tuning it on a stump near the common table, working through a string of notes that climbed and dropped and climbed again, searching for pitch.

"She arrived Tuesday," Samuel said, "from Philadelphia by way of Livingston."

"That's a fair number of particulars for a professional acquaintance."

"She's treating my patient. I keep track of who's involved in my patients' care."

"Of course you do."

Paul finished his chicken leg, set the bone on his plate, and wiped his hands on his trousers. Samuel turned his attention back to Eliza.

Timothy Pemberton had found his way to her. The boy had detached himself from Margaret's side and planted himself in Eliza's path, looking up at her with the absolute confidence of a five-year-old who'd decided this new person belonged to him. Samuel watched Eliza kneel. She went all the way down, her blue skirt spreading on the grass, and she listened to whatever Timothy was telling her with the same unhurried attention she'd given

Margaret. The boy spoke with his whole body, his small hands moving, and from thirty yards Samuel couldn't hear the words, but he could see Timothy's face bright with whatever story he was telling. Eliza's response was a nod, and then something spoken that made Timothy grin wide enough to show the gap where his front teeth had been. She reached out and straightened his collar, a small, absent motion, and Timothy didn't pull away.

Samuel set his plate on the ground beside the tree and picked up his cup.

Hattie Pemberton, Timothy's mother, called after him, and the boy went reluctantly, turning twice to wave at Eliza, who waved back both times.

He watched as Winnie and Eliza moved through the gathering after that, stopping at a cluster of homestead wives from the north end of the valley. Winnie handled the introductions. Eliza shook hands with each woman, and Samuel watched how she adjusted to them, a slight shift in her posture that brought her nearer to them. Ruthann Brennan laughed at something Eliza said, and two of the other women leaned closer, and within a few minutes the circle had closed around her as though she'd been standing in it for years.

Eventually, Winnie and Eliza crossed the grass toward them, and Samuel stood a little straighter.

"Mr. Higgins. I don't believe you've met Miss Miller. Eliza, this is Paul Higgins. He owns the livery and feed yard at the southern edge of town," Winnie said.

Paul removed his hat. "Miss Miller. Welcome to Providence Ridge. Your aunt is one of the finest women in this territory, and any kin of hers is welcome at my livery anytime."

"Thank you, Mr. Higgins. It's a pleasure. Aunt Leora speaks highly of you."

"She speaks highly of everyone she approves of and says nothing whatsoever about the ones she doesn't, which is how you know where you stand." He set his hat back on. "If you ever need to hire a horse or a buggy, I can accommodate you. I've got several good horses, a two-seat buggy, and a buckboard. The rates are fair. If you need to journey to Livingston, I can set you up with a team that won't give you any trouble and a driver if you require one."

"I appreciate that. I may have to make that trip before long for supplies."

"You come see me whenever you're ready."

"Dr. Porter," Eliza said, turning to him. "Good evening."

"Miss Miller. Good evening. Are you enjoying the celebration?"

"Very much. I don't think I've attended a gathering quite like this one. The whole town seems to be here, and the atmosphere is lively."

"That it is." He paused. "How's your aunt this evening?"

"She was well when I left. Edith offered to sit with her so we could attend. Aunt Leora told me to stay as long as I liked and bring her back a piece of whatever cake Mrs. Pemberton had baked," she said as she held up a tin plate covered in cloth. "I believe my aunt will be pleased; mission accomplished."

"Leora does have a sweet tooth, I've learned."

"That she does; I take after her in that aspect."

Winnie had turned to scan the crowd. She rose on her toes and shaded her eyes. "There's Luke." She turned back. "Eliza, do you mind if I go speak with him? I won't be long."

"Go and enjoy time with your beau," Eliza said. "I'm perfectly fine."

"You're sure?"

"Winnie. Go."

She smiled and was gone, crossing the grass toward a young man in a clean shirt who'd just reached the bottom of the path. Samuel watched her for a moment, then looked back at Eliza.

"She's been very kind to me," Eliza said. "Since the day I arrived, she's gone out of her way to make me feel welcome."

"Winnie's a delightful young lady. She was most welcoming to me as well when I first arrived."

Eliza looked out over the gathering. The fiddling had started in earnest, a slow waltz that drifted across the creek bank and mixed with the murmur of conversation. "This is a good community, Dr. Porter. I've only been here a few days, but I can feel it. People look after each other and genuinely like one another."

"They do. It's one of the things I noticed when I first arrived. A small town can go either way. It can close ranks against newcomers, or it can bring them in. This one brings people in."

"And have they brought you in?"

The question was direct, and he liked that she didn't talk around things. "They've been generous. Paul's been a good friend from the start, and most folks have been welcoming. I've got patients who trust me with their families, which is about the highest compliment a doctor can receive in a town this size."

"But?" she said.

"No, but at all. Just time. Roots take time. I haven't been here long enough to have history with anyone, and history is what turns a neighbor into something closer."

"Interesting thought, Mr. Porter... I can understand the truth in what you say," Eliza said.

"Give it a month, Miss Miller. By then you'll know more about this town than you wanted to, and the town'll know more about you than you intended, and the whole arrangement will feel perfectly natural," Paul said.

Eliza turned to look at him. "That's both reassuring and slightly alarming, Mr. Higgins."

"That's Providence Ridge."

Eliza laughed. This close, Samuel could see the way her eyes changed with it, the blue going brighter, and the way her shoulders eased a fraction.

"Miss Miller," Paul said, "I understand you've come from Philadelphia. That's a considerable distance. How are you finding the territory?"

"Larger than I expected. There is a wildness to it that I find interesting and terrifying at the same time. I feel so small in relation to the massive mountains that surround us. Everything here is expansive. There's so much wide-open country. Philadelphia has everything in a tight, confined space. Here, everything's spread apart, and there's more sky than I've seen in my entire life... it seems endless."

"I came from Ohio twelve years ago, and I still haven't gotten used to how much of it there is. You adapt, though. Eventually, you stop measuring in city blocks and start measuring by how long it takes a good horse to get there."

"I may need to learn to ride properly, then."

"You don't ride?" Paul looked at her with genuine surprise, the expression of a man who'd grown up on horseback encountering the concept of people who hadn't.

"I've ridden. Not well and not recently. Philadelphia doesn't require it."

"I've got a mare named Clementine who's gentle enough for a child and smart enough to bring you home if you fall asleep in the saddle. You come by the livery when you've got a free afternoon, and I'll introduce you."

"I'd like that, Mr. Higgins. Thank you. I've suddenly felt the need to explore, which is uncanny for me. I can't quite explain it, but I have a yearning to see more of what surprises this area holds."

The sky over the Gallatins had deepened to a violet wash, and the first stars showed above the Absaroka ridgeline to the east. Mica Hart was playing a melody Samuel didn't recognize, slow and sweet, and a few voices had joined in singing.

Eliza looked toward the path that led back to Main Street. "I should go soon and relieve Edith. She deserves to come and enjoy what's left of the evening."

"You could send word with someone," Paul said. "No reason to cut your evening short."

"I appreciate that, but I would rather not leave my aunt alone; she is quite restless as of late, and knowing her, she'd attempt to get out of bed again."

Samuel set his cup on the ground beside his plate and straightened. "I'll walk with you. I should look at her leg before the day's out. I want to see how that wound's closing."

"I'd welcome the company."

"I'll say good evening, then," Paul said. "Miss Miller, it was a genuine pleasure. Come by the livery anytime."

"I will. Thank you, Mr. Higgins. It was lovely meeting you."

"Doc... you go on, and I'll see that your plate and cup make it to the washtub and back to their proper owner. Have a good evening," Paul said.

"Thank you, Paul."

Chapter 8

The linen came away from her aunt's shin in a slow, careful pull, and Eliza kept her fingers steady against the skin beneath the wrapping, feeling for the give of tissue and the warmth that had worried her previously. Samuel stood at the foot of the bed with his arms crossed, speaking to Leora about the splint bindings while Eliza worked.

"I haven't shifted the splint, Dr. Porter. I haven't shifted anything. I've been lying here like a woman buried in sand, and if you ask me whether I've been resting, I may throw this pillow at you."

"I wasn't going to ask," Samuel said. "I can see you've been resting. You look like a woman who's ready to climb the walls."

"I passed ready two weeks ago. I'm now firmly in the territory of planning my escape."

Eliza removed the last strip of linen and set it in the basin on the bedside table. The wound along her aunt's shin still showed the raw pink of healing tissue. The discharge on the linen was lighter.

She pressed gently along the skin above the wound and felt only mild warmth.

"Dr. Porter, would you look at this?"

Samuel uncrossed his arms and came to the bedside. He bent and examined the wound, his large hands careful as he turned her aunt's ankle slightly to see the full wound in the lamplight. Eliza stepped back to give him room and found herself watching his hands instead of the wound. His fingers were gentle for their size. She could see a small white scar along the back of his right hand, old and well healed.

"This is good, Mrs. Hanscombe," he said. "The infection's responding. The tissue's granulating well, and the redness has pulled back considerably. I'd say we leave this uncovered for a while tonight. Let the air get to it."

"Does that mean I'm no longer at death's door?"

"You were never at death's door. You were at the door of a woman who doesn't listen to her doctor."

"I listen. I simply don't always agree."

"Those aren't the same thing, and you know it." He straightened and looked at Eliza. "Miss Miller, you've done fine work with these dressings. This wound's responding better than I expected at this stage."

"Thank you."

He pulled a chair from the corner and sat, which surprised her. She'd expected him to check the wound and leave. Instead, he settled into the chair and stretched his legs out in front of him. He was a tall man, broad through the shoulders, and the spindle-backed chair beneath him looked as if it were a child-sized chair.

"Now," Leora said, propping herself higher against her pillows with both hands, "you two have been out in the world tonight, and I've been lying here listening to the clock tick and having a one-sided conversation with a copy of Pilgrim's Progress while Edith drifted in and out of a nap. You're going to tell me everything."

"Everything about what?" Eliza asked.

"The celebration. The food. Who wore what? Who talked to whom? Who made a fool of himself?" Her aunt's voice had more life in it than Eliza had heard all week. The drawn, restless look she'd worn when they walked in had burned off, replaced by alertness.

"There were many people there, Aunt Leora. Blankets and quilts were spread along the creek bank. There was a lot of food that had been set out on a table made from sawhorses. Children were playing and running around... everyone seemed to be enjoying the evening."

"Was there music?"

"Mica Hart brought his fiddle," Samuel said.

"Of course he did. That man doesn't go anywhere without it. He once played three waltzes and a reel at a barn raising while the rest of us were still hauling timber, and I asked him whether he intended to help or serenade us, and he said he couldn't see why he was unable to do both."

Eliza laughed. "He was still playing when we left. Something slow I didn't recognize."

"Probably one of his own. He won't admit it, but I just know he composes a lot of his tunes. He plays some beautiful things I've never heard before anywhere else. My Harold used to say Mica

Hart had more music in him than conversation, and that was about right. The man can shoe a horse without uttering a word, but hand him a fiddle and you can't get him to stop."

"The food was exceptional," Samuel said. "Somebody brought a potato salad with fresh dill that I intend to track to its source."

"That's Nora Gallagher's. She puts dill and vinegar in it, and she won't tell anyone her proportions. I've asked twice. She just smiles and changes the subject." Leora shifted her weight and winced, and Eliza leaned forward, but her aunt waved her off. "I'm fine... just stiff. Everything's stiff. My back, my hip, and my patience." She looked toward the open window, where the last of the July evening had faded to a deep blue. "I'd give five dollars to sit on my own porch for twenty minutes."

"When your fracture's stable enough, we'll get you out there," Samuel said.

"When will that be?"

"A few more weeks, if you keep healing at this rate and stop trying to stand on it."

"A few more weeks." Her aunt closed her eyes and opened them with the expression of a woman swallowing a dose of medicine she knew was necessary and hated, anyway. "Do you know what I miss most? It isn't the porch, though I miss the porch something fierce. It isn't even the kitchen, though the Lord knows I miss that kitchen. It's walking through my dining room at supper and seeing people eating food I cooked, sitting at tables I set, in a room my Harold and I built with our own hands. That's what I miss. The being part of it."

Through the open window, faint and thinned by distance, the fiddle carried from the gathering by the creek. A slow melody like a pulse at the edge of the evening.

"They're still playing," Leora said. "Can you hear it?"

"Barely," Eliza said.

"When Harold was alive, we'd have been down there all evening. He loved a good gathering. He'd have been the first one there and the last to leave, and he'd have talked to every single person and remembered every word come morning." She looked at Samuel. "You remind me of him in some ways, Dr. Porter."

His eyebrows rose a fraction. "How so?"

"Harold was a big man, like you. Built like a brick house. He was quiet in the same way that you are. Not shy. Just a man who listened more than he talked and saved his words for when they'd do some good. People trusted him the minute they shook his hand because he carried himself like a man who didn't need your approval but would treat you well, regardless."

Eliza watched Samuel receive this. He didn't deflect it or turn it into a joke. "That's generous of you... and quite the compliment. Thank you."

"I don't give compliments I don't mean, young man. I once told a boarder his table manners would embarrass a barn cat, and I meant every syllable."

"Aunt Leora... my goodness," Eliza said.

"What? The man started using his napkin the next morning instead of his shirt sleeve. I also taught him the proper way to use a fork. He stayed here with me for three weeks while he waited for a bed to open up in the bunkhouse at the lumber mill. He learned quickly to use "please" and "thank you" as well to earn the respect of a lady, which was the real victory." Her aunt's humor had a restless edge tonight that Eliza recognized: the humor of a woman with too much energy and nowhere to put it, a sharp mind pacing inside a body that wouldn't cooperate.

"Tell me about the Pembertons," Leora said. "Was Margaret in her element... was she having fun and talking to everyone who would listen?"

"She was," Eliza said. "She introduced me to half the women in the valley before I'd gotten ten steps from the food table. And her grandson, Timothy, found me."

"Timothy finds everyone; he loves people. That boy has never met a stranger in his five years on this earth."

"He told me a long story about a frog he'd caught. I didn't follow all of it, but the frog was green and apparently the largest frog anyone has ever seen."

"Every frog Timothy catches is the largest frog anyone has ever seen. Making up tales is one of his finest qualities," Leora said. "Your turn, Dr. Porter. Tell me where you were before coming to our fine town."

"Wyoming, for a stretch. Various Colorado territories before that. I'm from Colorado originally. My family has a ranch near Trinidad."

"A ranch." Her aunt looked at him with renewed interest. "That explains your hands."

"Ma'am?"

"You've got a rancher's build, and you've got scars on your hands I've seen before on others. My Harold had hands like that. Capable of fine, careful work, but you could tell they'd gripped something rougher first and had done a lot of hard labor. You are quite gentle, but I can tell your hands have great strength in them."

Samuel looked down at his hands, spread wide on his knees, as if considering them for the first time. "I grew up doing ranch work. I learned to ride before I could read. My father always said, The ranch would teach me everything I needed to know about hard work, and medicine would teach me everything I needed to know about humility."

"Your father sounds like a wise man."

"He is. Stubborn as the ground he ranches, but wise."

"The best men are usually both." Leora turned to Eliza with an expression so carefully neutral it could have hung in a portrait gallery. "Isn't that right, Eliza?"

"I wouldn't presume to generalize about men, Aunt Leora."

"You wouldn't presume to generalize about anything. You're too careful for that. But I notice you haven't disagreed with me."

Eliza gathered the used linen strips from the basin and folded them into a tight, neat stack, one over the other, pressing each fold flat with her palm. She said nothing, which was the safest course of action when her aunt decided to fish.

"Tell me about the celebration some more," Leora said, turning back to Samuel. "Was Reverend Hale there and his wife Eunice?"

"They were. He said the prayer before the meal and gave a few words." Samuel glanced at Eliza. "I don't know if you were there at that time, Miss Miller. You and Winnie arrived after the prayer, I believe."

"We did. I haven't met the Reverend or his wife yet." She turned to her aunt. "I look forward to meeting them on Sunday."

"Webb Hale has been preaching in my dining room every other Sunday for as long as I can remember. He and Eunice always stay here at the boardinghouse when they're in town. They're practically family at this point." Leora adjusted her pillow behind her back. "Their daughter Sarah lives here, married to a young man named Levi Pruitt. Sarah's expecting her first child, and Eunice has been finding more and more reasons to visit Providence Ridge, which I suspect has less to do with Webb's preaching schedule and more to do with that grandchild on the way."

"Edith checked them in this morning while Winnie and I were prepping for lunch. I remember her mentioning it now that I think about it."

"You'll like Webb. He preaches like a man who's read the text and lived inside it, not like a man who's memorized it and is reading it back. There's a difference." Her aunt's expression sharpened with appreciation. "And Eunice is a force of nature. She'll have you on a volunteer committee within ten minutes of shaking your hand. That woman has a gift for putting people to work before they realize they've volunteered."

"She sounds like someone I'd enjoy."

"She sounds like you, is what she sounds like. You and Eunice Hale are cut from the same bolt of cloth. When the two of you meet, this town had better brace itself."

Samuel made a sound that was nearly a laugh, caught and held short. Eliza looked at him and found him pressing his thumb against the corner of his mouth, his eyes creased with the effort of keeping quiet.

"Something amusing, Dr. Porter?"

"Not a thing, Miss Miller."

Leora watched them both for a moment longer. Then she turned her head toward the open window, where the faint thread of the fiddle still carried from the creek, and her face changed.

"I wish I could've been there tonight," Leora said. "I've been to every Fourth of July gathering this town has held since Harold and I arrived. I always make a dozen pies to bring. Last year I stayed until the stars were thick and the children were asleep on the blankets. And this year I'm here, stuck in this bed. It's foolish, I know. A grown woman grieving over a picnic."

"It's not the picnic itself, is it?" Eliza asked.

"No, it's not the picnic. It's the feeling of being part of things. Of being useful for more than lying still."

"That's not foolish, Aunt Leora. That's honesty."

"It's both, sweetheart. Most honest things are a little foolish." Her aunt's mouth held a rueful line that Eliza knew as well as she knew her own handwriting. Her mother used to make that same expression when she admitted something she'd rather have kept inside.

"You'll be at next year's gathering," Samuel said. "You'll be on your feet, and you'll make those pies, and you'll stay until the stars are out."

"You promise me that, Dr. Porter?"

"I don't make promises I can't keep. But I'll tell you what I believe, and I believe you'll be standing at that picnic this time next year telling whoever arranged the food that they've done it wrong."

"No one arranges the food correctly. It's one of the great sorrows of my life."

"Then you've got a strong reason to heal."

She laughed, and the sound of it filled the entire room.

The conversation moved the way evening conversations do when the company is good and nobody's counting the hour. Leora wanted to know about the food in detail. Samuel described the ham and its dark glaze and the fried chicken that he thoroughly enjoyed. Eliza listed the cakes and the crocks of beans, and the pies. Her aunt pronounced judgment on each baker's strengths with the authority of a woman who knew this town like the back of her hand.

Leora told a story Eliza hadn't heard before, about the first winter after she and Harold arrived, when the pass road closed for three weeks and the town ran low on coffee. Harold had traded a man a smoked ham for two pounds of it, because Leora without her morning coffee was a woman Harold preferred not to live with.

"He wasn't wrong," Leora said. "I'm not fit for company before my first cup, and I've never pretended otherwise."

"That runs in the family," Eliza said.

"It does. Your mother was the same. Your grandmother was worse. Three generations of women who shouldn't be spoken to before breakfast, and the men who loved us learned that lesson quickly, or they learned it painfully."

Samuel laughed. Not the short, rationed sound she'd heard earlier, but something warmer and less measured, a laugh that came from a man who'd stopped thinking about whether to let it out. His face changed when he laughed like that. The straight lines of it, the strong jaw, and the serious brow that gave him the look of a man perpetually working something out rearranged into something less guarded. Less careful.

"Eliza, you've gone quiet," Leora said.

"I'm listening."

"You're always listening. Try talking. Tell Dr. Porter about the time your father tried to fix the cookstove while your Uncle Harold and I were living with you all, just before we left to come here to Montana."

"Aunt Leora."

"It's a wonderful story, and it reflects well on your father's character, if not his mechanical ability."

Eliza looked at Samuel, who was watching her with polite expectation and a faint curiosity underneath it. "My father is a printer," she said. "He's brilliant with type and ink and binding. He can set a page of Scripture in half the time it takes most men in his shop. But anything involving tools and physical repair is entirely beyond him. Our cookstove door wouldn't close properly, and instead of calling someone, he decided he'd handle it himself."

"This doesn't end well, does it?" Samuel said.

"It ends with the door off its hinges, soot on the ceiling, and my mother standing in the kitchen doorway asking my father if he'd like her to fetch someone who knew what they were doing."

"She didn't say it like that, though," Leora said. "Tell him what she actually said."

Eliza smiled. "She said, 'Henry, I married you for your mind, not your hands. Please go sit down before you set the house on fire.'"

Samuel's laugh was full this time, open and unguarded, and it filled the small bedroom the way Leora's laugh had filled it earlier. "I wish I could have met your mother," he said.

"She would've liked you, Dr. Porter. She had great respect for people who were good at practical things, since she'd married a man who wasn't."

"My father would get along with yours," Samuel said. "He can build a barn and shoe a horse and mend a fence line without breaking stride, but put a book in his hands and he holds it like it might bite him."

"So between our two fathers, we'd have one complete man."

"That's about the sum of it."

Eliza picked up the basin of soiled linen. "I'll take these to the kitchen and clean up this mess a bit. Aunt Leora, would you like tea or coffee?"

"I would love some tea. I'd love it even more if there were cake."

"I may have brought back a piece of Margaret Pemberton's cake for you."

"You are my favorite niece."

"I'm your only niece."

"And yet the statement holds."

Eliza carried the basin through the sitting room and down the short hallway to the kitchen. She set the basin beside the wash area and filled the kettle, setting it on the stove. She was unwrapping the cake when she heard the front door open.

Eliza wiped her hands and walked out of the kitchen to see a young man, not much older than herself, standing in the dining room.

"May I help you?"

"Ma'am, I'm sorry to bother you this late. My name's Jasper Cobb. I'm looking for Doc Porter. I went down to the celebration first, and Mr. Higgins told me I might find him here."

"He's here. Is everything all right, Mr. Cobb?"

"My wife is feeling poorly. I apologize for intruding."

"It's no intrusion. Let me take you to him."

She led Jasper through the hallway to her aunt's bedroom. Samuel looked up when they appeared in the doorway.

"Dr. Porter, this is Mr. Jasper Cobb; he's come for you," Eliza said.

"Sir... Miss Leora... I'm sorry for the intrusion," Jasper said. "I truly am."

"Hush now, Mr. Cobb," Leora said. "This isn't an intrusion. What's wrong? You look distressed."

"Thank you, ma'am." Jasper looked at Samuel. "It's my wife, Doc. She's been feeling poorly for two days. Headaches, exhausted, can't keep much down. She's warm to the touch. Not burning up, but warm enough to worry me."

Samuel stood. "Any other symptoms? Chills, stomach pain, anything in her joints?"

"She said her back's been aching. And she's been sleeping more than usual, which isn't like her. Ada's up before dawn most mornings, but these past two days I've had trouble getting her out of bed."

"Is there any chance your wife could be expecting?"

Jasper turned his hat another half circle. "She thinks she might be, Doc. She's suspected for a couple of months now."

"Any other children?"

"No, sir."

"Where do you live?"

"We live here in town... the row houses just to the west of this here boardinghouse. We're the first one you come to if you're headed south."

"You head back to your wife and tell her the doctor's on his way. I need to grab my medical bag from my office."

"Thank you, Doc. I appreciate it more than I can say. I'll leave a lantern lit on the porch for ya," Jasper put his hat on and looked at Leora. "Ma'am, I'm sorry again for the disturbance."

"Go look after your wife, young man. Don't you ever apologize for taking care of the people you love. That's never a disturbance."

Jasper nodded and left, his boots quick on the hallway floor and then on the porch boards outside.

Samuel buttoned his waistcoat and turned to Leora. "I'll check your wound tomorrow morning. Keep it uncovered tonight; a light sheet over it is fine. The air will do it good."

"Go, Dr. Porter. That young man's wife sounds like she needs you more than I do."

He turned to Eliza. "Miss Miller, thank you for the evening; I enjoyed your company and look forward to it again."

"It was a lovely evening, and thank you," she said. "I hope Mrs. Cobb is well."

He held her look for a moment, and then he nodded before leaving. She listened to his footsteps moving down the hallway. The front door opened and closed, and the boardinghouse settled back into its quiet.

"Well," Leora said. "Bring me my cake and tea, sweetheart. In fact, bring yourself a cup of tea as well, because I feel a good discussion coming on about our Dr. Porter. I'd very much like to hear your thoughts on him."

Eliza opened her mouth, closed it, and went to get the cake.

Chapter 9

Reverend Webb Hale's voice carried through the boarding-house dining room with the unhurried authority of a man who'd been preaching longer than some of the people in these chairs had been alive. The large table had been pushed against the far wall, where it held a coffee urn, a row of cups, and platters of baked goods that the women of Providence Ridge had brought to share. Chairs filled the room in neat rows with an aisle between them, and nearly every seat was taken.

Samuel sat in the third row on the right side, his hat on his knee, and his Bible open to the passage Webb had read.

Across the aisle, two rows forward, Eliza sat beside Edith Aldridge. She wore a light blue dress fitted simply at her waist, with her auburn hair pinned in a careful twist. She was listening to Reverend Webb with her hands folded in her lap, her attention entirely focused on him.

Reverend Webb was a tall man with deep-set eyes beneath a heavy brow and gray hair cropped short above his ears. He'd been reading from the book of Ruth, a passage about the harvest and the kindness of provision, and now he closed his Bible and set it on the chair beside him.

"I want to talk to you about July," Webb said. "Not this July in particular, though I'll get there. July in general. The month itself."

A few people shifted in their chairs. Owen Gallagher's youngest, a girl of about three, squirmed in Nora's lap two rows ahead of Samuel.

"July's a month of abundance. The fields are growing. The animals are fat. The days are long, and a man can put in a full day's work and still have light left over at the end of the day. It's easy to feel provided for in July. It's easy to look at a full garden or a healthy herd or a pantry with flour in it and think, the Lord has been good." Webb paused. "And He has. But I want to be careful with that thought, because it leads somewhere tricky if you follow it too far."

He took a step closer to the front row. "If we only see God's provision in the full months, we're going to have a hard time finding Him in February. If we measure His faithfulness by what's growing in our fields, we're going to lose track of Him come winter when the pass road closes and freight doesn't come. God's provision isn't seasonal. His faithfulness doesn't follow the weather."

"The Israelites learned this in the wilderness," Webb continued. "Manna came every morning. Fresh. Just enough. They couldn't store it. They couldn't hoard it against a day when it might not come. They had to trust that tomorrow's provision would arrive tomorrow. That's a hard lesson for people like us. We're planners. We're storers. We put up food for winter and stack wood before the snow flies, and we do it because we're wise and because the territory demands it. But somewhere underneath all that good planning, the Lord asks us to remember that the planning isn't what saves us. He is."

The room was quiet, and everyone's attention was focused on the Reverend at the front of the room. Amos Pemberton sat in the front row with Margaret beside him, her hands still in her lap. Hattie sat next to her mother, and Timothy was wedged beside her, his small legs swinging above the floor. He held a carved wooden horse in his lap, turning it over in his fingers with the infinite patience of a child who'd been promised he could play with it quietly if he sat still.

"I don't know what your February looks like," Webb said. "I don't know what season's coming that'll test your trust. But I know this: the same God who fills your garden in July is the same God who meets you in the cold. His faithfulness isn't measured by what you can see in your pantry. It's measured by what He's already given you. And that list, friends, is longer than any of us can count."

He picked up his Bible. "Let's pray."

Samuel bowed his head, and around him, the congregation did the same.

"Lord," Webb said, "we thank You for this July morning. For the sun on this valley and the water in the creek, for the food on our tables, and the people in this room. We thank You for the provision we can see and the provision we can't. We ask You to make us faithful in the months ahead, whatever those months hold. We don't know what's coming. You do. Help us trust You with it. In Jesus' name. Amen."

"Amen," Samuel and everyone surrounding him said in unison.

He had attended every service since arriving in Providence Ridge. He'd sat here faithfully every Sunday, bowed his head, and said amen. He'd done it because his mother had raised him to worship, because the habit was older than his grief, and because a town's doctor owed the community his presence on Sunday the same as any other day. But his praying came harder than it used to. Three years ago he'd prayed with the ease of a man who believed his prayers reached somewhere. Now his prayers felt more like letters posted to an address he couldn't verify. He still posted them. He'd stopped expecting a reply.

The congregation rose. Chairs scraped against the floor as people stood and stretched. The room shifted from worship to fellowship in the span of a minute, the formality of the service dissolving into handshakes and conversation.

Winnie had been standing near the kitchen doorway during the service, and she moved to the coffee urn now, pouring cups with quick, practiced hands. Eliza joined her, taking up a position beside the table. She set cups in a line as Winnie filled them. The two of them moved without speaking; it appeared they'd developed the coordination of women who understood each other's pace, and neither got in the other's way.

He was standing near the back of the room with Paul when Eunice Hale arrived at his elbow as though she'd materialized from the floorboards.

"Dr. Porter," she said.

Eunice was a woman of medium height with sharp brown eyes and silver-streaked hair pinned back snugly.

"Mrs. Hale."

"Good to see you. Are you feeling well? You didn't look like you were eating much Friday evening at the celebration."

"I ate just fine last Friday, ma'am."

"That's what every man says right before he falls over." She turned to Paul. "Mr. Higgins, you look like a man who could use a biscuit."

"I could always use a biscuit, Mrs. Hale."

"Then go get one. They won't last." She turned back to Samuel. "I've been meaning to tell you, Webb and I are grateful for the work you've done here. Leora speaks highly of you, and that woman doesn't speak highly of anyone she doesn't mean it about."

"I appreciate that."

"She also tells me her niece has been tending her wound under your direction. A fever hospital in Philadelphia, is that right? That seems like a mighty fine job for a woman of her age."

"That's correct. Miss Miller trained at the fever hospital auxiliary. She's been managing her aunt's wound care, and her work has been excellent."

"Good. I've been running around like a chicken with its head chopped off since we arrived on Friday, and I haven't gotten a chance to meet her yet. I plan to introduce myself to her properly. Any young woman who can impress Leora Hanscombe and earn the trust of a physician inside a week is someone I'd like to know."

She turned and started walking toward Eliza before Samuel could respond. She crossed the room, cutting through the milling congregation with the directness of a woman who didn't believe in circuitous routes, and he followed. Not because Eliza needed rescuing. Because Eunice Hale at full conversational speed was a force, he'd only been exposed to briefly in the past, and the prospect of watching her meet Eliza Miller was something he found he didn't want to miss.

He reached the table a few steps behind Eunice, arriving at the coffee urn just as she reached Eliza. He picked up the urn and poured himself a second cup with no particular hurry.

"You must be Eliza Miller," Eunice said. "I'm Eunice Hale. Your aunt has told me quite a bit about you, and I've been looking forward to meeting you."

Eliza extended her hand. "Mrs. Hale, the pleasure is mine. Aunt Leora speaks of you and Reverend Hale with great affection."

"She's too kind. I'm going to ask you a hundred questions, and I'd like you to answer honestly, because I can tell when people are being polite, and it wastes both our time."

Eliza pressed her lips together as if she were keeping a smile from becoming a laugh. "I'll do my best."

"Where in Philadelphia are you from? What neighborhood?"

"Germantown. My father runs a print shop on the main street."

"A printer. That explains why Leora says you always have a book within reach. What does he print?"

"Religious tracts, temperance literature, church bulletins. The occasional hymnal."

"A hymnal printer's daughter. Well, that settles it. I already like you," Eunice picked up a cup of coffee from the row Winnie had poured. "Now tell me, how's Leora, really? Not the version she gives me when I sit with her, the version where everything's fine and she doesn't need a thing. The real version."

"She's healing well. Dr. Porter is pleased with her progress." Eliza glanced at Samuel, a brief confirmation, and he nodded. "But the confinement is hard on her. She misses being part of the community."

"Of course she does. That woman has never sat still a day in her life, and lying in that bed is wearing on her spirit more than her leg is wearing on her body." Eunice took a sip of her coffee. "I intend to sit with her this afternoon. I've brought her three books from my own library to enjoy. I hear you trained at a hospital? A real hospital?"

"A fever hospital auxiliary. Eighteen months of clinical training, including wound care, fever management, and bedside assessment."

"And you left that to come manage a boardinghouse in Montana."

"I came because my aunt needed me."

"Hm." Eunice studied her over the rim of her cup. "I came to Montana years ago because Webb had a calling, and God was directing him here. So me being the good wife I am, learned really quickly how to cook over a campfire and sleep in a wagon bed. The day I married him, I told him I'd follow him anywhere God led him, and the Almighty led us straight into a snowstorm outside of Bozeman. I spent our first anniversary chipping ice off the wagon tongue." She set her cup down. "Never regretted a minute of it. You look like a woman who can handle whatever this territory throws at her. Leora thinks so. I'm inclined to agree. I think you and I will get along just fine, young lady."

Margaret Pemberton appeared beside them, carrying a plate with two slices of lemon cake. "Eunice, leave the poor girl alone. She's only been here five days."

"I'm not bothering her. I'm getting to know her. There's a difference."

"There's no difference when you're the one doing it." Margaret turned to Eliza and grinned. "Pay no attention to Eunice. She means well, but she has the conversational restraint of a locomotive."

"I take that as a compliment," Eunice said.

"You should, my dear friend... it was meant to be. Come, let's go visit with others and let Eliza recover from your directness a bit."

Eliza laughed, a quick, surprised sound.

"Please forgive Mrs. Hale; she means no harm. She's quite the character," Samuel said.

"She's delightful and quite the opposite of what I'd expect from a reverend's wife."

"That she is. That's my Eunice, though, and I love her more and more every day. She's a joy to me every single day," Webb Hale said, approaching with his Bible tucked under his arm. "Dr. Porter. Good to see you this morning."

"Reverend Hale. I enjoyed your sermon."

"I try to keep them short enough that folks don't lose interest and long enough that God gets His say." Webb turned to Eliza. "Miss Miller, I've heard a good deal about you from your aunt. She's a remarkable woman, and she speaks of you as though you hung the moon."

"She's generous with her affections."

"She's precise with them, is what she is. Leora's not one to waste words." He adjusted his Bible under his arm. "So Philadelphia. That's a considerable journey."

"It is. But Providence Ridge has made the distance feel worthwhile."

"Good. This town has that effect on people, though it takes some of them longer to notice than others." Webb glanced at Samuel. "We'll be here with you in this blessed boardinghouse through Friday, if the Lord sees fit to it. Eunice and I plan to visit two of our children who live here in Providence Ridge, and I'll look in on your aunt each day as well."

"She'd welcome that very much."

Webb nodded and moved on, drawn away by Amos Pemberton, who'd been waiting to speak with him nearby.

The fellowship crowd had thinned around them while they'd been talking, people filtering toward the door in the unhurried way of a Sunday congregation that had nowhere pressing to be. Samuel was still standing beside Eliza at the table, his coffee cup in his hand.

Winnie came through the kitchen doorway and crossed to Eliza's side.

"Have you seen Mr. Drumond today?" Winnie asked.

"I haven't," Eliza said.

"He didn't come down for breakfast this morning, nor did he attend Sunday service, which is not like him. Mr. Drumond has attended services faithfully every Sunday since his arrival a few weeks ago. During dinner yesterday, he told me he had a headache and was retiring early. He barely touched his food and looked a tad unwell."

"Does he have family in the area? Maybe he's gone visiting today."

"He moved here recently after being hired at the mill. He doesn't have family that I know of. He's boarding here while he waits for a bed to open up in the bunkhouses near the mill."

"Well, if he doesn't come down for dinner this evening, perhaps we should go up and check on him."

"I was thinking the same," Winnie said.

She moved back toward the kitchen, and Eliza turned her attention to the platter in front of her. She began selecting baked goods from what remained, setting each piece onto a cloth napkin. A slice of lemon cake. A biscuit with preserves. A small square of something dark that looked like gingerbread.

"Are those for Leora?" Samuel asked.

"They are. If I don't bring her something from fellowship to enjoy when I check in on her shortly, I'll hear about it for the rest of the day."

Eliza folded the napkin edges over and smoothed them flat. She looked up. "How was Mrs. Cobb when you saw her Friday night?"

"She's with child, just as she suspected. Roughly two months along, from what I could assess. She's been feeling poorly, and I've asked her to stay in bed for a few days. I plan to check on her after I leave here."

"I hope she improves. Her husband seemed quite worried."

"He was. But Ada's young and strong, and rest should help." He set his empty cup on the table. "Miss Miller, I was wondering if you might care to take a walk this afternoon. The valley's fine this time of day, and I thought you might enjoy seeing more of it beyond the boardinghouse and the mercantile. After I've finished my visit with Mrs. Cobb, of course."

Color came into her cheeks, and she looked down and began smoothing the folded napkin. "That's kind of you to offer, Dr. Porter. Perhaps not today. I'd like to spend the afternoon with my aunt."

"Of course. Another time, then."

"Perhaps. Good day, Dr. Porter."

"Good day, Miss Miller."

She turned and walked toward the hallway. Winnie was waiting near the kitchen, and she fell into step beside Eliza. He watched as they disappeared into Leora's quarters.

Samuel collected his hat from the chair in the third row where he'd left it and walked out of the boardinghouse. Halfway across the street, his stride slowed. He'd asked Eliza to walk with him this afternoon, hoping to spend time with her and to offer her a reprieve from the steady demands of caring for her aunt and running the establishment. He'd asked plainly enough, and he hoped he hadn't given offense. He turned their conversation over in his mind as he pushed open his office door.

His medical bag sat under the examination table. He checked the contents by habit, closed the clasp, and picked it up. He walked toward the front window and stood looking across the street toward the boardinghouse. Could she simply be reserved? Perhaps a walk alone with a man she'd known less than a week didn't sit well with her sense of propriety. She could have been taught by her parents that a gentleman and a lady didn't venture out unchaperoned without an understanding between them. Or perhaps the answer was simpler than any of that. Perhaps there was a young man back in Philadelphia waiting for her to come home.

Chapter 10

Winnie shook the tablecloth out in one clean snap, and Eliza caught the far end before it could settle crooked. The dining room had emptied twenty minutes ago, the boarders filtering upstairs or out onto the porch in the unhurried way of men who'd eaten well and had nowhere pressing to be on a Sunday evening. The dishes were washed and stacked on their shelves. The serving platters had been scraped and scrubbed and put away.

"Mr. Drumond didn't come down for dinner," Winnie said.

"I noticed." Eliza said.

Winnie tucked the tablecloth corners and stepped back. "He wasn't at church this morning. He didn't answer when I knocked this afternoon after Sunday service. I could hear him moving around in there, so I left him be."

"Did he say anything to you yesterday evening? Beyond the headache?"

"He said he was tired and his head hurt. I asked if he wanted me to bring him tea, and he said, No, he'd be right by morning." Winnie picked up the basin and settled it against her hip.

Eliza untied her apron and hung it on the hook beside the kitchen door. The dining room table was reset for Monday's breakfast, the chairs pushed in along both sides, the crockery stacked, and the flatware laid.

"I'm going to take him some broth, bread, and a cup of water. Perhaps his stomach is a bit sour," Eliza said.

They moved into the kitchen. Winnie ladled broth from the pot, still warm on the back of the cookstove, while Eliza cut two slices of bread and set them on a small plate. She filled a cup with water from the pitcher on the worktable and arranged everything on a wooden tray, wedging the cup into the corner so it wouldn't slide. Winnie added a clean napkin and spoon beside the plate.

"You want me to come up with you?" Winnie asked.

"Please."

They crossed the hallway to the stairs. The second floor was dim. The window at the far end of the corridor let in the last of the evening in a low band across the floorboards. Eliza counted doors. Mr. Drumond's room was the fourth on the left, near the middle of the hall.

She stopped outside his door and knocked with her free hand; the tray balanced against her hip.

"Mr. Drumond? It's Miss Miller and Miss Callahan. We've brought you something to eat."

A sound came from inside, low and muffled. Then the creak of bedsprings and a voice thinner than it should've been.

"Come in."

Eliza opened the door. The room was warm; his window was shut despite the July heat. Mr. Drumond was in bed, propped on one elbow as if he'd tried to sit up and gotten halfway before the effort stopped him. His shirt was damp at the collar and across his chest. His face was flushed in patches, high color on his cheekbones and forehead, while the skin around his mouth and jaw had gone the color of tallow.

"I brought broth and bread," Eliza said. She set the tray on the small writing desk beside his bed. "When did you last have something to drink?"

He blinked at her. "This morning. I think. Winnie left water outside the door."

Winnie stepped past Eliza and picked up the cup on his washstand. It was nearly full. She set it down and looked at Eliza.

"Mr. Drumond, I'm going to feel your forehead, if you'll allow me," Eliza said. She sat on the edge of the straight-backed chair beside his bed and pressed the back of her hand against his skin. Hot. Not the dry, searing heat she'd felt on patients in the worst ward at the hospital, but well above what a healthy man should be running. His skin was damp with the kind of sweat that came from a body working hard to cool itself, and the flush on his cheekbones had the uneven look of a fever that was climbing rather than breaking.

"How long have you had the fever?" she asked.

"I don't know that I have one. It's just a headache."

"You're warm, and you've been sweating. Has the headache been constant since Saturday?"

He rubbed his eyes with the heel of his hand. "It comes and goes. Worse at night. My whole body aches, like I've been hauling timber all day, but I haven't done a thing except lie here." He lowered his hand. "What day is it?"

"Sunday."

He frowned. "I thought it was Saturday."

Eliza kept her face steady. A lost day wasn't unusual for someone running a fever, especially if they'd been sleeping through most of it. But it told her what she needed to know. His body was fighting, and it had been fighting long enough to blur the hours into each other.

"Have you had any nausea?" she asked. "Stomach pains?"

"My stomach's been off for several days. I figured it was something I ate."

"Have you been able to get up to use the privy?"

"Yesterday I managed. This morning I used the chamber pot. My legs felt like they were made of sand."

Eliza looked at Winnie, who stood nearby with her arms folded, watching.

"Mr. Drumond, I want you to try the broth," Eliza said. "Even a few sips. You need to drink, and the broth has salt in it, which will help. I'm going to open your window to get some air into this room, and Winnie will bring up a basin of cool water and clean cloths. We'll get you more comfortable."

"I don't need fussing over," he said. "It's a stomach complaint. I'll be fine by morning."

"You said that last night, and here we are."

She crossed to his window. The sash stuck when she pushed it, swollen in its frame from weeks of summer humidity, and she pressed harder until it gave and slid upward. The air that came through was warm, but it moved, carrying the fresh, earthy scent of the valley.

"Drink the broth, Mr. Drumond. Winnie and I aren't going anywhere until you do."

Whatever argument he'd been assembling left him. He pushed himself up against his pillow and reached for the cup of broth on the tray. His hand trembled when he lifted it, a fine tremor he tried to steady by gripping tighter. Eliza watched him bring it to his lips and take a slow sip.

"Good," she said. "Small sips. Don't rush it."

Winnie had already gone downstairs. Eliza heard her footsteps on the stairs, and a few minutes later heard them coming back. Winnie came through the door carrying a basin of water with two clean cloths draped over her arm. She set the basin on his washstand and wrung out one of the cloths.

Eliza took the cloth and folded it into a long rectangle. "Lean back against the pillows for me and tilt your head back slightly."

She laid the cloth across his forehead, and he closed his eyes. Some of the tension left his face, the creased lines between his brows smoothing out the way they do when a body that's been bracing against discomfort is finally given one small relief. She wrung out the second cloth and laid it across the back of his neck.

"That's better," he said. "Thank you."

"You're welcome. Try to finish the broth if you can. I'll check on you again before I turn in tonight."

He nodded without opening his eyes. Eliza stepped into the hallway; Winnie followed and pulled his door shut behind them.

"He's worse than he's letting on," Winnie said.

"He is. The fever's been building since at least Saturday, I would assume, and he's not eating or drinking enough. He thought today was Saturday. It could be a stomach complaint that's run him down or a summer grippe. Either way, I think Dr. Porter should know."

"You want me to go fetch him?"

"No, there's no emergency. I'll walk over myself. Mr. Drumond's comfortable for now, and the cool cloths should help bring his temperature down."

"Dr. Porter's office will be closed. It's Sunday evening."

"I know, he mentioned he lives above the office. I'll go up and knock."

Winnie looked at her. "You want me to come with you?"

"No, stay here and listen for Mr. Drumond calling out. I won't be long."

"I'll keep an ear out."

Eliza washed her hands in the basin by the stove when they returned to the kitchen, dried them on a clean towel, and pulled the kerchief off her hair. She smoothed back her hair where the pins had loosened and caught her reflection in the small square of mirror beside the kitchen doorway. She stopped. She wasn't going on a social call. She was reporting on a sick boarder to the town physician, and the mirror couldn't tell her anything useful about that. She shook her head as she took her shawl from the hook near the back kitchen door and went out through the front entrance.

Main Street was quiet, and all the shops were dark. A cat sat on the mercantile steps across the road, cleaning its paw with the thorough disinterest of a creature that had not a worry in the world.

The doctor's office sat on the east side of Main Street, south of the mercantile. The building was narrow and plain, with a single large window facing the street, and the sign beside the door read DR. S. PORTER in neat black letters. His CLOSED sign sat in the glass.

She walked around to the south side of the building, where a set of wooden stairs climbed the exterior wall. They were narrow, built against the siding with a simple railing on the open side, and they creaked under her weight as she went up. At the top was a small landing and a door, and through the door's single pane she could see the flicker of lamplight.

She knocked and heard footsteps from inside, and then the door opened.

Samuel stood in his shirtsleeves, his collar unbuttoned at the throat and his sleeves pushed past his forearms. Beside him she could see a single room, small and spare: a narrow bed pushed against the far wall with a wool blanket folded at its foot, a washstand, a trunk, a table holding a lamp and a plate, and a chair pushed back. A book lay open and face down beside his plate.

"Miss Miller," he said.

"Dr. Porter. I'm sorry to bother you during your evening meal. I wouldn't have come if it weren't a medical matter."

"You're not bothering me." He stepped onto the landing and pulled his door mostly shut behind him. The small space put them close, no more than two feet apart, with the railing at her back and Main Street stretched out below them in the near-dark.

"What's happened?" he asked.

"It's Mr. Drumond. You may recall Winnie mentioned this morning at fellowship that he didn't come down for breakfast or attend church."

"I do."

"He didn't come for supper this evening either. That's three meals today on top of the dinner he barely touched last night before retiring with a headache. Winnie and I went up to check on him about half an hour ago. He's running a fever, not severe, and I suspect it's been building since at least Saturday. He's flushed, sweating, and aching through his whole body. His appetite's gone. He's not drinking enough. He's lost track of the day; he thought it was still Saturday when I asked him. His stomach's been off for several days. He couldn't get to the privy this morning. Winnie and I got a few sips of broth into him, opened his window, and applied cool cloths. He's resting now."

Samuel listened as she spoke, his arms crossed loosely, his head tilted toward her.

"You did the right things," he said. "Fluids, cool cloths, fresh air. That's precisely what I'd have done."

"I thought it was most likely a stomach complaint or a summer grippe. I didn't want to alarm him by sending for you on a Sunday evening, but I wanted you to know."

"You were right to come. Let him rest this evening. First thing tomorrow morning, I'll come by the boardinghouse. If you don't mind, keep the fluids going tonight if he'll take them. Broth, water, weak tea. Small amounts, frequently."

"I don't mind at all, and I understand."

"And if the fever climbs tonight, or if he becomes confused enough that he can't tell you his name, send for me immediately. I don't mind what hour it is."

"I will."

Below them, Main Street had gone nearly dark. A lamp had been lit at the livery on the south end of the street, its light falling in a narrow band across the road.

"Thank you, Dr. Porter," she said. "I'll let you get back to your supper."

"It wasn't much of a supper. I'm a better physician than I am a cook."

"I'll remind you that a boardinghouse is right across the street. Winnie Callahan is a fine cook. You're welcome at the table anytime."

"I may take you up on that." He reached behind him for his door, then paused. "Miss Miller, you gave me a thorough report tonight. I want you to know that I appreciate that, and I appreciate you caring enough to look in on Mr. Drumond."

"Good evening, Dr. Porter."

"Good evening."

She went down the stairs, her hand on the railing, her boots finding each tread by feel in the near-dark. She crossed Main Street toward the boardinghouse. Her shawl had slipped off one shoulder, and she pulled it back as she walked, her footsteps quiet on the packed earth. The porch was empty now; the two boarders had gone inside, and lamplight shone warm through the parlor window.

Eliza hung her shawl on the hook by the door after entering the kitchen.

Winnie was at the worktable, her sleeves pushed up and flour dusting her forearms, working the dough for tomorrow morning's bread with a steady, rocking rhythm.

"How did it go?" Winnie asked without looking up.

"He'll come first thing in the morning. Fluids through the night if Mr. Drumond will take them, and send for him immediately if the fever gets worse or if he becomes too confused."

Winnie folded the dough and pressed it flat. "I'll leave the broth on the back burner to keep it warm. You can take some up to him before you turn in if you'd like."

"Thank you, Winnie."

Eliza filled a cup with water from the pitcher and stood at the worktable while Winnie worked. The kitchen was quiet except for the soft rhythm of kneading and the tick of the cookstove as the fire settled lower in its firebox. Eliza thought about the past few days since her arrival and realized she was starting to settle in, and little by little she was becoming familiar with the rhythms of the boardinghouse. She knew which burner ran hotter on the stove, which drawer stuck if you didn't lift the handle, where Leora kept the good knives, and where she kept the everyday ones. She knew the fourth stair from the top creaked on the left side but not the right when she climbed the stairs to the second floor. Furthermore, she knew the front door latch needed lifting and pulling at the same time, or it wouldn't catch. She'd been in Providence Ridge for six days now, and the boardinghouse had closed around her the way a book closes around a pressed flower, gently and completely, until the flower forgets it was ever anywhere else.

She finished her water, washed the cup, and set it on the shelf.

"I'm going to check on him once more," she said. "Then I will check in on Aunt Leora and visit with her for a while."

"I'm going to finish up here, then retire to my room."

Eliza climbed the stairs to the second floor. The hallway was fully dark, and she moved through it by memory, counting doors with her hand trailing the wall. At Mr. Drumond's room she stopped and listened. Through the door she could hear his breathing, slow and heavy, with a rasp at the bottom of each exhale. She opened his door quietly, crossed to the washstand, wrung out a fresh cloth in the basin, and replaced the warm one on his forehead. He stirred, but didn't wake. The cup of broth on his bedside table was empty. She set the cup on the tray and picked it up to take to the kitchen.

She stood in his doorway and listened to three full breaths before pulling the door closed. The rasp caught low in each one, the sound of lungs working harder than they needed to. She'd heard that sound before, at the hospital, in patients who fought off a fever inside a week and sat up asking for breakfast. She'd also heard it in the ones who didn't recover. Eliza pulled his door shut and sent up a silent prayer as she descended the stairs.

Chapter 11

The second floor of the boardinghouse was dim, the single window at the far end of the hallway threw a narrow band of early morning light across the floorboards as Eliza led Samuel to Mr. Drumond's room.

"Mr. Drumond? Dr. Porter is here to see you,dim;" Eliza said after knocking on his door.

A voice, thick and slow, responded, "Come in."

She opened the door and stepped aside for Samuel to enter first. The room was warm despite the open window, carrying the stale smell of a body that had been sweating. Mr. Drumond lay with his head propped up on two pillows. His face carried the same uneven flush, high color across his cheeks and forehead, while the skin around his mouth and along his jaw had gone the color of old candle wax. His eyes were slow to find Samuel when he came to the bedside.

"Mr. Drumond, I'm Dr. Porter. How are you feeling this morning?"

"Tired... my head's bad off, doc," the sound of his voice came out dry and used up, as if the word had to travel a long way to reach his mouth.

Samuel set his bag on the writing desk, opened the clasp, and took out his stethoscope. "I'm going to listen to your chest and take a look at you. Try to stay relaxed."

He placed the bell-shaped head of the device against Mr. Drumond's chest. His lungs sounded clear in the upper lobes, but lower, near the base of each lung, a faint rasp surfaced on the exhale. Not fluid. Not the wet, heavy congestion that came with pneumonia. More like the dry, labored sound of a body running hard against a fever and wearing itself thin from the effort.

He folded the stethoscope and returned it to his bag. He pressed the back of his hand against Mr. Drumond's forehead and felt the heat radiating from the man.

"I'm going to press on your stomach," he said. "Tell me where it hurts."

He laid his hands flat against Mr. Drumond's abdomen, beginning high and working down with slow, even pressure. The man winced when Samuel reached his lower right side, and the muscles underneath tightened in a guarding reflex that told Samuel more than words would have. He moved his hands to the left. Less reaction, but the whole abdomen felt tight, mildly swollen beneath his palms. He checked both sides once more, mapping where Mr. Drumond flinched and where he didn't.

He picked up Mr. Drumond's wrist and counted his pulse against his pocket watch. The count came in at sixty-two. Samuel counted it again. Sixty-two. A man burning through a fever should be running a pulse close to ninety or a hundred, his body spending itself to fight the heat. Sixty-two was the resting rate of a man sitting in a chair after supper with a newspaper in his lap, not a man whose skin was hot to the touch. The mismatch lodged itself in Samuel's thinking the way a wrong note lodges in a hymn he knows by heart.

"Mr. Drumond, when did the stomach trouble start?"

"Friday, I think. Maybe Thursday evening. I remember feeling off at supper Thursday, but I ate anyway. I think, at least. Then, I think by Friday, my gut was churning. No... no... my stomach hasn't been right for quite a few days, I think..."

"And the headache?"

"Saturday morning it was awful; I remember that for certain. Before that, it came and went."

"Any blood when you use the privy?"

"No, sir."

"Any rash? Spots on your chest or belly that weren't there before?"

Mr. Drumond looked down at himself. "I haven't noticed any."

Samuel unbuttoned his shirt enough to check his chest and abdomen. No spots. No rash. His skin was flushed and damp, but there was nothing on the surface beyond sweat.

"Have you traveled recently? Before you came to Providence Ridge?"

"I came from Helena about five weeks ago. Took the stage to Livingston and then a stage here."

"Any illness on the journey? Anyone sick on the stage or at the stops along the way?"

"Not that I recall."

"Is anyone sick at the lumber mill?"

"I don't believe so."

Samuel buttoned his shirt and straightened it. Eliza had moved to the washstand during the examination and was wringing out a fresh cloth in the basin. She placed it on Mr. Drumond's forehead, and he closed his eyes when the cool fabric touched his skin, and some of the tension in his face eased.

"Miss Miller, would you hand me that cup of water?"

She passed it to him. He held it for Mr. Drumond. "Drink as much of this as you can."

Mr. Drumond took the cup in both hands. The tremor was there, a fine shake in his fingers that steadied once he gripped tighter. He drank slowly, four or five swallows, and handed it back.

"Good," Samuel said. He set the cup on the tray and turned to Eliza. "Can we talk in the hall for a moment?"

"Mr. Drumond, we'll check on you a little later," she said. "Try to rest."

They stepped into the hallway, and Eliza pulled his door closed. From the floor below, Samuel could hear the boardinghouse in its Monday rhythm: dishes being stacked, a chair pushed back from the dining table, and general chatter among the boarders in the dining room.

"Tell me how he was through the night; what did you observe?" he asked.

"I checked on him four times after you and I spoke yesterday evening. Once before I retired to bed, and he was sleeping at that time. Again around ten o'clock, and he was sleeping but restless. His pillow was soaked through with sweat, and I turned it for him. I changed his cloth and left fresh water on his tray. At two he was awake. He'd gotten himself to the chamber pot on his own, which he was proud of, but it cost him. His legs were shaking when I found him trying to get back into bed. I got him settled and got half a cup of water into him and a few sips of broth I'd warmed on the stove. His breathing was worse at two than it was at ten. The raspy sound had deepened. His skin was hotter, but I couldn't tell you how much without a thermometer. Then I checked on him around four this morning, and he was thrashing around in his sleep. I changed the cloth on his head and sat with him until around six because his fever worried me. He was mumbling in his sleep when I left his room."

"Was he lucid at two?"

"He knew who I was. He asked what time it was and whether it was still Sunday. I told him it was early Monday morning, and he accepted that. He didn't ask me the same question twice."

Samuel leaned his shoulder against the hallway wall.

"You got up three times in the middle of the night to check on this man," he said. "You're running this boardinghouse, looking after your aunt, and now you're keeping night watches on a sick man. That's a pace that'll wear you thin before you know it's happened. Be sure you are getting your sleep in."

"I'm fine, Dr. Porter."

"You are. Today. But I've seen those who care for others run themselves ragged. If this continues with Mr. Drumond, perhaps Winnie can also check in on him as well as assist you in caring for your aunt."

"I'll speak with Winnie," she said. "Winnie typically stays here at the boardinghouse throughout the week. Sometimes on Friday and Saturday nights she returns to her family's home; she misses them so much."

"Please do talk to her and accept her help if she's willing."

"What do you think is wrong with Mr. Drumond?"

"His fever's been building for at least. His stomach's been off for several days. His abdomen is tender and swollen somewhat on the right side. His lungs are working harder than they should be. It could be a stomach complaint that's run him down, or a summer grippe that's settled in deeper than most."

"But?"

He looked at her. "No 'but' yet. There are things I want to watch for. How his fever behaves over the next day or two. Whether new symptoms show up. Whether he responds to rest and fluids. For now, we treat what we see and continue pushing fluids, cool cloths, rest, and fresh air. Light food if his stomach will take it, broth and bread. No heavy meals. If the fever breaks in the next day or two, this was a grippe, and he'll mend."

She accepted this without pushing. He'd given her the truth as far as it went, and he was sure she recognized that his honesty was in the edges of what he didn't say as much as in what he did. The pulse had been sixty-two beats per minute. The tenderness in Mr. Drumond's lower right abdomen had produced a guarding reflex. Those two details sat in Samuel's mind like stones he'd picked up on a trail, not knowing yet whether they were landmarks or loose gravel.

"I'd like to check on your aunt while I'm here," he said. "Then I need to walk over to the Cobb house and check on Ada."

"Could you keep me updated on how she's doing? Two people are unwell in this town, and I'd like to remain knowledgeable about what is going on with Mrs. Cobb as well, just in case."

"I will. And you'll send for me if Mr. Drumond changes. Anything at all. Don't wait."

"I won't."

"I'll come back before supper to check on him."

They went downstairs. Eliza led him through the hallway past the kitchen, where Winnie stood at the worktable chopping ingredients for the soup she planned to make for lunch today. She glanced up as they passed and gave Samuel a nod.

Leora was propped against her pillows with a book in her lap and a cup of tea on the table beside her when they walked in.

"Dr. Porter. Good morning," Leora said as she set her book aside.

"Good morning, Mrs. Hanscombe. How's your leg?"

"My leg is the same stubborn nuisance it was yesterday and the day before that. It hurts when I shift and itches when I don't, and it's made me entirely dependent on the goodwill of two young women who have better things to do than bring me tea and spare me a few moments of company."

Samuel set his bag on the chair and crouched beside her bed to examine her leg. The wound along her shin was healing well; the tissue pink and granulating clean.

"Your leg's coming along," he said. "The wound looks good. Eliza's kept the dressings clean, and the tissue's responding the way I'd hoped."

"She's been doing more than dressings. She's been running my boardinghouse, managing my kitchen, and sitting with me when the walls start closing in, and now I hear there's a sick man upstairs on top of everything else."

Samuel glanced at Eliza. She gave a small nod.

"What is wrong with Mr. Drumond?" Leora continued.

"He's running a fever, and his stomach's troubling him. I examined him this morning. It looks like a stomach complaint or the grippe. I've given Eliza instructions for his care, and I'll be back later today to check on him again."

"How bad is he?"

"He's uncomfortable, but he's lucid and he can drink. We're keeping fluids in him and managing his fever with cool cloths and fresh air."

Leora picked up her teacup and took a slow sip, watching her niece over the rim.

"One of my boarders is sick under my roof," she said. "This is my house, Dr. Porter. I need to know everything that is happening with this young man and if there's something I ought to be doing to help him."

"You're doing exactly what you should. You're healing, and you've got two capable women looking after your boarders and your kitchen. The best thing you can do for Mr. Drumond is let the people on their feet do the work you'd be doing if you could walk."

"That's a miserable answer."

"Yes, ma'am. But it's the right one."

She set her cup down. "How is Ada Cobb?"

"I'm heading over to check on her now. She's with child, and she's been feeling poorly."

"That poor girl. She can't be more than twenty."

"About that."

"You'll tell Eliza how she is after you've seen her?"

"I already said I would."

"Good," Leora said as she set her teacup aside. "Dr. Porter, I don't care for the fact that two people in this town are ailing in the same week. I know it's likely nothing. People get stomach complaints every summer, and it passes, and nobody thinks twice. But I've lived in Providence Ridge long enough to know that when two folks fall ill close together, a person pays attention."

"I'm paying attention, Mrs. Hanscombe."

"I know you are. That's the only reason I'm not fretting over this more." She picked up her book. "Go see about Ada. Eliza, walk the doctor out and then come sit with me for a little while. I've barely laid eyes on you this morning."

"I'll be right back, Aunt Leora."

Eliza walked Samuel to the front door and out onto the porch. The morning was already warm, the air carrying the dry smell of packed earth baking in the July sun. Across Main Street, Pemberton's Mercantile had its door propped open, and Samuel could see Amos moving behind his counter. A freight wagon sat near the livery at the south end of the street, its team standing with their heads drooping in the heat, and the ring of iron from Mica Hart's smithy carried clear and sharp up the road.

"I'll be back before supper," he said.

"We'll be here."

He stepped off the porch and stopped. "Miss Miller."

"Yes?"

"Talk to Winnie about helping you care for your aunt and Mr. Drumond."

"I said I would."

"I know you did. I'm saying it again because you're the kind of person who agrees to rest and then finds six more things that need doing before she gets around to it."

Color rose along her jaw and spread to her cheeks. She looked past him toward the street. "You're assuming things about me, Dr. Porter. I'll talk to her this morning after I visit with my aunt. Good day."

"Good day to you as well, Miss Miller."

He put his hat on and crossed Main Street toward his office. Inside, he set his bag on the examination table and opened it. He cleaned his stethoscope with a clean cloth and then selected a paper of willow bark powder and a small bottle of peppermint water that helped with stomach complaints in expectant mothers.

He closed his bag and stood at his desk with his hands flat on the wood, looking at the wall where his medical certificate hung in its plain frame. Mr. Drumond's pulse had come in at sixty-two. He'd counted it twice to be certain. A man running a fever should have a pulse hammering away at ninety or a hundred, the body spending everything it has to fight the heat. Sixty-two was a man at rest.

One detail. It didn't explain anything on its own. Summer grippes presented in all manner of ways, and a slow pulse in a feverish man could come from half a dozen causes that would clear in a few days or a week. He'd treated enough illnesses to know that most of what looked troubling on day three or day four looked ordinary by day seven.

But he'd trained himself years ago, in those small Colorado towns where he was the only doctor for a day's ride in any direction, to hold on to what didn't fit. Even when he couldn't say why it didn't fit. Even when the answer might turn out to be nothing whatsoever.

He picked up his bag, locked his office door behind him, and walked south along Main Street to the path that cut behind the west-side buildings. The dirt track narrowed as it left the road, angling through open ground toward the row of small houses set back from town. Ahead, the first house showed a lantern still hanging on its porch post from Friday night, unlit and forgotten.

Chapter 12

The boarders were halfway through supper when Samuel came through the front door. Eliza saw him from the far end of the dining room, where she stood refilling the water pitcher at the sideboard. She set it down and walked toward him.

"Dr. Porter."

"Miss Miller." He hung his hat on the peg beside the door.

"Mr. Drumond hasn't improved. His fever's been creeping slowly since you left this morning, and he couldn't keep down the broth Winnie brought him just an hour ago."

"Let's go up."

She led him through the dining room, past the kitchen doorway, where Winnie glanced up from the worktable and gave a quick nod. They took the stairs to the second floor, and the air thickened with each step; the July heat collected under the roof and pressed down through the hallway.

Eliza knocked. "Mr. Drumond? Dr. Porter is here to see you again."

No answer.

She knocked once more, and a sound came from inside, low and formless, closer to a groan than a word.

She opened the door. His window was propped open as she'd left it, but the room still held the thick, sour smell of a body wringing itself out against a fever it couldn't break. Mr. Drumond lay flat on his back with both arms at his sides, his pillow soaked through, his shirt unbuttoned to the middle of his chest. His eyes were closed. The cloth she'd placed on his forehead a little over an hour ago had slid off and lay wadded beside his neck.

"Mr. Drumond," Samuel said. "Can you hear me?"

His eyes opened slowly. They found Samuel but didn't hold, drifting toward the wall and then back.

"Doc."

"How are you feeling?"

"Tired." His voice was thin, dried out, and hollow. "What time is it?"

"Just past six. Monday evening."

"Didn't you come this morning?"

"I did. I'm checking on you again."

"Oh." He blinked, the frown sitting on his face as though the information couldn't find a place to land.

Samuel pulled the chair to the bedside and took Mr. Drumond's wrist, his pocket watch in his other hand. Eliza watched his lips move faintly as the seconds passed. He counted, paused, and counted a second time. Then he set Mr. Drumond's wrist down with care and put the watch away.

"I'm going to listen to your chest," he said.

He drew the stethoscope from his bag and placed it against Mr. Drumond's chest. Eliza moved to the washstand and wrung out a fresh cloth in the basin. She folded the cloth and brought it to the bedside, waiting while Samuel listened.

He moved the stethoscope to Mr. Drumond's back and asked him to breathe deeply. Mr. Drumond tried. The effort produced a rasp on each exhale, coarser than it had been that morning.

Samuel folded his stethoscope. "I need to check your stomach again. And your chest."

He unbuttoned Mr. Drumond's shirt the rest of the way and laid it open. Eliza stepped closer with the cloth in her hand, ready to place it on his forehead, and stopped.

On Mr. Drumond's upper abdomen, just below his ribs, four small spots showed faint against his flushed skin. They were the color of salmon left too long on a plate, barely distinguishable, and if the light from the open window hadn't fallen across his body at the angle it did, she might have missed them.

Samuel pressed his fingertip against one of the spots. The color disappeared under the pressure and returned when he lifted his finger. He pressed a second one. The same. He checked the rest of Mr. Drumond's chest and found nothing else, then pressed his abdomen with the flat of his hands the way he had that morning. Mr. Drumond winced and pulled his knees up when Samuel reached his lower right side. The guarding was worse than it had been eight hours ago.

Eliza placed the cool cloth on Mr. Drumond's forehead and buttoned his shirt while Samuel wrote in the small notebook he'd taken from his bag.

"Mr. Drumond, try to drink some water for me," Samuel said. He held the cup while the man managed three swallows. Most of the water ran down his chin, and Eliza blotted it with the edge of the cloth.

"Rest now," Samuel said. "We'll be right outside."

Mr. Drumond's eyes had already closed.

They stepped into the hallway, and she pulled the door shut.

Samuel leaned against the wall with his notebook still in his hand.

"His pulse is sixty-four," he said. "His fever's higher than this morning. His lungs are worse. The right side of his abdomen is more distended, and his guarding reflex is stronger." He looked at her. "And you saw the spots."

"I did."

"What did they look like to you?"

"Rose spots," she said. "Four of them, salmon-colored, flat, blanching under pressure." She kept her voice level, reporting the way she'd been trained to report at the auxiliary when the supervising physician asked what she'd observed. "I saw cases in Philadelphia. The spots appeared in the late first week or early second week on the trunk. The patients who showed them ran a particular fever pattern. It didn't spike and break the way scarlet fever or influenza did. It climbed in steps, higher each day, and their pulses ran slow against the heat."

Samuel held her eyes for a long moment. What she read in his face wasn't surprise. It was the expression of a man who'd been carrying medical knowledge alone and had just found someone standing beside him who understood what he did.

"Typhoid," he said.

The word filled the hallway the way cold water fills a glass, settling heavily and still. She'd been turning the thought over in her mind since that morning, since she'd watched him count Mr. Drumond's pulse twice and then stand at the bedside with an expression that didn't belong to a simple grippe. She'd spent months at a hospital where typhoid moved through the wards often, claiming beds as fast as the nurses could strip and remake them. She knew the stepladder fever. She knew the slow pulse. She knew what rose spots meant, and she knew what followed them.

"How far along do you think he is?" she asked.

"If his symptoms started earlier than he's told us, and I believe they did, he could be seven or eight days in. The spots showing now fit that timeline. He was likely feeling poorly before Thursday and didn't pay it any mind."

"At the auxiliary, patients in the second week developed abdominal distension and tenderness. Some became delirious. The worst cases had intestinal complications early in the third week."

"That matches what I've seen." He closed his notebook and slid it into his vest pocket.

"What can we do for him that we aren't already doing?"

"Not much if it is typhoid; I'm sure you are aware of that. Fluids, constantly. Cool cloths for his fever. Keep his room ventilated. Light food only if his stomach will take it; don't force it if it won't. Watch his abdomen for any sudden rigidity or hardness that wasn't there before. And if his fever spikes or he becomes too confused to know where he is, send for me. Day or night." He rubbed the back of his neck. "There's no medicine that cures this, Miss Miller. We manage his symptoms and hope his body will fight this off."

"Dr. Porter, Winnie made venison stew this evening, and there's plenty. Stay and have supper."

He looked down the hallway toward the stairs, and she could see him weighing her offer against the habit of crossing Main Street to his rooms above his office and eating alone at his table.

"I'd be glad to," he said. "On the condition that you sit down and eat with me. You've been on your feet all day, I assume, and I'd guess you haven't had a proper meal since breakfast."

She hadn't. Half a biscuit at breakfast, a few bites of bread at noon, standing at the kitchen worktable. The rest of the day had gone to Mr. Drumond, to Leora, to the boarders, and to the steady work that didn't pause because a man upstairs was burning through a fever he couldn't shake.

"I will," she said. "We should discuss Mr. Drumond's care more fully, and I want to hear about Mrs. Cobb."

"Then we'll talk over supper."

They went downstairs. She asked Samuel to find a seat in the dining room and walked into the kitchen, where Winnie was wiping down the worktable with long, efficient strokes. The stewpot sat on the back of the cookstove, and the bread Winnie had baked that morning was wrapped in cloth on the shelf above the flour bin.

"I need two bowls of venison stew," Eliza said. She took a tray from the shelf and set it on the worktable. "And would you bring coffee out for us? Dr. Porter is staying for supper."

Winnie set her rag down. "Oh... this is new. He never comes for supper."

"We need to discuss Mr. Drumond's condition."

"Of course. I'll bring coffee to you both with two mugs shortly. You want cream?"

"Just the coffee. Thank you."

Eliza ladled stew into two bowls, thick with venison and potatoes, and carrots. She sliced bread from the loaf, arranged it on a small plate beside the butter crock and the jar of blackberry preserves from the pantry shelf, and set silverware and cloth napkins on the tray.

"Is Mr. Drumond worse?" Winnie asked.

Eliza set the tray down. "His fever's still climbing, and he's more confused than he was this morning. He's showing signs of a more serious illness than before. Colored spots on his abdomen. Dr. Porter intends to watch him closely."

"Should I be worried?"

"I think we should be careful." She met Winnie's eyes. "And if Aunt Leora asks you about him, don't provide her more information than she needs right now. I'm not asking you to lie. Just don't alarm her until we're more certain."

"I won't say more than the fever hasn't broken and the doctor's tending to him."

"That's enough for now."

She picked up the tray and carried it through to the dining room. The long table had been cleared at the far end, and Samuel sat in one of the chairs near the window with his medical bag on the floor beside him. Two boarders lingered at the opposite end over their coffee cups, their voices low, talking about timbering a large section of the woods next week for the lumber mill in which they worked. Through the open windows, the evening carried the dry heat of a

July day that hadn't yet surrendered to the cooler air coming down off the mountains.

She set a bowl in front of Samuel and another at the place across from him. The bread and butter went between them. She laid out the silverware and napkins. Winnie came through a moment later with the coffee pot and two mugs. She set them on the table and went back to the kitchen without a word.

Samuel picked up his spoon and tried the stew.

"Winnie is a fine cook," he said.

"She is. I've told her so, and she doesn't believe me. She thinks her sister's stew is better."

"Is it?"

"I haven't had it... in fact, I haven't even met any of her family yet. But Winnie's stew could hold its own against mine. I use my mother's recipe, and it's quite good as well."

He took another bite and set his spoon down. The two boarders at the far end pushed their chairs back and headed for the stairs.

"Tell me about Ada Cobb," Eliza said.

"Her nausea has increased, and the fatigue is deeper. She was in bed when I arrived this morning, and Jasper said she'd barely moved throughout the night. Her fever's still low, but it's persistent. Four days now, and it hasn't broken."

"Is it higher than Friday?"

"Slightly. Not by much, but the direction is wrong. In a healthy pregnancy at two months, a mild fever from overexertion or a stomach complaint should've resolved by now with rest and fluids."

"What about her appetite?"

"Jasper's been trying to get her to eat. She managed some broth and a few bites of bread yesterday, but this morning she couldn't keep the broth down."

Eliza spread butter across a piece of bread and ate slowly while she thought. At the fever hospital, the physicians had drilled into her the habit of watching for patterns across patients, not just within a single case. One sick man with a climbing fever and abdominal tenderness could be half a dozen things. Two patients worsening on nearly the same timeline was a different question altogether.

"Has she had headaches?" she asked.

"She told me her head's been aching for some time… she couldn't remember when it began. She assumed it was the pregnancy."

"And the stomach pain. When did that start?"

"Jasper thinks she first mentioned it Wednesday or Thursday of last week. She didn't make much of it. She thought it was the baby making her sick."

"So her symptoms and Mr. Drumond's started within a day or two of each other, possibly."

Samuel picked up his coffee mug and held it without drinking. He looked at her across the table.

"I assume so, yes," he said.

"Dr. Porter, at the auxiliary I assisted with intake assessments at times. The supervising physicians taught us to track onset dates across every patient on the ward and to map them against each other. When two or more patients presented with the same progression inside the same window, we treated it as a possible common source until we could rule it out."

"That's good training."

"It's what I'm thinking about right now." She set her bread down. "Mr. Drumond has a stepladder fever, a slow pulse, abdominal distension, and rose spots. Mrs. Cobb has a persistent low fever, nausea, fatigue, headache, and stomach pain that started within days of his, possibly. She's earlier in the course if it's the same illness, and she's smaller than Mr. Drumond by half. She's carrying a child. Her body has less to draw on."

"I know." He drank from his mug and set it down.

"Have you checked her for spots?"

"She showed none this morning. Friday night I was looking at a young expectant mother with what seemed like pregnancy complications. This morning I was still thinking along those lines, though her symptoms were troubling me."

The dining room had emptied except for the two of them. Eliza finished her stew and tore another piece of bread from her slice.

"This is the first time I've sat at this table," she said. "Normally I take my lunch with my aunt in her room; otherwise, I eat standing in the kitchen with Winnie. This is rather nice, sitting here in the dining room."

He wrapped his hands around his coffee mug. "Miss Miller, what did you do with your time in Philadelphia? Before you came west."

The question surprised her.

"I managed my father's household," she said. "The household fell to me after my mother passed, and I've run it for six years." She took a sip of her coffee. "I also volunteer with the Ladies' Benevolent Society as often as I can, visiting the sick in their homes. And the fever hospital auxiliary, of course."

"That's a full life."

"It's a busy life. There's a difference, though I didn't always know which one I was living."

"Does your father manage well without you?" he asked.

"He's never been without me. This is the first time I've been away from home, and I haven't received a letter from him yet. I assume I may receive word from him by next week."

"A man on his own tends to do okay... in time, I suppose."

"You are on your own; you seem fine... so I'll just assume my father will be okay as well. He may stumble for some time, but I'm sure instinct will kick in."

He glanced up, and the corner of his mouth twitched. "I'm sure it will. Since I've been on my own, I've graduated from bread and cheese to bread and whatever my cookstove doesn't ruin."

"You told me the other evening you're a better physician than you are a cook."

"I'll be honest... that's a low bar, Miss Miller. I'm a better physician than most things."

She smiled, and he looked down at his coffee.

"Will your father be expecting you home before winter?" he asked.

"He expects me to stay as long as Aunt Leora needs me," she said. "He didn't put a limit on it. My father trusts me to know when the work here is finished."

"And when do you think that'll be?"

"I don't know for certain. In my mind, I'm assuming I'll probably return home no later than the end of September to avoid incoming snow. That is... as long as my aunt is on her feet and managing well by then."

He looked up at her as she picked up her mug.

"More coffee?" she asked.

"No, thank you."

"I'll clear our supper dishes then."

She stood and stacked the bowls on the tray. Samuel pushed his chair back and picked up his medical bag. Eliza lifted the tray and turned toward the kitchen as the front door opened and Jasper Cobb appeared in the dining room doorway. He was hatless, his shirt dark with sweat at his collar, and his face carried the color of a man who'd been running. His eyes found Samuel across the room, and he crossed the floor in four strides.

"Doc." His voice was strained and barely held. "Can you come? Ada's taken a turn. She can't keep anything down, and she's burning up worse than before. Please, I don't know what to do for her."

His hands were shaking. His eyes were red, and the surrounding skin was drawn tight with worry.

"Let's go."

Eliza set the tray back on the table. She looked at Jasper's face, at the terror written plain across it, and she looked at Samuel.

"I'm coming with you," she said.

Chapter 13

Jasper pushed the door open ahead of them, and Samuel stepped through into the single room he'd been visiting since Friday. A cookstove sat against the left wall with its stovepipe running up through the roof boards. A table built from rough lumber held a basin, a tin plate, and a cup. A cotton curtain had been nailed across the corner nearest the stove to serve as a pantry. Against the far wall, Ada lay in a bed frame strung with rope and held a straw-tick mattress.

On Friday evening she'd been sitting up when he arrived, pale and tired but alert enough to answer his questions and describe her symptoms in full sentences. This morning she'd been lying down but tracking him with her eyes, following his voice, and managing a few words between bouts of nausea. Now she lay flat on her back with one arm across her stomach and the other at her side, her dark hair loose against a pillow. Her skin carried the mottled flush of a body spending itself against heat it couldn't bring down. Her eyes opened when Jasper said her name, but didn't stay open.

"Ada," Samuel said as he pulled the chair to her bedside and sat. "Can you tell me how you're feeling right now?"

"Tired. My head hurts. My stomach won't settle." She swallowed. "I can't keep water down."

"When did the vomiting start today?"

"This evening."

Samuel pressed the back of his hand to her forehead. Hotter than this morning. He drew his stethoscope from his bag and placed the bell against her chest. Her heartbeat was strong but slow. He counted against his pocket watch. Fifty-eight. He counted again. Fifty-eight beats per minute in a woman whose fever should've been driving her pulse well above ninety.

"I need to listen to your back," he said. "Miss Miller, would you help Mrs. Cobb sit forward?"

Eliza crossed to the bed and sat on its edge, placing one hand behind Ada's shoulders and easing her upright. Ada leaned on her arm, and the effort of sitting drew a low sound from her, more weariness than pain. Samuel placed the stethoscope against Ada's back and asked her to breathe. She tried. Her lungs sounded cleaner than Drumond's, no rasp on the exhale, but her breathing was shallow and quick, a body that didn't have the strength for anything deeper.

"Good," he said. "You can lie back."

Eliza lowered her gently. Ada's head settled into the pillow, and her eyes closed.

"Mrs. Cobb, I need to check your stomach. I'm going to press on your abdomen, and I need you to tell me where it hurts."

She nodded without opening her eyes. Samuel laid his hands flat against her upper abdomen and pressed with even, measured pressure, working down the way he'd done with Drumond. Ada flinched when he reached her lower right side. Her muscles tightened, and she pulled her knees toward her chest.

He pressed her left side. Less reaction, but the tenderness was there. He moved back to her right side and pressed again, lighter. The guarding came again, involuntarily.

He unbuttoned the top of Ada's nightgown enough to see her upper chest and lifted the fabric over her abdomen. Her skin was flushed from the fever, pink and warm, but clean. No spots. No rash. He checked both sides of her body. Nothing.

He buttoned her nightgown and drew the sheet back over her.

"Her fever's higher than this morning," he said to Jasper. "And she isn't keeping fluids down, which concerns me more than anything else right now. Her body needs water."

Jasper stood with his hat in his hands, turning it by the brim. "Is it the baby making her this sick?"

"The pregnancy makes it harder, yes. But the fever and the stomach tenderness go beyond what I'd expect from pregnancy alone. She's fighting an illness, and the pregnancy is making that fight harder for her body."

"What illness?"

"I'm not ready to name it yet. I need to watch how her fever behaves." He met Jasper's eyes. "I need to change one of my instructions from this morning. This is important."

"Tell me."

"Boil all her drinking water. Every drop. Don't give her water straight from the pail anymore. Boil it first and let it cool before she drinks it."

"All right."

"Everything else stays the same. Bed rest. Cool cloths. Small sips of broth, a few spoonfuls at a time, not a full cup. I'll keep coming twice a day. If her fever spikes suddenly or she can't be roused, come get me."

"I will."

Eliza had moved to the washstand. She wrung out a cloth in the basin, folded it, and brought it to Ada's forehead. She looked so small and fragile. Eighteen years old, two months pregnant, and lying in a bed in a one-room house at the edge of a town that didn't have a hospital or a telegraph.

Three years ago, in a cabin outside Trinidad, Colorado, he'd stood in a room not much bigger than this one. Ruth had been in bed, and his brother Caleb had been standing nearby.

Samuel closed his bag and dismissed the thoughts of Colorado rising in his mind.

"Mr. Cobb, one more thing. Is there anyone else nearby who's been feeling unwell?"

"My neighbor, actually. Mr. Thompson, the next house over. Name's Zeb. He came to our door yesterday and asked if I could fetch him a pail of water from the well. He said he wasn't sure he had the strength to walk down and draw it himself. He's an older fellar who lives alone."

Samuel looked at Eliza. She'd gone still near Ada's bedside, her hand resting flat on the sheet.

"Did he say what was wrong?" Samuel asked.

"Just that he felt poorly. I asked if he wanted me to send for you, but he said he'd be fine with a night's rest." Jasper shifted his weight. "This evening I checked on him, and he was worse. In bed. Hot to the touch. I couldn't get him to drink not a single drop. I brought him another fresh pail of water and put a damp cloth on his forehead."

"How long ago?"

"A couple of hours, I'd say."

Samuel picked up his bag. "We're going to look in on him."

They stepped outside. What remained of the evening had settled into the valley while they'd been inside; the last band of light behind the Gallatin ridgeline gone to a thin yellow line below clouds that were already blending into the dark above them. The air had dropped ten degrees since they'd left the boardinghouse, the way July evenings did at this elevation, the day's heat lifting off the valley floor as soon as the sun dropped behind the western range.

The row of homes stretched south along the wagon road, six structures set close to the ground, each built from the same milled lumber in the same plain design. A tiny porch with a single step. A plank door and a single window on each side of the home. The Cobb home sat at the north end of the row houses, behind Main Street's west-side buildings. The next home was twenty feet south, its windows dark.

Samuel knocked on Zeb Thompson's door.

No answer.

He knocked again and pressed his ear to the door.

"Mr. Thompson," he called. "I'm Dr. Porter. I'm coming in."

The room was the same size and shape as the Cobbs', but where theirs had held the signs of two people starting a life, this one belonged to a man who'd been living alone a long time. A coat hung on a nail beside the door. A pipe sat on the table next to a well-used Bible. A pair of boots stood beneath the chair.

Each window was shut. The room smelled sour with the smell of unwashed bedclothes and a body writhing with a fever, with no one to change the linens. Samuel crossed to the nearest window and shoved the sash up. Eliza went to the other, on the south wall and did the same. A cross breeze found its way between the two openings, and the worst of the air began to move.

Zeb Thompson lay with his blanket pulled to his chin despite the heat. He was older than Samuel had pictured, perhaps sixty or more, with thin white hair flat against his skull and a deep flush across his face. His eyes were shut. His breathing carried the labor of a body working against something it didn't have the reserves to fight, each exhale audible.

"Mr. Thompson." Samuel set his bag on the table and moved to the bed. "Can you hear me?"

His eyes opened. Pale, watery, confused.

"Who's that?"

"Dr. Porter. The town doctor. Jasper Cobb told me you weren't feeling well, and I've come to check on you."

"I didn't send for a doctor."

"I know. I'm here anyway."

Zeb looked past Samuel's shoulder to where Eliza stood near the foot of the bed. "Who's she?"

"Miss Miller. She's a nurse. She's helping me tonight."

"A nurse?"

"Mr. Thompson, when did you start feeling poorly?"

"Thursday, maybe. Friday... I don't recall. I had a headache the other day, and it laid me flat. Thought it'd pass."

"Has it?"

"Does it look like it's passed?"

The irritation was a good sign. A man who could muster annoyance wasn't as far gone as Samuel had feared. "I need to check you over. I'm going to feel your forehead and take your pulse."

Zeb's skin was hot, hotter than Ada's, and his pulse counted at sixty.

"I'm going to press on your stomach," he said. "Tell me if anything hurts."

He pulled the blanket down and laid his hands on Zeb's abdomen. The man winced on his right side but didn't guard the way Drumond and Ada had. The tenderness was early and diffuse, without the focused distension he'd found in the other two. He checked Zeb's chest and stomach for spots. Clean skin beneath the fever's flush.

He pulled the blanket back up and looked at the water pail on the floor beside the bed. Full to the brim. Untouched. A tin cup beside it, dry.

He looked at Eliza, and she walked to the bedside and lifted Zeb's head enough to turn his pillow to the dry side.

"Mr. Thompson, I'm going to bring you some broth from the boardinghouse," she said. "It'll give your body what it needs. Do not drink water from that pail. When I return, I need to boil it first, and then you can use it for drinking water. Understood?"

"You don't have to trouble yourself."

"It's no trouble."

She wrung out a cloth from his washstand basin, folded it, and placed it on his forehead. His eyes closed.

"Try to rest," she said. "Leave those windows open. The air will help you."

They stepped outside. Jasper was waiting on the path between the two homes, his arms folded.

"How is he?" Jasper asked.

"Running a high fever as well. I've opened his windows, and Miss Miller's bringing him broth shortly. Can you look in on him until she returns?"

"I've been doing that already. I'll keep at it."

"Good man. Go be with your wife for now and check on Zeb in about ten minutes. We've left his windows open, so if you prefer not to walk into his home, listen at the window if you could for signs of struggling to breathe."

Jasper nodded and went inside his home.

Samuel and Eliza walked north along the wagon road toward town. There were no streetlamps and no lanterns marking the doorways. Just the packed earth under their feet, the cooling air, and the moon providing just enough light to see where they were going.

Three patients. Mr. Drumond upstairs at the boardinghouse. Ada Cobb in the first house. Zeb Thompson in the second. Three people, each of a different age, a different body build, and fairly close in the timeline of possible infection.

"I'll go back to Zeb immediately with broth. Is there anything else you'd like me to do for him?" Eliza asked.

"Now, the broth will be enough, and remember to boil his pail of water. Eliza, don't walk back to his home alone. It's late."

"I've walked alone in Philadelphia at later hours than this."

"Philadelphia has streetlamps and constables on every corner. Providence Ridge has neither."

"I'll ask Winnie to walk with me, but Dr. Porter, I have no fear here. I feel quite safe in this town."

They reached the edge of Main Street, and the boardinghouse stood ahead of them, its ground-floor windows lit. Samuel's office was across the road, dark.

Eliza stopped and turned to look back the way they'd come, toward the row of homes along the wagon road barely visible now. The Cobb home still had the lantern lit on the front porch and a faint light showing from inside. Zeb's home was lit faintly by lantern as well. Beyond those two homes, four more sat spaced along the road, each one a shape without a window showing light. No lamps. No movement. Four dark homes, and it wasn't even nine o'clock on a July evening.

"Dr. Porter, the other four homes. Are they all occupied?"

"To my knowledge. I've been told people live in all six. In fact, Edith Aldridge resides in one of them. The last home, I believe."

"They're all dark except for the Cobbs' home and Zeb Thompson's."

"It's late. They could be sleeping."

"All four of them at nine in the evening?" She was quiet for a moment, looking at those houses.

"Tomorrow morning," he said. "After I check on Ada and Mr. Thompson, I'll check the rest of those homes."

"And I shall come with you."

He looked at her. She stood at the edge of the road with her arms at her sides, her face turned half toward him and half toward those dark houses. What he could read in the set of her mouth and the stillness of her hands wasn't fear. It was the same expression he'd seen on the faces of the senior physicians at the hospitals he'd trained in when they recognized the shape of what was coming before anyone else in the room could name it.

"I'd be glad of it," he said.

At the boardinghouse steps, Eliza paused with one hand on the porch railing.

"The well," she said. "Zeb and the Cobbs draw water from the same well as does the boardinghouse."

"I know."

"We could be wrong about what we're both assuming, but we could be correct. We need to spread the word and tell people to boil their water."

He nodded. "Marshall Callahan's office still has a light shining from it. That's where I'm headed next," he said.

"I'm going to speak with Winnie and Aunt Leora and tell them what we suspect. Be safe, Dr. Porter."

"You as well, Miss Miller."

Chapter 14

Two Days Later...

Leora's bedroom hadn't been built to hold several people at the same time. That was plain enough from the way the chairs crowded against one another at the foot of the bed, borrowed from the dining room. Marshal Tom Callahan stood against the wall near the window with his arms crossed and his hat pushed back. Winnie had pulled the straight-backed chair from Leora's writing desk to the doorway, where she sat with her spine straight and her hands folded.

Eliza stood beside the washstand, close enough to her aunt's bed to pass a cup of water if it was needed. Samuel stood at the foot of the bed with his notebook open in his hand. She'd watched him fill those pages over the past two days—at kitchen tables and bedsides and once on the Cobbs' front step—his handwriting small and deliberate, each entry a name and a date and a list of symptoms that grew longer every time he opened the cover.

Reverend Webb Hale sat in the chair nearest Leora's head-board, his Bible resting closed on his knee. Beside him, Eunice had claimed a stool Eliza had taken to using when changing her aunt's dressings. Edith Aldridge sat in a chair between Eunice and the door, a shawl drawn over her shoulders despite the July warmth, her hands resting in her lap.

"Webb," Leora said from her pillow. "Would you lead us in prayer before we begin?"

Webb bowed his head, and everyone in the room followed.

"Lord, we come to You this morning with heavy hearts and uncertain days ahead. We ask for wisdom where we lack it and strength where ours falls short. Steady the hands that will do this work. Clear the minds that must make decisions for people who can't make them for themselves. Remind us, Father, that You are present in the sickrooms as surely as You are in the sanctuary. We trust You with what we can't see. Amen."

Samuel opened his notebook.

"As of this morning, I've confirmed illness in at least twelve people in Providence Ridge." He let the number land before he continued. "Four boarders upstairs in this building, which includes Mr. Drumond, who has been ill the longest and is the most seriously affected. Ada Cobb and Zeb Thompson are in the first two row houses. A young couple, Nolan and Clara Fitch, in the fourth house. Emmett Sloane in the fifth. Jessie Wicks, who lives above the saloon he owns. His waitress, Miss Pardee, who lives out on Culver Road by herself. And Peter Hart, Mica's brother, who lives with him behind the blacksmith shop."

"I want to be direct about what I believe we're dealing with and equally direct about what I can't prove." He looked at each person in turn, unhurried, giving each of them a moment for the information to sink in before he proceeded. "The pattern of illness across these patients is consistent with typhoid fever. The fever climbs in steps over several days rather than spiking and breaking the way influenza or scarlet fever would. The person's pulse runs slow against high temperatures, which is the opposite of what a body normally does when fighting illness. Several patients show abdominal distension and tenderness, particularly on the right side. And Mr. Drumond has developed rose-colored spots on his body that, in my training and experience, are associated with this particular illness."

He closed his notebook and held it against his leg. "I can't confirm this with certainty. There's no test I can administer. What I can tell you is that the pattern is consistent, the timeline fits, and Miss Miller has observed the same pattern independently, based on her experience at the fever hospital auxiliary in Philadelphia. Miss Miller... share with us your experiences."

"The fever hospital treated typhoid cases often," she said. She kept her voice level and her language plain. These weren't physicians. They were neighbors who needed to understand what was happening to people they loved, and precision mattered more than vocabulary. "I assisted with intake assessments and bedside care for patients presenting with the same progression Dr. Porter has described. The stepladder fever. The slow pulse running counter to high temperatures. The abdominal symptoms. The spots. I've seen numerous cases before, and what I've observed in the patients we visited the past few days matches what I saw in that ward."

The room was still. Eunice hadn't moved on her stool. Webb's face had gone grave. Tom Callahan's expression hadn't changed, but something in the set of his jaw had tightened—a lawman's jaw, already working three steps past the conversation.

"Explain how it spreads, Doc Porter," Tom said. "I want everyone to understand what you've told me already so they hear it straight from the horse's mouth, so to speak. Can a person who is not ill catch it from being near a sick person?"

"Thank you, Marshal Tom, for bringing that up," Samuel said. "This illness doesn't travel through the air the way some fevers do. It travels through contaminated water and through filth—soiled linens, waste, anything that carries contamination from a sick person into water or food that someone else consumes. A person caring for the ill isn't at risk from sitting at the same bedside, so long as they're careful. Hands must be washed with soap after tending to each patient. All drinking water needs to be boiled. Soiled bedding handled with care and laundered separately."

"Miss Miller," Tom said, turning to her. "Does that match what you saw in Philadelphia?"

"It does. The nurses at the auxiliary followed strict cleanliness measures, and the rate of illness among the nursing staff was low. The physicians I worked under believed the contamination traveled through water and waste, not the air we breathe. Clean hands and boiled water were the two things they insisted on above all others."

Tom nodded.

Eunice leaned forward on her stool. "Dr. Porter. Everyone in this room has been drinking water from that well. My daughter and her husband draw from it daily." She paused. "She's expecting her first child. Will everyone who has been drinking that water fall ill?"

"No," Samuel said. "Not everyone who drinks from a contaminated source develops the illness. Some sickened and some don't, and I cannot tell you why one person falls ill while another is spared. What I can tell you is that the risk increases the longer people continue drinking contaminated water. Which is why the well must be sealed right away and every drop of drinking water must be boiled from this moment forward, regardless of where you are getting it from, to be on the safe side. We believe the well behind this building is the source of the problem, but cannot be one hundred percent sure. We have nothing to test the water with."

"How long?" Webb asked. "How long does this sickness take to run its course?"

"Weeks, and it can vary. Patients who are going to recover will take two to four weeks from the onset of symptoms. Some will worsen extremely before they improve. The second and third weeks are the most dangerous, when the fever reaches its peak and the body is under the greatest strain." Samuel's voice didn't soften, but it slowed, and the slowing was its own form of honesty—a man making certain every word was heard. "Some patients may not recover. I won't stand here and tell you otherwise."

"Samuel, how bad could this get?" Leora asked.

"If there are people ill in this town that I don't yet know about—and I believe there may be—this could very well be the worst thing Providence Ridge has faced."

"Then tell us what you need and what we as a community need to do," she said.

Samuel looked at Eliza. In the look was the conversation they'd already had—last night in the kitchen, standing at the worktable with cups of coffee gone cold and the list of names spread between them, talking through what had to happen next and how to say it to a room full of people who trusted them to know. They'd planned this together and would stand together in their decision.

"Miss Miller and I are recommending that the sickest patients be moved to the boardinghouse dining room," he said. "Right now, the people who are ill are scattered across seven different locations—row houses, upstairs above the saloon, the blacksmith's home, and four here upstairs. I can't provide adequate care to patients in that many places, and neither can Miss Miller. Half our time is spent walking or riding between locations, and the other half is spent providing care that isn't as thorough as it should be because we're always needed somewhere else."

"Centralizing patients in one location allows Dr. Porter and me to monitor everyone under one roof," Eliza said. "The kitchen is right there, which gives us constant access to boiled water, broth, and clean supplies. Volunteers can work more efficiently in a single space than scattered across town. And if new patients present, they come to one place rather than adding another location we have to go to."

"You're asking for my dining room," Leora said.

"I am."

"You have it." Her aunt's voice carried no hesitation. "That room has served as a church and a meeting hall, and a place where this town gathers when gathering is what's needed. It will serve as a sick ward now. Winnie and Eliza, the boardinghouse is shut down immediately. We take on no new boarders until this illness is finished."

Winnie spoke from her chair by the door. "I'll manage the kitchen. Broth, boiled water, bread, tea—whatever's needed, for as long as it's needed. I'll stay here in my room that you've so kindly given me, Leora, the entire time and not return home until we see this thing through."

"You won't do it alone," Eunice said. She straightened on her stool, and Eliza watched something shift behind her eyes—the look of a woman whose mind had already moved past the crisis in front of her and into the logistics of meeting it. "I'll coordinate the women in this community who are willing and able to help. Laundry, linen, cooking, washing, and sitting with the ill through the night so Miss Miller and Dr. Porter can rest when they need to. We can read scripture to ease the patients' minds and give them a sense of peace. I'll have a rotation organized as fast as I can."

"I can help as well," Edith said. "I'm no nurse, but I can sit with patients, read to them, and keep them company. I can man a stove as well as any of you youngins, so I can be a relief cook. Whatever's useful."

Eliza looked at Edith. Her voice was steady, but her face was pale beneath the frame of her silver hair, and her shawl was wrapped tighter than the warmth of the room required. Eliza filed it away in her mind—the pallor, the shawl, the careful way Edith had lowered herself into her chair earlier—beside the other observations her training had taught her to collect without speaking.

"Thank you, Edith," she said. "Every pair of willing hands will matter."

Tom pushed off from the wall and stepped closer to the center of the room.

"I've got a recommendation of my own," he said. "I want to shut the town down. Block the bridge to the north and the south road past the mill. No travelers coming in, nobody going out, until Dr. Porter says the danger's passed."

The room shifted. Eliza could see the ripple of it—Winnie's hands pressing tighter in her lap, Webb's eyes moving to Eunice.

"It's a strong measure," Tom continued. "I know that. But we've got an illness moving through this town whose full scope we can't yet see. I won't have it carried to Tomblin or Sutton's Ridge because a traveler drank tainted water on his way through. And I won't have more people riding into Providence Ridge not knowing what's waiting. If there's any possibility that this could be something other than typhoid fever, by shutting down the town we take no chances whatsoever, and please, Doc Porter, I mean no ill thoughts against you... I trust you and your medical knowledge, but only God knows what we are up against."

"I agree," Samuel said.

"As do I," Eliza said.

Tom looked at Webb. The reverend's face was troubled in the way of a man who understood both what was being proposed and what it would cost the people it protected.

"My daughter lives here," Webb said. "She's carrying her first child, and she has been drinking from that well. I wouldn't ask anyone in this room to accept something I wouldn't accept for my own family. I support the marshal's recommendation."

"Leora?" Tom asked.

"Shut the town, Tom. Do what needs doing."

Tom took his hat from the windowsill and set it on his head. "Before we can move patients and seal the well, I need the town committee behind us. I'm calling a meeting tonight. Seven o'clock, my office next door. I'll ride out this morning and tell Owen

Gallagher and anyone else I can reach. I'll speak with Amos and Margaret as well."

"The sooner that meeting happens, the better," Samuel said. "Every hour that well stays open is another hour someone could drink from it."

"Then I'd best be riding. I'll see every one of you tonight," he said, and then turned and left the room.

Webb rose and laid his hand on Leora's shoulder. "I'm going to sit with any of your ill boarders who'd welcome the company. And I'll pray with anyone who asks, is that all right with you?"

"Yes, please do so," Leora said.

Webb took his Bible and went.

Eunice crossed to Winnie, and within seconds the two of them were talking in low, rapid voices—kettles, linen stores, and how many pails of water the boardinghouse stove could boil at once. Eunice produced a pencil from her apron pocket and began writing on the back of an envelope she'd pulled from somewhere Eliza couldn't account for. The woman operated like a supply depot of opinions, and at this moment Eliza could have kissed her for it.

Edith excused herself. She said she'd check the linen stores in the hallway closet and then start washing the soiled linens. She rose with one hand on the arm of her chair, her movements careful and measured, and left the room. Eliza watched her go and said nothing.

Samuel slid his notebook into his vest pocket, picked up his bag, and looked at her.

"I need to check on Mr. Drumond before the others. His fever's extremely high... I'm concerned."

"I'll come. I want to assess the other three boarders upstairs and see how they are as well."

They moved toward the door.

"Eliza."

She turned. Her aunt was watching her with an expression that held neither worry nor instruction—the expression of a woman seeing someone she loved walk into something large and finding in that person what was needed to bear it.

"Yes, Aunt Leora?"

"You and Dr. Porter will see to this. I know you will. I will pray like you've never seen a soul pray before. Whatever I can do to help from this bed, bring it to me and I'll see it's done.

"We'll do everything we can, Aunt Leora. Your prayers can do the most at the moment."

"God be with us all."

Samuel was already in the hallway. Eliza pulled Leora's door shut and followed. She could hear Eunice and Winnie still talking behind the closed door, their voices a low, efficient murmur.

At the foot of the stairs, Samuel stopped. He set his bag on the bottom step and pressed his thumb against the bridge of his nose—a gesture she'd come to recognize the way she recognized the fourth stair's creak or the kitchen drawer that stuck. He dropped his hand and looked at her.

"What you told them in there needed saying," he said. "About the auxiliary. The pattern. They needed to hear it from someone who'd seen it, not just from a doctor telling them what he suspects."

"They needed the truth. That's all I gave them."

"That's what I mean. I appreciate you more than you know. I believe God brought you here for a reason, and that reason was far beyond maintaining a boardinghouse while your aunt is down in bed."

He held her eyes a moment longer than the words required, and something in his expression shifted—a softening at the edges that wasn't professional and wasn't practiced and disappeared before she could be certain she'd seen it at all. Then he picked up his bag, and the moment closed like a book returning to its shelf. She took the railing and climbed the stairs behind him. The slow, labored breathing of people whose bodies were spending everything they had fighting a serious illness could be heard throughout the entire hallway.

She had heard those sounds in Philadelphia. She'd heard them in wards where the windows stayed open all summer and the sheets were changed multiple times a day. She'd heard that sound in her mother's bedroom, where her breathing had grown shallower by the week until the week it stopped, and a sixteen-year-old girl discovered that the absence of a sound could be louder than any sound she'd ever heard.

She pushed the thought down. Not now. There were patients to see, and the morning was not going to wait for the girl she'd been at sixteen to grieve in a hallway in Montana.

Samuel had stopped outside Mr. Drumond's door and was waiting for her, his hand raised to knock, his face already shifting into the expression she'd come to know as his working face—attentive, composed, and careful. But he didn't knock. He waited until she reached him, until she was beside him, and only then did his knuckles meet the wood.

It was a small thing. The kind of thing a person could dismiss as courtesy or habit, or nothing at all. But Eliza had spent several days watching this man work, and she knew the difference between a doctor who walked into a sickroom alone because he'd always done it that way and a doctor who waited at the door because the person beside him had become part of how he chose to work.

"Mr. Drumond?" Samuel called through the door. "It's Dr. Porter. Miss Miller is with me."

A sound came from inside. Low. Formless... a mumble. The sound of a man whose body had been fighting for numerous days now and was running out of what it needed to keep fighting.

Eliza straightened her shoulders, and they went in.

Chapter 15

Marshall Tom's desk had been shoved against the wall to make room for the committee meeting, and there weren't enough chairs for half the people who'd come. Eliza stood near the open door with Winnie beside her, her back against the frame, her hands clasped. Samuel stood opposite, near the desk.

Tom stood in front of his desk with his marshal's badge catching the lamplight when he moved. He didn't call the meeting to order. He began talking, and the room went quiet because Tom Callahan didn't waste words, and Providence Ridge had learned long ago that when he spoke, it was worth hearing.

"Most of you know why you're here. For those who don't, I'll keep it plain." He looked at Amos Pemberton, who stood near the window with Margaret beside him, then at Owen Gallagher, who'd come in from the mill with sawdust still on his trouser cuffs. Paul Higgins leaned against the wall near the gun cabinet with his hat in his hands. Eunice and Webb sat in two chairs Tom had managed to find. Edith Aldridge sat beside Eunice with her shawl pulled close. Several people Eliza didn't know stood around the room.

"Dr. Porter believes we've got typhoid fever spreading through Providence Ridge because of the water in the well here on the west side of town," Tom said. "As of this morning, twelve people are sick. Every one of them either lives on the west side, works there, or draws water from that well. Nobody on the east side who uses creek water has fallen ill. Dr. Porter and Miss Miller have been tending patients across numerous locations, and they're asking us to transport the ill to the boardinghouse dining room where they can be cared for properly. I'm asking us all to agree to shut the town down. Block the bridge over the river and the road heading south out of town. Keep people from entering town, and everyone who is already here stays here until we know this thing is over. I also want to shut the town down as a safety measure. Dr. Porter and Miss Miller are both educated medical professionals, and I trust them, but as they mutually agreed, everything is in the hands of God. No one but him truly knows what we are facing."

He stepped back. "Doc. Tell them what you told me."

Samuel moved forward. He spoke the way Eliza had watched him speak that morning in Leora's bedroom: direct, measured, each sentence carrying meaning and information that needed to be heard. He laid out the symptoms, the pattern, the slow pulse running against a high fever, and the rose-colored spots on Mr. Drumond. He told the room he believed this was typhoid but couldn't confirm it with one hundred percent accuracy. He told them the illness traveled through contaminated water, not through the air. He said weeks, not days. He said some patients might not recover, and he said it without softening the blow, because the people in this room deserved truth more than comfort.

When he finished, the room held still for three full seconds before Amos Pemberton spoke.

"Dr. Porter. I don't question your medical judgment. I've watched you treat people in this town since you arrived, and I trust you're telling us what you believe. But I've got questions, and I need honest answers before I agree to anything that shuts down the roads leading into our town."

"Ask them," Samuel said.

"How long will this quarantine last? A week? Two? A month? Because I need a number, and I need it before we close that bridge."

"I can't give you a fixed number. The illness typically runs two to four weeks in each patient from the time symptoms begin. If new cases stop appearing, the quarantine could lift sooner. If they don't, I'd recommend it hold until they do."

"That's not a number, Doc. That's a maybe."

"It's the most honest answer I can give you, Amos."

Amos crossed his arms. He wasn't angry. Eliza could read that much from across the room. He was scared, and the fear wore the coat of practicality the way a man buttons up against a winter storm he knows is coming.

"There's a freight wagon due across that bridge next Monday," Amos said. "Flour, sugar, coffee, nails, lamp oil. Supplies this town needs. Families here depend on my store for everything from salt to soap. You close that bridge, you'll cut off our supplies." He looked at Owen. "And every day the mill doesn't ship lumber out of this town is a day Owen's men might not get paid."

"Amos is right," Owen said. "I've got eighteen men at that mill. They work, or they don't eat. Their families don't eat. I need to know how I'm supposed to look those men in the eye when their children go hungry over an illness that might or might not be typhoid."

The word might have stayed in the room after Owen's voice left it. Eliza watched Samuel take it without flinching.

"Owen, I understand what you're facing," Samuel said. "And Amos, I understand what the freight schedule means to this town. I wouldn't be standing here asking you to shut the town down if I didn't believe the alternative was worse. But I've examined twelve people in three days, and every single one of them drank from the same well. That isn't a coincidence. That's a pattern, and the pattern is telling me that until we seal that well and stop people from carrying this illness beyond our roads, we're going to keep adding names to the list."

"You said you can't prove it's typhoid," Amos said.

"I can't. But I can tell you what I've seen, and what I've seen matches the illness in every particular. Miss Miller observed the same pattern in a hospital in Philadelphia where typhoid was treated often. We could be wrong. But if we're right, and we do nothing, people will die who didn't have to."

Amos looked at Margaret. She stood beside him with her hands folded at her waist, and whatever passed between them in that glance was private and practiced, the quick shorthand of two people who'd been reading each other's expressions for years. Margaret didn't nod or speak. But when Amos turned back, the edge in his resistance had softened into something closer to negotiation.

"What about the freight?" he asked. "If we shut the bridge, what happens to supplies coming in?"

"I'm not proposing we starve ourselves," Tom said. "Incoming freight gets unloaded at the bridge by the drivers on the opposite side of the river. Crossing the bridge will not be possible. Our men carry it into town from there. No outside drivers may enter. Outgoing shipments are held until the quarantine lifts."

"That'll slow everything down," Amos said.

"It will. But it's better than the other option."

Amos went quiet. Owen looked at the floor and then the ceiling, running numbers that didn't have a good answer regardless of which way he turned them.

"Owen," Samuel said. "I know nothing about the lumber mill you run... absolutely nothing. I recommend you keep your men working and do what you can. Keep cutting timber, keep milling the lumber down, create a stockpile, and pray to God in the meantime we can open our town back up and business can resume as usual."

Eliza hadn't spoken. She'd been standing at the doorway through every exchange, her hands clasped, listening the way the supervising physicians at the auxiliary had trained her to listen: tracking not just words but what lived behind them. Amos wasn't fighting the quarantine because he didn't care about the sick. He was fighting because he could see two disasters bearing down on Providence Ridge at once: the illness and the economic ruin, and he was trying to find ground between them that wouldn't collapse. She respected that. But respect didn't change what she knew.

"Mr. Pemberton," she said.

The room turned. She stepped away from the door and stood where she could see Amos and Owen and the rest without turning her head.

"I understand your concerns, and they're fair. This town's livelihood matters, and I wouldn't dismiss it. But I want to tell you what I've seen, because I think everyone in this room should understand what we're dealing with before a decision is made."

She kept her voice level. She wasn't asking permission, and she wasn't performing authority. She was a woman who'd spent months in a fever ward where this illness killed people, and she was going to tell them what that looked like, because they needed to hear it from someone who'd been standing in the room when it happened.

"Typhoid fever doesn't end in the first week. The first week is the beginning, and those infected often think they have a stomach bug, or occasionally the symptoms seem as if it's nothing, and they brush it aside. In the second week, the fever climbs past a hundred degrees and does so steadily and holds there. Patients become delirious. They don't recognize the people caring for them. They can't drink, and they can't eat. Their bodies waste because the illness burns through everything they have." She paused. Not for effect, but because what came next was worse, and she wanted them steady for it. "In the third week, the intestines in some patients weaken. In the worst cases, they hemorrhage. In the very worst cases, they perforate. When that happens, there's nothing a doctor can do. Not here, not in Livingston, not in the finest hospital in Philadelphia. The patient dies."

"I saw fifty-nine cases end that way in just over a year's time," she said. "Fifty-nine people who were alive at the start of their second week and in the ground before the end of their third. I don't say this to frighten anyone. I say it because you deserve to know what's at stake before you decide. Dr. Porter is a doctor. I am a nurse. We know the signs and symptoms of typhoid fever, but we are not God. We do not know for certain this is what we are facing because it could quite possibly be something else—some new illness or disease that hasn't been studied yet. We simply do not know. It's best to err on the side of caution and prevent innocent people from getting sick. It's best to keep this contained. Furthermore, it's the smart thing to do."

She stepped back to the doorway, and when she turned to face the room again, Samuel was looking at her from across the room.

"What's the compromise?" Amos asked in a quiet tone.

Tom laid it out. The well gets sealed tonight. All drinking water is boiled, with no exceptions. The bridge blocked, and two men stationed there at all times around the clock. The same for the south end of town; the road is blocked and men stationed. Freight handled at the bridge by local men once the delivery is dropped and the freight drivers have driven away. The people who are sick will be moved to the boardinghouse dining room beginning tomorrow morning, with volunteers to assist. The quarantine holds until Dr. Porter says otherwise.

"The mill stays open; I'll follow Dr. Porter's suggestion," Owen said. "If any of my men become ill, I'll transport them to the boardinghouse myself."

"I'm glad you will keep the mill running, Owen; it will help morale and reduce worries among some people. But if you hear of anyone who develops symptoms out that way, or any family members of your crew, send word to me immediately," Samuel said.

"Fair enough," Owen said.

Amos was still thinking. Eliza could see him working through it, a man who loved his town trying to calculate how to keep it alive from two directions at once and coming up short on both.

"I'll support the quarantine," he said. "On the condition that we revisit the terms in one week. If the situation has improved, we loosen up. If it hasn't, we hold. But I want a voice in that decision, Tom. The committee's, not just the doctor or yourself... no offense to either of you."

"None taken, and I agree. Revisit in a week, consider all options, and put our people and those living outside of Providence Ridge as top priority," Tom said.

"Then we're agreed?" Samuel asked.

Tom looked around the room. Webb nodded. Eunice nodded. Paul gave a brief dip of his chin. Everyone in the room nodded in agreement. Margaret touched Amos's arm, and he covered her hand with his, the way a man reaches for the person he trusts most when the ground is unsteady, and they both nodded in unison.

"We're agreed," Tom said. "The well gets sealed tonight. I'll see to it myself. Paul, can you get a wagon and two men to the bridge and the same at the other end of town?"

"Consider it done," Paul said.

"Eunice, you offered this morning to coordinate volunteers to help the sick at the boardinghouse. Still willing?"

Eunice rose from her chair with the energy of a woman who'd had her answer ready before Tom finished asking. "I've already spoken with Alma Jessup and Della Raines. We'll go door-to-door at daylight collecting spare bedding and blankets. We'll need pallets for the ill to lie on, washcloths, and every clean sheet and blanket this town can scrape up."

"Margaret?" Tom asked.

"I'll be at the boardinghouse before dawn with everything we can spare," Margaret said. "Blankets, quilts, linens. Whatever medicines Amos has in the store that Dr. Porter can use. And I'll supply the coffee. It sounds like many of us will be working through the night in the near future, and I'm firm that we do it properly."

A low laugh moved through the room, brief and grateful.

"Winnie and I will have the dining room cleared, disinfected, and ready by midmorning at the latest," Eliza said.

"I'll have men organized for moving patients by then," Tom said. "Owen, can I count on a few of your mill workers who are fit and willing?"

"You'll have them," Owen said.

Tom looked at Samuel. "Anything else, Doc?"

"One thing. When the patients arrive tomorrow, Miss Miller and I will assess each one and place them where they can be properly watched. Anyone helping with the transfer, respect the cleanliness rules. Wash your hands with soap after touching a patient. Don't drink water that hasn't been boiled. Handle soiled bedding carefully. The rules are simple, and they work. Follow them."

"You heard the man, let's go," Tom said. "Most of us will begin at first light. Get what rest you can tonight. Paul, if you encounter any problems locating men, just say the word and I'll rally a few from the more distant homesteads of Providence Ridge."

The room began to loosen. People moved toward the door the way any gathering breaks apart, conversations splitting into twos and threes as they went. Owen shook Samuel's hand and told him that he was confident many of his men would help with anything he needed. Paul clapped Samuel's shoulder and said something Eliza couldn't catch that made Samuel exhale through his nose in what was almost a laugh. Eunice had her pencil out and was writing notes on a sheet of paper.

Eliza stayed near the door as people filed past. Margaret stopped in front of her, took both her hands the way she had the first time they'd met at the mercantile counter, and held them.

"You were brave tonight, young lady," Margaret said. "What you said tonight needed to be said, and you said it with more grace than most men in that room could've managed."

"I told them the truth, Margaret."

"Yes, you did. That's precisely what I mean." She squeezed Eliza's hands once more before letting go. Then she glanced across the room to where Samuel stood speaking with Tom, and when she looked back at Eliza, her expression carried a warmth that had nothing to do with typhoid or quarantine or freight schedules.

"You two make a fine team, and I feel safe with both of you leading us through this illness that has affected our community," Margaret said.

She was through the door before Eliza could form an answer.

The office emptied. Tom straightened his desk with unhurried, deliberate movements, putting his papers back in order the way a man puts his world back in order, one stack at a time. Winnie touched Eliza's arm.

"I'm heading back to start preparing the kitchen," Winnie said. "I'm going to wash every pot and pan and be ready to start boiling water come morning. I'm too on edge right now to go to sleep."

"Thank you, Winnie. I'll be right behind you."

Winnie left. Tom looked up from his desk.

"You two did well tonight," he said. "Get some rest while you can."

"Good night, Marshal," Samuel said.

"Good night, Tom," Eliza said.

They stepped out into a night that had come down fully while they'd been inside. The air had dropped the way July evenings did at five thousand feet, the valley's heat lifting and leaving something cooler against her arms and the back of her neck. Stars crowded the sky above the Absarokas, close and thick, and Providence Ridge lay quiet in every direction except for Winnie's footsteps on the boardwalk ahead of them.

They stood outside Tom's office, ten feet from the boarding-house steps. Eliza folded her arms against the cool air.

"I admire the way you spoke truth tonight and addressed the room with honesty," he said.

"I didn't plan to," she said. "I heard what Amos was saying and what he wasn't saying. I assumed many in the room needed to hear the truth, not to instill fear but to bring the reality of what we're facing front and center. It needed to come from someone who'd witnessed it, and I have. I'll never forget some of the things I've seen."

"I believe your speaking up changed the opinions and thoughts of many and brought the situation we are facing front and center. It had to be said."

"I agree."

He was quiet for a moment. She could feel him looking at her the way she'd felt him look at her that morning at the foot of the stairs, with an attention that had crossed past professional and settled into territory she hadn't yet mapped.

"Eliza."

"Yes?"

"Thank you. For what you did in there. For all of it."

"You don't need to thank me, Dr. Porter. We're in this together."

"I know we are." He adjusted his grip on his bag. "I meant it when I said it this morning, and I mean it now."

The boardinghouse was ten steps away. The lamp Winnie had left burning threw a wash of pale yellow across the porch boards. South of town, out past the mill, a coyote called from the ridgeline, high and thin, and another answered from the benchlands above the valley.

"We should go," Eliza said. "Tomorrow starts early, and we both should try to rest as much as possible."

Neither of them moved. They stood on the boardwalk with the cool air settling between them and the weight of what was coming. For a span of seconds that would stay with Eliza longer than the meeting or the speeches or anything Amos Pemberton had said, they were two people standing side by side at the end of a day that had asked everything of them, not yet willing to walk through separate doors into separate rooms.

"Good night, Dr. Porter," Eliza said and hurried up the boardinghouse steps and went inside.

Chapter 16

Two of Owen's mill workers carried Emmett Sloane through the boardinghouse door on a litter built from pine slats and a wool blanket. Eliza directed them to the fourth pallet from the window without looking up from the cloth she was wringing into a basin.

"Set him down easy," she said. "Lower his shoulders first, then his legs. Don't jar him."

The men obeyed. Emmett groaned when his back met the pallet but didn't open his eyes. He was flushed from his collarbones to his hairline, his shirt soaked through at the chest. His wife, Nell, walked beside the litter with her hand on his arm, her face carrying the particular emptiness of a woman who hadn't slept and had been crying for hours.

The dining room Eliza had known for ten days as the place where Providence Ridge worshipped on Sundays and boarders ate their suppers had been changed dramatically. The long table was shoved against the far wall, covered with a clean sheet, holding basins of boiled water, stacked cloths, Samuel's medical supplies in the order she'd arranged them, and a row of tin cups. Eight pallets lined the floor in two rows, spaced far enough apart to walk between, each one assembled from the quilts and blankets the women of the town had collected that morning. The air smelled of carbolic and lye soap, and beneath that, the warm yeast smell of bread dough from the kitchen, where Winnie hadn't stopped moving since before sunrise.

Margaret Pemberton knelt beside a pallet, tucking a clean sheet around Ada Cobb. Ada had arrived an hour ago, carried by Jasper and one of Owen's men. She lay on her side with her knees drawn up, her dark hair loose against the pillow, her face mottled with the uneven flush of a body spending everything it had. Jasper sat on the floor beside her with his hat in his lap and his back against the wall, watching his wife.

Across the room, Zeb Thompson lay on the pallet, irritable and making sure everyone knew it. He'd arrived thirty minutes ago, carried by two men, and had spent most of that time telling anyone within earshot that he didn't need to be carried anywhere and could've walked himself if people would stop treating him like an invalid. Samuel, who'd been checking Zeb's pulse when the complaints started, had said, "Mr. Thompson, the fact that you've got the energy to argue is the best sign I've seen all morning." Zeb told Samuel that he could keep his opinions to himself. Samuel had smiled, and it was the first time Eliza had seen him smile since yesterday evening on the boardwalk outside Tom's office.

Nell Sloane stood at the foot of her husband's pallet, her hands twisting in her apron, her body caught between staying and not knowing what to do if she stayed. Eunice crossed the room before Eliza could reach her.

"Mrs. Sloane," Eunice said. "Come with me to the kitchen. Winnie could use a pair of hands, and there's fresh coffee. Your husband is right where he needs to be, and Miss Miller will look after him."

Nell looked at Emmett and then followed Eunice to the kitchen.

Eliza knelt beside Emmett's pallet and pressed the back of her hand to his forehead. Hot. She counted his pulse against the small watch she'd taken to wearing pinned at her waist. Sixty-four beats per minute. She checked his abdomen with careful pressure, working from the top down. His right side was tender and distended, and he guarded it when she pressed.

"Emmett Sloane," she said to Samuel, who was crossing from Zeb's pallet with his stethoscope in his hand. "Pulse sixty-four. The fever's high. Right-sided tenderness and guarding."

Samuel knelt beside her. He placed his stethoscope against Emmett's chest and listened, his face still, his breathing quiet so the instrument could do its work. He moved it to Emmett's back. "Breathe for me, Mr. Sloane."

Emmett did, and his exhale rattled low.

"Water," Samuel said. "Small sips, a spoonful at a time. Broth when Winnie has it ready. Cool cloths, changed every half hour."

He stood and moved toward the door just as two more of Owen's men carried Clara Fitch on a litter. She lay still with her eyes closed. Her husband, Nolan, walked beside them, upright but gray-faced, sweat running down his temples. He held Clara's hand and wouldn't release it, not even when the men set the litter down.

"Mr. Fitch, I need you on the pallet beside your wife's," Eliza said. "You're ill, too. You shouldn't be on your feet."

"I'm fine," he said. His voice cracked on the second word.

"You're running a fever, and you need to lie down. Please."

He looked at Clara as he lay down on his pallet, and before Eliza had finished arranging his pillow, he'd reached across the narrow gap between them and taken Clara's hand again. Their fingers laced on the bare floor between the pallets, and Eliza had to look away for a moment because the tenderness of it reached a place she wasn't braced for. It nearly brought tears to her eyes. Two young people, married less than a year, held on to each other across three feet of pine flooring while their bodies tried to fight off something neither of them understood.

The morning passed in arrivals and assessments. Samuel examined each patient as they came in, checking pulses, pressing abdomens, and unbuttoning shirts to look for rose spots. Eliza worked alongside him, reporting what she'd observed before he reached each pallet, handing him instruments before he asked, adjusting blankets, and replacing cloths between examinations. They'd developed a shorthand over the past few days that didn't need full sentences. She'd say, "Pulse sixty," and he'd nod. He'd say, "Spots?" and she'd tell him where or shake her head. They moved through the makeshift sick ward the way two people move through a kitchen they've shared long enough to know where the other will be without looking.

By midday the dining room held eight patients on pallets and four more upstairs in their rooms. Della Raines sat beside Zeb Thompson, reading aloud from the Bible in a low, even voice. Alma Jessup moved between patients with a basin of cool water, replacing the cloths on foreheads with the calm hands of a woman who'd raised children through summer fevers and didn't need to be told what to do. Margaret had gone to the kitchen to help Winnie put a meal on the worktable for the volunteers, because Eunice had announced that hungry helpers were useless helpers, and nobody had argued.

Edith sat near the sideboard in the chair Margaret had vacated, a folded blanket across her lap. She wasn't working. She was sitting, her hands flat on the blanket. A fine dampness lay along her forehead near her hairline.

Eliza crossed to her. "Edith, are you well?"

Edith looked up and gave her the warm, reassuring smile Eliza had first received on the day she'd arrived in Providence Ridge. But the face wearing it now was paler than it should've been.

"I'm fine, dear. Just tired. I didn't sleep much last night, and the morning's caught up with me."

"Can I get you something to eat or drink?"

"I will go in a moment and fetch my own tea, dear; I'm quite capable. Please don't fuss over me, Eliza. There are people in this room who need your attention far more than I do."

Eliza studied her. Edith's shawl was pulled tight against a room that held July warmth even with both windows open. Her hands, wrapped around the blanket, were still in a way that didn't match the Edith who'd been folding linens and carrying water all morning. Eliza's training filed it beside the pallor she'd noticed yesterday morning in Leora's bedroom and the careful way Edith had risen from her chair at the committee meeting last night.

Eliza turned around to observe the activity in the dining room. Samuel was crouched beside Ada's pallet, his fingers on her wrist, his watch in his other hand. Jasper watched from his place against the wall. Samuel set Ada's wrist down gently and drew the sheet back over her arm.

"How is she?" Jasper asked.

"Her fever's holding steady," Samuel said. "That's not improvement, but it isn't worse, and right now I'll take it. Keep talking to her, Jasper. Let her hear your voice. It helps, even when she can't answer."

Jasper took his wife's hand and held it against his chest and began speaking to her in a voice too low for Eliza to hear.

Samuel stood, and his eyes found hers. He smiled, tired and small and honest, and it loosened a knot she'd been carrying between her shoulders since before dawn.

Then Della called her name from Zeb's pallet because his cloth needed changing, and she went.

The afternoon settled into a rhythm. Eliza moved between pallets, checking temperatures, coaxing sips of water into patients who refused them, changing cloths, and adjusting sheets. Winnie appeared every so often, bringing cups of broth or boiled water.

Samuel went upstairs twice to check on the boarders. Both times he came back with his jaw tight and his notebook open, writing as he walked. Both times he didn't say what he'd found. After the second visit, she asked.

"Mr. Drumond's worse," he said. "His breathing's heavier, and his fever climbed another half degree since this morning. I've done everything I know to do for him right now." He closed his notebook. "I don't like the direction it's headed, Eliza."

By late afternoon Clara slept with Nolan's hand still in hers. Zeb had stopped complaining, which worried Eliza more than anything. Ada was managing small sips of broth from the cup Jasper held to her lips. Emmett's fever hadn't broken, but he was keeping water down, and she counted that as a small mercy in a day that hadn't offered many. Della and Alma sat near the window, tired, resting their bodies for a moment.

Eliza stood at the supply table, rolling a strip of clean linen between her hands. She'd been on her feet since four that morning, and her body knew it, even if her mind kept adding to the list of things that still needed doing. She could help Winnie in the kitchen. She could check on Leora, who'd been alone all day except for Webb's visit. She could go upstairs and look in on the boarders. She could mix more carbolic solution. Any of those tasks would keep her hands busy and her thoughts aimed forward, which was where she preferred them pointed. Still hands invited still thoughts, and still thoughts had a way of drifting toward things she'd rather not think about: Mr. Drumond's worsening. Edith's pallor. The fact that she hadn't eaten since the half biscuit Winnie had pressed into her hand before dawn.

Samuel appeared in the doorway between the dining room and the kitchen. He carried two cups, steam rising from both, and walked toward her with the stride of a man who'd made up his mind about something and didn't plan to negotiate.

"Sit down," he said.

"I should help Winnie with supper for the volunteers."

"Winnie and Margaret have supper well in hand. I just came from the kitchen. Sit down."

"I should mix more carbolic. We'll need it by late evening, and I'd rather have it ready than scramble when we run out."

"The carbolic can wait twenty minutes. You can't." He held out one of the cups. "You haven't sat down once today. You haven't eaten since the biscuit Winnie put in your hand at seven this morning, and I know that because I watched you eat half of it and set the other half aside. Sit down and drink this coffee."

He stood there with two cups of coffee and a look on his face that said he wasn't moving until she sat. The certainty of it was so complete and so uninterested in her objections that her resistance folded.

She sat in the chair, and Samuel sat beside her and held out the cup.

"Thank you," she said.

"You're welcome."

They sat with the makeshift sick ward quiet around them, patients sleeping, the late-afternoon light coming through the west-facing windows in long slats that fell across the pallets and the tangled sheets and the floor. From the kitchen she could hear Winnie and Margaret's voices and the knock of a pot being set on the stove.

"You need to rest tonight," Samuel said. "Actual rest. Sleep. Eunice and I can handle the overnight."

"I'll rest when the patients are stable."

"You're no help to anyone if you're worn down to nothing."

She turned her cup in her hands. "I'll try," she said.

"That's all I'm asking."

He drank from his cup and then rested it on his knee.

"Samuel, tell me honestly. How bad is Mr. Drumond in your opinion?"

He was quiet. "Bad," he said. "His fever's climbing, and his breathing's getting worse. His body's running out of what it needs. I'm doing everything I know to do." He paused. "I'm not sure if it's going to be enough. He's progressing more quickly than the others."

The honesty cost him. She could see it in the way he held his cup, both hands wrapped around the tin, his thumbs pressed hard enough against the sides to whiten his knuckles.

"Then we keep doing everything we know," she said. "And we pray for the rest."

"Yes," he said. "We do."

<h1 style="text-align:center">Chapter 17</h1>

Eunice had already taken the chair beside Zeb Thompson's pallet when Eliza crossed the dining room for her final round, checking each patient in the order she'd kept since morning. Zeb slept with his breathing ragged but even. Ada lay on her side with Jasper's hand wrapped around hers, and Jasper had finally dozed off sitting up against the wall, his chin tipped toward his chest. Clara and Nolan Fitch slept facing each other across the gap between their pallets, their fingers laced on the bare floor between them. Emmett Sloane's fever hadn't broken, but his breathing had eased in the last hour. The cup beside his pallet was half empty, which meant he'd managed water while she'd been upstairs with the boarders.

Della Raines sat near the window with a lamp turned low and her knitting needles working a rhythm so soft it could barely be heard.

"Go on," Eunice said without looking up from the cloth she was wringing into a basin. "Della and I have everything covered. You've been upright since before the sun came up, and I don't want to hear one word about how you aren't tired."

"I wasn't going to say that."

"You were thinking it. Go."

Eliza laid the back of her hand against Emmett's forehead one final time. Still warm, but the fever had stopped climbing. She set the cloth back on his forehead and turned toward the kitchen.

The kitchen was lit by a single lamp on the worktable, its flame turned low enough that the shelves of crockery and the hanging pots were only dark shapes above the worktable. The cookstove held a banked fire, its iron still warm to the touch, and the window over the washbasin showed nothing but a July night, black and cool.

Samuel sat at the far end of the worktable with his notebook open and his pencil moving. His waistcoat hung unbuttoned, his sleeves were shoved past his elbows, and a cup of coffee sat beside his notebook.

Eliza gathered the instruments she'd left soaking in the carbolic basin near the stove and carried them to the washbasin. She cleaned them one at a time, running a cloth along each surface, drying them, and laying them on the clean linen she'd spread across the counter.

"Emmett's keeping water down," she said as she turned toward Samuel. "His fever's holding, not climbing. Ada took broth from Jasper not long ago. Zeb stopped talking three hours ago, which worries me more than his complaining did."

"Zeb went quiet?" Samuel's pen stopped.

"Della noticed first. She said he closed his eyes mid-sentence when he was speaking to her."

"I'll check on him in a few moments."

He wrote two more lines, closed his notebook, and looked at her. In the low lamplight, the day showed on him plainly. Stubble lined his jaw. His hair had gone uncombed, the dark waves falling where they'd pulled loose. The lines beside his mouth ran deeper than they had a week ago.

"Any thoughts on Mr. Drumond?" she asked.

"He's the same. His breathing's heavier and his abdomen's more distended than this afternoon. I was able to get him to swallow a few small sips of broth."

She set the last instrument on the linen and dried her hands. "And Edith?"

"What about Edith?"

"You've noticed... I'm sure."

"I have."

Eliza pulled out the chair across from him and sat down . Her legs ached from the soles of her feet to her hips and sitting sent a wave of relief through her. "Yesterday morning in Leora's room, I noticed her color was off, and she had her shawl pulled tight in a room that was plenty warm enough. Today she couldn't rise from her chair without gripping the armrest, and her hands were cold when I brought her tea."

"Her color's been off since the committee meeting," Samuel said. "She's moving slowly and carefully. I noticed the same things you did."

"I don't believe it's just tiredness."

The lamp on the worktable flickered as its wick settled, and the shadows across the kitchen walls shifted and steadied.

"Let's let her be and keep an eye on her; we'll know when we need to insist she join the sick," Samuel said.

Eliza nodded. She picked up his cold coffee, carried it to the washbasin, poured it out, and went to the stove where the pot still sat on the back burner. She poured two fresh cups and brought them to the table.

"Thank you," he said.

"You're welcome."

He took a drink and closed his eyes for a moment as if he were relishing the taste of fresh coffee, then he set his cup down. "May I ask you something?" he said.

"Yes."

"The hymn you hum when you're working. I've been trying to place it all day."

Her hands stilled on her cup. "What?"

"You hum at times while you work... the same melody almost every time. I've heard it at least a dozen times today, and I can't quite name it."

She hadn't known he'd heard. "It's 'Abide with Me,'" she said. "Henry Francis Lyte."

"That's it. I knew I'd heard it in church, but I couldn't catch enough to be certain."

"My mother used to sing it. She sang hymns the way some women hum lullabies, without thinking about it, while she was cooking, or hanging laundry, or sitting with her mending. 'Abide with Me' was her favorite. She said the words felt like a prayer she could carry through the day without stopping to kneel."

"That's a good way to think about a hymn."

"When she got sick, she couldn't sing anymore after a while. The consumption took her voice before it took the rest of her. Near the end, I'd sing it to her at night because it calmed her when nothing else could. She'd close her eyes, and her breathing would slow, and I'd keep singing until she fell asleep." Eliza turned her cup on the table a quarter turn, then another. "I hum it and other hymns at times when I'm caring for someone who's struggling."

Samuel watched her across the table. "Your mother sounds like she was a remarkable woman," he said.

"She was. Everyone who knew her said so, but it wasn't the kind of remarkable that announces itself. She was the person who noticed when you were carrying something you hadn't spoken about, and she'd find a way to lighten it without you even knowing. My Aunt Leora reminded me the other day of something I had either almost forgotten or never realized. My mother could walk into a room where someone was suffering, and the room got quieter. Not because she said anything. Because her presence made the pain less lonely."

"You have that same quality."

Eliza looked down at her hands on the table. She spread her fingers against the scarred wood, studying them the way she studied a patient's skin for signs of change. Reddened knuckles from carbolic. Short nails trimmed for nursing. The small callus on her right middle finger.

"Have you written to your father since all this started?" Samuel asked.

"Yes, I've written to him twice. With the town shut down, I'm not sure when or if we'll receive mail." She turned her cup on the table. "I told you at supper the other day that he's never been on his own before. I keep wondering how the household is faring without me there to manage it."

"A man on his own tends to find his footing, eventually. Though I wouldn't hold up my own housekeeping as proof of that."

"You told me your cookstove is your adversary. I haven't forgotten."

"Is there anyone else in Philadelphia, Eliza?" He turned his cup a quarter turn on the table, a gesture she'd seen him make before when he was approaching something carefully.

He wasn't looking at her when he asked the question. He was looking at his cup on the scarred wood.

He was asking if she had a beau. She looked at his profile in the low lamplight, the line of his jaw, the way he kept his eyes on his cup as if the answer might cost him something he couldn't afford. The fact that it mattered to him enough to ask sent warmth climbing the back of her neck and into her cheeks.

"No," she said. "There's no one waiting for me. There was someone a few years back. A young man from our church, Thomas Caldwell. He courted me when I was eighteen, while I was training to become a nurse. He was kind and patient, and he wanted a wife who'd be ready to keep a home and start a family. I was spending twelve hours a day in a ward full of sick people, learning how to dress wounds and manage fevers, or studying, and I couldn't make myself want the life he was offering. Not because it was wrong. Because something in me needed to do this work, and Thomas needed someone whose heart was ready to make a home." She picked up her cup and drank. "He married a girl from our congregation the following year. I was glad for him. I was truly. But it taught me that what I wanted for my life didn't fit easily beside what a man expects from a wife. Since then my life revolves around that of my father, his household, the Society, and the auxiliary."

"I'm glad you told me," he said.

"You could've asked days ago."

"I wasn't sure it was mine to ask."

"It was."

Eliza watched him as he drank from his cup. He was an intriguing man, and she didn't know much about him beyond medicine and the handful of stories he'd offered in passing. She had questions stacking up that needed answers. What had brought him to this small frontier town when the world was wide open to a qualified and experienced doctor? Did he plan to stay here? Had he traveled beyond Colorado and Chicago and this valley? What did he do with his evenings after the day's work was finished, in the quiet hours? She wanted to know all of it, and the wanting surprised her, because she couldn't remember the last time she'd been this curious about another person's life.

"Samuel, what made you want to be a doctor?"

"I grew up on a ranch. My father raises cattle outside Trinidad, Colorado. When I was twelve, one of our mares went down during foaling, and the foal was turned wrong. My father sent a rider for help, but the nearest man with any skill was a day out, and the mare was dying. I sat with her all night. I couldn't do anything for her, not really, but I stayed, and I talked to her, and I kept her calm, and by morning the foal had turned on its own, and she delivered. My father said it was the Lord's doing. I thought it was the Lord's doing and the mare's stubbornness in equal measure." The trace of warmth that crossed his face made him look younger, briefly, and less tired. "After that, I started paying attention to every sick animal on the ranch, every injury, and every ailment. My mother said I was born noticing things that hurt, and she was right. I went to medical school in Chicago because I wanted to be the help that doesn't come too late."

"And you became that."

"Most days I hope so."

"You are. I've watched you this week. I watched you sit with Ada and calm her fears. I watched you talk to Zeb when he was angry because you knew the anger was hiding the fear, and you spoke the words he needed because that helped him more than anything. You're a good doctor, Samuel."

He turned his cup. "You know more about working with the sick than you learned in any training program, I can tell. The way you anticipate what a patient needs before they've asked, before I've asked. That isn't months of instruction, nor did it come from a medical book. That's older than the auxiliary. Closer to home." He set his cup down and looked at her straight on. "There's more to you than you've let on, Eliza. I want to know what shaped you. What made you who you are?"

She took a slow breath. This man wanted to know her. Not her schedule, not her training credentials, not her plans for returning home. He was asking her to open the door she'd kept shut for six years, the one she'd boarded up with competence and long hours and the steady rhythm of work that never ran out. No one had ever asked her this. Not Thomas, who'd wanted her company but never her history. Not the supervising nurses at the auxiliary, who valued her skill without questioning where it came from. Not even her father, who knew the answers already and loved her too much to make her say them aloud.

"My mother was diagnosed with consumption when I was four-teen," she said. "Dr. Ashford came to the house on a Tuesday in October. My father was there, and I was in the hallway because I'd been told to wait outside the bedroom, but I could hear everything through the door. Dr. Ashford spoke the way I've heard you speak with families this week: carefully and plainly, giving them the truth without making it worse than it already was. When they came out of the bedroom, my father's hands were shaking. I'd never seen my father in the state he was in, and it scared me. My mother was standing in her room, and she was perfectly still." Eliza paused. "My mother was never still. She stood there, and she didn't move, and her stillness frightened me more than anything Dr. Ashford had said."

She looked at the lamp's flame. It held steady on its wick, a small orange point doubled in the glass chimney.

"Before the consumption, my mother was the most amazing person I knew. She laughed at my father's terrible jokes. She brought meals to every sick neighbor in our parish and forgot to eat her own supper while doing it. She taught Sunday school and led the sewing circle, and could make a room full of frightened people feel safe just by being in it. She brought joy and peace into the room. She was literally an angel on earth to everyone that knew her. She was everything I wanted to grow up to be, and I got two more years with her after her diagnosis. Those years changed me in ways I'm still learning."

"What happened in those years?" Samuel asked.

"I became her caretaker. Not because my father wasn't willing. He worked long hours at the print shop because the bills didn't stop, and when he was home, he did everything he could. But I was capable, and my mother trusted me, and I was there. I choose to be by her side through it all, and I'll never regret that."

She set her cup down.

"I kept her laudanum schedule written on a card tucked inside her Bible, because I'd forget the times without it, and forgetting meant she'd be in pain she didn't have to bear. I changed her linens while she was still in bed by the second year because she couldn't stand on her own, and it was easier than moving her to a chair. I read Scripture to her every night until she slept, and then I'd sit beside her and count her breaths because I was afraid if I stopped counting, the breathing would stop too. I sang 'Abide with Me' when the coughing kept her awake, and sometimes it helped and sometimes it didn't, but I sang it anyway because it was all I had left to give."

"Eliza, that must have been very hard on you," Samuel said.

"One afternoon, just before she became completely bedfast, I came home from the grocer and found her on the hallway floor. She'd tried to reach the parlor window because she wanted to see and feel the sun. She was lying there in her nightgown, and she was so thin that when I picked her up, I could feel every rib through the cotton. I carried her back to bed. My mother, who had carried me as a child, who had lifted me onto kitchen counters and swung me around the room when I was small enough to swing. Samuel... she weighed nothing in my arms. I laid her down and tucked her quilt around her and sang until she slept, and then I went to the kitchen and stood at the sink and couldn't make myself move for twenty minutes. I cried the entire time and begged God to stop and rewind what was taking place. I begged Him for a miracle."

She pressed her fingertips against the table. The wood was solid beneath them, knife-scarred and worn, and real.

"She died in the spring of 1878. April. I was sixteen. I was holding her hand. Her breathing had changed around midnight, and I knew what that meant. I don't know how I knew it because I had never experienced death before. Her breathing grew slower and fainter, and then it stopped, and I sat there holding her hand for a long time afterward because I wasn't ready. I kept waiting for one more breath. I kept listening for it, and it didn't come."

Her eyes burned and her throat ached, and she didn't hide it from him. She let him see the tears she was holding, and the holding was an offering she hadn't given anyone besides her father in six years.

"The hardest part wasn't losing her," she said. "The hardest part was what came after. The question I couldn't stop asking. Whether I'd done enough. Whether there was a dose of medicine that I could've timed better or a sign I should've seen sooner. The question whether I had done enough drove me to study to become a nurse and the auxiliary. The auxiliary gave me training, and the training gave me skill, and every patient I've cared for since is my answer to that question. Was I enough? Could I have done more? I went into nursing because I never want to stand beside someone and wonder again whether my hands could've saved them if they'd only been better."

Samuel set his cup on the table. "You were enough," he said. "You were sixteen years old, and you kept your mother comfortable and loved and cared for until the very end. The illness took her life . Not any failure of yours."

"I know that now."

"You know it in your head. You don't know it in your heart." He pressed his hand flat against his chest briefly and let it fall. "I understand that. I carry the same kind of knowing and not knowing."

She waited as he studied his hands on the table in front of him. The ink on his fingers. The scar across his right hand. Broad hands that had held instruments and had taken pulses for hours today.

"I left Colorado because of a patient," he said. "Someone in my family. A woman my brother loved dearly." His voice held level, but the effort showed in the way his thumbs pressed hard against the table's edge, whitening at the knuckles. "She needed help I couldn't give her by myself. I knew what she needed. I didn't have the instruments or the hands to do it alone, and help was too far away. She didn't survive."

He stopped. He looked at the lamp, then at her.

"I came to Providence Ridge because a town needed a doctor and didn't ask where I'd been or why I'd left. I wanted a place where I could practice medicine and be useful and not walk into a room and see her in every patient I treated." He turned his cup without drinking from it. "Some days I manage that. Some days I don't. I believe you and I both experienced things in our past that will never leave us, and they continually shape our thinking as we move forward in life."

Eliza reached across the table and laid her hand over his. His fingers were warm against the wood, and when her palm covered his knuckles, he turned his hand so their palms met.

"Samuel," she said. "I think we should pray."

He looked at her.

"For our patients. For Mr. Drumond, Ada, Zeb, the Fitches, and Emmett. For everyone in this town who's frightened tonight." Her fingers tightened around his. "I'm afraid of what tomorrow's examinations are going to show us, and I would rather not carry that into the morning without giving it to God first. We should pray for you and for me. Because we're both holding things we can't set down on our own."

"All right," he said.

They bowed their heads over the worktable, their hands clasped between the lamp and the closed notebook and the two cups of coffee gone cold. Eliza prayed, and her voice was steady and plain.

"Lord, we come to You tonight tired and uncertain, and we bring You the people in this house who are fighting for their lives. Watch over Mr. Drumond. Keep him breathing, Lord; help him fight this. Be with Ada and Jasper, and the Fitches, and Emmett, and Zeb. Give their bodies the strength to heal, and give us the wisdom and the steady hands to care for them well. Be with Edith. We don't know what's coming for her, and we're scared, and we need You to be braver than we are. Help Samuel and me to ease the pain in our hearts from things we've experienced in the past. Guide our hands tomorrow and every day we're asked to do this work. We don't have enough strength on our own. You do. You always have. Help us. In Jesus' name. Amen."

"Amen," Samuel said.

He lifted his head, and she lifted hers. Their hands remained joined on the table, and neither moved for a time.

Eventually, Samuel let go and stood. He picked up both cups and carried them to the washbasin, and on his way back past her chair, he stopped. His palm came to rest on her shoulder. Flat against the cotton of her dress, the full warmth of his hand pressed through the fabric. A touch that carried everything he hadn't been able to say and placed it where she could feel it.

Jasper Cobb appeared in the doorway of the kitchen. "Dr. Porter? Ada's restless. I can't get her to drink, and she feels hotter than she did."

"I'm coming." Samuel said as he moved away from her, but before he reached the doorway, he stopped. He turned and looked at her across the kitchen, the lamplight catching one side of his face and leaving the other in shadow.

"Eliza," he said.

She waited. She could see him working toward something, the words gathering and not arriving.

"We'll talk more later, Samuel," she said.

He nodded and then turned and went into the dining room. She heard him kneel beside Ada's pallet, heard Jasper's low reply, and heard Samuel's voice settle into the calm, measured cadence he used with frightened patients and family members. Eliza sat alone in the kitchen with the lamp burning low, and she pressed her own palm against her shoulder where his hand had been, her fingers finding the place, holding it.

She could hear him telling Jasper that Ada's pulse was steady, that her temperature hadn't climbed past where it had been earlier, and that he should try to rest. Jasper said something too quietly to catch.

Eliza stood and walked to the kitchen doorway. She watched Samuel crouched beside Zeb Thompson's pallet with his fingers on Zeb's wrist, steady and sure, a man who'd handed her something tonight he'd been carrying alone for three years but was still struggling to put into words.

Chapter 18

Samuel was lifting the cloth from Emmett Sloane's forehead to check his temperature against his wrist when the boarding-house front door struck the wall hard enough to rattle the tin cups stacked on the dining room table.

Hattie Pemberton came through the dining room doorway with Timothy against her shoulder, and the sight of them stopped him. The boy hung limp, his dark hair plastered to his forehead, his cheek flat against his mother's collarbone, one arm dangling. Hattie's skin was the color of tallow and slick with sweat, and her hand on Timothy's back shook clear to her elbow.

"Dr. Porter," she said. Her voice came out thin, scraped dry. "Help."

Samuel reached her in four strides and took the boy from her arms. Timothy was burning. The heat came through his nightshirt and into Samuel's palms, and the boy's body was slack, his head rolling against Samuel's forearm. Timothy's brown eyes opened halfway, unfocused, searching for something they couldn't find.

"Mama," Timothy said.

"I'm right here, sweetheart," Hattie said, and reached for his hand.

Her knees buckled as she reached. She went down hard, both kneecaps hitting the floorboards, her palms slapping flat against the wood, her braid falling over her shoulder.

Eliza had been a few steps away, wringing cloths at the washbasin near the front window. She'd dropped everything the instant Samuel had reached for Timothy, but she wasn't fast enough to catch Hattie before she fell.

"Reverend Hale," Eliza yelled.

Webb had been reading aloud from the Psalms to Zeb Thompson in the far corner. He set his Bible on the chair and crossed the room without a word. He slid his arm under Hattie's left side, and Eliza took her right, and between them they got her upright. Hattie tried to help, tried to work her legs beneath her, but her body refused, and the sound she made was a small, staggered cry.

"The pallet beside the window," Eliza said to Webb. "The one we made up this morning."

They carried Hattie across the room, and Samuel watched them settle her onto the pallet while he held Timothy against his chest, one hand cradling the boy's head. Timothy's fist had found the front of Samuel's shirt and gripped a handful of fabric, the reflexive grab of a child who didn't know where he was and needed to hold on to something solid.

"Reverend," Eliza said, kneeling beside Hattie and drawing the sheet up over her legs. "Amos and Margaret need to know. Would you go to the mercantile?"

He was through the doorway and out the front door before Samuel had reached the empty pallet beside Hattie's.

Samuel lowered Timothy onto the bedding. The boy's grip tightened on his shirt, then released, as Samuel eased his head onto the folded blanket that served as a pillow. Timothy's cheeks were blotched and burning, his nightshirt soaked through at the chest and under his arms.

Samuel placed two fingers against the inside of Timothy's wrist. He counted against his pocket watch. The boy's pulse was slow for the fever, the same dissociation he'd tracked in every typhoid patient in this room, the body's rhythm failing to rise with its temperature. Timothy's skin was dry and papery beneath his fingertips, and his lips had cracked at both corners.

"Timothy," Samuel said, keeping his voice level. "I'm Dr. Porter. I need to look at your belly. It might feel a little tender, but I'll be as careful as I can."

Timothy's brown eyes opened. They were glassy and unfocused, and the boy looked up at Samuel and then past him, searching.

"Mama?"

"Right beside you. See?" Samuel turned the boy's head on the pillow so he could see Hattie. Eliza was pressing her palm to Hattie's forehead as Hattie turned her head to face her son.

"Mama's sick," Timothy said.

"Your mama's going to rest right there next to you," Samuel said. "And I'm going to take care of you both."

He lifted the hem of Timothy's nightshirt and pressed his fingers against the boy's abdomen, starting at the upper right quadrant and moving slowly across. Timothy flinched at the first touch and pulled his knees up. His abdomen was distended and hard under Samuel's hand.

"I know," Samuel said. "I'm sorry. Almost done."

Timothy whimpered when Samuel's fingers reached the lower right. Rose-colored spots marked his chest in a scattered pattern, each the size of a lentil. Samuel counted seven. He checked behind each of Timothy's ears, then ran his thumb along the boy's jawline, then lifted his eyelid and checked the white of his eye. He looked at his tongue.

"Can you drink some water for me, Timothy?"

The boy shook his head. His lower lip trembled, and two tears tracked from the corners of his eyes into the blanket beneath his head. "I want home."

"I know you do." Samuel pulled his nightshirt back down and tucked the sheet around him. "But you're going to stay here so I can help you feel better. And your mama will be right next to you the whole time."

He picked up his notebook and wrote. *Pulse 68 against fever exceeding 101. Abdominal distension with tenderness concentrated in the right lower quadrant. Seven rose spots across the chest and trunk. Dry mucous membranes, cracked lips, and dehydration.*

Samuel moved to Hattie's pallet as Eliza held a cup of cool water to her lips. Hattie managed three small sips before lowering her head and turning her face away.

"How long have you been unwell?" Samuel asked.

"Three days, I think." Her voice was hoarse. "I thought it was a summer cold. I had a headache, and my stomach wasn't sitting right. I kept working because Timothy needed meals and clean clothes, and I had a dress to finish for a customer by Saturday." She closed her eyes. "He started running hot last night. I kept putting wet cloths on him and giving him water, and this morning he couldn't get out of bed."

Samuel placed his fingers on her wrist and counted. Her pulse was faster than Timothy's; her body's fever response was still in its earlier pattern. He checked her abdomen. Tender but less distended, and no spots. Her skin was feverish and damp, and she shivered when the sheet shifted off her shoulders.

"When did your fever start?"

"Yesterday. I think."

"You need to drink," he said. "Small sips, as often as you can manage."

Hattie reached across the gap between the pallets and found Timothy's hand.

"Dr. Porter," she said. "I can't lose him. I've lost everything I was given. My husband, my home, every plan I had for my life. If I lose my boy, there's nothing left of me to save. So you tell me what to do, and I'll do it. Whatever it takes. Whatever it costs."

"I'm going to take care of your son, Hattie," Samuel said. "And I'm going to take care of you. You aren't alone. You have a room full of people who are here to see you and your boy through this."

She held his gaze for a beat longer, and then her grip on Timothy's hand loosened, her eyes closed, and her body surrendered to the exhaustion she'd been fighting since before she walked through that door.

Samuel moved back to Timothy's pallet. Eliza was already there, kneeling beside the boy with a fresh cloth wrung in cool water. She folded it with her quick, precise hands and laid it across his forehead. Timothy stirred but didn't wake.

She tucked the sheet closer around his shoulders and brushed his damp hair off his forehead with the backs of her fingers.

"Timothy," Eliza said. Her voice dropped to a register Samuel had never heard from her before, warm and unhurried, almost musical. "Can you hear me?"

His eyes opened.

"My name is Eliza. Do you remember me? We met at the big picnic by the creek. You told me about the frog you caught."

His brow creased. "A... green one."

"That's right. The biggest frog anyone's ever seen, you told me. I'm going to sit right here beside you while Dr. Porter takes care of you and your mama. I'm not going anywhere. And while I'm here, I'd like to tell you a story. Would you like that?"

He nodded. A tiny motion against his pillow.

"Once there was a boy who lived near a creek, and this boy was the best frog catcher in the whole territory. He could catch frogs nobody else could even find because he knew their hiding places. He knew which rocks they sat under and which patches of moss they liked best, and he was so quiet and so patient that the frogs didn't hear him coming until he'd already scooped them up." She rested her hand over Timothy's on the sheet. "One morning this boy found a frog sitting on a rock in the middle of the creek. And this wasn't an ordinary frog, Timothy. This frog was bright green, the greenest green you've ever seen, greener than the grass after a rainstorm."

Timothy's eyes stayed on her face. His breathing slowed. The crease between his brows loosened.

"And this frog could jump higher than any frog in Montana Territory," she said. "He could jump so high that when he jumped, he could see all the way over the mountains. And the mountains were covered with snow on their peaks even though it was summer, and the frog thought the snow was the most beautiful thing he'd ever seen."

Samuel stood at the foot of Timothy's pallet and watched. He'd seen Eliza with every patient in this room over the past several days. He'd seen her hold Ada Cobb's hand as she sobbed with worry over her unborn child. He's watched her manage Zeb Thompson's irritability with patience that never frayed.

This was different.

Her thumb moved across Timothy's small knuckles in a slow, absent rhythm while she talked. When his eyes started to drift, she leaned closer and brought her voice down, not to a whisper but to the quiet murmur a mother uses when her child is falling asleep and she wants the last sound he hears to be her voice. The story she was inventing as she went along was to keep a frightened boy tethered to something kind while his body fought, and she spun it without hesitation, one scene flowing into the next. The frog jumped from rock to lily pad to the branch of a cottonwood tree, each new detail drawn from whatever she could read in the boy's face about what he needed to hear next.

Samuel turned away. He picked up his notebook and completed his entries on Timothy and Hattie. He checked Emmett Sloane's temperature and replaced his cloth. He walked to Zeb Thompson's pallet and took his pulse, which was steadier than yesterday but weaker than he wanted. He checked on Ada, who was sleeping with Jasper still beside her. He crossed to the Fitches, who were both awake, watching Hattie and Timothy with worry on their faces.

"How are you both feeling?" he asked, kneeling beside Clara's pallet.

"Better when I lay still," Clara said. "Worse than I'd like to."

"That sounds about right for where you are. Nolan?"

"The same." Nolan said as he closed his eyes. Clara's hand found his across the gap between their pallets, and she closed her eyes as well.

Samuel made his way back toward Timothy. The green frog had found a friend, a smaller brown frog who couldn't jump as high but could swim faster, and the two frogs had decided to explore the creek all the way to its source. Timothy's eyes were half-closed. His grip on Eliza's hand had loosened, but held.

The front door opened. Boots struck the entryway floor, and Amos Pemberton came through the dining room doorway with Margaret behind him and the reverend following.

Amos looked nothing like the man who'd stood in Tom Callahan's office days ago, struggling to understand what was happening in this town. His face was drained of color. He scanned the room, found Hattie's pallet and Timothy beside her, and stopped moving.

Margaret rushed past him. She walked to the gap between her daughter's pallet and her grandson's, gathered her skirt, and lowered herself to the floor. She took Hattie's hand in her left and Timothy's in her right and bowed her head. Her lips moved without a sound.

Amos came to Samuel.

"How bad?" His voice was low and stripped of everything except the question.

"Timothy's showing the same pattern I've seen in every patient here. Fever and abdominal tenderness. He's dehydrated and has been symptomatic longer than Hattie knew. Children are resilient, but they're small, and the illness hits them hard."

"And Hattie?"

"Earlier in the course. My best guess is that her symptoms are a few days behind Timothy's. She pushed through it for his sake, and the exhaustion on top of the fever is what brought her down quickly."

Amos looked at his daughter on the pallet. Hattie's eyes were closed. Margaret was stroking her hair.

"Tell me what you need," Amos said. "Supplies, hands, anything I've got at the store. I'll have it here within the hour."

"Fresh linens. Whatever light blankets you can spare. More stew bones and raw vegetables for the broth if you've got them. And clean water. We can always use more boiled water."

Amos held Samuel's gaze for a few moments. "You take care of them, Dr. Porter."

"I will," Samuel said, and then went to the kitchen. Winnie was at the stove, stirring the broth pot with a long wooden ladle she favored, and she looked up when he came through the doorway.

Winnie set the ladle across the rim of the pot. She pressed her palms flat on the worktable for a moment, steadying herself.

"I'll have broth ready for them both in a few moments. Doc Samuel, my heart is breaking. I don't know what else to do besides stand here at this stove and keep making broth and boiling water. The sight of Timothy hurts Doc. It is tearing me apart. What else can I do?"

"Continue doing what you're doing. Pray, keep yourself busy so your mind doesn't have time to think about things that are out of our control." He looked at her. "And, Winnie, eat something yourself. You've been in here since before sunup."

"I ate."

"When?"

She pulled a biscuit from the cloth-covered plate on the shelf and took a bite.

Samuel filled a tin cup with cool water from the boiled supply and carried it through the dining room.

Eliza was still sitting cross-legged on the floor beside Timothy. Timothy had fallen into a restless sleep, his flushed face turned toward his mother. Eliza held his hand. Her other hand rested on his forehead, her fingers curved against his skin. Not checking for a fever. Resting there, the way a person rests a hand on something precious and breakable that she's promised to keep safe.

Samuel lowered himself to the floor beside her. He held out the cup of water.

"Drink," he said.

She took the cup and drank. A trace of moisture caught on her lower lip, and she wiped it with the back of her hand, a quick, absent gesture, and gave the cup back.

"Thank you," she said.

He set the cup on the floor between them. Timothy stirred and made a small sound, and Eliza's hand moved across his forehead, a slow pass that settled him back into sleep. On the other side of Timothy's pallet, Margaret sat with Hattie's hand in one of hers and Timothy's in the other. Her lips still moved. Her prayer was a quiet current running beneath the sounds of the room.

The dining room held the breathing of nine patients in various stages of illness and rest. Della Raines had returned to her post near Emmett's pallet with her knitting, the needles working their soft, steady rhythm. Eunice had appeared and was changing the cloth on Zeb's forehead with the brisk efficiency of a woman who'd been doing this for hours and intended to keep doing it until every last patient walked out on two good legs. Webb stood near the doorway with his Bible under his arm, watching the room.

Samuel looked at Eliza beside him. Her auburn hair was coming loose from its pins, strands falling along her neck. Her sleeves were rolled up past her elbows. Her apron was creased and spotted with drips of bone broth. Her hand on Timothy's forehead was steady, and the boy slept beneath it with his small fist curled against his chest, trusting her completely.

Eliza's blue eyes were bright with tears she wasn't shedding. She was holding herself in place by will alone because there was a child under her hand who needed her to stay steady. She was hurting for this boy; he could see it in the careful control of her breathing, and in the way her jaw tightened each time Timothy shifted and whimpered.

Last night in the kitchen, she told him about her mother. About being fourteen and becoming a caretaker. About counting breaths and singing hymns and carrying a woman who'd once carried her. About the question that had driven her into nursing. Was I enough? Could I have done more?

That question was alive in her face right now, sitting beside him on the floor of this dining room. Eliza would give Timothy everything she had, the way she'd given her mother everything, and the same question would follow her home if the worst happened.

He knew it because she'd trusted him enough to share a part of herself, and the trust had changed what he saw when he looked at her.

"Eliza," he said. Quiet enough that only she could hear.

She turned and looked at him.

"He's going to get the best care we can give him," Samuel said. "Both of them are. We'll watch them through the night and do everything we humanly can for them."

"I know," she said. "But this hurts. This is breaking my heart."

Timothy's fingers opened and closed around Eliza's hand in his sleep. Her thumb traced a line across his knuckles. Margaret's lips moved on the other side of the pallet, her prayer a steady current beneath everything else.

Samuel sat beside Eliza on the floor of the boardinghouse dining room, with July heat pressing through the open windows and the sharp smell of carbolic in the air. He couldn't look away from her hand on Timothy's forehead. The instinct that lived in her fingers and in her voice, and the story she'd pulled from nothing to ease a frightened child into sleep. He'd watched her steady, competent, and compassionate with every patient in this room, and none of it had prepared him for this. For watching her love a child who wasn't hers with a tenderness so fierce and so careful and so natural, she didn't seem to know she was doing it.

Margaret prayed. Eliza kept watch. Timothy's small body lay still on the pallet between the two women who'd claimed him. And Samuel, who hadn't prayed honestly and deeply in three years, who posted his prayers like letters to an address he couldn't verify, closed his eyes and asked God to let this boy live.

Chapter 19

Eliza was wringing a cloth over the basin beside Timothy's pallet when Samuel crossed the dining room and stopped in front of her. She'd been at the boy's side for hours.

"Eliza."

She didn't look up. She laid the fresh cloth across Timothy's forehead and smoothed it with her fingertips. The boy was sleeping, his breathing shallow but steady, his small fist curled against his chest. Hattie slept on the pallet beside him. Margaret sat between them on the floor, her Bible open on her lap, her hand resting on her daughter's arm.

"Eliza," Samuel said again. "Come outside with me."

"Not right now."

"Timothy's sleeping. Hattie's stable. Margaret's right here, and Eunice and two other volunteers have the room covered." He kept his voice low. "You haven't eaten anything that I've seen. You're no good to anyone if you wear yourself into a pallet of your own."

She set the cloth in the basin. Her fingers were red from the wringing, her knuckles tight and raw. She looked at Timothy, then at Margaret, who glanced up from her Bible and gave a small nod.

"Twenty minutes," Eliza said.

"Thirty minutes... longer if we need it, so we can come back in here and feel refreshed."

She rose, and she took a moment to straighten after so long on the floor. Samuel put his hand under her elbow as they moved toward the dining room doorway to steady her. His thumb rested against the inside of her arm where her sleeve had bunched above her elbow, and the warmth of her skin against his hand sent a thread of awareness through him.

They walked out the front door together, and the fresh air hitting his face brought welcome relief. After hours in the dining room with its carbolic and lye and the close warmth of too many bodies in a room built for eating, outside was a blessing in disguise. Fresh, clean air, carrying the faint mineral smell from the river.

Eliza stopped on the porch and closed her eyes. She stood with her face turned up, and the tension in her shoulders slowly eased.

He let go of her elbow. "Sit down. I'll get us coffee."

"I should be the one getting the coffee."

"You should be the one sitting on that bench and letting somebody do one thing for you."

She sat on the bench to the right of the door and leaned against the boardinghouseFor two wall. Samuel went to the kitchen, where Winnie was ladling broth into tin cups lined up on the worktable. He poured two cups from the pot on the stove and took a biscuit from the cloth-covered plate on the shelf.

"Is she eating?" Winnie asked without turning.

"She's about to."

"Good."

He carried the coffee and the biscuits out to the porch. Eliza took the cup and held it in both hands. He sat beside her. The bench was warm from the sun, the wood smooth where hundreds of people had sat before them and worn the grain flat. Across the street, the mercantile stood closed, its porch empty, Margaret's geraniums curling in their tin window box. No wagons on the road. No horses at the hitching rail. The quarantine had stripped Main Street to its bones.

"Eat this," he said as he held the biscuit out to her.

She looked at it.

"Eat it, or I'll tell Winnie you refused, and then you'll have her to answer to instead of me."

She took it, bit into it, and chewed slowly. Her grip on her cup loosened as her body remembered food and adjusted from holding herself so tightly wound for hours with little relaxation.

"I keep thinking about his face when she carried him through the door," Eliza said. "His empty eyes. He was looking for his mama, and he couldn't find her." She took a sip of coffee. "Children break me, Samuel. I've nursed men twice my age through fevers that should've killed them, and I've held women's hands through pain I can't imagine, and I manage. I do what needs doing. But a child hurting... a child with a fever raging through his little body and his mother too sick to hold him." She stopped. "That's where my training runs out."

"I know," he said.

"You can't know. You're a doctor. You're built for this."

"I'm not built for it. Nobody is." He held his cup on his knee and looked out at the empty street. "Once, a rancher brought his daughter to me on a board. Seven years old. A horse had spooked and thrown her onto a fence post. Broken collarbone, three cracked ribs, and a punctured lung. I worked on her for six hours. Her father sat outside my door the entire time with his hat in his hands, and every time I came out for water or supplies, he stood up, and I could see his whole world was crumbling. He begged me to keep her alive and make her well again."

"Did she live?"

"She walked out of my office two weeks later with her arm in a sling and her father carrying her boots because she refused to put them on. She told me my bed was too hard and my peppermint candies were terrible." He looked at Eliza. "I went home that night and sat on my porch and thought about those two weeks she had recovered under my care. For two weeks her father and I both never left her side. That first night back in my home, I couldn't hold a cup; I was shaking so hard thinking about that little girl. I was unable to do anything but sit and think about the what-ifs, about her small, little body lying there broken. That first night home, I cried; I knew she was going to be okay, but my mind and body had collected every bit of what I'd held back. The stress, the anxiety, the fear, and the worry. I had held it in for so long that all I could do was cry. That was the release I needed."

Eliza held her coffee and watched the steam thin and curl above it. She took another bite of the biscuit.

"Tell me about something that isn't focused on anything medical. Tell me a story... anything to take my mind off what is going on inside this building because I'm reaching my breaking point, and I can feel it. Tell me about your family. The ranch. Tell me something good."

He leaned back against the wall and stretched his legs out on the porch boards. His boots were scuffed, and he looked at them while he gathered where to start.

"My mother's kitchen was the center of everything on our ranch," he said. "My mother, Esmi, cooked as if feeding people was her way of praying. Breakfast was the meal she took most seriously. She'd be up before any of us, and by the time my father came in from the barn, the table would be covered. Eggs, biscuits, ham, potatoes fried with onions, preserves she'd put up the summer before, and coffee so strong you could stand a spoon in it."

"How many of you were at that table?"

"Eight. My parents, Caleb, Marian, me, Gerald, Rachel, and Bonita."

"Six children," Eliza said with a smile. "I hope to someday have a home full of children as well."

"My father always said the ranch needed hands, and the Lord provided. My mother says the Lord provided, and the ranch gave her somewhere to put them all." He smiled. "She's funnier than she lets on. She keeps her humor for the kitchen and the supper table. In public she's proper and composed, the way a rancher's wife is expected to be. At home she'd catch my father's eye across the table and say something so dry he'd choke on his coffee, and the rest of us would fall apart, and she'd sit there eating her supper like she'd said nothing at all."

Eliza turned on the bench to face him. "What is your father like?"

"Patient and firm. He rarely raises his voice." He turned his cup in his hands. "He taught every one of us to work. Not just the boys. Marian could rope a calf before she was ten. Rachel could mend a fence line as well as Gerald could. Bonita was the youngest, and she could ride anything with four legs by the time she was eight. My father believed every person on a ranch earned their keep, and he believed it equally. He sat us each on a horse before we could read a book. He taught us how to read the sky for weather, how to tell if a pasture was overgrazed, how to dig a well and fix a gate, and how to pull a calf. He'd say, 'The Lord gave us this ground, and He expects us to tend it. If you can't tend what you've been given, you don't deserve to keep it.'"

"He sounds like a wonderful father."

"He is. Stubborn enough to argue with a fence post and patient enough to wait it out. My mother says she married the most hard-headed man in Colorado and has the gray hairs to prove it."

Eliza laughed. The sound was small and tired but real, and it loosened the tight line of worry she'd worn since Timothy's arrival.

"Do you miss them?" she asked.

"Every day. I don't write home as often as my mother would like. She sends letters four pages long, filled with every detail of what my nieces and nephews have done since her last one. I write back two paragraphs and call it correspondence. She hasn't forgiven me for it."

"How many nieces and nephews?"

"Fifteen. Marian's got four. Bonita's got three. Caleb has one. Rachel's got three, and Gerald's got four. They're all under the age of ten, and when they're at the ranch at the same time, my mother says the noise carries clear to the county line."

"Fifteen children running through a ranch house. Your poor mother."

"She loves every minute of it. She told me in her last letter that if she'd known grandchildren were this much fun, she'd have skipped the children and gone straight to the good part."

Eliza smiled and took a sip of her coffee. The Absaroka Range filled the sky above the rooftops across the street, its timbered slopes banded in late-afternoon light that turned the lodgepole stands from green to near-black where the ravines cut deep. The bare peaks above the timberline stood pale against a sky that had faded toward white near the horizon, the heat pressing the blue out of things.

"What brought you to Providence Ridge?" She asked.

"I'd been moving between small towns for a little over a year. Railroad camps, mining settlements, and ranching communities. Good work, needed work, but nothing held me." He looked at his hands around his cup. "Providence Ridge was a town that needed a doctor. I'd been told that this town was small and close-knit and that good people lived here. I heard that there was plenty of space to build a home and start a new life. That was enough."

"What were you running from?"

He turned to look her straight in the eye. "That's a conversation for another time," he said. "Not now. Right now is for good things."

He saw the question in her eyes, but she let it go and simply nodded.

"Then tell me more good things... funny things from your childhood, maybe."

"My younger sister, Bonita, got thrown from a horse when she was nine. Landed in the irrigation ditch, soaked from head to boots, covered in mud, and came up swinging because she was angry at the horse for embarrassing her. My father pulled her out and set her on her feet, and she marched back to that horse and climbed on before anyone could stop her. My mother came out of the kitchen, took one look at Bonita on the horse covered from head to toe in mud, shook her head, and went back inside."

"I would like your mother very much."

"I'm sure she would like you as well. She'd take one look at you and put you to work in her kitchen, and she'd have your life story out of you before the biscuits were done. People tell my mother things they don't tell anyone else, and I've never figured out how she manages it. My father says it's because she doesn't pry, but she listens like she's got all the time in the world, even when she doesn't."

The front door opened, and Reverend Hale stepped onto the porch. His Bible was tucked under his arm, his sleeves rolled to his forearms, and he looked tired.

"It's good to see you both out here taking a break; you deserve it," Webb said. He lowered himself onto the bench on the other side of the door. "Eunice banished me out of the dining room... told me I needed to take a break myself."

"She's not wrong; you deserve a break too, Reverend," Samuel said.

"She's rarely wrong, which is a fact I've accepted over thirty years of marriage." Webb set his Bible on his knee. "Timothy's sleeping well. Hattie woke for a bit and took some broth. Margaret hasn't moved from her position on the floor between the two of them."

"Thank you for spending your time with all of them," Eliza said. "And for reading bits of scripture to them. I truly believe it's helping them."

"It helps me, too. When I'm not sure what else to do for someone, I read and I pray. It's all I've got sometimes, and most times it turns out to be enough."

Eliza looked at his Bible. "Would you read something now? For us?"

Webb opened his Bible and turned the thin pages with care, found what he was looking for, and held the book flat on his lap.

"Psalm 145," he said. "Verses eight through sixteen. 'The Lord is gracious and full of compassion; slow to anger and of great mercy. The Lord is good to all, and his tender mercies are over all his works. All thy works shall praise thee, O Lord, and thy saints shall bless thee. They shall speak of the glory of thy kingdom and talk of thy power; to make known to the sons of men his mighty acts and the glorious majesty of his kingdom. Thy kingdom is an everlasting kingdom, and thy dominion endureth throughout all generations. The Lord upholdeth all that fall, and raiseth up all those that be bowed down. The eyes of all wait upon thee, and thou givest them their meat in due season. Thou openest thine hand and satisfiest the desire of every living thing.'"

He closed the Bible.

Eliza sat with her cup in both hands. Her breathing had slowed, her fingers resting loosely around the tin instead of gripping it. Samuel had watched as the Scripture reached her, the way water reaches cracked ground, not flooding but soaking in, settling into the places that needed it most.

"Lord," Webb said as he bowed his head, "we put these two in Your hands tonight. They've given this town everything they have, and they'll give more before this is over. Renew their strength. Steady them when they falter. Remind them that the work is Yours and they are Yours and the people in that room are Yours, and none of it rests on their shoulders alone. We ask for Your mercy over Timothy and Hattie and every soul in that ward. In Jesus' name. Amen."

"Amen," Eliza said.

Webb stood and tucked his Bible under his arm. "I'm going back in. I promised Zeb I'd finish the chapter of Job we started this morning. He's got opinions about it, which is a good sign." He looked at them both. "Stay out here a few more minutes; we've got everything inside covered."

Samuel and Eliza sat alone on the porch and enjoyed a few more minutes of relaxation. Samuel leaned against the boardinghouse and closed his eyes, taking in deep breaths as he cleared his mind.

"I love this view," Eliza said. "When I arrived, I thought the mountains were beautiful the way a painting is beautiful, something to admire and walk past. I look at those ridges now, and I think about how long they've been standing. Thousands and thousands of years. And every patient I've lost sleep over, every night I've spent wondering if I'm doing enough, all of it is the blink of an eye to those mountains. They don't know my name, and they don't need to. I'm one small person in a valley God carved before anyone was here to see it." She was quiet for a moment. "That should make me feel small. It doesn't. It makes me feel held. Like whatever I'm carrying, He's carried bigger, and He'll carry this too."

"That's the best sermon I've heard since I came to Providence Ridge," Samuel said. "Don't tell Webb."

She smiled, and the smile reached her eyes, and the sight of it did something to him that a medical textbook couldn't diagram and his notebook couldn't record. He held his cup and looked at the mountains with her.

"Samuel."

"Yes?"

"Edith." She sat up straight and turned to him. "I haven't seen Edith today."

He ran through the morning in his mind. Timothy in his arms, burning. Hattie on the floor. Webb running for the Pembertons. Eliza at Timothy's side for hours. Winnie in the kitchen. Eunice directing the volunteers. Della. Alma. Margaret. Every person accounted for, every patient tracked, and he hadn't once looked for the one person who he knew had been looking slightly under the weather as of late.

"She wasn't well yesterday, Samuel. You saw it. I saw it. She was pale and cold in a room that was too warm."

He stood quickly, and she did the same. Every trace of the fatigue she'd carried onto this porch was gone, burned away by the focused urgency of a nurse who'd just understood that someone had slipped through while she was tending to everyone else.

"Her home," Eliza said. "We need to go now."

Chapter 20

Eliza knocked on Edith's door and waited. The small home sat at the far end of the row houses, past the Cobbs' place and Zeb Thompson's, the last of the small homes that lined the dirt path. A garden plot ran along one side, its herbs going leggy and unwatered in the July heat, and a rocking chair sat on the narrow porch.

"Edith," Eliza called. "It's Eliza and Dr. Porter. We've come to check on you."

A voice came from inside, thin and hoarse but clear. "The door's not latched. Come in."

Samuel lifted the handle and pushed the door open. The cottage was a single room divided by a half-wall of rough pine into a living space and a sleeping area. Everything in the front half was ordered and clean, the home of a woman who kept things where they belonged. A cookstove stood against the far wall with a kettle centered on the cold burner. A shelf held a row of books, their spines cracked and well-handled, beside a tin of tea and a jar of dried lavender. A teacup sat upside down on a cloth beside the basin, washed and set to dry.

Edith was in bed behind the half-wall, propped against her pillows with a quilt pulled to her waist and her shawl wrapped around her shoulders despite the warmth trapped in the cottage from the closed windows. Her silver hair had come loose from its pins and lay against her neck in thin strands. Her face was pale, her skin damp at her temples and along her jaw. Her hands rested flat on the quilt with the stiffness that came from her arthritis.

She looked at them, and her mouth trembled before it found its shape.

"I've been talking to the Lord all day," she said. "Told Him if He was going to send somebody, He'd better do it before suppertime because I wasn't getting any younger lying here." Her eyes moved from Eliza to Samuel and back. "I've been too weak to get out of this bed. I tried twice. My legs wouldn't hold me." She pressed her lips together. "I'm sick. I've done everything I could think of to fight it off. I drank boiled water. I made some vegetable broth last night. I prayed the Lord would take this from me, and He saw fit not to. So I'll go through it, and I'll go through it with whatever dignity He lets me keep."

Eliza knelt beside the bed and took Edith's hand. Her fingers were hot, her joints swollen tighter than usual beneath the fever's grip, and her palm dry and papery.

Samuel set his bag on the floor and sat down in the straight-backed chair he'd brought from the table. He placed his fingers on the inside of Edith's wrist.

"How long have you had the fever, Edith?" he asked.

"It started late last night. I came home early from the boarding house yesterday because I couldn't keep my eyes open, and by the time I got here, my whole body ached even more. I made a bit of broth, and then I laid down to rest."

"Have you been able to drink anything at all today?"

"I managed about half a cup of water early this morning. My stomach won't settle."

"Any pain in your belly?"

"Low. On the right side. It started this morning."

He pressed his palm to her forehead. He checked her abdomen for extreme tenderness and her chest for spots, finding none, and looked at her tongue and the whites of her eyes.

"You're early in this, Edith," he said. "The fever's real, and you're getting dehydrated, but you're lucid and answering every question I'm asking, which tells me your body's fighting well. I want to bring you to the boardinghouse where Eliza and I can be with you at all times and keep fluids in you."

"I expected you'd say that."

"I'm going to go to the livery and get Paul and a wagon. Eliza will stay with you until I get back."

"Dr. Porter." Edith looked at him. "I know what this illness does. I'm old, and I'm not as strong as I used to be, and I'd appreciate it if you treated me like a grown woman and didn't spare me the truth."

"The truth is what I just told you," he said. "You're early. You're coherent. You're fighting. Those are good things. I don't spare anyone the truth. I'm not starting with you."

She studied him for a moment and nodded. "All right. Go get the wagon."

Samuel left, and the cottage was quiet except for Edith's breathing and the tick of a small clock on the shelf that Eliza hadn't noticed before.

"Edith, is there anything you'd like to bring with you? Anything from home that would comfort you?"

"My Bible," Edith said. "It's on the shelf beside the tea tin. You'll know it by the state of it. I've loved that book near to pieces."

Eliza crossed to the shelf. The Bible was smaller than she'd expected, bound in brown leather that had gone soft at the spine and dark at the corners from decades of handling.

"And the photograph on the shelf above the stove. In the tin frame."

Eliza found it. A carte de visite in a small tin frame, the image faded. A man with a broad face and kind eyes, his hair combed back, his collar buttoned, his expression the stiff stillness of someone who didn't sit for portraits often and wasn't sure what to do. He looked like the sort of man who'd be more comfortable holding an axe handle than a coat lapel.

"That's my Arthur," Edith said.

Eliza brought the photograph and Bible to Edith and set them beside her on the bed.

"And the quilt at the foot of the bed, Eliza. Would you bring that too?"

Eliza unfolded it and laid it across Edith's lap. The fabric was cotton, faded in places to the soft colors of something washed many times. The pattern was a nine-patch, each square pieced from scraps in blues and whites and a pale yellow that had once been brighter. The stitching was even and close, done by hands that knew their way around a needle.

"My mama made this quilt," Edith said. "She started it the winter before my wedding and finished it in time to fold it across the foot of my bed the morning Arthur and I were married. She told me a wife needs three things in her home: a Bible for her soul, a good cookstove for her family, and a quilt made by someone who loves her for the nights when the world feels cold." She smoothed the fabric with her palm. "My mama's been gone thirty-one years. My cookstove hasn't been lit since yesterday. But I've still got the Bible she and Daddy gave me and this quilt. I suppose two out of three is more than most people get to keep."

Eliza sat in the chair Samuel had pulled to the bedside and took Edith's hand again.

"Tell me about Arthur," she said.

Edith's thumb moved across Eliza's knuckles. "Arthur Aldridge was a carpenter. He could build anything. Tables, chairs, doorframes, cabinets. He helped to build a few of the businesses in town and these homes here on this wagon road. He built our first home, which was a bit further south of here, tucked into a hillside and near the river." She looked at the photograph of her husband. "He was a quiet man and a deep thinker. But when he talked, people listened, because Arthur never said a word he hadn't already turned over twice and decided was worth saying. And he had a sense of humor like you wouldn't believe."

"How did you meet?"

"At a church social in Cheyenne," Edith said. "I was twenty-one and helping my father run his general store. Arthur was twenty-five and working carpentry jobs wherever the railroad was building. He came to the social because the preacher's wife told him there'd be pie. I was standing near the pie table, and he decided he needed a slice just so he could speak to me. Then he had a second slice."

Eliza smiled.

"He courted me for four months," Edith said. "Came to the store every Saturday and bought something he didn't need just to have a reason to talk to me. I knew what he was doing by the second week, but I let him keep at it because I liked watching him pretend he needed another box of nails."

"He sounds like a good man."

"He was the best man I ever knew. Not perfect. He couldn't carry a tune, and he burned everything he tried to cook, and he'd forget to come in from his workshop until I went out and told him his supper was cold. But he was faithful, and he was kind, and those two things will carry a marriage further than anything else." Edith's words came slower now, with more space between them. "We were married for forty-two years. He died three years ago this October. His heart gave out on a Tuesday evening. He was sitting in his rocking chair on the porch of our home out by the river, and I brought him his coffee the way I did every evening, and he was gone."

"That was a hard time for me. I grieved him something fierce, but the good Lord brought me through it," Edith said. "The hardest part after the Lord took him home was the quiet. Forty-two years of someone sitting across your table and sleeping beside you and calling your name from the other room, and then one day the house goes silent and stays that way. I had to learn how to live in a quiet house, and it took me longer than I'd like to admit." Her thumb had stilled on Eliza's hand. "Your aunt saved me from that, Eliza. Leora came to my door two days after Arthur's funeral and said, 'Edith Aldridge, I need you at the boardinghouse tomorrow morning. I've got more boarders than I can handle and a dining room that won't set itself, and I refuse to do it alone when you're sitting here with nothing but four walls for company.' She didn't ask if I was ready. She told me where to be."

"That sounds exactly like my aunt."

"She and the good Lord saved me. Leora pulled me out of the state I was in by giving me a reason to get up every day and somewhere useful to go. She was the person who convinced me to sell my home and move closer to town, and that's how I came to live here." Edith's eyes were heavy now, her blinks longer, her lids slow to open. "She's going to be frightened when she hears I'm sick. You'll have to tell her gently, Eliza. She acts as if she's tough as old leather, but Leora Hanscombe loves with her whole heart, and she's lost too many people already. You be gentle with her when you tell her."

"I will."

"And you take care of yourself, too." Edith's fingers loosened in Eliza's. "I've watched you these past few days, child. You pour yourself out for everyone else, and you forget that your pitcher needs filling too. Your mama and daddy raised a good woman... Leora's as proud as a peacock of you, Eliza. She loves you so."

"Thank you, Edith."

"I'm not finished." Her voice was thinner now, each word arriving from further away. "Don't let this illness take your joy. Don't let it take the good things God's putting in front of you. You've got work to do here, and people who need you, and a life that's growing in ways you haven't let yourself look at yet. Promise me you'll keep looking."

"I promise."

Edith nodded. Her eyes closed. Her breathing slowed, each exhale longer and softer than the one before, and her hand went still in Eliza's, her fingers loose but holding. She'd fallen asleep the way the sick do, between one breath and the next, her body making the decision her mind was too tired to make.

Eliza sat beside her and held her hand. The clock ticked. The light through the window had dimmed to the blue-gray of early evening, and the home held the quiet Edith had described, the quiet of a house with only one person awake in it.

She'd been holding everything together inside her since Timothy arrived that morning. Since she'd knelt beside a five-year-old boy and invented a story about a frog to keep him from being afraid. She'd held it through Hattie's collapse and Margaret's whispered prayers, through hours of wringing cloths and counting pulses and coaxing broth into mouths that didn't want it. She'd held it on the porch with Samuel while he talked about his mother's kitchen and his sister in the irrigation ditch. She'd held it while Webb read Scripture and prayed over them both.

She couldn't hold it anymore.

The tears came, and she let them fall because there was no one awake to see and no reason left to stop them. They tracked down her cheeks and fell from her jaw, and she didn't wipe them away.

She bowed her head over Edith's hand and closed her eyes.

"Lord," she said, her voice low and rough in the quiet room. "I'm so scared. I'm asking You for mercy tonight. I'm asking for Edith. She's been Your faithful servant longer than I've been alive, and I'm asking You to carry her through this. Please don't take her from us. Don't take her from Leora." She pressed her forehead against their joined hands. "I'm asking for Timothy. He's five years old, Lord, still a babe. He's lying on a pallet fighting something his little body shouldn't have to fight, and his mama's beside him fighting the same thing. Be with them. Be with Hattie. Be with Ada and her unborn babe, and Zeb and the Fitches, and Emmett and Mr. Drumond. Be with all of them Lord, they need your touch. I don't have enough hands for all of them, and I don't have enough hours, and I'm running out of strength."

She breathed deeply. Her tears soaked Edith's knuckles, and she didn't lift her head.

"And Samuel. Watch over him. He carries so much by himself because he thinks that's what You require, and it isn't. Show him that. Give him rest. Give him peace. Give us all Your tender mercy tonight. In Jesus' name. Amen."

Chapter 21

Eliza woke with her cheek pressed against the back of Edith's hand and her neck bent at an angle that sent pain down her left shoulder the moment she tried to lift her head.

She hadn't meant to fall asleep. She'd been praying while lying on the floor beside Edith's pallet.

Edith's face was slack, her silver hair spread across the makeshift pillow in thin strands. Her breathing was shallow but steady, each exhale carrying a faint rasp. The flush of fever sat high on her cheekbones, darker than it had been before she'd fallen asleep.

Eliza eased her fingers free and sat up. Her back protested. Her hip ached, and the muscles along her ribs felt cinched. She pressed her fingers to the inside of Edith's wrist. The pulse was there, thin and quick beneath her papery skin.

The dining room was quiet. The light through the dining room windows was the colorless gray that came before dawn in the mountains, when the sky had begun to pale but the sun hadn't yet cleared the Absarokas. It turned the room into shapes without edges. The pallets lay in rows across the floor, each one holding a body beneath a sheet or a thin blanket.

She moved through the room quietly and stood before Hattie's pallet with Timothy's beside it. Both of them were sleeping with their hands joined across the narrow space between them.

Samuel was on the floor beside Timothy's pallet.

He'd made a bed of sorts from a folded quilt and a blanket pulled from the linen shelf. He lay on his side with one arm bent beneath his head and the other resting across his chest, his hand open and loose against his shirt. His boots were still on. His vest was unbuttoned, and his notebook lay open on the floor beside his shoulder, the pencil still caught in its spine. His face in sleep appeared younger, lacking the visible signs of stress and concern it normally held. The concentration gone from his brow, his jaw loosened.

She stood in the gray light and watched him sleep. She looked at his fingers resting open against his shirt, broad and relaxed in a way she'd never seen them during the day, when they were always holding a pencil or pressing a pulse point. She looked at his dark hair that had fallen across his forehead.

Timothy stirred on his pallet. His head turned on the pillow and his lips parted, but he settled again with a small sound that was more breath than word, and his fingers tightened once around Hattie's hand before going slack.

She turned and walked to the kitchen. The cookstove was still warm, a low orange glow visible through the draft door. She fed two pieces of split pine into the firebox and adjusted the damper, and the coals caught the new wood with a soft crackle.

She filled the coffeepot with water from the boiled-water bucket on the table, measured grounds from the tin, and set it on the stove. While the coffee heated, she washed her face and hands at the basin, scrubbing with the carbolic soap, which stung the cracks in her skin from washing her hands so often. She unpinned her hair, combed it with her fingers, and twisted it back into a low knot at her nape.

When the coffee was ready. She poured two cups and carried them down the hall to her aunt's room.

The door was open, and she was happy to see that she was awake. She sat up against her pillows with her quilt pulled to her waist and her shawl around her shoulders, and she was looking at the window where the first thin light was beginning to show. She turned when Eliza came through the door.

"You haven't been sleeping enough, my dear," Leora said.

"I slept for aboutEdith, an hour." Eliza said as she handed a cup of coffee to her aunt. "On the floor. Beside Edith's pallet."

Leora's cup stopped halfway to her mouth.

"Beside Edith's pallet," she said.

Eliza pulled a chair close to the bed and sat down . Leora set her cup on the bedside table. Her hands came back to her lap, and her knuckles went white where her fingers locked.

"Edith has fallen ill. Samuel and I went to check on her last evening at her home. She was too weak to stand. We brought her here in Paul's wagon, and I sat with her through the night."

Leora didn't move. She sat against her pillows with her hands pressed flat against each other and her face perfectly still. Then Leora's mouth pressed into a line so tight the color left her lips, and she closed her eyes.

"How bad?" she asked.

"She has a fever. She's dehydrated, and her stomach hasn't been able to keep much down. Samuel examined her thoroughly. He said she's early in this, and she's lucid, and her body's fighting."

"How bad, Eliza?" Leora opened her eyes, and they were full of moisture. "Tell me the truth."

"She's sick, Aunt Leora. She has the same illness the others have, and she's sixty-six years old, and her body isn't as strong as it once was. She was alert when we checked on her last night at her home and could speak clearly and knew what was happening. She told me which things to bring from her cottage. She asked for her Bible, Arthur's photograph, and the quilt her mama made." Eliza reached across and took her aunt's hand. "She asked me to be gentle with you when I told you. She said you act tough as old leather, but you love with your whole heart, and she didn't want you frightened."

Leora's face broke.

It wasn't the slow crumbling Eliza had watched in patients' families, the gradual loosening of composure. It was sudden and complete. Leora pressed her hand over her mouth, and her shoulders drew in, and the sound that came from behind her fingers was low and raw.

Eliza set her cup on the table and climbed onto the bed beside her aunt. She wrapped her arms around Leora's shoulders and drew her close, and Leora turned into her, her forehead pressed against Eliza's collarbone, her hand gripping the front of Eliza's dress.

"She's my dearest friend," Leora said, her voice broken against Eliza's shoulder. "She's been my dearest friend for years. She came to me when Harold died and sat with me, and she didn't leave my side for a week. She's been coming to this boardinghouse every day for three years. Every day, Eliza. Through snow and July heat, and her hands hurting so bad some mornings she could hardly button her coat." She drew a breath that caught, and her tears continued to fall. "And I'm lying in this bed with this useless leg, and I can't even go to her. I can't sit beside her and hold her hand. I can't do one single thing for the person who has done everything for me."

"You are doing something," Eliza said. "You're trusting me and Samuel to take care of her the way she'd want to be taken care of. That isn't nothing, Aunt Leora."

"It feels like nothing." Leora pulled back enough to wipe her eyes with the heel of her hand, impatient with her own tears the way she was impatient with her own leg. "I lie here day after day, and people bring me reports, and I listen and I nod and I say the right things, and the whole time I want to scream because I should be out there. I should be standing at that stove in my kitchen making broth and boiling water and doing something useful instead of sitting in this room waiting for news."

"You're not sitting here waiting for news. You're recovering from a broken leg so that when this is over, you can walk back into your boardinghouse and run it the way only you can run it. Edith would tell you the same thing if she were sitting where I'm sitting, and you know it."

Leora looked at her with wet eyes, and the ghost of what might have been a smile. "She would. She'd tell me to stop carrying on and drink my coffee before it gets cold, and she'd be right."

"Then drink your coffee."

Leora picked up her cup. Her hands trembled, and the coffee shivered against the tin, and she took a sip.

"Tell me about the others," Leora said. "All of them."

Eliza told her. Timothy was holding on. His fever hadn't broken, but he was keeping small sips of water down, and he'd slept through most of the night. Hattie was fighting the way Hattie fought everything, with a stubbornness that came from the same place her love for her son did. Ada was stable, her fever lower than the day before, and Jasper hadn't left her side. The Fitches were holding steady, Clara's hand still finding Nolan's across the gap between their pallets every time one of them shifted in the night. Emmett was improving, slowly, in degrees so small they were almost invisible unless you were watching for them.

"And Mr. Drumond?" Leora asked.

"He's worse. Samuel's doing everything he can. We both fear we will lose him."

Leora was quiet. She drank her coffee and looked at the window, where the light had strengthened enough to put a line of sun across the foot of her bed.

"And you?" she said. "How are you, Eliza?"

"I'm tired. But I'm all right."

"You slept one hour on the floor beside my best friend."

"I've slept less before."

"That isn't the reassurance you think it is."

"I'm scared," Eliza said. "I'm scared for Edith and for Timothy, and for Mr. Drumond... all of them. I'm tired... I'm frightened... I feel all twisted up inside. I'm not sure if I'm coming or going half the time. This is all hitting me hard, and my body is feeling it."

Eliza looked toward the window again. Beyond it, the sky was turning the particular shade of blue that happens in Montana in the minutes before full sunrise, deep and clean, as though someone had washed it in the night and hung it up new.

"I don't know how to talk about this," she said. "I've never had anyone to talk to about it. I'm not even sure how to say what I need to or if it's proper for a young woman to ask some of the questions that are on my mind."

"You have me."

Eliza looked at her hands in her lap, at the reddened knuckles and the small cracks along her fingers, and she thought about how many things those hands had done over the past several days. How many cloths they'd wrung, pulses they'd felt, and cups they'd held to fevered lips. None of that work had prepared her for what she was about to say.

"It's Samuel," she said.

Leora's expression didn't change. Not a flicker, not a twitch. "Go on," she said.

"I don't know when it started. I don't know if it was one particular day or if it's been building since the first time he walked into your room and I saw the way he treated you, the care he took, and the respect he gave you even when you were trying to run him off." She folded her hands in her lap and turned to look at her aunt. "When I'm near him, something in me settles. I can't explain it better than that. Everything is pressing in from every direction—the patients, the fear, and the work that doesn't stop—and when he appears, I can breathe again. Not because he fixes anything or says anything in particular. Just because he's there."

"And when he isn't?" Leora asked.

"I look for him. I listen for his voice, and when I hear it, my chest does something I can't account for. It tightens and then it opens, like a fist letting go, and I don't understand why a man's voice is doing that to me." She looked at her aunt. "I watch him with the patients. The gentleness in his hands when he checks a fever, the way he tells people the truth even when the truth is hard because he respects them too much to lie. And I find myself caring about him in a way that goes past what I should feel for someone I'm working beside. I notice when the strain of all this is pressing on him and he won't say so, and I want to do for him what he keeps trying to do for me, which is make him stop and sit down and take a break."

"And the worst of it," she continued, "is that I don't know if any of this is proper. I'm not certain if I should be feeling this way about a man I've known for less than two weeks while people are lying in the next room fighting for their lives. I feel selfish even thinking about it. People are sick, Aunt Leora. Edith is sick. Timothy is still a babe and burning with fever, and here I am talking about the way a man's voice makes me feel. What kind of woman does that make me?"

"A living one," Leora said. "A living woman with a beating heart. And the fact that you think it makes you anything less tells me everything I need to know about how long you've been putting yourself last."

"I haven't been putting myself last. I've been doing what needs doing."

"Those are the same thing, child, and you've been doing them both since you were fourteen years old and began caring for your mother." Leora adjusted the pillow behind her back and turned toward her niece. "Now you listen to me, because I'm going to say things your mother would have said if the Lord had seen fit to leave her here with us long enough to say them, and I'm not going to soften a word of it because you don't need soft right now. You need the truth."

"There's nothing selfish about your heart recognizing a good man in the middle of a hard time. That isn't selfishness. That is God's timing, and God's timing has never once cared about what we find convenient. Do you think love waits until the circumstances are comfortable? Do you think your uncle Harold courted me during a peaceful, easy time? He courted me during a drought year when my father's store was barely making its accounts and half the town was worried about whether they'd eat come winter. My Harold showed up every day to visit me, and I let him keep at it because even in the middle of hard times, especially in the middle of hard times, the heart knows what it knows."

"But how do I know it's real?" Eliza said. "How do I know this isn't just the closeness and the crisis and the fact that we're spending every waking hour in the same building? What if this is nothing more than exhaustion and fear making me reach for the nearest steady thing?"

"I don't have an answer to that, Eliza. Not a certain one." Leora turned her cup between her palms. "I can't see what's between you and Samuel. I'm in this room, not out there. But I can tell you what I've noticed from right here in this bed, and you can make of it what you will." She paused. "He asks about you. Every time he comes to check my leg, every time he stops in this doorway to give me his reports, somewhere in the conversation, if your name is brought up, he'll look for ways to learn more about you. He perks up if your name is mentioned. Just the way his expression changes, or the way he speaks of you; if you are brought into the conversation, his entire demeanor changes. His voice changes. Gets quieter, maybe a bit more emotional. More carefule, as if he were choosing his words the way a person chooses where to step on uncertain ground. I've been married, child. I know what a man sounds like when a woman has gotten under his skin and he isn't sure yet what to do about it."

"He hasn't said anything to me."

"He wouldn't. He's the kind of man who shows his interest by doing. The kind who puts a cup of coffee in your hands before you've asked for one and makes you sit down when you won't do it yourself. Those aren't the actions of a man who sees you as a colleague. Those are the actions of a man who cares about you and doesn't know what to do with it any more than you do."

"I don't know how to do this," Eliza said. "I don't know how a woman is supposed to respond when she feels this way. I never had the chance to learn. Thomas courted me for five months, and I liked him well enough, but I never felt anything close to what I'm feeling now. When the courtship ended, I wasn't heartbroken, and the fact that I wasn't heartbroken frightened me.... I thought there was something wrong with me. This is different. This is something I don't have a word for, and I don't have a mother to sit me down and tell me what it means."

"You have me," Leora said. "And I'm telling you what it means. It means your heart is waking up. Eight years, Eliza. For eight years you've poured every last drop of yourself into caring for your mother first, then your father, caring for sick strangers, running a household, volunteering at hospitals, and doing everything on

God's green earth except stopping long enough to ask yourself what you want from life. And now the Lord has put you in a place where you can't outrun it anymore, and He's put a good man in front of you, and your heart is answering. That isn't weakness. That isn't selfishness. That is the most natural and God-given thing a woman's heart can do."

"But what do I do about it? Do I carry on as we have been and hope he says something? Do I behave differently so he knows I'd welcome his attention? Do I push it all aside until this illness has passed and people are well again?"

"You do not push it aside." Leora's voice was firm as she reached for Eliza's hand. "I'm going to tell you something, and I want you to write it on your heart. Life doesn't stop for crises. It can't, and it shouldn't. If the only time you allow yourself to feel joy is when there's no sorrow anywhere in sight, you'll go your whole life without it. 'To everything there is a season. A time to weep, and a time to laugh; a time to mourn, and a time to dance.' Seasons of life don't always come one at a time, and I speak from experience. They can come tangled up, all of them at once sometimes, and the measure of a life isn't whether you can sort them out but whether you can hold them all."

Eliza was quiet. The line of sun across the foot of the bed had moved while they'd been talking, climbing from the quilt's edge toward Leora's folded hands.

"As for how to let him know," Leora said, her voice settling from firmness into something gentler, "you don't need to do anything dramatic or improper. You be yourself. You speak to him the way you speak when you aren't guarding every word. You let him see that his company brings you joy. A woman doesn't need to announce her feelings to a man who's paying attention, and from what I gather, that man is paying attention."

"I'm not certain he knows what I feel."

"Then give him a chance to find out somewhere besides a sickroom." Leora drank from her cup. "I've got a horse stabled at Paul's livery and a wagon that hasn't moved since I broke this leg. There's no reason you couldn't go to Paul and ask him to hitch it up. There's no reason you couldn't ask Samuel to ride out with you for an hour. Just an hour, Eliza. Get out of this boardinghouse and breathe air that doesn't smell like carbolic. See the country. Talk to each other without a patient between you."

"I can't leave like that... just take off when people are ill."

"Can't or won't? Those are different things. You and Samuel have been in that dining room nearly every minute of every day. Eunice is capable. Winnie is capable. The rest of the volunteers know what to do. Everything that can be done for the sick is being done, and the rest is in God's hands. It has always been in God's hands. All you and Samuel can do is keep them comfortable, keep them hydrated, and offer prayers, and those same things can be done by any one of the people who are already standing beside you in that dining room."

Eliza pressed her lips together. Her aunt was right, and the rightness of it sat in her chest alongside something that surprised her, because she hadn't expected to feel guilty about wanting an hour of peace.

"There's something else," she said as she looked away. "He lives here. I live in Philadelphia. It would be unfair to pursue something such as this. My whole life is in Philadelphia. My father is there. His business, his home, everything I've ever known."

"Your life so far is in Philadelphia," Leora said. "That isn't the same thing as your whole life. You know very well that I packed my life up and Harold and I moved here because we chose to. We chose to pursue the life we wanted. Your mother did the same when she married your father and moved from Ohio, where we grew up, to Philadelphia. The women in this family have never been the kind to let geography decide their future."

"But I can't just leave my father. No dutiful daughter would leave her father on his own so she could chase after her own wants."

"Eliza Constance Miller." Leora set her cup down with a firmness that made the table ring. "Your father is a fifty-four-year-old man who runs a successful printing business. He is not a child. He's quite capable of feeding himself and taking care of himself. He isn't helpless. He isn't infirm. He loves you with his whole heart, and because he loves you, he'd be the first person to tell you that he didn't raise a daughter to spend her life keeping house for a man who's perfectly capable of keeping his own. Henry Miller would want you to find your own way, Eliza. He'd want you to find your purpose and your joy, and he'd be ashamed to know you were holding yourself back from both because you believed it was your duty."

Eliza opened her mouth and closed it again.

"You're a strong, capable woman," Leora said. "You have a gift for healing and caring for others. God made you for this work. That much is as clear to me as the nose on my face. And I believe with my whole heart that God brought you here for more than running my boardinghouse while I mend. He brought you here to show you that your life is bigger than your father's household and the streets you grew up on. Maybe He brought you here to open your eyes to a world you didn't know was waiting for you. Perhaps He brought you here to plant your feet in a place where you can grow into the woman He made you to be." She reached over and took Eliza's hand. "Your life is just beginning, child. If you'll reach out and take hold of it."

They sat with their hands joined on the quilt between them, and the line of sun moved from the foot of the bed toward their fingers, slow and unhurried. From the kitchen came the first sounds of the house waking: a pot set on the stove, water poured from a bucket, the rhythm of someone beginning the day's first work.

"Could you see yourself here?" Leora asked. "If everything else fell away, if Philadelphia wasn't waiting, and your father, let's say, was courting a woman and planning to marry again, and the question was simply, what does Eliza want? Could you build a life in this place?"

Eliza looked at the view outside the bedroom window. "I've been here less than two weeks," she said. "And I know that isn't long enough to know anything for certain. But I like it here, Aunt Leora. I like the quiet. I like the way the mountains change every time the light moves. I like the way the air smells clean and fresh, and the feeling of renewal that it gives me. I haven't seen any of this area properly, not the way I want to. I haven't walked along the creek or the river, nor stood somewhere high enough to see how far this land goes. There's so much I haven't seen, and I want to see it. All of it." She paused, and when she spoke again, her voice was lower, closer to the one she used when the truth surprised her. "I want to know what this place could be if I stayed long enough to find out."

Leora squeezed her hand.

"Then don't you dare let fear make decisions for you," Leora said. "Not fear of leaving your father, not fear of what people might think, and not fear of giving your heart to a man who deserves it. The Lord didn't bring you fifteen hundred miles to show you something beautiful and then ask you to walk away from it."

Chapter 22

A few days later...

Samuel stood at the foot of Mr. Drumond's bed with his note-book open and his pencil still, looking at the man who'd been lying in this room for nearly two weeks. He was no longer fighting in any way Samuel could measure.

Eliza stood beside the washstand, wringing a cloth into the basin. She'd come upstairs with him after the patients in the dining room had been checked, leaving Eunice, Reverend Hale, Winnie, and Margaret stationed among the pallets below.

He moved to the bedside and set his notebook on the chair. Mr. Drumond's face had a pale grey pallor, and the hollows beneath his cheekbones had deepened. His lips were cracked white at the corners. Each breath came slow and costly, a labored draw that pulled his ribs inward and released with a thin rattle. His abdomen was rigid when Samuel pressed his fingers against it, and the rigidity hadn't softened at all.

Samuel lifted Mr. Drumond's wrist. His pulse ran faint and thready. He pressed his palm to Mr. Drumond's forehead, and his skin was dry and hot.

The man stirred, turned his head on the pillow, and his right hand lifted from the mattress in a searching arc, fingers closing around Samuel's wrist. Not a grip. A reflex, the blind reaching of a man deep in the fog his fever had built. His lips parted. A single word came out.

"Constance."

His fingers went slack. His hand fell to the mattress, and his eyes, which had opened to a slit, closed. His breathing resumed its heavy, slow rhythm, and he was gone from them again, pulled back into whatever place the fever kept him.

Samuel straightened and looked at Eliza.

She stood with the cloth in her hands, her eyes on Mr. Drumond's face.

"Who's Constance?" she asked.

"I don't know."

Constance? Was she his wife, a sister, or a sweetheart? Someone, somewhere, didn't know this man was dying in a boardinghouse he'd only come to because the lumber mill had no room in the bunkhouse.

Samuel pulled the second chair from the corner near the window and set it beside his at the bedside. Eliza came and sat down . She laid the cloth across Mr. Drumond's forehead and rested her hands in her lap.

The room held the close heat of a July night, the air thick. The single flame from the lamp threw their shadows against the wall behind them, long and wavering when either of them shifted. Mr. Drumond's breathing was the only sound in the room.

Samuel opened his notebook, turned back through the pages, and found the first entry. He read it aloud.

"July second. Boarder, Mr. Drumond. Headache two days, poor appetite, and fatigue. Temperature one hundred point one. Pulse steady. Abdomen soft. Instructed rest and fluids. Will re-examine tomorrow." He turned the page. "July third. Temperature one hundred and two. Headache worsening. Rose spots observed on the abdomen. Stepladder pattern suspected." He flipped forward. "July seventh. Temperature one hundred and three point six. Confusion intermittent. Unable to take solid food. Abdomen tender to palpation." Page after page, his handwriting grew tighter as the entries multiplied. Temperature readings, pulse counts, fluid intake—each observation noted with the precision of a man who believed that thorough records could make the difference between a patient saved and a patient lost.

He closed the notebook.

"Six weeks he's been in this boardinghouse," he said. "I've examined him nearly every day for two of them. Multiple pages of notes about his body. His temperature, his pulse, his abdomen, and his breathing." He set the notebook on the bedside table, beside the lamp. "And I don't know this man's first name. I don't know who Constance is. I know he came from Helena for a job at the lumber mill. That's it. I don't know what his life was like in Helena. I don't know if he has a family waiting for a letter. I don't know what he did before the lumber mill or what he wanted his life to be. I don't know the first real thing about him."

"His name is Titus," Eliza said. "Titus Drumond. I checked the register after we knew typhoid was his illness. I needed to know his name."

"Titus," he said. The name sat strangely in his mouth.

"This is the part of medicine nobody teaches," he said. "Not in lectures, not in training, not in any textbook I've ever read. They teach you to observe symptoms. Track a fever, read a pulse, and note the progression of a disease. They train you to keep your distance from the person in the bed because distance keeps your judgment clear and your hands steady. And it works. It keeps you able to walk into the next room and do it again." He looked at Titus Drumond's still face. "But it costs you the person. You start seeing the illness instead of the man. You treat the symptoms and push the human being into the background, and you save them or you lose them, and either way you never knew them. And the training tells you that's correct. That not knowing them is what makes you effective."

"I know nothing about this man. I don't know whether he has a mother alive or a brother or a sweetheart, wife, or sister named Constance."

"Samuel." She waited until he looked at her. "I sat beside dying patients in Philadelphia who had a room full of family. Children and spouses and parents who'd known them their whole lives, and those rooms were full of love and full of knowing, and it didn't change the outcome. Not once." She folded her hands in her lap, and he could see her reddened knuckles and the small cracks along her fingers. "My mother had me and my father at her bedside for two years. We knew everything about her. Every favorite hymn, every recipe she loved, every story from her childhood in Ohio. We knew her completely. And she still died."

The floorboards creaked beneath her chair as she shifted forward.

"The thing that took me longest to accept was that presence doesn't have to be perfect to matter. You don't have to know someone's whole story to sit beside them while they fight for their life. You just have to be willing to stay in the room."

She looked at Mr. Drumond, then back at Samuel. "You're here now. You come up and check on him multiple times a day. He's the first person you check on at first light, and you think I haven't noticed, but I have. You care about him. You care about every person in this building." Her voice was steady and clear. "That isn't a failure, Samuel. That's who you are. It is not your fault that you didn't know this man's first name nor understand who Constance is to him."

He sat with those words as the lamplight caught the side of her face, the line of her jaw, and the loose strand of auburn hair that had pulled free from her nape. Her eyes were tired. Her sleeves were rolled past her elbows, and the skin of her hands and forearms was dry and chapped from days of carbolic and hot water and work that hadn't stopped.

She was right here. Alive and present, sitting in this room with him while a man they'd both fought for slipped further from their reach. And Samuel couldn't keep pretending. He couldn't sit beside her day after day any longer and call what he felt partnership. He couldn't keep lying to himself about the way his whole body went still and quiet when she walked into a room, as if some part of him was listening for her even before she appeared.

"Tell me something about yourself that has nothing to do with nursing," he said. "Something more that I don't already know."

Her hands went still, and she glanced away from him.

"I myself am a serious person… far more serious than I'd like at times," he continued. "I've spent days beside you, and I know how you take a pulse, how you mix carbolic, and how you coax broth into a man who won't drink. I know you're competent and steady, and I know you hum 'Abide with Me' when you work because you learned it from your mother, and it brought her peace in her last days. But I don't know what you wanted to be before nursing. I don't know your favorite room in your father's house. I don't know your favorite color, or what God means to you when you're not standing in a sickroom, or what your dreams are." He placed his hands on his knees. "I'm sitting in this room, and I realize now that I didn't ask a man his story while he could still tell it. He's dying, and I didn't even know his first name until now. I won't make that mistake again. Not with you."

She studied him, and he watched her composure loosen.

"My favorite room in my father's house is the back parlor," she said. "It's small. Barely enough space for the settee, the bookshelf, and the lamp table. My mother called it the reading room. The window faces east, and in the morning the light warms the settee cushions. When I was a girl, I'd curl up there with a book and have the whole room to myself. After my mother died, it became the place I went when I needed to talk to God and didn't have the words for a proper prayer. I'd just sit, and I'd trust that He knew what I meant."

"And your father's shop?"

"There's a corner in the print shop, near the back wall, where my mother kept a chair by the window. She used to sit there and read to my father while he worked. Poetry, mostly. Sometimes Scripture, sometimes a story from the lending library. He'd be setting type or binding pages, and she'd just read, and then they'd talk about it. She'd read, and he'd work, and it was the most beautiful thing to observe. She loved him so much and spent as much time as she could with him. They brought out the best in one another." Eliza's voice grew quieter. "That chair's still there. When I have time, I go sit in it and read to him the way she did. He never asks me to. I just do it."

"What do you read him?"

"Poetry at times, just as my mother did. Scripture when he's heavy or troubled. Occasionally I'll pull a book off his shelf and start the first chapter, and if it catches us both, I'll continue to read." She smiled, and it was small and unguarded, and it made her look younger than the woman who'd been wringing cloths and counting pulses for days now. "He pretends he's too busy to listen. But his hands get quieter on the press, and he tilts his head toward my chair, and I know he's hearing every word."

Samuel let the image settle. Eliza sat in a chair by a window, reading aloud to a man who loved her enough to slow his hands so he wouldn't miss a syllable. Samuel found himself wanting to know more. He wanted all of it.

"What did you want to be?" he asked. "Before nursing. Before your mother got sick. When you were a girl and the world was wide open."

"A wife and a mother," she said. "I wanted a house full of children. I wanted what my parents had: a home where people were kind to each other and laughed at the supper table, and read aloud in the evenings. I hoped for more than one child; they were never blessed with more than me. I wanted a house full of children. I wanted a garden with vegetables and herbs, and I wanted to learn my mother's bread recipe, the one she got from her mother in Ohio." She looked at her hands. "Then my mother got sick, and I wanted to be whatever would keep her alive the longest. And after she died, I didn't want to be anything for a few months. The world felt flat, as if someone had taken the depth out of it. Then I started nursing, and it gave me a reason to get out of bed and use what I'd learned at her bedside for people who needed it."

"And now?"

"Now I want both," she said. "The nursing and the family. I didn't think a person could want both. Thomas, my former beau, didn't think so, and maybe that's why I felt nothing when he left, because he wanted me to choose, and I didn't believe I should have to." She looked toward the window, dark with the July night. "I still want the house full of children. I still want the garden. I still want that bread recipe. But I also want to walk into a room where someone's sick or hurting and be the person who knows what to do. I want to comfort the ill and bring them moments of peace and reduce their fears just by being present with them."

"What's your favorite color?"

She laughed. Quiet and brief, and it surprised them both in this room where a man lay dying three feet away.

"Blue," she said. "Not pale blue. The blue the sky turns right before full sunrise here, that deep, clean color like someone washed it and hung it up new. I saw it from Aunt Leora's window my first morning, and I stood there watching it change for five minutes." She tilted her head. "Your turn."

"My turn for what?"

"I've been answering your questions. Now you answer mine." She turned in her chair. "What don't I know about you? When the last patient's seen and your notebook's closed and you're alone in your rooms above the office, what does Samuel Porter do with himself?"

He rubbed the back of his neck. "I read. Medical journals, mostly, but my mother sends novels with her letters because she thinks I don't read enough that isn't about medicine, and she's right. I've got a copy of Ivanhoe on my desk that she sent in April. I'm only halfway through because I keep falling asleep while I'm reading."

"You fall asleep while reading?"

"Every time. I open the book, find my place, read a few paragraphs, and I'm out. I've read some paragraphs so many times I could recite them."

She laughed, fuller this time. "What else?" she said.

"I write letters home that are too short, and I feel guilty every time I seal the envelope. I like mornings better than evenings. I drink my coffee black and hot, and I've burned the roof of my mouth so many times I've probably scarred it. I can't cook anything worth eating except eggs and bacon, and even the bacon I burn more often than not." He looked at his hands on his knees. "I pray, but not the way I used to. When I was younger, prayer felt like a conversation. Now it feels more like sitting in a room and hoping God's in the next one and can hear me through the wall."

"I miss singing," he continued. "At church. Growing up, my whole family sang. Loudly and badly. My father can't carry a tune in a bucket, but he sang every Sunday like the Lord had given him a gift and he intended to use it. My mother stood beside him, trying not to laugh, and by the end of the hymn, half the congregation would be hiding smiles behind their hands. I haven't sung in church since I came to Providence Ridge. I stand there and mouth the words, but nothing comes out."

"Why?"

He looked at the lamp on the bedside table, at the way its flame bent sideways with the draft and straightened again. "Because the last time I sang, I was standing beside my brother Caleb at his wife and children's funeral. We sang 'Amazing Grace,' and I couldn't get past the second verse. Caleb put his arm around my shoulder and sang it for both of us." He stopped. "I haven't been able to sing since."

From downstairs came the faint creak of floorboards as someone crossed the dining room, and then Eunice's voice murmured to one of the patients, steady and low.

"I don't know why I told you that," he said as he looked at Titus, still asleep, his breathing labored.

"Because your heart is heavy, and you needed to tell someone."

He looked at her, and she looked back without flinching and without pity.

"My heart is heavy at times, so heavy it hurts. Tell me something else about yourself... what don't you miss about Philadelphia?" he asked.

"The noise," she said. "The constant press of carriages and vendors and people calling across the street. The city never held still long enough for a person to hear her own thoughts. I'd walk to the market and come home exhausted, not from the walking but from the sound. And the air. You can't see the sky properly in Philadelphia. There's always smoke and soot sitting on everything. When I stepped off the coach here and looked up and saw those mountains against the sky, I couldn't breathe for a moment. Not because I was scared. Because I'd never seen that much open space, and I didn't know what to do with it."

"What do you miss?"

"My father's laugh. He laughs with his whole body. He tips his head back, and his shoulders shake, and he slaps whatever surface is nearest. And the smell of ink and paper from the shop on a warm day. His entire office building smells of ink and paper, and binding glue. I've smelled it every day of my life, and I didn't know I loved it until I couldn't smell it anymore. Now it's your turn; tell me about a Christmas in Colorado with your family," she said.

"Christmas on the ranch was my mother's production. She started planning in November. My father, Caleb, and I would cut a tree from the stand of pines north of the house and drag it back on a sled a week or so before Christmas, and she'd have the front room cleared and ready. She made ornaments out of whatever she had. Dried apple slices, ribbons, and bits of tin my father cut into star shapes with his snips. One year she made gingerbread ornaments, and Gerald ate three off the tree before Christmas morning, and she didn't scold him. She just baked more and hung them higher."

"Your mother is a saint."

"She'd tell you she's a sinner who cooks well, and that's close enough." He rested his hands on his knees. "Christmas morning was the one day my father didn't go to the barn before breakfast. He sat in his chair by the fire, and my mother brought him coffee, and the six of us came down and opened our gifts. Simple things.

A pocketknife, a book, and a pair of gloves she'd knitted in secret. Bonita got a doll one year my father carved from a piece of pine, and she carried that doll until the paint wore off and the arms came loose."

"I want to meet your family," Eliza said. Her cheeks colored, and she looked at the basin on the washstand. "I mean. The way you describe them. They sound like people I'd enjoy knowing."

"They'd like you. My mother would claim you inside of ten minutes, and my father would respect you because you work hard and say what you mean. Bonita would try to put you on a horse. Caleb would tell you every embarrassing story from my childhood before I could stop him."

"Tell me one of those embarrassing stories."

"When I was fourteen, I tried to impress a girl at a church social by jumping a fence on my brother's horse. The horse stopped at the fence. I didn't. I cleared the top rail on my own and landed in a water trough on the other side, in front of every family in the congregation."

"Samuel."

"My father didn't say a word, just shook his head and grinned. My mother waited until we were inside the church and alone, and then she laughed. She laughed until she cried as she helped me wring out my church clothes. Then we went home, and she made me biscuits and put honey on them, and she never once made fun of me or brought up the incident again. The girl never spoke to me again."

Eliza pressed her hand over her mouth, and her shoulders shook, and the laughter she tried to hold came through anyway, quiet and warm.

Eventually her laughter eased, and she looked at Mr. Drumond. His breathing hadn't changed. The cloth on his forehead had gone warm, and she rose and wrung a fresh one in the basin and laid it across his brow with the same gentleness she gave every patient.

"Why are you asking me to tell you things about myself?" She asked as she sat back down and looked at him. Her blue eyes were steady and open, and the composure she carried like a second skin was gone.

Samuel looked at Titus Drumond in the bed and then back at her.

"Because you're the first person who's made me want to know more," he said. "I've kept people at a distance for a long time, Eliza. Professional distance is what I know, and it's what keeps my work manageable. Then one day I walked into your aunt's room, and you looked at me like you expected me to either be competent or get out of your way, and I haven't been the same since. I've tried to put it back where it was. It won't go. I'm drawn to you, and I would rather not explain it away anymore. I want to know everything about you."

He looked at Titus again, at the man whose story they'd never fully hear.

"I don't want to be the man who stands in a room with you for weeks and never asks who you are. I don't want to know you the way I know a colleague. I want to know you the way a man knows someone who matters to him." He turned to look at her. "You matter to me, Eliza. You've mattered to me for longer than I've had the courage to say so."

She didn't look away. Her lips parted, and her eyes grew bright in a way that wasn't tears but was close.

"I need you to know something," she said. "I've never felt this before. Not like this. I was courted in Philadelphia by a good man, and I liked him well enough, but I never once sat in a room with him and felt what I feel sitting here with you. I don't have experience with this. I don't know the rules or the steps or what a woman's supposed to say when a man tells her she matters to him." She pressed her palms flat against her skirt. "All I know is that when you walk into a room, I can breathe again. Everything pressing in—the patients and the fear and the work that doesn't stop—it eases when you're there. And when you leave, I count the minutes until you come back. I've been carrying that for days without knowing what to do with it." She looked at him. "I apologize for my inexperience. But I have to tell you the truth. This is new to me. All of it."

He offered his hand toward hers, where it rested on her knee. She looked at his hand, open and waiting, and placed hers in it. Her fingers were rough and dry, her knuckles cracked from carbolic, and he closed his hand around hers and felt the strength in those worn fingers.

The lamp burned low. Titus Drumond breathed his slow, heavy breaths, each one a labor, each one a measure of time in a life they hadn't known and couldn't save. The July heat pressed against the window. From downstairs, the creak of floorboards and the faint clink of a tin cup being set on a table.

Her thumb moved once across his knuckles. A motion so small he almost missed it, and it undid him more completely than anything she'd said.

He still had things to tell her. Things that lived in Colorado, in a room he couldn't leave, and a loss he hadn't spoken aloud to anyone in this town. She deserved to know why he held himself at a distance. She deserved the whole of it.

That was for another night. Tonight, her hand was in his, and a man lay before them who reminded them both that the time to know a person is while they're still here to be known.

Chapter 23

Three days later...

Eliza wrung a fresh cloth in the basin and laid it across Titus Drumond's brow. His skin beneath her fingertips was papery and hot. Each breath pulled his ribs inward and released with a thin rattle.

His face in the lantern's reach had thinned again since morning, the hollows deepening beneath his cheekbones. His lips were cracked despite the water she'd been pressing to them every hour with a soaked cloth, coaxing what drops she could into a body that had stopped accepting what it needed.

Somewhere beyond this room, beyond this valley, and whatever distance separated this dying man from the life he'd lived before a lumber mill brought him here, someone named Constance existed. A wife, perhaps. A sister. A sweetheart who expected a letter that would never come.

Eliza dried her hands on her apron. She adjusted the wick on the lantern until the flame steadied and stood a moment longer in the small room.

"I'll be back."

She stepped into the hallway, and the slight breeze through the open window at the end of the hall moved against her face and neck. Her shoulders ached, and a deep, persistent throb had settled into the muscles along her spine and wouldn't shift. Her hands were so dry that when she flexed her fingers, the cracks along her knuckles pulled and stung.

From below came the sounds of the boardinghouse holding its night watch. Eunice's voice, low and measured, reading scripture in the dining room—the words indistinct at this distance, but the cadence unmistakable, unhurried and certain. A floorboard gave beneath someone's step, and then Margaret's voice murmured something Eliza couldn't catch, followed by the faint clink of tin on wood.

They were all still here. Eunice, Reverend Hale, Margaret, Della, Alma, and Winnie, each stationed among the pallets like sentinels who'd volunteered for a watch they hadn't been trained for and refused to abandon. The boardinghouse had become something Eliza hadn't anticipated when she stepped off the coach two and a half weeks ago.

She pressed her palms flat against her apron—an old habit, one she'd developed in the early days of her mother's illness when her hands needed something to do and her mind needed a motion small enough to hold itself to. Then she went downstairs.

The kitchen was lit by a single lantern on the table, and Samuel was there.

He sat in the chair nearest the stove with his notebook closed in front of him and his hands resting flat on either side of it. His coffee cup sat empty.

Eliza paused in the doorway. She'd always been observant—her mother's illness had taught her to watch for changes the way a sailor watches weather, constantly and without rest, because the shift that mattered was always the one you missed. But reading Samuel was different from reading a patient. With a patient, she watched for decline or recovery. With Samuel, she watched for the moments when the man beneath the doctor surfaced, and the surfacing had come more often since the night he'd taken her hand and told her she mattered to him.

She could see it now. The muscles along his jaw were tight, his focus fixed on one thing; his stillness was the stillness of a man lost deep in thought.

She crossed the kitchen and poured herself coffee from the pot on the stove. Hot and bitter, brewed hours ago, she drank it anyway. She brought the pot to the table and refilled his cup without asking, and he looked up.

"Thank you," he said.

She sat across from him. Her Bible was on the table where she'd left it.

"How is he?" Samuel asked.

"The same. His breathing hasn't changed much, and his fever's holding."

Samuel nodded. He picked up his cup and drank.

"He's not going to recover," Samuel said.

"I know," she said.

He looked at his notebook. "I've been thinking about what you said the other night. About presence not needing to be perfect to matter." He turned the notebook a quarter turn with his fingers, the same restless motion she'd seen him make when his mind was outrunning his hands. "You were right. I believe that. But there's a part of me that still measures everything by whether it was enough. Whether I did enough. Whether knowing more, or acting faster, or being better would've changed the outcome."

"I know that part," Eliza said. "I live in it."

He looked at her across the table. What she saw in his face wasn't the guarded steadiness he wore like a coat. It wasn't the warmth that had started breaking through—the warmth that surfaced when he looked at her and didn't look away. What she saw was a man standing at the edge of something he'd carried alone for a long time, deciding whether to set it down.

"I told you once that there was something I wasn't ready to talk about," he said. "On the porch. You asked what I was running from, and I said it was a conversation for another time."

"I remember."

He was quiet for a long moment. He stared at her open Bible on the table and worked his jaw. She could see that he was struggling to put into words whatever it was he'd held inside for so long.

"My brother Caleb—his first wife's name was Ruth," he said. "She was the kind of person who made a room brighter just by being in it. She laughed easily. She teased Caleb in front of the whole family, and he loved her for it. We all adored Ruth."

He picked up his cup. Drank. Set it down.

"The winter of 1881, Ruth was pregnant with twins. Caleb rode to my door in the middle of the night. I had a small home not far from his ranch—about a thirty-minute ride in fair weather. That night the weather wasn't fair. A snowstorm had been building since afternoon, and by the time Caleb reached me, the passes were filling. He'd ridden through it because Ruth was laboring early and something was wrong."

"I rode back with him. It took us an hour through a storm that was turning the landscape around us white. I had my medical bag with me and every medical instrument I owned. I remember thinking during that ride that I should have brought more... which was a strange thought because I had left nothing behind. Every single thing I owned was in that bag and had served me well for years. I've thought about that ride every day for three years and wondered why that thought came to mind that night. It was as if I already knew that what I was riding toward would require more than what I had on hand. It's one of those odd memories that stays with you."

"When we reached his cabin, Ruth was laboring hard. Caleb's nearest neighbor, an older woman named Mrs. Hensley, was with her. She'd helped many women in the area during a birth, and she was capable. When I walked in, she looked at me, and all I saw was fear. I could see in her face that she knew something was gravely wrong."

He rubbed the back of his neck, and Eliza could see the tendons standing taut beneath his rolled sleeve.

"I examined Ruth, and I knew within minutes. The labor was obstructed. The first twin was positioned in a way that prevented delivery, and she'd been laboring for hours without progress. She was exhausted. She was bleeding more than she should've been. I knew what she needed." His voice went quieter—not softer, but thinner, as if the words were being pressed through a space that was narrowing. "She needed a cesarean section. Surgical intervention. And I knew how to perform one. I'd studied it. I'd assisted on one during my training in Chicago. I didn't have chloroform because my supply had not reached me yet."

"I sent a rider—Caleb's neighbor, Mr. Hensley. The nearest surgeon was a full half-day's ride in clear weather. I knew when I sent him that help wouldn't arrive in time. I sent him anyway, because not sending him meant accepting that Ruth was going to die in that room, and I wasn't willing to accept it."

His palms were flat on the table again, pressed against the wood as if he were steadying the room itself.

"I did everything I could. I tried to reposition the baby. I managed the bleeding with what I had. I kept her conscious. I talked to her. I told her she was strong, and she was—she was so strong, Eliza. She fought for hours. Caleb held her hand, and she looked at him between the pains, and she was still trying to smile at him, because that was who Ruth was."

He was quiet for a few moments. The muscles along his jaw worked once, twice, and then he gathered himself the way she'd watched him gather himself at every bedside since she'd known him—the steadying of hands, the squaring of attention, and the refusal to let the shaking take hold.

"The bleeding worsened, and I couldn't stop it. I tried everything, and it wasn't enough. She looked at me, and then she looked at Caleb, and I think she knew before either of us did. She died just before dawn, just after the second babe was born." He stopped. "Both twins had been born still. A boy and a girl. They never drew breath. And Ruth's final breath came within seconds of the little boy's arrival."

"I held that still little boy in my arms," he said. "Caleb was on the floor beside the bed, holding his little girl. I could hear the wind howling outside as if it were mourning the deaths that had just taken place, and I thought to myself. What did I do wrong? What should I have done to prevent this? How could God have allowed this to happen? I stood in that room and begged God to forgive me for whatever I had done wrong."

He looked at his hands on the table. Large hands, square-tipped, scarred across two knuckles.

"Later that day the neighbor arrived with the surgeon. The surgeon examined Ruth and reviewed my notes and told me I'd done everything correctly. Textbook management of an obstructed labor under impossible conditions. He told me that I should assume that Ruth had a condition that was not known and had not shown itself during her pregnancy. He said that most doctors would've lost the mother sooner." Samuel's voice leveled into something flat and clinical. "He meant it as comfort. It wasn't."

"Caleb didn't blame me. Not that night, not the next day, not in the weeks after. He stood at the funeral—two small graves beside the fence line on my father's property and one for Ruth—and he never once looked at me with accusation. He looked at me with grief, but not blame. My mother and father came to my home three days after the funeral. She sat on my bed and held me the way she'd held me when I was a boy, and she said, 'You did everything God gave you the ability to do.' My father gripped my shoulder and didn't say a word. He just stood beside me. That was his way."

"And it worsened it," Eliza said.

He looked at her. The guarded steadiness was gone. What was left was the man underneath all of it—the man who'd walked into her aunt's room on a June afternoon and looked at her with those same blue eyes and who'd been carrying this behind them every moment since.

"Yes," he said. "Because if everyone forgave me and I still couldn't forgive myself, then the failure wasn't something anyone else could reach. It lived inside me, and there was nowhere to set it down. Caleb could tell me it wasn't my fault. My mother could hold me. My father could stand beside me. None of it touched the place where I'd decided I should've been enough and I wasn't."

"I left Colorado because the grief was in every room. At every meal. At church on Sundays, when Caleb sat in the pew without Ruth. In the face of every pregnant woman who came to my door, because every one of them was Ruth, and every complicated symptom was that night." He looked at the lantern flame where it bent with a draft from the kitchen window and righted itself. "Providence Ridge was a town that needed a doctor. I could be Dr. Porter, the new physician. No history. No graves. No brother who looked at me across the supper table with a kindness I couldn't accept."

Eliza leaned forward. "The worst part wasn't the losing, was it? Yes, it hurt—it hurt badly, losing Ruth and two precious babies. But even worse was having people all around you who loved you and forgave you and couldn't reach the place inside you where guilt, doubt, grief, pain, and the constant questions of why and what if lived."

He looked at her. His mouth opened and closed without sound, and then something in his face stilled—not hardened, not eased—stilled the way a person's face stills when they hear a language they thought no one else spoke.

"Yes," he said.

Eliza looked at her Bible on the table, its leather cover worn from age and use. Her mother's Bible. The one her father had pressed into her hands at the train station the morning she left Philadelphia. "Your mother would want you to have this with you," he'd said.

She pushed her chair back. The legs scraped against the floor, and Samuel looked up. She lifted the chair, carried it around to his side of the table, and set it beside him and sat down.

She reached for his hand, which rested on the table. His fingers opened, and she slid hers between them—her rough, carbolic-cracked skin against his scarred knuckles—and held on.

"We needed this," she said. "We both needed to speak our worst moments out loud. Thank you for listening to mine days ago when I told you. You didn't judge me, nor did you walk away, and that means so much to me."

"Thank you for staying while I told you the one thing that's defined my entire life since the night it happened."

"There's nowhere else I'd rather be. I truly believe God wanted us to lay our burdens down."

He lifted their joined hands from the table and pressed them against his chest, just left of center, where she could feel his heartbeat through his shirt—steady and strong beneath her knuckles. He held them there, his fingers tight around hers, and didn't let go.

Chapter 24

Titus Drumond lay beneath the sheet with his face turned toward the window. She'd drawn the curtain back an hour ago because the sky beyond the glass was beginning to change. Morning was coming. She'd wanted him to have it, if any part of him could still receive what his eyes no longer opened to see.

She held his hand. His fingers were cool and dry against hers, his knuckles prominent beneath skin that had gone thin.

"Morning's coming, Mr. Drumond," she said. "The sky's starting to turn."

He didn't stir. His chest rose and fell in shallow, measured draws, each one further apart than the last.

She started humming. The hymn moved through the room, softening the silence.

The lantern on the bedside table had burned low. She'd trimmed it twice during the night but hadn't refilled it, and now the flame was small.

Eliza looked at Titus's face as she hummed. The hollows beneath his cheekbones had deepened past gauntness into something closer to sculpture—bone pressing through from underneath, the living warmth of a man's face slowly being replaced by its architecture.

She thought about Constance. She'd thought about this mystery woman every day since she'd first heard her name—that single word spoken in delirium, a name that belonged to someone they didn't know. A wife. A sister. A mother. Someone who might never know that Titus Drumond had died in a boardinghouse in a town where he'd simply come to work and took a drink of water that would shorten his life, tended by people who'd done everything they could.

The door opened behind her, and she turned to see Samuel. He'd shaved. His shirt was clean, his sleeves already rolled to the forearm, and he carried with him the faint scent of soap and coffee. He looked at her first, then at Titus, then back at her.

"Good morning," he said. "Winnie's got breakfast ready downstairs. Eggs and biscuits and gravy, enough for every volunteer in the territory. She asked me to come up here and tell you it's hot and it's ready, and she doesn't want to hear any arguments."

Eliza smiled. "He doesn't have much time," she said. "Minutes, I think. His breathing's been getting shallower."

Samuel closed the door behind him.

He crossed to the bed and lifted Titus's wrist. His fingers found the pulse point with the sureness of a man who'd done this thousands of times. Then he lowered it gently onto the bed.

He pulled the second chair from the corner and sat down facing Eliza from the other side of Titus's bed.

Eliza kept hold of Titus's hand, and neither of them spoke.

Titus's next breath came, a whisper of air drawn through parted lips, his chest barely rising.

The pause after it was long.

She waited. Her fingers tightened around Titus's hand. She watched his chest for the rise that would mean she'd been wrong, that there was more time, that the pauses between breaths had simply grown so long her counting had lost its rhythm. But the sheet didn't move. His chest didn't rise. His parted lips stayed parted, and his face was still.

Samuel stood and placed his fingers against Titus's neck, pressing gently beneath his jaw. He held them there. His face was composed; his attention narrowed to the single task of confirming what they both already knew. After a long moment, he withdrew his hand.

He pulled his notebook from his vest pocket. The scratch of his pencil on paper was the only sound.

"Seven fifteen," he said.

Eliza released Titus's hand. She laid it on the bed beside him, straightening his fingers against the sheet.

She stood and drew the sheet up over his chest, over his shoulders, and then over his face.

Samuel closed his notebook. He stood at the foot of the bed, looking at the shape beneath the sheet. His jaw worked once, then stilled. His hands hung at his sides. Then he walked to the door.

"I'll get Reverend Hale," he said.

Eliza stood alone in the room and bowed her head.

"Lord," she said. "Receive your servant Titus into Your rest. Whatever his life held—whatever joys, whatever sorrows, whatever he carried that we never knew—let it be met with Your mercy now.

Wherever Constance is this morning, be near her. Be near her if the news ever reaches her. Please don't let her bear it alone."

She stood a moment longer. Then she picked up the basin from the bedside table, emptied it into the pail by the door, and carried both downstairs.

***

Reverend Hale stood near the front window in the dining room, speaking with Amos and Margaret. His Bible was in his hand, held loosely at his side, and his face wore a sober steadiness. Amos stood with his arms folded and his hat in his hand. Margaret stood listening, her mouth pressed thin.

She searched the room for Samuel, past the pallets where the sick lay in various stages of rest and wakefulness, past Della adjusting a pillow beneath Emmett Sloane's head. Past the table where Winnie had set out plates and a basket of biscuits covered with a cloth.

She set the basin and pail beside the kitchen door and crossed to where the Reverend stood with Amos and Margaret.

"Eliza," Webb said. He reached out and clasped her hand firmly. "Samuel told us."

"He passed away peacefully," she said.

Margaret's eyes were bright with the shine that grief puts in a woman's eyes before the tears fall. "God bless him," Margaret said.

"Amos, can you gather men? We'll need a grave dug," Webb said.

"I'll have Paul send word to a few of the mill hands," Amos said. "Owen's boys will come. They knew Drumond better than any of us; I'm sure they'd be honored to help."

"Margaret, would you speak with Leora? She may know something we don't. If Mr. Drumond ever mentioned family or a friend. Anything... just anything that may be useful to help us find his family."

"I'll go to her now," Margaret said.

"I'll sit with Titus," Webb said. "Until the men come for him."

Eliza nodded. "Has anyone seen Samuel?" she asked.

Margaret turned to her. "He came down and told us about Mr. Drumond. Then he said he needed some air and time alone, and he walked out the door."

"All right," Eliza said.

She watched the three of them separate—Margaret toward the back hall and Leora's room, Amos toward the front door with his hat settled on his head, and Webb toward the stairs with his Bible held against his chest. Each of them carried a portion of what needed to be done.

***

Hattie was asleep beside Timothy, her hand resting on his chest. They'd move the two pallets closer to each other, sensing it would bring comfort to them both to be nearer one another. Timothy's color was better this morning. Not good. But better. The flush that had burned so high across his cheeks for days had faded, and his breathing was even. She adjusted his sheet without waking him.

She passed the Fitch's. Nolan was sitting up against the wall, Clara's hand in his lap. He looked at Eliza as she passed and gave a small nod—the nod of a man too tired to speak but wanting her to know he'd seen her and was grateful for her. Clara slept beside him, her face turned toward his shoulder.

She knelt beside Edith's pallet.

Edith lay on her back with her eyes closed and her hands folded across her stomach. The shawl that Margaret insisted on keeping around her friend's shoulders had slipped, and Eliza drew it back into place. She lifted the warm cloth from Edith's forehead, wrung a fresh cloth in the basin beside the pallet, and laid it across Edith's brow.

She stirred, her eyes opened halfway, unfocused, and her lips moved.

"Leora?" she murmured.

"It's Eliza, Miss Edith. Leora's resting. She's fine."

"Tell her…" Edith's eyes drifted. Her hand moved on the sheet, reaching for something that wasn't there. "Tell her I'll be over for coffee…"

"I will," Eliza said.

She took Edith's hand and held it until the restless motion stilled and Edith's eyes closed again. Her pulse was steady, but slower than yesterday. The fever was holding. Not spiking, not breaking. Holding, the way a storm holds over the mountains before it decides whether to build or pass.

She laid Edith's hand on the sheet.

***

The fresh air hit Eliza's face when she stepped onto the porch. She closed her eyes and stood there for a few moments to breathe in deeply and clear her mind.

She hadn't been outside in over forty-eight hours.

The street was quiet; the only sounds she heard were birds, the distant clang of someone at the livery, and the river running its low, constant course nearby.

She looked across the road toward the mercantile, its doors still closed. She looked down toward the bridge across the river, where two men sat on an overturned crate, both with a rifle across their knees. She looked in the opposite direction, toward the south end of town.

Samuel stood outside the livery with Paul Higgins beside him. Paul leaned against the doorframe with his arms crossed. Samuel stood a few paces away with his hands in his pockets, his face turned toward the sky.

She felt a tightening in her chest, a small tug, the way a thread pulls when it's sewn through fabric that shifts. Tiredness and tenderness coursed through her. The memory of his hand holding hers a few nights ago and the plain fact that he was standing over there and not here with her hurt a bit. He'd come downstairs and told the Reverend and Margaret and Amos, and he'd walked out the door, and he hadn't come back to her, nor had he waited for her.

She didn't begrudge him. Death was hard for anyone, regardless of training or temperament. She'd watched seasoned nurses at the auxiliary step outside after losing a patient and stand with their faces turned toward the sky, needing nothing but air and a moment where nobody asked them for anything. She'd seen nurses crumble to the floor and weep after losing a patient. She'd even witnessed a doctor walk out of the very hospital that employed him after losing a patient, never to return. Samuel had fought for Titus Drumond for weeks. He'd sat beside the man day after day and filled pages of his notebook with observations and the careful record of a physician who refused to stop trying. This morning all of those pages had ended the way they'd both known for days they would end.

He needed fresh air. He needed a moment alone. He needed his friend.

She understood that.

But standing on the porch, watching him from a distance, she wished he'd come to her instead. She let the thought sit. She didn't push it down, didn't chase it, and didn't smooth it into something more reasonable. She stood with her hands at her sides and the July air moving against her neck, and she let the ache be what it was—not a grievance. Not a fear. Just the tender feeling of caring for someone and not knowing yet what that caring would ask of her.

She turned and went back inside.

Chapter 25

Reverend Webb Hale's voice carried through the dining room with the unhurried authority of a man who'd been speaking truth into difficult rooms for years. But the room he spoke into bore no resemblance to the one that had held Sunday worship three weeks earlier, when chairs had been arranged in neat rows with an aisle between them and the coffee urn steamed on the back table beside platters of baked goods.

In place of the congregation, pallets lined the floor in rows, each holding a body beneath sheets fighting off a vicious illness. Reverend Hale stood near the front windows with his Bible open in his hands. He wasn't preaching from behind a pulpit or a lectern. He was standing among the sick the way he'd been standing among them for days, reading Scripture and praying over them all.

Samuel sat in one of the straight-backed chairs pushed against the wall. Eliza was across the room near Hattie and Timothy's pallets, seated on a stool. Her hands were folded in her lap, her attention on Webb. Samuel could see the line of her jaw, the careful twist of her auburn hair, and the peace that shone across her face.

Edith lay on the pallet nearest the front window, the shawl Margaret kept wrapped around her shoulders bunched beneath her chin. Her eyes were closed.

Edith's fever had climbed half a degree since yesterday evening. Her pulse was thinner than it had been the morning before. She'd managed a few sips of broth at dawn, and when he'd pressed his fingers to her abdomen an hour ago, the rigidity had deepened. She was sixty-six years old, with hands stiffened by arthritis she'd never once complained about in his hearing, and her body was spending everything it had fighting an illness that had already taken one man in this building.

Titus Drumond had died in the room directly above them, over twenty-four hours ago. He'd witnessed the man's burial yesterday afternoon and couldn't help but think how sad it was that not a soul who knew him outside of Providence Ridge was aware of his passing. On the walk back from the cemetery yesterday, he thought deeply about how quickly a life could end.

Now he sat in the dining room, and Webb was reading from Ecclesiastes.

"'To every thing there is a season, and a time to every purpose under the heaven,'" Webb read. "'A time to be born, and a time to die; a time to plant, and a time to pluck up that which is planted; a time to kill, and a time to heal; a time to break down, and a time to build up; a time to weep, and a time to laugh; a time to mourn, and a time to dance.'"

He closed his Bible partway, holding his place with one finger, and looked out across the room. Nolan Fitch sat up against the wall with Clara sleeping beside him, her hand in his lap. Zeb Thompson lay on his pallet with his eyes open, watching Webb with the wary attention of a man who listened harder than he let on. Ada slept with Jasper's coat beneath her head. Emmett Sloane's color was better than three days ago, and he lay still, listening. Eunice sat beside Della near the kitchen doorway with her back straight and her hands folded. Margaret stood near the supply table. Winnie had come out of the kitchen and leaned on the doorframe, listening.

"I'm not going to stand here and tell you that God's timing makes sense," Webb said. "I'd be lying if I did. We lost Mr. Drumond yesterday. A man who came to this town to work at the lumber mill and drank water from a well that made him sick. He fought as hard as a man can fight, with people beside him who did everything they could." Webb looked at Samuel, held there a moment, then moved on. "There's a woman named Constance somewhere in this country who doesn't know yet that the man she'd made an impression on had spoken her name out loud near the end of his life. And some of you lying in this room are still fighting the same illness that took him, and you're frightened, and you have every right to be."

"The passage I just read isn't meant to comfort the way a warm blanket comforts. It's harder than that. Solomon is saying that grief has a place. That weeping has a season. That mourning is part of the order God built into the world, not something that breaks it. When you bury a neighbor or a family member, and even if you bury someone you don't know, the sun comes up the next morning anyway, and that can feel cruel. Like the world didn't notice." Webb set his Bible on the windowsill and folded his hands.

"But that sunrise isn't indifference. It's God's promise that the seasons keep turning. That this one, the hard one, the one where we bury and we weep and we sit beside people who are suffering, this one has its purpose, and it won't last forever. Because the same God who made a time to mourn also made a time to dance. He put them in the same verse because they live in the same world. Sometimes in the same room. Sometimes in the same heart, on the very same day."

Samuel looked at his notebook, which was sitting in his lap. The cover had gone soft from being carried in his vest pocket through weeks of heat and the damp that settled into everything in the boardinghouse after days of boiling water on the stove. Its edges had curled. Inside were pages of his handwriting: patient names, dates, temperatures, pulse counts, fluid intake, and treatment notes. Every decision he'd made since the first morning he'd examined Titus Drumond and written a line about a headache and a low fever that hadn't yet seemed alarming. On the last written page, a time of death.

Seven fifteen.

Webb bowed his head. "Let's pray."

"Heavenly Father," Webb said. "We come to You this Sunday morning not in a church building, but in a room where Your people are sick and Your people are serving and Your people are grieving. We pray for the soul of Titus Drumond. Receive him into Your rest, Lord. Whatever his story held that we never knew, let it be met with Your grace."

"We pray for Edith. We pray for Timothy and Hattie. We pray for Ada and the child she is carrying. We pray for Nolan and Clara. We pray for Zeb and Emmett and for every person on the second floor of this building whose name You already know. Strengthen those who are fighting. Steady the ones who are serving. Hold the ones who are afraid." Webb's voice dropped lower. "We pray for Dr. Porter and Miss Miller. They've given this town everything they have. Renew them, Lord. Sustain them. Remind them that the work is Yours and they are Yours and the people in this room are Yours, and that none of it rests on their shoulders alone. In Jesus' name. Amen."

"Amen," said several voices across the room.

Samuel opened his eyes, and across the room, he watched as Eliza moved toward Edith. He watched her wring a cloth, lay it across Edith's brow, and smooth a strand of silver hair from Edith's temple.

He stood and slid his notebook into his vest pocket, picked up his hat, and walked through the dining room toward the front door.

He stepped onto the porch, put his hat on, descended the steps, and turned south on Main Street.

Samuel walked with his hands in his pockets. He didn't have a destination. He thought about Edith's abdomen, the rigidity that had spread since Friday, and the tenderness in her lower right quadrant that he didn't like. He thought about her pulse, thin and quick beneath skin that felt like old paper. He thought about Timothy's fever, which had held steady for two days without breaking, and about Hattie beside him, whose fever had dropped a quarter degree yesterday, a change so small it could've been a flaw in the thermometer but which he'd recorded, anyway.

He thought about Ada and the child she carried, about the danger typhoid posed to a pregnancy, and about the limits of what he could do for a woman whose body was fighting on two fronts.

He walked through his list of treatments. Fluid replacement. Cool cloths. Willow bark tea for fever. Rest. Broth when they could take it. Patient, steady, repetitive care that followed the best practices he'd been trained in and that amounted, in the end, to supporting the body while the body fought its own battle. There was no cure for typhoid. There was no medicine that could reach into the blood and kill the fever at its source. There was only management, vigilance, and time.

"Samuel."

He turned to see Webb walking toward him, his Bible tucked under his arm, his hat settled on his head.

Webb reached him, and they both walked together side by side.

"Good breeze today," Webb said.

"It's a fine day," Samuel said.

"Eunice told me this morning she's been praying for rain because the garden behind our daughter and son-in-law's home is drying out, and I told her we've got people in that dining room who could use her prayers more than tomato plants, and she told me the Lord is perfectly capable of answering more than one prayer at a time and that I should mind my own sermons." Webb chuckled. "I love that woman. Through many years of marriage, she's never once let me win a theological argument."

Samuel smiled as they walked past the last building, and the creek came into view. A dragonfly hovered above the water, its translucent wings catching the afternoon in brief flashes before it darted upstream.

"How's Edith doing today?" Webb asked.

"Her fever's climbing. Her body's fighting hard, but she's six-ty-six years old. I'm worried for her." Samuel watched the water move over the stones. "I'm doing everything I know to do for her... for all of them."

"I know you are, Samuel. Nobody in that building questions whether you've done enough."

"I do."

Webb glanced at him. "You are wrong, then."

They walked without speaking for a stretch. The creek ran beside them. A meadowlark called from somewhere in the grass beyond the road; two sharp notes followed by a tumbling phrase that dissolved into the air above the valley.

"Has there been word from anyone who works at the lumber mill?" Samuel asked.

"None that I know of. Marshall Tom told me yesterday that the homesteaders south of town are well. The families on the east side haven't reported a single case. It's been ten days, maybe eleven, since the last person fell ill."

Samuel turned that over. Ten days without a new case. He'd been so consumed by the patients already in the ward, by Titus's decline and Edith's worsening, and by the daily labor of managing multiple sick people that the absence of new cases hadn't fully registered.

"That's significant," he said.

"I thought the same. There'll need to be a committee meeting soon. Tom will want to discuss how much longer to keep the town closed. What would you recommend, Samuel?"

"Another week at minimum. Better to keep the town closed a week too long than open it a day too early."

Webb nodded. "I'll mention it to Tom."

They'd reached the place where the road bent nearest the creek. The water ran close enough that Samuel could hear individual notes of current against stone, each one distinct, each one lasting only a moment before the next replaced it. He stopped walking, and Webb stopped beside him.

"Anything else sitting heavy on you, son?"

Samuel looked at the creek. "Plenty, Reverend."

"Then let's hear it. We're out here in the fresh air with mountains God himself carved standing all around us, a beautiful creek singing a tune all its own, and there's nobody within earshot but the Almighty and a meadowlark. Whatever you're carrying, set it down for a minute. Let somebody else hold it with you."

Samuel took his hands out of his pockets. He pressed the heel of his palm against the back of his neck, the tendons taut beneath his collar. He looked at the mountains for a long moment. Then, at the creek.

"I've grown close to Eliza," he said. "What I feel for her isn't something I'm confused about. I know what it is. It isn't professional admiration. It isn't gratitude, though I'm grateful for her every hour of every day in that boardinghouse as we tend the ill." He looked at his hands. The knuckles scarred across two fingers, the broad, square tips. The hands that held pulses and mixed medicines and had held his stillborn nephew in a cabin in Colorado three years ago. "It's the kind of feeling a man has once in his life if God is generous enough to give it to him. I know that. I'm not trying to push it aside or pretend its something smaller than it is."

"What I can't make sense of is the timing. There are several people in that building fighting for their lives, and this town is sealed off from the world because the water poisoned its people. Edith is lying in the dining room, getting worse by the day. We buried a man yesterday. My attention, my focus, everything I have should be aimed at those patients. At finding something I've missed, some adjustment I haven't tried, some way to ease their suffering or speed their recovery. That's what God called me to do. That's why I became a physician."

He looked east toward the Absarokas. "So why now? Why would God open my heart to a woman in the middle of all this? Why would He let me fall in love during a time when people are so sick and death is knocking at the door, and I can barely keep my hands steady from the strain of it? Is it a test? Something I'm supposed to resist?" He picked up a stone from the bank and turned it between his fingers. "I've tried, Reverend... I've tried to resist it, and I can't. She's in every room I walk into, and every time I look at her, I know. Yesterday I sat with Titus as he took his final breath, and I couldn't help but wonder what kind of man falls in love in the midst of all this sadness."

Webb looked at the creek for a while, his deep-set eyes beneath their heavy brow taking in the water and the stones.

"Let me tell you something, Samuel," Webb said. "I've been preaching for many years. I've buried more people than I've married. I've sat at bedsides where the fever won, and I've stood at gravesides where the words I said felt thin as paper against what those families were carrying. And in all those years, I have never once stood somewhere God was not present. Not once."

He turned to Samuel. "You're asking the wrong question. You're asking why God would give you this feeling in the middle of a hard season. As if love is a luxury that belongs to peacetime. As if your heart is supposed to shut down when your hands are full." He shook his head slowly. "Son, God doesn't wait for the easy season to give you what you need. He gives it to you in the hard one. Because the hard one is when you need it most."

"Miss Eliza didn't arrive in Providence Ridge accidentally," Webb said. "She arrived while this outbreak was already brewing. She was already here, already trained, already capable, already the exact person this town would need when the crisis was right in front of us. You think that was chance? You think God sent a woman with fever hospital training to a boardinghouse in a Montana lumber town mere days before the signs of typhoid became clear to us. Do you really think his timing with all this was just fortunate?"

"I've considered it."

"Consider it harder. God put the two people this town needed most together, at the same time, with the same calling, and then He gave them hearts that recognized each other. And you're standing beside this creek asking me why He'd do that during an epidemic instead of during a picnic."

Samuel turned the stone over in his palm. The meadowlark called again from the grass, the same tumbling melody as before.

"I preached about seasons this morning," Webb said. "You were listening. I know you were. So hear the part you didn't let in. Solomon didn't write about a time to mourn and then, in a separate chapter, a time to love. He put them together. Same passage. Same breath. Grief and love sharing the same roof. That isn't a contradiction, Samuel. That's the way a faithful life is built. You don't get to choose which season the good things arrive in. You get to choose whether you receive them when they come."

Webb looked at the mountains, then back at Samuel. His face held the joy and the steadiness of a man who'd chosen faith, not because it was simple but because it was true.

"Love isn't a distraction from the work you are deeply buried under right now. It's provision for it. You've been shouldering this burden of illness on your own for weeks, even with Eliza beside you, because that's what you do. You shoulder it. You contain it. You measure yourself by whether your hands were sufficient." Webb set his hand on Samuel's arm. "And God is standing beside you saying, 'I didn't ask you to be sufficient on your own. I sent you someone. I sent you a gift... receive it.'"

The creek ran over its stones. The cottonwoods continued to move in the breeze. The meadowlark had gone quiet. Samuel stood with the stone in his palm, and he turned it once more before he slipped it into his trouser pocket.

Webb gripped his arm firmly, the way Samuel's own father gripped his shoulder when words weren't needed.

"Come," Webb said. "Let's walk back. Eunice will want to know where I've gone, and if I'm not careful, she'll organize a search party, and I'll never hear the end of it."

Chapter 26

*T*hree days later...

Eliza was sitting on the floor beneath the front window with her back against the wall, her legs drawn to one side, and her hand resting on Edith's forearm. Her eyes were fixed somewhere across the room.

Samuel crossed the room and knelt beside Edith's pallet. Eliza turned her head toward him, and her eyes took a moment to find him, as though she were coming back from some place that had nothing to do with this room.

"Good morning," he said.

"Good morning, Samuel."

He lifted the cloth from Edith's forehead and set it in the basin. Her skin beneath was flushed, but not the deep, angry flush of a fever climbing. He placed his palm against her forehead. Warm. Persistently, stubbornly warm, the way her fever had held since

Sunday, lodged at a height that worried him but hadn't moved in either direction.

He took her pulse. His fingers found the thread of it beneath her wrist. Steadier than he'd expected.

"Edith," he said. "Can you hear me?"

Her eyelids moved. She didn't open them, but her lips parted and a sound came that was near enough to acknowledgment.

He drew her sheet down to her waist and pressed his fingers against her abdomen, beginning at the upper left and working across with care. Her belly had softened. Not much, not everywhere, but the rigidity that had alarmed him since Friday, the hardness in her lower right quadrant, had eased. The tissue beneath his fingertips gave more than it had on Sunday. More than it had on Monday.

He checked the spot again. Pressed with two fingers, held, and released. Edith's face tightened, but she didn't pull away.

He pulled her sheet back into place and wrung a fresh cloth in the basin. He laid the cloth across Edith's forehead and tucked its edge along her temple, where her silver hair had come loose from whatever pins remained.

"Her abdomen has changed," he said.

Eliza looked at him.

"The rigidity in her lower right side has softened. She still has tenderness, and she's still running a fever, but the guarding reflex that was deepening through last week has reversed. Her body isn't shutting down." He sat back on his heels, his forearms resting on his knees. "She's fighting. Whatever her body is doing, it doesn't match the common patterns; it's different."

"Different how?" Eliza said.

"I can't explain it fully. Typhoid follows a course. The textbooks describe it in stages, and I've seen those stages hold true in most patients. Edith isn't following the textbook. She reached a point where every indicator I was tracking suggested she'd continue to decline, and she stopped declining. Her fever hasn't broken, and she's very sick, but her body has drawn some line I didn't expect it to draw."

Eliza looked down at the sleeping woman.

"She's strong," Eliza said.

"She is."

Samuel looked at Edith. Sixty-six years old. Hands thickened by arthritis, she'd never once complained about. Her body was reduced slightly by days of fever, and her skin was translucent at her temples, where the veins showed blue beneath the surface. And beneath all of it, something wouldn't yield. Something that Edith Aldreidge held at her very center had nothing to do with logic and what was known about this illness and everything to do with her.

He pulled his notebook from his vest pocket and turned to a blank page and recorded the date, the time, Edith's temperature, her pulse, and the change in her abdominal examination. He wrote, Rigidity reduced. Guarding reflex diminished. Patient responsive to voice. Fever is holding but the decline trajectory has not materialized. Course atypical. Etiology of improvement is unclear.

He closed his notebook and looked at Eliza.

She hadn't moved. Her hand was still on Edith's arm, her body still settled against the wall in the same position. Her hair was twisted and pinned, but the twist had loosened until it sat low on her neck, half-undone, held by two pins doing the work of six.

He could see the terrible state her hands were in; one on Edith's arm, the other resting on her lap. Her knuckles were split along three fingers of her right hand, the cracks dry and deep from carbolic and lye and the relentless wringing and scrubbing that hadn't stopped since the first morning they'd moved patients into this room. The skin along the backs of her hands was rough and reddened past anything a twenty-two-year-old woman's hands should show.

He'd seen hands like that before. Ranch women in Colorado whose knuckles bled through winter from washing and the cold. His mother's hands in February cracked across every joint, and she'd worked bacon grease into them at the kitchen table before bed and been back at the washboard by six.

"Eliza."

She looked at him.

"When did you last sleep more than an hour?"

"Monday afternoon," she said. "I sat down in the kitchen after the noon meal and put my head on the table. Winnie woke me when the broth was ready."

"Monday."

"Yes."

"That was two days ago."

She didn't answer. She looked at Edith and adjusted the cloth on her brow, her fingers moving from habit, sure and gentle.

"I need you to go sit with your aunt and take a break," he said.

"I'm fine."

"You're not fine. You've had less than an hour of sleep in two days."

"I want to be near Edith and Timothy in case they need me... or anyone else for that matter."

"Eliza... look at me. I examined Edith; her abdomen has improved, and her fever is holding rather than climbing, and she's as stable as she's been since she took ill. Timothy is doing fine. Margaret will be here within the hour to help. Della and Alma are already here . I have plenty of help; go sit with Leora and take a break and try to sleep."

"Samuel, there are patients who need—"

"There are patients who need a nurse who has slept. I just came from your aunt's room. She was asking after you. She hasn't seen you since yesterday morning. She's in good spirits. I just told her I'm going to start allowing her to get out of bed. The longer she stays flat, the harder it'll be for her to regain her strength and mobility. Her fracture has healed well enough to bare light support, and I want her upright and moving. I spoke with Amos moments ago, and he's going to speak with Owen at the mill today and ask him to send one of his men to the boardinghouse to take measurements for a pair of walking sticks."

Eliza straightened against the wall.

"Walking sticks... I imagine she's pleased," Eliza said.

"Go and see for yourself."

Eliza looked at Edith. She drew the shawl closer across the older woman's shoulders, and her fingers rested there for a moment against the worn wool.

"I'll be in Aunt Leora's room if you need me; if I'm not back in an hour, please come get me," she said.

"I know where to find you."

She rose from the floor, and the rising was slow. She put one hand on the wall and pushed herself up. He watched the effort it cost her to straighten; the way her back held stiff for several seconds before it released. She pressed her palm against her hip where the joint had locked from hours on the hard floor. After a moment she drew herself up straight as a board and ran her hands down the front of her skirt.

She walked toward the hallway that led past the kitchen to Leora's quarters. Her step was steady. It was also the slowest pace he'd ever seen her keep in this boardinghouse.

Chapter 27

Leora's door was open as Samuel approached. He'd come to check on her and to find Eliza, whom he hadn't seen since he'd sent her away from the dining room that morning.

The afternoon had been long. He'd changed Edith's cloths multiple times, taken temperatures across the makeshift sick ward, helped Della carry fresh linens upstairs, and spent twenty minutes coaching Emmett Sloane through a bowl of broth the man's stomach didn't want. Margaret had arrived at ten and stayed through the afternoon, freeing Samuel to move between the dining room and the second floor without worrying about who was watching over whom.

Now it was past four o'clock, and the boardinghouse had settled into its late-afternoon quiet. From the kitchen came the soft clank of a lid being set on a pot and the scrape of Winnie's spoon against iron.

He stepped into Leora's doorway and stopped.

Leora was propped against her pillows with a book resting in her lap, her reading spectacles low on her nose.

Eliza was on the bed beside her aunt, asleep.

She lay on her side with one arm tucked beneath her pillow and the other resting across her waist. Her shoes were still on. Her hair had come completely unpinned, auburn and wavy, spread across the pillow.

Leora looked up from her book, saw him, and smiled. She waved him in and pointed to the chair beside her bed.

He crossed the room and sat down. "How is she?" he whispered.

"Samuel Porter, don't bother whispering on her account. Eunice came and visited with me earlier. We ate and talked and carried on for a good hour and a half, and Eliza didn't move once. Didn't stir, didn't turn over, didn't so much as twitch. Eunice said she hadn't ever seen anyone sleep that hard." She shook her head. "The poor thing is completely worn through."

Samuel glanced at Eliza. Her breathing was deep and even, the slow rhythm of someone who'd been running on nothing and had finally stopped.

"How long has she been out?" he asked.

"Since this morning, shortly after she came in. She lay down right here beside me and started telling me about how everyone was doing. She got about three sentences in, and she was gone."

"Good," he said. "She needed it."

"She needed it days ago, and you and I both know it." Leora looked at him over her spectacles. "Now. Tell me about Edith."

"Her fever dropped two degrees this afternoon," he said. "I checked her just before I came back here. She's still sick, but her body is doing something I can't account for. The trajectory she was on should've continued downward. It hasn't. She's reversing course, and the textbooks I studied in Chicago don't describe what I'm seeing."

Leora closed her bookmade; around one finger to hold her place. "God doesn't consult medical textbooks, Samuel. He wrote the body those books are trying to understand. I've been praying for Edith. If she's defying what you were taught, maybe that's not a mystery. Maybe it's an answer."

He didn't argue with her. "I hope you're right," he said.

"I usually am. Ask anyone in this boardinghouse." Her mouth twitched. "Except possibly Edith, who would tell you I'm right about half the time and stubborn the other half, and she'd be correct about both."

He smiled at that. "I have news for you," he said. "Mark Willard is coming from the mill this afternoon. His shift ends at five. He's going to take your measurements for a pair of walking sticks."

Leora's hands went still on her book.

"I am so pleased," she said.

"I'll have Margaret or Eunice here when he arrives to help you stand so he can take the measurements properly."

Leora took her spectacles off and set them on top of her book. She blinked twice, pressed her lips together, and when she spoke, her voice had gone rough.

"Six weeks I've been in this bed, Samuel. Six weeks. I've run this boardinghouse through a flood and multiple Montana winters. I buried my husband and kept my doors open. And having to stay in this bed has been just as difficult as any of those things." She looked at him. "Walking sticks. Lord have mercy."

"After Mark finishes, I'll carry you to the dining room if you'd like. You could sit and visit with folks. Or I could take you to the kitchen, and you could speak with Winnie while she cooks. Whatever you want."

"Whatever I want," she said. "I want to sit in my dining room and see my boardinghouse with my own eyes. I want to see the people in those pallets. I want to see Edith with my own eyes. I want to help however I can. Even if that means sitting and reading to any of them. I'll fold linens. I'll do whatever you need me to."

"Your wants will be granted soon."

She put her spectacles back on and picked up her book, but she didn't open it. She held it and looked toward her window, and the breeze came through, warm and green-smelling, and her chin trembled several times before she could set it firm.

Samuel let her have the moment. He sat in the chair and looked at Eliza.

Her face on the pillow was more still than he'd ever seen it. The freckles across the bridge of her nose stood out against her fair skin. Her auburn hair lay in loose waves against the pillowcase.

He'd been watching her for weeks. Watching her mix medicines and carry broth to patients who couldn't lift their own heads. Watching her hum while she worked and stop humming when she was thinking deeply or praying over someone. He'd watched her hold Titus Drumond's hand while the man took his final breath.

He'd never watched her peacefully at rest.

"Samuel."

He turned his head.

Leora was watching him. She'd set her book aside entirely, and her face held a look he recognized from his own mother. The same look Esmi Porter had given each of her children at the exact moment she'd figured out what they were trying not to say when any of them were hiding something from her.

"You're smitten," Leora said.

"Yes, ma'am. I am."

"Well," she folded her hands in her lap. "What are you going to do about it?"

He shook his head slowly, but a grin came to his face that he couldn't have stopped if he'd wanted to. "I don't know yet. I've never done this before."

"What do you mean?" she said.

"I've never fallen in love before... and in the middle of all this chaos to boot. I didn't come to Providence Ridge looking for this, and I certainly didn't expect to find it in a boardinghouse during a typhoid outbreak."

"My sister Caroline, Eliza's mother, fell in love with Henry Miller in less than a month. She married him right away, and they had several years of the happiest marriage I've ever seen outside my own. Speed doesn't make it less real, Samuel. Sometimes it just means the Lord didn't see any reason to waste time."

He looked at Eliza sleeping on the bed beside her aunt. The breeze from the window moved a strand of her hair across her cheek.

Leora glanced toward her window. "What time does the mill shift end?"

"Five o'clock."

"Then Mark Willard will be here soon." She looked at Eliza, then back at Samuel. "Carry her into her room. It's right next door. When Mark gets here and you and Margaret or Eunice help me stand, the commotion is going to wake her... I just know it will, and that girl needs to sleep until her body decides it's finished sleeping."

"Yes, ma'am." Samuel stood up from his chair and moved to Eliza's side of the bed.

He bent and slid one arm beneath her shoulders and the other beneath her knees. When he lifted her, her head fell against his chest, and her loose hair slipped across his forearm. She felt tiny and fragile in his arms.

He carried her through the doorway into the short hall between Leora's room and the small bedroom next door. Her door was open. Her narrow bed was made, the patchwork quilt smooth.

He laid her on her bed. Her head settled onto her pillow, and her hair fanned across it, auburn against the white cotton. Her hands came to rest at her sides, her fingers open and still.

She never woke.

Samuel stood watching her sleep for a few moments before turning away.

Chapter 28

The window was on the wrong side. That was the first thought to surface, slow and blurred, through whatever thick place she'd been sleeping in. She'd been lying beside Leora, and Leora's window was on the opposite wall.

Eliza sat up, and her body announced itself in stages. Her back first, locked tight along her spine from weeks of bending over pallets and basins. Then her shoulders, seized between the blades and across the tops. Her hands ached when she opened them, and the cracks along her knuckles pulled against skin that had gone stiff while she slept. She looked down at herself. Yesterday's dress, wrinkled and creased from sleeping in it. Her shoes still on. Her hair loose on her shoulders and down her back, every pin gone.

The last thing she remembered was Leora's bed. She'd gone to sit with her aunt after Samuel sent her away from the makeshift sick ward. She'd lain down and started telling Leora about the patients.

She swung her legs off the bed and stood up. The room tilted with a slow, heavy sway that made her grip the edge of the washstand until the floor steadied beneath her feet.

She poured water from the pitcher into the basin. It was cool against her face, against the creases the pillowcase had pressed into her cheek and along her jaw. She washed her hands, working the water carefully over the cracked skin along her knuckles, and dried them on the cloth beside the basin. Her comb was in the top drawer of the dresser, and she pulled it through her hair, easing the tangles loose from the waves that a night of sleeping on one side had pressed flat in some places and knotted in others. She twisted the length into a low knot at her nape and pinned it. She smoothed her dress. Wrinkled and slept-in and not at all what a proper young woman from Philadelphia ought to look like at any hour, but her hair was pinned and her face was clean.

She walked through the short hallway to Leora's room, and her aunt's door was open.

Leora sat propped against her pillows with her reading spectacles low on her nose and a book resting in her lap.

Leora looked up when Eliza appeared in the doorway and set her book aside.

"There she is," Leora said. "I was starting to wonder if you'd sleep through to Friday."

Eliza came in and sat on the edge of the bed. "What time is it?"

"Just past seven. Thursday morning. You've been asleep since yesterday around noon."

"Since noon." She pressed her palms against her knees. "I don't even remember falling asleep. I remember lying down beside you and talking about the patients, and then nothing."

"You got about three sentences out," Leora said. "I was listening and nodding and waiting for the fourth, and when I looked over, you were gone. Sound asleep in the middle of a word. I don't think you finished the sentence."

"And you just let me sleep?"

"I wasn't going to wake you. Nobody in this building was going to wake you. Eunice came in around one o'clock to visit with me, and we talked and carried on for a good hour and a half, and you didn't stir. Didn't turn over. Didn't so much as twitch."

Eliza looked down at her wrinkled skirt. "How did I get to my room?"

"Mark Willard came by yesterday evening to take measurements for my walking sticks, and I was worried the commotion would wake you. So I had Samuel carry you to your room."

Samuel carried her. He'd lifted her off this bed and walked her through the hallway and laid her in her own bed on her own pillow, and she'd been so deeply gone she hadn't felt his arms go beneath her. She hadn't woken when he picked her up. Her body had simply quit, and while she was sleeping, while she was nothing but slack limbs from exhaustion, he'd gathered her up and carried her.

She pressed her palms flat on her lap and looked at her aunt.

"How's Edith?"

"Samuel checked on her this morning before dawn. Her fever dropped again overnight; she is making good progress."

"And Timothy?"

"He's doing fine. Yesterday I read to him, and it was such a blessing. The poor child fell asleep with a smile on his face while I was reading."

"You read to him?"

"Eliza... Samuel carried me into the dining room yesterday evening after Mark left. I spent the evening watching over the ill myself, and it was a wonderful thing to present and do something useful. Samuel, himself came this morning to check on me, and he told me everyone is still doing just fine. The whole building kept moving while you slept, Eliza. Winnie cooked. Margaret sat with patients. Eunice and Della washed the linens. I sat with patients and I also read to Timothy. Samuel did his rounds. Nobody was neglected. Nobody went without."

Eliza looked at her hands in her lap. The reddened knuckles, the dry skin, the small cracks that stung when she flexed her fingers.

"You're angry with yourself," Leora said.

"I'm not angry."

"Then tell me what that look on your face is about, because to me it's the look of a woman who thinks she's failed at something."

Eliza turned her hands over in her lap, palms up.

"I slept for nearly nineteen hours," she said. "People were sick. Edith was fighting for her life. Timothy's five years old and still running a fever, and I was asleep in my bed while other people did what I should've been doing."

"What you should've been doing is exactly what you did. Sleeping. Resting. Letting your body have what it's been begging you for since this outbreak started."

"My body betrayed me and shut down."

"Because you wouldn't shut it down yourself. So it did the job for you. Since the day you stepped off that wagon here in Providence Ridge, you've taken care of everything. You kept this boardinghouse running. You had a supply list written and an order placed. You took charge of everything, and the boardinghouse was running smoothly, and you hadn't even been here but a few days. I thought to myself, Lord, my niece is capable. And you are. You're the most capable person I've ever known, Eliza."

Leora paused.

"But capable isn't the same as well. And you haven't been well in a long time. Not just since the outbreak. Since before you came to Montana. Since before your father put you on that train. You learned during your mother's illness that the one thing you could control was how well you cared for her. You couldn't stop the consumption. You couldn't fix what was happening to her body. But you could change the linens and brew the tea and sing the hymns and count her breaths and make sure every single thing within your reach was done right. And when she died anyway, you didn't stop giving. You gave more. You gave to your father. You gave to the Society. You gave to that hospital. You gave to me the minute I wrote and asked. You've given to every patient in that dining room." She squeezed Eliza's hand. "And you've never once, not one single time, allowed another living soul to give back to you."

"You told me a few days ago that you felt all twisted up inside," Leora continued. "That you were scared and tired and frightened and didn't know if you were coming or going. Do you remember saying that?"

"I remember."

"I listened to you that day, and I held my tongue on half of what I wanted to say. Well, I'm not holding back any longer, and you're going to hear it now." Leora took Eliza's hand. Her grip was firm, her fingers warm and strong around her niece's cracked knuckles. "What happened yesterday wasn't weakness. Your body did what your will refuses to do. It stopped. It received. It let someone carry you when you couldn't carry yourself. And the fact that it was Samuel who carried you, that it was a man who loves you whether he's said the words or not, that isn't a thing to be ashamed about. It's a mercy, Eliza. The kind you don't earn and can't arrange and wouldn't have asked for, and it came anyway, because that's how God works when His children won't stop long enough to let Him work."

Eliza sat on the edge of her aunt's bed and didn't speak. She held Leora's hand, and she let the words find their footing inside her, and the finding hurt in a good way.

"Being human isn't a failure of faithfulness," Leora said. "It's the very thing God made you to be."

Eliza sat and didn't argue, nor did she stand and reach for something to do to keep herself busy. She let herself be held by a woman who loved her, and for the first time in longer than she could measure, she didn't try to earn it.

After a while, Leora squeezed her hand and let go. "Go eat your breakfast. Winnie's been up since five, and she'll have your head if you don't eat something after sleeping that long."

Eliza stood and kissed her aunt's forehead, and Leora's hand came up and cupped the back of her head for a moment before releasing her.

The hallway opened into the dining room, and Eliza paused at the threshold. The sick ward lay quiet in its early-morning stillness. Hattie lay on her side, facing Timothy, her hand resting on his small shoulder. Ada's pallet was nearest the window, and Jasper sat beside her on the floor with his back against the wall, his chin dropped to his chest, dozing. Edith lay beneath her shawl with a cloth across her brow, her silver hair spread thin against her pillow.

Margaret sat in a chair near the supply table with a cup of coffee balanced on her knee.

"Everyone's resting," Margaret said. "Samuel was through here not forty minutes ago. Checked every one of them. Edith's fever came down another half degree overnight, and Timothy kept a full cup of water down before he fell back asleep." She waved toward the kitchen. "Go eat. Winnie made eggs."

"Thank you, Margaret," she said.

She turned and walked into the kitchen.

Winnie stood at the cookstove with a wooden spoon in one hand and a cloth in the other, turning something in the skillet. The room carried the warm smell of butter browning in the pan.

Winnie looked over her shoulder. "Sit down. Don't touch any-thing. Don't help. Just sit."

"I wasn't going to help."

"You were thinking about it. I saw your face. Sit."

Eliza sat in the chair nearest the stove. Winnie set a plate in front of her. Eggs, two biscuits, a spoonful of preserves from the jar Margaret had brought from the mercantile. A cup of coffee, poured hot and set beside her hand.

She picked up her fork and took the first bite, and her stomach answered with a hunger so sharp it startled her. She hadn't eaten a real meal in days.

Winnie poured herself a coffee and sat across the table. "You look better."

"I slept for nineteen hours."

"I know. Samuel told us not to wake you under any circumstances. He said if anyone knocked on your door before you came out on your own, he'd have words with them, and I believe he meant it."

"He carried me to my room, Winnie... I was so tired I don't even remember it."

Winnie took a sip of her coffee.

"He's a good man, Eliza," Winnie said. "I know you know that. But I'm saying it out loud because someone ought to, and I'm tired of watching the two of you circle around what everybody in this building already sees."

"What does everyone see?"

"Two people who are in love with each other and too stubborn or too scared to say so."

Eliza looked at her friend across the table. Winnie's expression was plain and open, and unapologetic. She'd said what she meant, and she was letting it sit the way Winnie let everything sit, with the patience of a woman who'd already decided she was right and wasn't in a hurry about it.

"You're a blessing, do you know that, Winnie? Thank you for being exactly who you are and for everything you've done these past few weeks to help us all."

"You're welcome. Now finish your eggs before they get cold."

Eliza picked up her fork and finished eating. Winnie rose and carried her cup to the basin, then turned back to the stove where a pot of broth had started to simmer. The kitchen filled with the small sounds of her work. The scrape of her spoon against iron. The soft knock of a lid being set on a pot. The creak of a floorboard beneath her step as she moved between the shelf and the stove.

Eliza pushed her plate aside after she'd finished.

Her mother's Bible was on the table in front of her, and she drew it toward her. She held it in both hands and ran her thumb along the spine where the binding had gone soft from years of opening and closing.

She opened it to where the pale blue ribbon lay. It marked a page in Lamentations. Beside the text, a thin pencil line ran in the margin, drawn with the light and careful hand of a woman who treated books with reverence. Her mother's mark.

Eliza read the words.

It is of the Lord's mercies that we are not consumed, because his compassions fail not. They are new every morning; great is thy faithfulness. The Lord is my portion, saith my soul; therefore will I hope in him. The Lord is good unto them that wait for him, to the soul that seeketh him. It is good that a man should both hope and quietly wait for the salvation of the Lord.

She read it again. Her lips moved with the words the second time, not quite speaking them, not quite holding them silent.

It is of the Lord's mercies that we are not consumed.

Her mother had marked this passage in the months when her voice was gone, when the consumption had taken the singing and the speaking and left only her hands and her eyes. Caroline couldn't say the words. But she could hold her Bible open on her lap and press her finger against this verse and close her eyes.

Mercies that don't fail. Compassions that arrive without being earned. New every morning, whether the morning is deserved or not.

They are new every morning.

This was a new morning. She'd woken in a bed she hadn't put herself in. She'd been fed by a friend who asked nothing in return. She'd been loved by an aunt who spoke the truth she needed to hear. She'd been carried by a man whose hands were gentle with her when she couldn't know they were there. None of it earned. All of it is given.

Eliza sat at the kitchen table with the Bible open in her hands and her mother's faded ribbon between the pages, and for the first time in years, she didn't reach for anything else.

Chapter 29

Zeb Thompson was arguing with Della Raines about whether she was holding his water cup at the correct angle, and Samuel stood at the foot of his pallet and let it happen.

"I can drink from a cup, Mrs. Raines. I've been drinking from cups since I was old enough to hold one, and I don't need somebody tilting it for me like I'm a yearling calf at a trough."

"Mr. Thompson, if you'd quit squirming and hold still, the water would go into your mouth instead of down the front of your shirt, and we wouldn't be having this conversation."

"The shirt was already wet."

"It was clean five minutes ago."

"Well, it ain't clean now."

Samuel wrote in his notebook. Pulse seventy-four. Temperature down a full degree since this morning. Appetite returning. Patient argumentative. He underlined the last word and closed the cover.

Last week Zeb couldn't lift his head off his pillow. He'd stopped talking for several days and could hardly mumble. Now he was fighting over the angle of a water cup, and Samuel considered that a victory.

"Zeb, drink the water," he said. "All of it. I don't care if Della holds the cup or you hold the cup. I care that you finish it."

"I'd finish it faster if she'd let me do it myself."

Della set the cup in his hands with the careful restraint of a woman resisting the urge to pour it over his head. Zeb took a long drink and set the cup on the floor beside his pallet with a deliberate thump.

"There," he said.

"Thank you," Samuel said. "I'll check on you again before supper."

He moved to the next pallet. Emmett Sloane sat upright against the wall with a cup of broth, spooning it to his mouth with the careful effort of a man rebuilding the simple act of feeding himself. His color had improved. The grayish cast that had clung to his skin through the worst days of his fever had given way to something warmer, and his eyes tracked Samuel with the clear look of a man who knew where he was.

"How are you feeling?" Samuel asked.

"Tired," Emmett said. "But I kept bread down this morning."

Samuel pressed the back of his hand to Emmett's forehead. Warm, but the sustained heat of the past weeks was gone. His body was cooling in the slow, gradual way that signaled genuine recovery rather than a temporary dip. "You're mending, Emmett. Another few days and I expect you'll be ready to go home."

Emmett nodded.

Samuel crossed to the Fitches. Nolan was sitting up with Clara's hand in his lap. She lay on her side beside him, her breathing even, her face turned toward his knee.

"She ate this morning," Nolan said. "Broth and a few bites of biscuit. She kept all of it down."

"Good. And you?"

"Same. My legs are shaky when I stand, but I'm standing."

"Don't rush it. That'll pass."

Nolan looked down at his wife. His thumb moved across her knuckles. "When can I take her home?"

"A few more days. I want to see both of you keeping solid food down and walking the length of this room before I'm comfortable with it."

"I imagine I can walk the room now."

"Then show me tomorrow morning, and we'll talk."

He moved to Ada's pallet. Jasper sat on the floor beside her, one hand resting on her arm above the quilt. Ada was sleeping, and her sleep was the deep, restful kind. Her face had lost the tight, drawn lines of a body spending everything it had. She looked like a young woman asleep in the middle of the afternoon.

He checked her pulse. Steady, seventy-two. Her forehead was cool under his hand. Her fever had broken yesterday and hadn't returned.

"She's doing well," he told Jasper.

Samuel straightened and looked across the room.

Hattie Pemberton sat on the edge of her pallet with Timothy beside her. The boy was propped against his mother's side with a picture book open in his lap, turning pages with the slow care of a child who wasn't reading the words but was studying the pictures with full attention. The angry flush that had burned across his cheeks for days had faded to a warmth that looked closer to health than fever. He turned a page, pointed at something, and looked up at Hattie. She bent her head to his and said something Samuel couldn't hear, and Timothy nodded and went back to his book.

Margaret sat in a chair at the foot of their pallets with a cup of coffee balanced on her knee.

He crossed to them. "How's our patient?"

Timothy looked up. "I'm reading."

"I can see that. Good book?"

"It has horses in it."

"That's the best kind." Samuel knelt beside the pallet and pressed his hand to Timothy's forehead. Warm, but not hot. He checked the boy's pulse, counting against his pocket watch. Stronger than yesterday. The small wrist beneath his fingers carried more life in it than it had a week ago. He'd spent nights beside this pallet counting each of Timothy's breaths, and every morning he'd checked this same pulse with the same question running beneath his training: was he doing enough? Would this young boy survive? He knew the answer snow. The knowing loosened his grip on the watch, and he slipped it back into his vest pocket.

"He ate breakfast," Hattie said. "A full bowl of Winnie's porridge. He wanted more, and Winnie told him he could have a second bowl at noon, and he did."

"Two bowls of porridge. That's a very good sign." He straightened and looked at Margaret. "He's mending."

Margaret pressed her lips together and nodded once.

Samuel moved to Edith's pallet. She lay on her back beneath her shawl, her silver hair combed and pinned loosely at her nape. Her breathing was even. A cloth lay folded across her brow, and her hands rested on the quilt with the stiffness of her arthritis.

He knelt and lifted the cloth. Her skin beneath was warm, but not the deep, angry heat that had frightened him through the worst days. He took her pulse. Nice and steady. He pressed his fingers to her abdomen through the quilt, gentle, checking the quadrants he'd been monitoring for weeks. Soft. The rigidity that had alarmed him was gone.

Samuel no longer had any fear that Edith wouldn't survive this vicious illness. He'd been cautious with the word recovery because he'd learned what it cost to let hope run ahead of evidence. But looking at Edith now, at the steadiness of her breathing and the color returning to her face, he let the caution go.

He wrote in his notebook. Temperature, pulse, and the change in her abdomen. Recovery trajectory holding. He closed the notebook and slid it into his vest pocket.

He stood and turned toward the far side of the room where Leora sat.

She'd been there since just after noon, when he'd carried her from her bedroom and settled her in the wooden armchair Margaret had positioned between the supply table and the window. She'd spent the afternoon talking with Margaret, instructing Eunice on the state of the linen supply, which was, according to Leora, inadequate and in need of her personal attention the moment she could stand long enough to sort it properly. She had Della bring her a cup of coffee and then sent her to tell Winnie to step away from the kitchen and take a coffee break herself.

Leora sat with her hands folded in her lap and her reading spectacles tucked into the collar of her nightgown, watching the room the way a woman watches a house she built with her own hands being used for purposes she didn't plan and approves of, anyway. Six weeks in bed had thinned her face and taken the sturdiness from her frame. But her eyes were sharp, and her jaw carried the same iron Samuel had recognized the first time he'd treated her.

Eliza sat in the chair beside her aunt.

He'd been watching Eliza all afternoon, and something about her today was different. The difference had been working at him since she'd come into the dining room after breakfast and taken the chair beside Leora instead of picking up a cloth or checking a pulse or doing any of the hundred things she'd done every other day since the outbreak began.

As of this moment, Eunice was directing the volunteers. Della was changing cloths. Margaret was sitting with Hattie and Timothy. Winnie was in the kitchen. The ward was functioning, and Eliza was watching it function, and she was letting it.

In the many weeks of working beside her, Samuel had never seen Eliza Miller sit still when there was a task within reach. But today she had been checking on patients regularly and taking breaks either sitting with her aunt or walking outside for fresh air.

He crossed the room to them.

"How are the patients?" Leora asked.

"Improving," he said. He pulled up the chair Margaret had been using and sat across from them. "Zeb's complaining again, which I consider a medical milestone. Emmett's keeping solid food down. Ada's fever is gone. Timothy ate two bowls of porridge."

"I know about the porridge," Leora said. "Margaret told me. She said Winnie tried to cut him off after the first bowl, and Timothy told her he was still hungry in a tone that sounded exactly like Amos, and Margaret couldn't help but laugh."

"That sounds right."

He looked at Eliza. "How are you?"

"Good," she said. "I feel well rested. I feel like myself again. No worries, Dr. Porter, Winnie insisted earlier that I join her for the afternoon meal. We ate together in the kitchen."

"I know. I told her to."

Her mouth curved into a smile. "You told her to watch after me as if I were a child?"

"I told her not to let you skip meals."

Leora glanced between them. "Well. I'm glad someone around here listens when they're told to eat, because the Lord knows I've been telling this girl the same thing for days and she hears me the way she hears rain on the roof. Present but unattended to."

"That's not true," Eliza said.

"It's approximately true, and approximately is close enough for my purposes."

Samuel looked at Edith's pallet across the room, then back at Leora. "I checked Edith. The rigidity in her abdomen is gone. Her fever's lower than yesterday. Her pulse is steady."

Leora pressed her palms flat against her knees and looked at the ceiling. Her chin trembled. She drew a breath, held it, and let it go. When she brought her face back down, her eyes were wet, but her jaw was set firm.

"Thank you, Samuel," she said. "For everything you've done for her."

"Edith did the fighting. I just kept the cloths cool."

"Don't sell yourself short in my presence. I don't tolerate false modesty from people who've earned the real kind." She wiped the corner of her eye with the back of her hand, quick and impatient. "Now. I've been sitting in this chair for far too long, and I'd like to try standing."

"I think that's a fine idea," he said. "Eliza, take her left side. I'll take her right."

Samuel positioned himself on her right, his hand beneath her elbow. Eliza stood on the left, her arm threaded through her aunt's, her free hand braced against Leora's forearm.

"Whenever you're ready," Samuel said.

Leora gripped the arm of the chair with her right hand. She set her good foot flat on the floor. She looked straight ahead at the window across the room, took a breath, and pushed herself up.

Her legs shook. Samuel could feel the trembling through his hand on her arm, the fine vibration of muscles that hadn't borne weight in six weeks trying to remember what standing required. Eliza's grip tightened on her left side.

"My goodness," she said. "My legs feel like they belong to someone else."

"They'll remember. Give them a minute."

She stood still, breathing, adjusting to the height and the balance and the simple, enormous fact of being upright. Across the room, Margaret looked up from Timothy's pallet. Eunice set her pencil down. Della stopped mid-stride with a basin in her hands.

"One step," Leora said. "Just one."

"One step," Samuel said.

She slid her right foot forward. No more than four inches, toes dragging against the floorboard before her heel settled flat. She shifted onto it, and Samuel felt the transfer through his arm, the way her body leaned and found its balance on the new footing. Then her left foot followed.

Two steps. Leora looked at the pallets. She looked at her dining room, at the ward it had become, at the people lying in beds that didn't belong here in a room meant for supper and conversation and fellowship.

"Turn me around," she said. "I want to go back."

They turned her carefully, Samuel pivoting on her right side while Eliza guided the left. Leora took two more steps back to her chair. She sat, and the sitting was heavy, and she gripped the arms of the chair.

"Four steps," she said.

"Four good ones," Samuel said.

"Four is a start." She opened her eyes and looked at the room again. "This evening I want six."

He sat back down. Eliza returned to her chair, and the three of them stayed beside the window while the ward moved around them. Della carried her basin to Zeb's pallet. Eunice returned to her writing. Margaret leaned down and said something to Timothy that made the boy laugh, a small, bright sound that carried across the room.

Samuel watched Eliza. She sat with her hands in her lap, her attention moving from one person to the next. She watched Margaret with Timothy. She watched Jasper holding Ada's hand. She watched Della press a fresh cloth to Zeb's forehead while Zeb complained that the water was too cold, and Della told him he'd survive. She watched Winnie appear in the kitchen doorway, scan the room, and disappear again.

She wasn't rising from her chair to take the cloth from Della's hands. She wasn't crossing the room to check on Ada or adjust Timothy's blanket. She was sitting beside her aunt and simply observing.

"You're quiet today," he said.

She turned to him. "Am I?"

"You haven't gotten up from that chair in over an hour."

"I got up to help Aunt Leora walk."

"Other than that."

She looked down at her hands folded in her lap. "I've been thinking."

"About what?" Samuel asked.

Eliza was quiet for a moment.

"About everything," she said. "About how much has happened since I came here? About what it's meant to be part of this. I keep thinking about how precious all of it is. Every bit of it. The hard parts and the good parts, and the parts I wouldn't have chosen. I came here to run a boardinghouse and care for my aunt, and I did those things, or at least I started to and then this terrible illness struck this town. Life is precious, Samuel. Things can change so quickly. My life is changing. Those are the things that are on my mind right now."

She looked at him. Her blue eyes were steady, and there was nothing careful in the way she held his attention. She wasn't composing herself. She was just looking at him, and the openness of it was so unlike the woman who'd met him at Leora's bedside weeks ago with clinical vocabulary and a composure so thorough he'd mistaken it for coolness.

Leora reached over and took her niece's hand.

Chapter 30

A few days later...

Through the dining room windows, Eliza could see the mercantile doors standing open across Main Street, both of them propped wide. A wagon sat at the hitching rail with its tailgate down, and a man she didn't recognize was loading sacks of flour onto its bed. Two women came out carrying parcels wrapped in brown paper, and their voices carried faintly through the glass, ordinary and unhurried.

The bridge and the road on the southern edge of town had opened this past Saturday. The quarantine had been lifted. She'd watched the first freight wagon cross the bridge this morning from the boardinghouse porch, the wheels drumming on the timber planks, and the sound had traveled up Main Street to where she'd stood with Winnie. Neither of them had spoken.

The makeshift sick ward in the dining room had thinned. The Fitches had gone home yesterday morning, Nolan walking slowly with Clara's arm through his. Emmett had left the day before. She and Samuel had walked Zeb home this morning. It had been a slow walk, but he had done it on his own and quarreled the whole way home. Ada and Jasper had gone home Saturday evening, and she and Samuel had checked on her twice since. The three boarders upstairs had all recovered steadily, and each of them needed another week before returning to their jobs at the lumber mill. Peter Hart had returned to his home behind the blacksmith shop, where his brother promised to make him take it easy for a few days. Jessie Wicks had returned to his home above the saloon and had no plans to open his doors for at least another week. He was still weak, but insisted on returning home. His employee, Miss Pardee, had left the boardinghouse as well; her sister had taken her home with her yesterday after church.

Timothy and Hattie were still here. Hattie was well enough to leave, but Samuel wanted to keep Timothy here for a day or two more as a precaution. Edith was in her chair beside Leora, the two of them carrying on a conversation about the plans to build a proper school building here in Providence Ridge that would also serve as a church.

Eliza sat in her chair near the window with a cup of coffee, watching the town go about its Monday through the glass. The dining room had begun to feel like a room again rather than a ward. Most of the pallets were gone. The long table had been uncovered at one end, and Winnie had set a jar of purple asters on it that morning, picked from the strip of ground behind the kitchen.

The boardinghouse doors stood open to the afternoon, letting the warm air move through the dining room. Boots crossed the entry, and Amos Pemberton appeared in the doorway with two envelopes in one hand and his hat in the other.

"Miss Miller," he said. "These came in on the freight wagon this morning. Both were postmarked from Philadelphia. I sorted the mail this afternoon and saw them and thought I'd bring them over straight away."

He crossed the room and handed them to her, and she recognized her father's handwriting on both envelopes.

"Thank you, Amos. That was kind of you to bring them over."

"You're welcome."

Eliza looked at the two envelopes in her hands. The first was postmarked July eighth. The second, July sixteenth.

Eliza crossed the room and sat by her aunt and Edith.

"Letters from my father," she said, holding them up.

"Oh, that's wonderful. Hurry and open them," Leora said.

She turned the first envelope over, slid her finger beneath the seal, and unfolded the single sheet inside.

Dear Eliza,

I hope this letter finds you well and that the Montana Territory has not proven too wild for a Philadelphia girl. I suspect it has, and I suspect you are managing it with the same competence you bring to everything.

The shop is busy. Mr. Hargrove brought me a rush order for two hundred temperance pamphlets last Thursday, and I had them set and printed by Saturday, which I consider a personal triumph given that I've been doing my own bookkeeping in your absence and the ledger is suffering for it. Mrs. Abernathy has been bringing supper three evenings a week. She brings enough for two meals, which I believe is her way of ensuring I eat on the days she doesn't come. I have not told her this is unnecessary because the food is excellent and I am not a foolish man.

I found one of your mother's recipes last week. It was tucked inside the back cover of the Fannie Farmer, written on a piece of the shop's notepaper in her hand. Her chicken and dumplings. I read it through twice and decided I would attempt it, because I thought it would be a fine thing to eat something Caroline had made often, even if it was my hands doing the making. I will spare you the details and say only that the dumplings did not hold together, the broth was thin, but I ate every bite because it was her recipe. I will try again. Your mother would have laughed at me and then shown me what I'd done wrong, and I'd give anything for that.

The church is well. Reverend Pratt delivered a fine sermon on the book of Ruth last Sunday, and I thought of you, not because you are Ruth but because you are the kind of woman who goes where she is needed without being asked twice. The Ladies' Society sends their regards. Mrs. Whitmore told me to tell you that the Benevolent fund is in order, though she says it with a look that suggests she'd prefer you were the one keeping it.

I miss you, daughter. The house is quiet without you.

I am managing fine, but I miss you.

Your loving father, Henry

Eliza folded the letter and held it in her lap.

"Well?" Leora said.

"He's fine," Eliza said. "The shop sounds busy. Mrs. Abernathy's been feeding him three nights a week, and he tried to make Mama's chicken and dumplings."

"Lord help us all," Leora said. "Henry Miller in a kitchen is a danger to himself and others."

"He said the dumplings didn't hold, and the broth was thin, and he ate all of it because the recipe was hers."

"That man," Leora said with a grin. "He loved my dear sister from the day they met. He has never stopped."

Samuel came through the front door. He'd been across the street at his office checking on supplies, and he carried his medical bag in one hand and a small brown bottle in the other. He set the bottle on the supply table, saw the three of them sitting close, and crossed the room.

"Letters from her father," Leora said.

"Good news?" Samuel said.

"Mrs. Abernathy, our neighbor back in Philadelphia, is feeding him; the shop is busy, and he attempted to cook my mother's chicken and dumplings," Eliza said.

"How'd that go?"

"About the way you'd expect from a man who has never really cooked all that much."

Samuel sat in the chair across from her. "At least he tried. That's more than I'd attempt with a chicken and dumplings recipe."

"You've told me your cookstove is your adversary."

"It is. We've reached an uneasy truce. I don't ask it to do anything ambitious, and it doesn't set my supper on fire."

Leora looked at Edith. "These two," she said.

Edith took a sip of her tea and said nothing.

Eliza opened the second letter.

My dear Eliza,

Your letter arrived yesterday, and I read it three times before supper and once more before bed. I am glad you are safe. I am glad Leora has you. I am glad the journey was without serious difficulty, though I suspect you have edited the account for my benefit.

You described the mountains, the sky, and all the beautiful things your eyes had witnessed, and I could hear your voice on the page.

I've been praying for you every morning. I read a passage in Romans last week, the eighth chapter, and I sat with it a long time because it made me think of your mother and of you. "And we know that all things work together for good to them that love God, to them who are the called according to his purpose." Your mother believed that verse with her whole heart, even at the end when believing it was the hardest thing she did. I believe it too. I believe God has you where He wants you, and I trust Him with you, even when the trusting is hard for a father who'd rather have his daughter under his own roof where he can see for himself that she's well.

I won't pretend I'm not missing you. I know you said you'd stay as long as Leora needs you, and I meant it when I said I trust you to know when the work is finished. But I'd be lying if I told you the house doesn't feel like a coat with one sleeve missing. It fits, but it doesn't fit right.

Come home when you're ready, Eliza. Not before. But come home.

All my love,

Father

She read the last line again. Come home when you're ready. Not before. But come home.

She folded the letter along its crease and set it on top of the first one in her lap.

"He misses me. He wants me home," Eliza said.

"Of course he does," Leora said. "He's your father."

"He said the house feels like a coat with one sleeve missing."

"That sounds like Henry. He's a man who speaks in pictures when he means it most."

Samuel sat across from her with his hands resting on his knees, a calm expression on his face.

She looked down at the letters. "He asked when I'm coming home."

Home. Her father's house on Chestnut Street, the rooms she'd managed since she was a young girl, the church with its bell tower two blocks east, the market where she bought vegetables on Thursday mornings. That was home. Twenty-two years of it.

Sitting in this dining room with Leora and Edith sitting beside her and Samuel across from her, the word arrived and kept going, like a key slid into a lock that no longer fit.

She had told Samuel in early July that she'd possibly return by September's end. She'd said it over bowls of Winnie's stew, back when September was a distant, abstract thing. The quarantine was lifted now. Leora was on the mend.

What would she go back to? The household. The Society. The auxiliary. The Thursday market and the Sunday sermon and the careful, steady rhythm of a life built around usefulness. She'd go back to managing her father's house and visiting the sick and teaching Sunday school and filling every hour with purpose, and none of it would be wrong, and all of it would be the life she'd already lived.

She couldn't go back and pretend she hadn't stood in Tom's office and told a room full of frightened people what typhoid did to a body because the truth mattered and she was the one willing to say it. She couldn't pretend she hadn't held Titus Drumond's hand while his fever took everything he had. She couldn't pretend she hadn't sat with a man who poured her coffee and told her she mattered and meant it, or that he hadn't carried her to her bed while she slept because her body had given out.

Leora was watching her. Eliza could feel her aunt's attention, steady and close and patient.

"I don't know what to write back," Eliza said.

"You don't have to write back today," Leora said.

"I know. But he's waiting. He's been waiting since I left, and every day I don't write is a day he worries."

"Henry Miller has survived worse than waiting for a letter. He survived your mother's illness and her death and years of grief, and he's still standing. He can wait a few more days while his daughter figures out what she wants to say." Leora put her hand on Eliza's arm. "The question isn't what to write, Eliza. The question I have for you is: What do you want? And you don't owe anyone that answer until you're ready to give it."

Eliza looked at the letters in her lap.

Come home when you're ready.

She wasn't ready. Not for the going and not for the staying.

She stood and tucked both letters into her apron pocket. "I'm going to check on Timothy," she said.

Leora let her go. She could feel Samuel's eyes on her as she crossed the dining room, and she didn't turn around, because turning around would mean looking at him, and looking at him right now would make the question louder than she could bear to hear it.

Chapter 31

A *few days later...*

Samuel was kneeling beside Linden's bed when Eliza came through the upstairs hallway with a fresh pitcher of water and a stack of clean cloths over her arm. Linden sat propped against his pillow, working through a bowl of broth with the slow, measured attention of a man whose appetite had only just come back after weeks of refusing everything but sips of water.

"His color's better," Eliza said, setting the pitcher on the night-stand.

"It is." Samuel pressed two fingers to Linden's wrist and counted silently, his lips moving once before he let go. "Pulse is steady. Appetite's returning. I'd say five or six more days before light work, and even then I'd want him on half shifts at the lumber mill."

Linden looked up from his broth. "Half shifts won't pay my room and board, Doc."

"Half shifts will keep you out of this bed for good. Full shifts too soon and you'll land right back in it."

"He's right, Mr. Linden," Eliza said. "Your body spent weeks fighting this illness. It needs time to rebuild what it lost."

Linden grumbled into his broth but kept eating.

They checked the other two boarders on the second floor of the boardinghouse. Jenkins was sleeping, his breathing clear and unhurried. Monroe sat in the chair beside his bed, reading a book. Samuel made his notes, slid his notebook into his vest pocket, and they left the room and walked down the stairs.

The dining room looked like a dining room again. The remaining pallets had been cleared; the long dining table was back in its normal place. The room carried the clean bite of lye soap.

Leora sat in her armchair near the window, her walking sticks propped against the wall within reach. Her reading spectacles rested on the small table beside her, next to a half-empty cup of coffee and her book.

Edith was in the chair beside her.

"There they are," Edith said.

Eliza crossed the room and knelt beside Edith's chair. She took Edith's hand, careful of the swollen joints, and closed her own fingers around it. Edith's skin was cool and papery, her bones too near the surface, but her grip closed around Eliza's and stayed.

"You look wonderful," Eliza said.

"I look like I've been dragged behind a wagon for a month, and I know it, so don't flatter me."

Samuel pulled a chair across from the women, and Eliza took the one beside him. The four of them sat near the window and watched as a freight wagon rattled past.

"Winnie," Leora called toward the kitchen.

Winnie appeared in the doorway, her sleeves shoved past her elbows and flour dusting her forearms. She carried a large wicker basket in the crook of her arm, covered with a blue-checked cloth tucked neatly around a generous mound of whatever was inside. She set it on the table and smiled.

"Oh, that was fast," Leora said. "I wasn't going to call for you for another five minutes."

Eunice walked toward them with a folded quilt over her arm and held it out to Eliza.

Eliza took the quilt and recognized it as one of her aunts'. "Why do I need your quilt, Aunt Leora?"

"This is your afternoon. Both of you." Leora said as she looked from Eliza to Samuel. "Winnie has packed a lunch. You're going to walk down to the river, find a nice spot, spread that quilt on the ground, and eat a proper meal together away from this boarding-house."

Samuel looked at the basket. Then at Leora and grinned.

"We have patients to check on this afternoon," Eliza said. "Aunt Leora, I appreciate this, but there's still work that needs doing."

"There's always work that needs doing. There will always be patients to check on. There has always been work that needs doing since the day Harold and I opened these doors, and there will be work that needs doing long after I'm in the ground." She leaned forward in her chair. "The two of you have been drowning in work for weeks, and I'm telling you, as the woman who loves you both, that the work will wait."

"She's been planning this since yesterday," Winnie said. "She made me promise not to breathe a word."

"Winnie packed fried chicken," Eunice said. "Biscuits. Pickled beets. And I believe there's lemonade in there as well."

"Two jars," Winnie said.

Leora settled her hands in her lap. "So. You can walk out that door with the basket and the quilt and enjoy a beautiful afternoon by the river. Or you can argue with me, lose, and walk out the door five minutes later, anyway. I'm not above locking the front door behind you and refusing to open it until suppertime if you even think about eating quickly and rushing back here, and every woman in this room will back me up."

"I certainly will," Edith said.

"Without hesitation," Eunice said.

Samuel looked at Eliza. "I think we've been outmaneuvered."

"You have," Leora said. "Accept it gracefully."

Eliza looked at her aunt.

"Go," Leora said, quieter now. "Enjoy yourselves. You've earned a quiet afternoon, and I'd like to give you one."

Eliza stood and tucked the quilt under her arm, and reached for the basket. It was heavier than she'd expected.

"I'll carry that," Samuel said, and took the handle before she could shift her grip.

"Perfect. Now leave and enjoy your afternoon," Leora said.

Eliza bent and kissed her aunt's cheek.

"Have a lovely time," Edith said.

Chapter 32

The quilt lay spread on the grassy bank and the Yellowstone River ran wide and steady, its current pulling fast over the stones near the center where the water broke white and slowed where it spread thin across the shallows on the far side. Upstream, cottonwood trees lined the bank, their leaves catching a breeze. Beyond the far bank, the mountains climbed steeply from the valley floor.

Samuel was eating a piece of fried chicken as he watched the river. The afternoon was warm; the food was still hot from Winnie's kitchen, and Eliza was beside him on the quilt.

Eliza sat beside him with her boots tucked beneath her skirt.

"Winnie outdid herself," Eliza said, holding up a biscuit. "These are perfect."

"She did. She's an exceptional cook." A trout rose in the shallows near the far bank, a silver flash that broke the surface and vanished.

Eliza uncapped her lemonade and took a sip.

"Can I ask you something?" she asked.

"Of course."

"What does fall look like here? I imagine it's similar to what you grew up with in Colorado," she said as she leaned forward slightly with the biscuit half in her hand, her eyes on the mountains across the river as if she were trying to picture them wearing a different season.

"The aspens turn first," he said. "Back home near Trinidad, they'd go all at once. You'd wake up one morning in late September and see gold covering every mountainside overnight. The cottonwoods follow a week or two later, and by October the whole valley looks like a different country. Deep reds, browns, and rich shades of gold. I would imagine this area is similar to Colorado in many ways. Same elevation, same kind of mountains, same kind of sky. But every valley has its own way of doing things. I'm curious to see how this one handles fall myself."

"What about winter?"

"Cold. The pass roads between some of the mountains here will more than likely close, probably in November if the snow comes early. Could be later if the weather holds. Once the roads close, freight stops running, the world slows down, and folks settle in for a long winter." He turned his lemonade jar in his hands. "My father used to feed cattle in snow that came up past the horses' chests. My mother kept the cookstove burning day and night from November clear through March. Winters in Colorado tested everything a family had, and Montana's supposed to be harder, so I've been told."

"Do you think the river will freeze?"

"Most of it will more than likely if it's a bad winter. You'll see it build out from the banks in the cold weeks, thicker every morning.

But a river this size, running this fast, won't freeze solid. The creeks will, though. Providence Creek will ice over."

She was quiet. She turned her lemonade jar in her hands, one slow rotation, and looked downstream toward where the road curved back toward town. The bridge was visible from here, its timber planks pale against the darker water.

"Philadelphia gets cold. The snow comes, and you put on your coat and walk to the market and walk home. It's an inconvenience, not the way I suspect it is here," she said.

"It can be plenty dangerous here," he said. "I won't pretend otherwise. But people prepare for it. They stack wood and put up food, and look after each other. It's a different way of life."

"When I came here, I thought I'd be here through the summer and go home at the end of September or October at the latest. I'd help Aunt Leora get the boardinghouse running properly and go back to Philadelphia and pick up where I left off."

"And now?" he said.

"Now I'm sitting on a riverbank asking you what fall and winter look like here because I'm curious. I genuinely like it here and would enjoy seeing the seasons change."

Samuel set his lemonade down.

"Eliza, I need to tell you something. I've been looking for the right words, and I've decided there aren't any, so I'm going to say it plain."

She set her jar down too.

"Before you came here, I had a life that worked," he said. "I had my practice and my routine, and I'd convinced myself that was enough. Most days I believed it. I came to Providence Ridge looking for a fresh start, and I found one. I filled my days with work and didn't look too hard at what was missing." He looked at his hands resting on his knees. "Then you arrived. And the parts that were missing became the only parts I could see, because you showed me what my life could look like with someone in it, and I couldn't go back to pretending that didn't matter."

"I love the way you laugh when something catches you off guard," he said. "That quick sound you make before you can stop it, like joy snuck past you when you weren't looking. I love the way you talk to people when they're frightened. You have this gentleness that makes a scared person believe they're going to be all right." He looked at her. "I love the way you care about people. Not because it's your training or your obligation. Because you can't do otherwise. Because it's who you are at the center of yourself, and I have never in my life known anyone like you."

She was still. Her hands rested in her lap, and she hadn't looked away from him.

"You make me want things I'd stopped wanting," he said. "A home that's more than rooms I sleep in. Someone to talk to at the end of a hard day. A future with more in it than work and solitude." He held her eyes. "I'm in love with you, Eliza, and I don't want you to go back to Philadelphia."

"Stay," he continued. "Stay in Providence Ridge. I'm not asking because the town needs a nurse, or because your aunt needs help. I'm asking because I need you. Because my life is better with you in it, and I don't want to go back to what it was before."

She reached over and took his hand where it rested on his knee, and she closed her fingers around his.

"Samuel," she said. "I care for you. Deeply. What I feel for you isn't nothing. It's the furthest thing from nothing. It's so full I don't have a word for it, and the fullness is what I'm learning to trust, because I've never felt it before and I need to be sure it's real."

"It's real," he said.

"I believe it is." She looked at the river. "I want to stay. When I look at these mountains and this town and the people I've come to love here, I can see a life. I can see myself in it. Not visiting or passing through. I can clearly imagine myself waking up every day and feeling as if I belong here. I never expected that to happen. I expected to do my duty here and go home. But everything I've seen and done since I stepped off that wagon has changed me, Samuel. My world is bigger now than it was."

She paused. Her hand stayed in his, and he could feel her pulse against his thumb, quick and steady.

"But my father is alone," she said. "He's all I have, and I'm all he has. His letters are full of missing me. I need time. I need to pray about this and write to my father and sit with it long enough to trust myself. I've made every decision in my life based on what I ought to do. Being asked to make one based on what I want is new ground for me, and I need to stand on it long enough to believe it'll hold." She looked at him. "Can you give me that?"

"Take all the time you need," he said. "I'm not going anywhere. I'm here."

"What about you? Do you plan to stay here?" She asked after a while. "Or do you think about going back to Colorado to be near your family?"

"I have no plans to leave," he said. "I like it here. My work feels right in a way it hasn't in a long time. I intend to build a home and a life here. I'd like to visit my family. I miss my mother and father more than I let on."

She nodded.

"We should head back soon," Eliza said. "Before Leora sends a search party. I'd like to finish checking on our patients this afternoon with you; we have many homes to visit. Then I'm going to spend my evening thinking about my future and what I want for myself."

"Miss Leora would send a search party out eventually, I believe. If you'd prefer, I can check on our patients alone... take the afternoon off if you'd like."

"No, Samuel. I'd like to spend my afternoon by your side, visiting our patients together, and perhaps if we finish up a bit earlier, you could take me for a buggy ride. I'd like to see what's south of town."

"Miss Miller, that sounds like a mighty fine plan. I'd enjoy a buggy ride with you, and I promise to have you home in time for supper."

Chapter 33

The bridge timbers were cool beneath Eliza's hands where she leaned against the railing, and the river ran below her. She'd left the boardinghouse before anyone else stirred, slipping through the front door in her shawl and walking the half mile north along Main Street while the town slept.

To the east, the Absarokas were still in shadow, their ridgeline barely separated from a sky that hadn't decided yet whether it was gray or blue. To the west, the Gallatins stood dark and patient against a paler band of sky. Between them the valley floor lay quiet, the grassland and the benchlands and the scattered shapes of homesteads all waiting for the light to find them.

She'd come here to think. She'd come here to watch the sun rise over the mountains, because this bridge was where her life in Providence Ridge had begun the day she first crossed it, and it felt like the right place to decide whether it would continue here in this place she'd come to love..

The last time she'd been on this bridge, she'd been sitting on the bench of a mail wagon with dust on her collar and a trunk full of books and dresses. She'd crossed this river and watched the town take shape beyond it, a handful of wood-frame buildings and swept boardwalks and a mercantile with red geraniums in a tin planter.

She'd felt small that day. Not frightened, but aware in a way she'd never been before of how much world existed outside her father's neighborhood. She'd grown up beneath a sky that ended at rooftops and church steeples. Here the sky had no boundary. It went on past the mountains and past the valley and past everything she'd ever learned about the size of her own life, and she'd sat on that wagon bench feeling like a thumbtack pressed into the edge of a very large map.

She'd been nervous too. The wildness of this country had thrilled her and scared her in equal measure, because it was vast and unfamiliar, and she had no map for living in it. She'd told herself on the road from Livingston that she knew exactly why she was here. Her aunt needed her. The boardinghouse needed managing. She had a job, and she'd do it, and when it was done, she'd go home. That had been the plan, the kind of plan Eliza Miller made and kept.

She'd kept it. She'd arrived and taken stock of the kitchen and the linens and her aunt's stubbornness. She'd learned the rhythms of the boardinghouse in days, which drawer stuck, which burner ran hot, which stair creaked on the left side but not the right. She'd cooked and cleaned and managed, because that was what she did. The woman who showed up and got to work, and didn't stop until the work was done.

Then the fever came, and when it arrived, her training took over, and she served. She served the way she'd served her mother through two years of consumption and her father through six years of grief and the strangers at the fever hospital and the families in the Benevolent Society homes. She poured herself out because people needed her, and being needed was the only language she'd ever learned for being alive. She'd served once again for the needs of others.

She'd done what she had to do. She wasn't sorry for any of it.

But standing here on this bridge in the quiet before dawn, she could see what she hadn't been able to see while she was inside it. Serving had been her hiding place. Not a lie, because the work was real and good, Ridge, and necessary. But a hiding place all the same, because as long as she was busy being useful, she didn't have to sit still long enough for the wanting to reach her. She didn't have to answer the question of what Eliza Miller wanted for herself.

The sky was changing. Along the eastern ridgeline, the gray had warmed to a thin line of pale color where the sun was pressing up behind the Absarokas. The mountain's edges were sharpening against it, each ridge growing more distinct as the light climbed. A bird called from somewhere on the railing downstream, two sharp notes she didn't recognize.

She thought about Philadelphia. She thought about it honestly, with the love it deserved, because that life had earned her honesty.

Her father's house on Chestnut Street, with the parlor where he read his Bible every evening in his chair by the window. His laugh, the one that came from deep in his chest and filled a room like a bell fills a steeple. The church two blocks east, where she'd been baptized and where her mother's funeral had been held and where Reverend Pratt still preached every Sunday from the same oak pulpit. The Thursday market where she bought vegetables from Mrs. Cortland, who always slipped an extra bunch of carrots into her basket and told her she was too thin. Her friends in the Ladies' Society. The familiar streets she could walk with her eyes closed.

That life was real. It was hers, and it had held her well for twenty-two years.

But standing between two mountain ranges, with the river running beneath her and the valley opening in every direction and a sky above her that had no ceiling, she understood what she hadn't been able to understand from inside her father's house. Her life in Philadelphia was complete. Not finished the way a book is finished when the last page is read, but complete the way a chapter is complete when the story needs to move forward. She'd grown up there. She'd buried her mother there. She'd learned to cook and nurse and manage a household and keep her grief so occupied it never had time to sit down. Philadelphia had given her everything she needed to become the woman standing on this bridge.

She was here in a valley between mountains that had been here long before any map was drawn, and the life she was discovering was open and wide and unwritten, and it was hers to fill.

Her father would be fine. She knew that with a certainty that had taken weeks to arrive but had settled into her like bedrock. Henry Miller was a grown man with a successful business, good neighbors, and a church family he loved. He loved his daughter. He missed her. But he hadn't raised her to spend her life tending his house because she was afraid to build her own. He'd raised her to be brave, and brave meant being where her heart felt at home, not staying in a place because it was all she'd ever known.

She'd write to him. She'd tell him the truth, all of it. She'd tell him about the mountains and the people and the work she'd done and the woman she'd become doing it. She'd tell him about Samuel. She'd tell him she wasn't coming home, and she'd tell him why, and she'd trust him to understand, because Henry Miller was a man who loved his daughter enough to let her go.

She thought about Samuel.

Not the doctor who'd checked her aunt's splint or the man who'd stood beside her through weeks of sickness. She thought about Samuel, the man himself, the one she'd discovered underneath the profession.

The man who burned beans on his cookstove and confessed it with a sheepishness that made her want to laugh and fix his supper at the same time. The man who loved horses and visited the livery with a regularity that Paul Higgins found endearing. The man who read his mother's four-page letters twice and wrote back two paragraphs and felt guilty every time he sealed the envelope. The man who fell asleep reading Ivanhoe every night without making it past the same page. The man who'd sat on a quilt beside the Yellowstone two days ago and told her he was in love with her, plainly and without rehearsal, and then told her to take all the time she needed, because he respected her enough to let her come to her answer on her own.

She loved him. The word had been circling her for weeks, and she let it land now on this bridge in the quiet before dawn. She loved the way he made her feel safe without making her feel small. She loved his patience, the unhurried way he listened when someone talked to him, as if their words mattered more than whatever he'd been about to say. She loved his tender heart, the one he'd carried through three years of grief and still kept open despite everything it had cost him. She loved spending time with him. She loved that when she imagined her life five years from now, ten years from now, he was in every version of it.

She wanted to learn this country with him. She wanted to see the aspens turn, and the river ice at its edges, and the snow come down over the valley. She wanted to ride south toward Yellowstone National Park and discover what was there. She wanted to build a life with him here, something new and theirs, full of things neither of them had seen yet. She wanted to grow old beside him, Lord willing, in a place where the sky went on forever and the mountains stood steady through every season.

The sun crested the Absarokas. It came over the ridgeline in a clean, bright line that caught the river first, turning the dark water to silver, then reached the bridge and touched the railing and her hands. The valley floor lit up in pieces, the grassland going from gray to green, the sagebrush silvering, the rooftops of Providence Ridge catching the light a half mile south where the town sat small and solid against the mountains.

She closed her eyes. She folded her hands on the railing and bowed her head.

Lord, you've placed me here in Providence Ridge and you've opened my eyes and my heart. I clearly see what you've put in front of me, and I'm not ready to let it go. I'd been so busy serving others that I forgot to stop and listen. I'm listening now. I'm standing on this bridge and I'm asking You. Is this where You want me? Is this the life You've been leading me toward? Because I want it. I want this place and these people and this man you've placed in my life, and I need to know that wanting isn't selfishness. I need to know that You brought me here for more than duty. I want to stay here, Lord. And I'm trusting You with that.

Chapter 34

Leora was sitting up in her bed with her reading spectacles on and her coffee in her hands when Eliza entered her room. Her aunt looked up from her book, studied Eliza's face for a long moment, and set her cup on the side table.

"You're flushed, child." Leora said.

"I walked to the bridge." Eliza sat on the edge of her aunt's bed and folded her hands in her lap. "I watched the sun come up."

"That's a half-mile each way. At this hour. Alone."

"I needed to think."

Leora took off her spectacles and set them on her book.

"I'm going to write to my father today," Eliza said. "I'm going to tell him I'm not coming home."

Leora looked at her.

"Are you asking my permission or telling me your decision?"

"Telling you."

"Good. Because I would've given my permission, but you didn't need it." Leora reached over and took Eliza's hand. Her grip was warm and firm. "Your mother would be proud of you, Eliza. I know that as surely as I know anything. And your father will be too." She squeezed Eliza's hand. "God has a purpose for you, child. I think you've finally let yourself see what it is."

Eliza held her aunt's hand.

"I love you, Aunt Leora."

"I love you too. Now go write your letter before you lose your nerve."

"I'm not going to lose my nerve."

"I know you're not. But go right now and write it anyway." Leora picked her spectacles up from her book. "And when you've finished, you march across the street and mail it."

Eliza kissed her aunt's forehead and left the room.

***

Eliza sat at the writing desk beneath the window in her room. She looked out onto the grassland behind the boardinghouse, the ground rising in long slopes toward the timbered foothills. She opened her stationery box and withdrew writing paper and an envelope.

She unstoppered her bottle of ink. Dipped the pen and set the nib to the paper.

Dear Father,

I've started this letter multiple times in my mind and tossed many openings aside because I kept trying to find a careful way to say what I need to say, and there isn't one. So I'm going to just say what I need to without dilly-dallying.

I'm not coming home.

I know those words will hurt you, and I'm sorry for the hurt, but I won't be sorry for the decision, because it's the most honest one I've made in such a long time.

I imagine you are quite concerned that you haven't heard from me since my first letter, and there is a reason for that.

Providence Ridge was hit with typhoid fever in early July, just days after my arrival. The town's shared well was contaminated, and within days people were falling ill. The marshal shut the town down. The roads were closed, and the boardinghouse dining room was turned into a sick ward where Dr. Samuel Porter and I cared for patients around the clock for weeks.

We lost a man. His name was Titus Drumond. He was a boarder here, a quiet man who worked at the lumber mill and paid his room and board on time, and kept to himself. Samuel and I, and the many hands of community members that helped during this terrible crisis, did our best to save this man, but in the end, we lost him. I held his hand while he was dying. I'll carry that with me for the rest of my life, not as a wound but as a reminder that life is precious.

Edith Aldridge, Aunt Leora's dearest friend, became very ill as well. Samuel and I both worried over her, as she is sixty-six years old and riddled with arthritis. I saw the hand of God working through her; she defied all medical books that I've ever studied. She is a living, breathing miracle, Father. She's recovering now.

A five-year-old boy named Timothy was gravely ill. Seeing this poor, sweet child so gravely ill hurt my heart. He also made me stop and think about dreams I had once had as a child. Dreams of filling a home of my own with children and a husband by my side. I haven't thought of such things since mother became ill. He's home with his mother, Hattie, now, healthy and recovering in leaps and bounds. There were many others. They all survived through the grace of God.

Father, I can do good work here. I know that now in a way I didn't know when I arrived. The training I received in Philadelphia, every hour at the fever hospital, every skill I learned at Mama's bedside, all of it prepared me for what this town needed. I didn't come here expecting to be needed in this way. But I was, and the work mattered, and I want to continue doing it. Providence Ridge needs someone with my training, and I want to be that person.

But I'm not staying only because the town needs me. I've spent my life making decisions based on what's needed and serving everyone else except myself. I came here because Aunt Leora needed me. I nursed Mama because she needed me. I managed your household because it needed managing and I felt a duty to you to do so. Every choice I've made for as long as I can remember has been built on duty and serving, and the duty was real, and I don't regret a moment of it, nor do I regret ever helping others and tending to others' needs.

But I've learned something about myself in this valley. I've learned that duty and serving others can become a hiding place. I've learned that filling every hour with usefulness is a way of never having to ask what I actually want for my own life. And I've learned that wanting something for myself isn't selfishness.

I want to stay in Providence Ridge and build a life for myself. I want to fulfill the dreams and desires I have for myself. I can see a life here that is mine. Not a life I'm managing for someone else. A life I'm choosing.

There is a man here, Father. His name is Dr. Samuel Porter. He's the town's physician. He's a good man, an honest man, and a faithful man. He grew up on a ranch in Colorado, and he came to

Providence Ridge because the town needed a doctor and he needed a fresh start. We worked side by side through the outbreak, and in those weeks I came to know him better than I've known anyone outside of our family. He's patient and kind and steady, and he makes me laugh, which you know doesn't happen easily with your serious-minded daughter.

He told me he's in love with me, and I believe him.

I care for him deeply, Father. I've prayed to God for guidance, and I feel in my heart that he is my future.

I'm not leaving you. I will never leave you. You're my family and you'll always be my family, and Philadelphia will always be the place where I grew up and learned to love God and buried my mother and became who I am. I'll visit. I'll write. I'll send letters that are longer than they need to be and shorter than you deserve, and I'll miss you every day.

But Montana isn't what I expected, Father. It's better. It's wider and harder and more beautiful than anything I could've imagined from the maps in your parlor. The mountains here have been standing long before any map was drawn, and the river runs fast and clear over stones you can see from the bridge, and the sky above this valley has no ceiling. I've fallen in love with this place, and it has changed me, and I'm grateful for every bit of it.

Please don't worry about me. I am well. I am strong. I am exactly where God wants me to be.

I love you with my whole heart. Give Mrs. Abernathy my regards and please try the chicken and dumplings again. Mama would want you to get them right.

Your daughter,

Eliza

She set her pen down and read the letter through from beginning to end.

She folded the paper along its creases, slid it into the envelope, and wrote her father's address in her careful hand.

Her mother's Bible sat on the nightstand beside her, the blue ribbon resting between its pages. She picked it up, opened it to the marked passage, and read the words her mother had underlined in the months when her voice was gone and her faith was the only language she had left.

It is of the Lord's mercies that we are not consumed, because his compassions fail not. They are new every morning; great is thy faithfulness.

New every morning. This was her new morning.

She closed the Bible and picked up the envelope and held it in both hands, her father's name in her own handwriting looking up at her.

Eliza smiled.

Then she stood up from the desk and walked out of the room with the letter in her hand.

Chapter 35

The bell above the mercantile door rang once as Eliza pushed it open. Margaret stood behind the counter, sorting a crate of thread spools into the glass-fronted display case. Amos was bent over his ledger with his spectacles low on his nose and a pencil behind his ear.

"Good morning, Eliza," Margaret said.

"Good morning to you both."

Amos glanced over his spectacles. "Morning, Miss Miller."

"I need to post a letter," she said, and set the envelope on the counter.

Amos marked his place in the ledger and came forward. He picked up the envelope, turned it to read the address, and reached for the postal scale beside the mail rack. "Philadelphia," he said. "That'll be three cents."

She took the coins from her pocket and placed them on the counter. Amos put them into the cash drawer, stamped the envelope, and set it in the outgoing mail slot beside the postal window.

It slid into the wooden rack and settled against the others, waiting for the next freight wagon north.

Margaret stood with both hands flat on the counter, studying Eliza's face.

"Eliza Miller, I've known you a month and I've never once seen you smile like that. What on earth has got you in such high spirits this morning?"

"I'm staying," Eliza said. "I'm staying here in Providence Ridge."

Margaret's hands came off the counter. Her mouth opened, closed, and then gave way to everything she was feeling at once. She came around the end of the counter so fast the thread spools rattled in their case, and before Eliza could say another word, Margaret had both arms around her in a fierce embrace.

When she pulled back, tears were running down both her cheeks.

"I'm so happy," Margaret said. "You've no idea how pleased I am."

"Margaret, you're going to make me cry."

"Good. Cry. We'll cry right here in my store and Amos can mind his own business."

Behind the counter, Amos took off his spectacles and folded them carefully. "I'm minding my own business," he said. "But I'm also glad to hear it, Miss Miller. Very glad."

Margaret gripped Eliza's arms and held her at arm's length. "I imagine Leora is beside herself."

"She is. As soon as I told her I was staying, she told me to go write to my father before I lost my nerve."

"That sounds exactly like Leora." Margaret laughed and wiped her cheeks with the back of her hand. "That woman's been praying you'd stay since the day you arrived, I guarantee it. She told me herself just last week, "Margaret, that girl belongs here' I told her I thought so too."

Margaret released her arms and straightened her apron, composing herself with the speed of a woman who could go from tears to commerce in ten seconds flat. "You'll come for supper this week. You and Leora and Winnie, and Edith too. I'll make a good roast. We're going to celebrate this properly."

"I'd like that."

"Amos, put a note in the ledger. Supper for the boardinghouse ladies, Friday evening."

"I'll remember without a note, Margaret."

"Put a note anyway."

Eliza hugged Margaret and turned toward the door. The bell rang again as she pushed it open.

As she was crossing Main Street, she heard Samuel's voice.

She turned to see him walking toward her from the direction of his office, his medical bag in his hand.

He stopped a few paces from her and tipped his hat back. "You look rather happy this morning," he said. "And beautiful, if I might add."

Warmth climbed into her cheeks. "You might," she said. "And I am happy. Very happy. I'd like to tell you why, if you have a moment."

He tilted his head, the same way he studied a patient's face when he wanted to understand what he was looking at before he spoke. "I have several moments. All of them are yours."

"I mailed a letter to my father this morning," she said. "I told him I'm not coming home. I've decided to stay here. In Providence Ridge. I'm---."

His medical bag hit the dirt. His hands found her waist, and then her feet left the ground, and the sky swung above her, and she was turning, lifted and held, his arms tight around her and the August morning wheeling past.

She giggled like a schoolgirl, which turned into a full laugh before long. Her hands gripped his shoulders. Her skirt fanned out as he turned her, and she laughed some more because the joy of the moment was the most beautiful thing she'd ever experienced.

He set her down. Her boots found the road, and his hands steadied her waist until she had her balance, and she looked up at him. She'd seen his face tired and his face grieving, and his face composed over a dying man's bed. She'd seen it by lamplight in the kitchen the night they'd prayed with their hands clasped over cold coffee. She'd never seen it like this. The lines beside his mouth had relaxed, the furrow between his brows gone smooth, and he was grinning at her.

"Eliza Miller," he said. "You've just made me the happiest man on the face of this earth."

Chapter 36

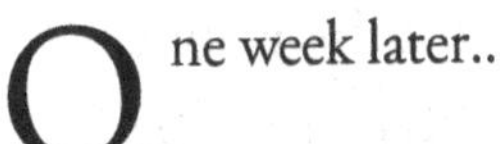

One week later...

Samuel knocked on the open door of Leora's bedroom.

Leora looked up and smiled. "Come in, Samuel."

He stepped through the doorway. She was sitting in her arm-chair beside the window with a cup of coffee on the small table and her walking sticks propped against the wall within reach. Her reading spectacles sat on top of a closed book in her lap.

"Miss Leora," he said. "Would you mind if I spoke with you? In private."

She looked at his hat in his hand, then at his face, then back at his hat. "Should I be worried?"

"No. Not worried."

"Then close the door, young man, and sit down."

He closed the door. He pulled the straight-backed chair from beside her writing desk and set it facing her, with his medical bag on the floor between his boots.

"How's your leg today?" he asked.

"My leg is the same as it was when you checked it two days ago. It's healing. I'm walking with my walking sticks. I'm not fast, but I'm upright, but you didn't come here to discuss my leg, now did you."

"Well... I intend to, and then I wanted to speak with you about something else."

"Hmm... speak to me privately behind a closed door. In my experience, that means a person has something important to say." She picked up her coffee. "I've got all afternoon, Samuel. But you look like a man who'd rather be anywhere else, so I'll do you the kindness of not pretending I don't suspect what this is about."

"I'd like to ask for your blessing," he said. "To marry Eliza."

He'd rehearsed three different versions on the walk from his office to the boardinghouse, each one more elaborate than the last, and all three had fallen apart as soon as he walked into the boardinghouse.

Leora set her coffee down and stared at him.

"I want to be clear about something first," he said. "I know I should be asking her father. Henry Miller is alive and well in Philadelphia, and he's the man whose permission I ought to be seeking. The proper thing would be to travel east, or at the very least to write and wait for his reply. I know that."

"But?" Leora said.

"But I can't make the trip right now. I'm the only doctor in this town, and leaving for the weeks it would take isn't responsible. I intend to write to him. I'll write today if you give me your blessing. I'd even travel to Livingston to send him a telegram if you insist." He turned his hat in his hands.

"How long?" she asked.

"How long what, Miss Leora?"

"How long have you known that you wanted to marry her? When did you know?"

"I knew for certain the day I stood outside Titus Drumond's door the morning he passed away. I stood outside listening to her hum a hymn to a man she'd known less than a month because she didn't want him going to heaven without someone singing him through it. We sat with him as he passed." He stopped turning his hat. "I knew I loved her before that. But that day. I knew I wanted to spend my life with her. I can't put into words what we experienced that day, and I don't fully understand why God put it on my heart that day to ask her to be my wife as a man lay taking his final breath, but I can tell you that a man named Titus Drumond left an impression on me."

"Do you plan to stay in Providence Ridge?" she asked.

"Yes."

"Permanently?"

"I've been looking at land southeast of town. A piece of property near the river. I want to build a home."

"Can you provide for her?"

"I can. I won't pretend a frontier doctor's salary makes a woman rich, but I'm not in debt. I've got savings, plenty to buy the property and build a home. I can keep a roof over our heads and food on the table. The property I'm looking at has good soil, flat ground, and room enough for a nice home. I'll build it myself if I have to. My father raised me to work with my hands before he sent me to medical school, and I haven't forgotten how."

"What kind of life are you offering her?"

"A life here," he said. "In this valley. I'll practice medicine for as long as this town needs a doctor, and I expect that'll be a good while yet. She'll have a home of her own. She'll have work that matters to her if she chooses it, whether that's nursing or helping you run this boardinghouse or whatever she decides she wants to do. I won't decide for her. I'll give her room to choose, and I'll stand beside whatever she chooses." He set his hat on the floor beside his bag. "And I'll love her. Every day. I can't imagine my life without her in it."

Leora pressed her lips flat. Her chin moved once, a small tremor she didn't try to hide. She gripped the arms of her chair, her knuckles white against the wood.

"My sister, Caroline," she said, "was the finest woman I've ever known. She married Henry Miller because he was kind and steady, and because he loved her in a way that showed up every single day, not just on the days it was easy. She raised Eliza to be brave and faithful and good, and then she got sick, and a fourteen-year-old girl watched her mother disappear over two years." She paused. "I promised Caroline right after she was diagnosed that I would watch over Eliza as best as I could. It hasn't always been easy living so far away, but I tried my best to travel back east once a year to visit Eliza and her father. I made a promise to my sister and I've carried it every day since. So when a man sits in my room and tells me he wants to marry my niece, I don't ask my questions lightly. I ask because Caroline would have asked, and she's not here to do it, and I ask because I know her father would want to know the same things."

"I know," he said.

"My sister would have liked you, Samuel."

He looked at his hands on his knees, at the old scar across his right knuckles. He swallowed and looked back at her.

"I hope so," he said.

"She would have adored you, Samuel, because you're honest, a hard worker, and because you love Eliza in a way, that's evident when she's in your presence. You wear your heart on your sleeve, young man, and I'm certain my sister would have seen all those qualities as clearly as I have.

"You have my blessing," Leora continued.

"Thank you, Leora."

"Don't thank me. Marry her. And don't you dare wait." She leaned forward in her chair. "I buried my husband four years ago. I nearly lost my closest friend a few weeks ago. I've spent weeks flat on my back with a broken leg while the world kept turning without me. Life is short, Samuel, and the good Lord doesn't promise us a single day beyond the one we're standing in. If you're certain, act. Write to Henry tonight and tell him your intentions. Tell him I gave you my blessing, and I assure you that will be enough for Eliza's father. He trusts me. Ask Eliza soon. Don't let propriety or timing or any other excuse rob you of a single day you could've had with her."

"I intend to ask her this Sunday after church. I thought I might take her for a buggy ride."

Leora picked her spectacles up from her book. She put them on and looked at him over the rims. "A buggy ride. Southeast of town, by any chance?"

He looked at her and grinned. "Yes, Ma'am."

"Smart boy. And if she doesn't like this piece of property you have your eyes on?"

He rubbed his hand across the back of his neck. "Well... I hadn't considered that, but if she doesn't like it, then I guess we'll have to find one she does like."

"Good thinking, Dr. Porter," Leora said with a wink before she adjusted her spectacles and picked up her book. "Now go write your letter to Henry. Tell him everything you told me. And Samuel?"

"Yes?"

"Don't you dare make my niece cry from sadness. You make that woman happy. You take care of her the way she's spent almost most of her life taking care of everyone else. She doesn't know how to let someone do that for her yet, not fully. Teach her."

"I will," he said.

"And one more thing before you go... I expected a passel of nieces and nephews running around this town sooner rather than later."

"I'll do my best, Miss Leora."

Chapter 37

The buggy rolled south past the lumber mill with the August sun full on their shoulders and the two-horse team pulling steady on the packed road. Samuel held the reins loosely in his hands while Eliza sat beside him with her bonnet shading her face, her church dress smoothed beneath her, watching the valley open as the last of the town buildings fell behind them.

"You still haven't told me where we're going," Eliza said.

"Southeast," he said. "Just a bit further."

"You've been saying 'just a bit further' for half a mile."

"And I've been right every time."

She smiled and turned back to the valley. The road had narrowed past the mill; the ruts were less worn this far south of town. To the east, the Absarokas rose in their full height, bare rock ridges above dark timber. Grasshoppers kicked up from the road as the wheels passed over dry grass that had crept in from both edges.

A quarter mile past the mill, he pulled the team off the road and turned them east through open ground. The grass was thick here;

the stems bleached pale at the tips from weeks of heat but still green at the base where the roots held moisture. The buggy rattled over uneven ground, finding the dips between tussocks.

"Samuel, we're off the road."

"I know."

"Is there a road where we're going?"

"Not yet."

She put her hand on the seat rail as the buggy swayed. He liked the way she didn't ask him to slow down or turn back. She just braced herself and rode it.

Providence Creek appeared ahead, running low in its late-summer bed. The water was still clear enough to count the smooth stones on the bottom, but the flow had thinned since July, pulling back from its banks and leaving pale lines of dried silt on the exposed rocks. He guided the team to a shallow crossing where the water barely covered the horses' fetlocks. The wheels splashed through the riffle, climbed the far bank, and they were across.

The ground rose ahead. Not steeply, but in a long, steady slope toward a rise that stood above the surrounding bottomland. A stand of cottonwoods grew along the south edge, their leaves thick and still full, not yet touched by the turn toward fall. Beyond the trees, the ground leveled into a broad, flat stretch that opened to the sky.

He pulled the team to a stop at the top of the rise and set the brake. He climbed down and came around to Eliza's side, offering his hand. She took it and stepped down beside him, and they stood on the flat ground with the buggy behind them and the whole valley laid out.

The view had stopped him the first time he'd ridden out here on his own. It stopped him again now. To the west, the Gallatins formed a long, timbered wall. To the east, the Absarokas climbed steep and jagged, their highest draws still holding patches of old snow. Below them, forty yards down the gentle slope, the Yellowstone River curved wide and steady around the base of the rise, its current running fast over gravel bars in the shallows, slowing where the channel deepened against the far bank. North and slightly west, a mile and a half away, he could make out the rooftops of Providence Ridge clustered along its single road. The boardinghouse and the mercantile were the two tallest shapes among them.

"Samuel," Eliza said. "This is beautiful."

"It is. And I wanted you to see it."

He walked her across the flat ground, and she came beside him with her hand still in his, her skirt brushing the tops of the grass. He showed her where the land leveled, where the soil was dark and deep, and where the cottonwoods along the south edge would break the winter wind coming up the valley. He pointed northwest toward town.

"My office is a mile and a half from here," he said. "On horseback I could be there in under ten minutes. Close enough to get to a patient fast. Far enough to have a home that's separate from my work."

"You've been thinking about this," she said.

"Yes, I have." He stopped walking and turned to face the river. "The land's got good water access from the creek and the river both. The flat ground up here is high enough to stay dry even if the river floods in spring. There's room for a house and a barn, eventually. A garden on the south-facing side where it'd get sun most of the day."

"A garden on the south side," she said. "You'd want raised beds with soil this deep. You could grow potatoes and beans and most of the root vegetables Margaret stocks at the mercantile." She stopped. She looked at him and then away, back toward the flat ground she'd been studying. "I'm sorry. You're telling me about your plans, and I'm rearranging your garden."

"Eliza."

"It's a wonderful piece of land, Samuel. I'm happy for you. I think it's a fine place to build a home."

She turned towards the river. The Yellowstone ran below them in its wide curve, the current breaking white over stones near the center and slowing against the willows on the far bank. A pair of ducks worked the shallows downstream. The valley stretched south toward the mountains that closed around Yellowstone country, and the distance between this rise and those far ridges was so vast it made everything between feel like possibility.

He took his hat off and held it in both hands.

"Eliza," he said.

She turned.

He looked at her. The blue of her eyes beneath her bonnet's brim, the auburn hair at her temples where the pins never quite held, and the freckles across the bridge of her nose that the Montana sun had brought out. At the hands that had wrung cloths and mixed medicines and held a dying man's fingers and gripped his own across a kitchen table the night she'd taught him to pray again. He'd been in this woman's presence for weeks, and he'd watched her give everything she had to a town full of strangers and never once stop to ask for anything back. He'd carried her to her own bed when her body finally quit on her, and he'd stood in her doorway and known, with the certainty of a man who'd spent his life diagnosing what was wrong with people, that nothing had ever been more right.

"I can't buy this property," he said, "without knowing that you'll be standing beside me when the house is being built."

Her lips parted.

"Eliza Miller, will you marry me?"

She didn't hesitate. She didn't look away or step back. She stood on that rise of ground with the river below and the mountains around her and the town they'd fought for visible in the distance, and she said, "Yes."

Her voice was steady. Her eyes were wet.

"Yes, Samuel. I will marry you."

He closed the distance between them in two steps. His arms went around her, and she came into him, her hands pressed flat against his chest, her forehead against his collar. He held her and felt her shoulders shake once before she steadied, and then she laughed, a small, wet sound muffled against his shirt.

"I love you, Eliza," he said. The words came out low, spoken into her hair.

She pulled back enough to look up at him. Her cheeks were wet, and she was smiling.

"I love you too."

He brought his hand up and rested his thumb against her cheekbone, brushing the tears from her skin. She leaned into his palm, and the warmth of her face against his hand was so simple and so complete that he couldn't think of a single thing to add to the moment.

"May I?" he asked.

She nodded.

He leaned down. She tilted her face up. He kissed her, gentle and brief, his lips against hers for a span of seconds that held every week they'd spent side by side in a sick ward and every night they'd sat across a kitchen table too tired to speak and every morning she'd been there when he needed her, steady and sure and refusing to leave.

When he lifted his head, her hand was resting on his chest, where she could feel his heartbeat through his shirt. She didn't move it. He covered it with his own and held it there.

Chapter 38

Eliza sat at the writing desk in her bedroom and bowed her head.

"Lord," she said quietly, "thank You for this life You've given me. Thank You for bringing me here and for the man You've put in my path. Help me find the words to tell my father. Help him understand. And be with him when he reads this, because I know it'll change his world the way it's changed mine. Amen."

She lifted her head, dipped her pen, and began.

Dear Father,

I have news that I expect won't surprise you entirely, given my last letter.

Samuel Porter has asked me to marry him, and I said yes.

I told you in my last letter that he's a good man, and he is. But I want you to know more about the man your daughter has chosen, because if you were here, I'd sit you down at the kitchen table and tell you every bit of it over coffee, and since I can't do that, this letter will have to serve.

He grew up on a cattle ranch near Trinidad, Colorado. His father, Phillip, raised six children on that ranch, and his mother, Esmi, kept them all fed and faithful through every kind of weather the territory could throw at them. Samuel learned to shoe horses and mend fences before he ever learned to read a pulse. He went to medical school in Chicago because he felt called to healing, and his family supported that calling even though it meant losing a strong pair of hands on the ranch. He has five siblings, Father. An older brother, three sisters, and a younger brother. He comes from a large, close family, and I can hear in the way he talks about them that their family bond is st rong.

He came to Providence Ridge in June because the town needed a doctor and he needed a place to do honest, steady work. He's been here one month longer than I have, and in that time he's become the kind of doctor people trust with their lives. Not because he's perfect, but because he shows up. Every time. For every patient. In any weather, at any hour.

I wrote to you about the outbreak and about how Samuel and I worked side by side through it. What I didn't tell you, because I didn't have the words yet, is what I saw in him during those weeks that made me certain he's the man I want to spend my life with. I watched him fight for Titus Drumond for days, even knowing the fight was likely lost because Samuel doesn't stop trying. I watched him sleep beside Timothy, a five-year-old boy burning with fever, because he wanted to make sure he was nearby if the boy struggled through the night. He carried me to my own bed when my body gave out from exhaustion, and I didn't wake, Father. I was so spent I didn't feel his arms beneath me. Aunt Leora told me about it the next morning, and I sat on the edge of her bed and couldn't speak, because no one had carried me since I was small enough for you to lift

.

He asked me to marry him yesterday, on a piece of land southeast of town near the Yellowstone River. He wants to build us a home there. The property sits on a rise with a view of the river curving below and the mountains on every side, and when he showed it to me he talked about where the house would stand and where a garden could go and how quickly he could reach his office on horseback. He was so excited, Father. He looked like a boy showing someone a treasure he'd found in a creek bed. And then he took his hat off and told me he couldn't buy this land without knowing I'd be beside him while the house was built, and he asked me to be his wife.

I know you'll want to meet him. I want that too. Which brings me to the part of this letter that I need you to read carefully.

Father, I'd like to be married in September. I know that's soon. I know the journey from Philadelphia to Montana Territory is long and hard, and I wouldn't ask if it weren't important to me. But the pass roads close when heavy snow comes, sometimes as early as October, and Reverend Webb Hale and his wife Eunice, who travel between towns to preach, won't be able to reach Providence Ridge reliably once winter sets in. Reverend Hale is the man I'd like to marry us. He prayed over Samuel and me during the darkest days of the outbreak. He read scripture to our patients and sat with them daily. I can't imagine anyone else speaking the words over our wedding.

I want you to walk me down the aisle. I want you to place my hand in Samuel's. I want you to see this town and this valley and the boardinghouse where Aunt Leora has kept her doors open through everything life has asked of her. I want you to meet Margaret Pemberton, who hugged me and cried when I told her I was staying. I want you to meet Winnie Callahan, who kept us all fed during the typhoid outbreak and never once complained. I want you to meet Edith Aldridge, who survived a fever that should've taken her and is sitting in her chair beside Aunt Leora right now, the two of them arguing about whether the new schoolhouse should face east or west.

Please come. Aunt Leora and I will have a room ready for you. You'll have clean sheets and a warm meal and family waiting at the door.

Now, before I close, I want to tell you a few things so you know that your daughter's life here isn't all work.

Samuel has been teaching me to fish. Last week we sat on the bank of the Yellowstone, and he showed me how to bait a hook and cast a line. I tangled the line twice and caught nothing, but Samuel caught two trout, and Winnie cooked them for supper that evening. They were the best fish I've ever eaten, though I suspect the company had something to do with it.

He also took me hiking into the foothills east of town and taught me which plants are safe to eat and which are poisonous. I didn't realize I needed this knowledge until I was standing on a mountainside surrounded by things that could either feed me or make me very ill. He was patient about it, Father. He's patient about everything.

Samuel and I went berry picking last week with Winnie and her beau, a kind young man named Luke. We picked huckleberries, which grow wild here in the mountains. I'd never seen a huckleberry before I came to Montana, and that day we picked enough to fill three baskets. Aunt Leora taught me how to make huckleberry jam, and I'm pleased to report the jam turned out well on my first attempt.

Leora said that was a small miracle, and I choose to take it as a compliment.

Aunt Leora is recovering steadily. She uses her walking sticks and grows stronger each day. She informed Samuel and me that she intends to be standing on her own two feet at our wedding without assistance from sticks or human beings.

I'm also looking forward to learning how to garden here. The soil on the property Samuel's buying is deep and dark, and Winnie has promised to teach me what grows well at this elevation and when to plant. I've never grown my own food, Father, and I'm excited to learn. Here, I'll put seeds in the ground and tend them and eat what they produce, and the thought of it makes me happier than I can put into words.

I love you, Father. I miss you. I miss the sound of your press running in the shop and the smell of ink on your hands at supper. I miss the way you used to read the newspaper aloud to me over breakfast, whether I asked you to or not.

But I'm building a life here that Mama would recognize. A life of faith and service, and love, beside a man who loves God and loves me, and isn't afraid of hard work.

Come to Montana, Father. Come and see what God has done in my life.

Your daughter,

Eliza

EPILOGUE

Reverend Webb Hale stood beside Samuel at the front of the room, his Bible held loosely in one hand, its pages soft from decades of turning.

"You okay, son?" Webb asked.

Samuel's hands hung at his sides, and he wasn't sure what to do with them. He'd delivered babies and set compound fractures, and right now the prospect of standing still in a clean shirt while a room full of people watched him marry the woman he loved was turning his palms damp in a way that no medical emergency ever had.

"I'm fine," he said.

"You look like you're about to perform surgery."

"Surgery, I know how to do."

Webb's mouth twitched. "Just stand there and mean what you say. The Lord will handle the rest."

The long table in the dining room of the boardinghouse had been pushed against the back wall and laid with Leora's best cloth. Chairs, some of them borrowed from community members, filled the space in two groups with an aisle between them, the same arrangement the room took on Sundays for worship.

People were filling the chairs. Margaret Pemberton sat in the front row on the left side, her silver-streaked hair pinned tight, her face already shining with the tears she wasn't the least bit sorry about. Amos sat beside her, his spectacles folded in his breast pocket, his posture as upright as a man at a town committee meeting. He'd shaken Samuel's hand that morning and said, "You're getting a good woman, Dr. Porter."

Hattie sat beside her mother with Timothy on her lap. His cheeks were round with the health of a child who'd been fed steadily by women who remembered what he'd looked like on a pallet with his skin the color of old paper.

Behind them, Owen Gallagher and Nora sat with their seven children. Owen caught Samuel's eye and gave a single nod.

Edith Aldridge was in the second row, her silver hair combed and pinned, her hands resting in her lap on top of her Bible.

The Fitches were there. Nolan and Clara, side by side the way they'd been side by side on their pallets through the worst of the fever, Clara's hand finding Nolan's across the gap between them every day as naturally as breathing.

Ada Cobb sat with Jasper beside her, her pregnancy showing now. Jasper's arm rested along the back of her chair with the quiet possession of a man who'd watched his wife fight for her life and intended to stay close for the foreseeable future.

Zeb Thompson sat near the back, his thin white hair combed flat, his expression suggesting he had opinions about the seating arrangement and was keeping them to himself with visible effort.

Paul Higgins leaned against the wall near the kitchen doorway, one boot crossed over the other, watching the room fill. He caught Samuel's eye and held it. Paul didn't nod or smile. He just looked at him, and the looking said everything that needed saying, because Paul Higgins didn't waste gestures any more than he wasted words. When Samuel had told Paul he was going to ask Eliza to marry him, Paul had stood in the livery yard for a long time with a halter in one hand and a lead rope in the other. Then he'd said, "About time."

Eunice Hale sat in the front row on the right side, directly across the aisle from Margaret, positioned like a general surveying a field she'd helped organize. She'd been in the kitchen since noon directing traffic, and Samuel had heard her tell Winnie that if anyone touched the wedding cake before the ceremony was over, she'd have words with them, and the words would not be gentle.

Winnie stood near the foot of the staircase, her hands clasped in front of her, her face holding the shining composure of a woman who loved her friend and was about to watch her walk down a set of stairs and into a different life. She'd been crying off and on since breakfast. She was also the reason the flowers were arranged, the bread was baked, the dining room was clean enough to eat off the floor, and every logistical detail of this afternoon had been handled so thoroughly that Samuel suspected she'd written a list, checked it twice, and then written a second list to make sure she hadn't forgotten anything on the first one.

Leora sat beside Eunice. Her splint was gone. The bone had healed well. Samuel had confirmed it himself two weeks ago. Leora had received the news with the restraint of a woman who didn't believe in making a fuss, and then cried for ten minutes in Eliza's arms while Eliza held her and said nothing because nothing needed saying.

Leora's face today was the face of a woman preparing to watch the niece she'd called West with a letter because of a broken leg. She stood straight. Her hair was pinned in its practical twist. Her dress was her best one, dark blue with a lace collar Hattie Pemberton had sewn for the occasion.

Henry Miller was upstairs with Eliza.

He'd arrived four days ago on the freight wagon from Livingston. He was a man of medium height with a printer's careful hands. He'd studied Samuel on the boardinghouse porch that first evening with the quiet assessment of a father who understood that his daughter's life was about to change and wanted to know whether the man responsible deserved her.

Samuel had expected a formal conversation, and he'd gotten one. Henry had asked to speak with him privately that evening, and they'd sat in the parlor. Henry had asked about his family, his practice, his plans for the house he intended to build on the property southeast of town. He'd asked about the outbreak, and the morning a man named Titus Drumond had died.

Henry had listened to all of it without interruption. Then he'd been quiet for a long time, sitting in Leora's parlor chair with his hands on his knees. Samuel had let the silence stand because what Henry was doing in that silence was more important than anything Samuel could say to fill it.

"My daughter," Henry had said at last, "has spent years taking care of everyone around her and forgetting to take care of herself. She did it because her mother died and someone had to hold things up, and Eliza decided she was that someone. I let her. I'm not proud of that. I needed her, and she was there, and I didn't look closely enough at what it was doing to her. The letters she sent me from Providence Ridge were beautiful to read. Not in what she said. In what she didn't have to say. I believe you're a good man, Dr. Porter. And I believe God brought my daughter here for a purpose far greater than we could ever imagine, and I'm happy that you'll be by her side through it all."

Samuel had taken Henry's hand, and Henry's grip was firm, and neither of them said anything more

Now footsteps sounded above, and the room went still.

Samuel looked at the staircase. The conversations stopped. Margaret reached for Amos's hand. Eunice sat up straighter. Timothy looked up from his carved horse.

Henry appeared at the top of the stairs first. He wore his pressed suit and his spectacles, and the face of a father arriving at the moment he'd been preparing for since his daughter was born. He paused at the landing and looked down at the room full of people who'd become his daughter's community, and then he stepped to the side.

Eliza came into view.

Samuel forgot everything. He forgot Webb beside him and the chairs full of people. He forgot everything except the woman descending the staircase with her hand on her father's arm and her eyes on his.

She wore a dress of ivory cotton with lace at her collar that Hattie had made by hand, fitted at her waist, the fabric simple and fine. Her auburn hair was pinned up, but softer than her usual arrangement, with a few strands left loose at her temples. She carried a small bouquet of the same asters and goldenrod that sat on the table, tied with a ribbon.

She was the most beautiful thing he'd ever seen, and the beauty had nothing to do with the dress or the hair or the way the afternoon sunlight fell across her face as she came down the stairs. It was the walking toward him. It was the choosing. She'd arrived in this town carrying her mother's Bible and a trunk. She'd knelt beside sick people and mixed medicines and held his hand across a kitchen table at midnight and prayed with him when he'd stopped believing his own prayers reached anywhere. Now she was here, walking toward him, and she was smiling.

Henry brought her down the last step and across the aisle between the chairs. Henry's face was composed; his eyes were bright, and his hand over Eliza's on his arm was the hand of a man letting go of the most precious thing he'd ever held.

They stopped in front of Samuel. Henry looked at him. Then he lifted Eliza's hand from his arm and placed it in Samuel's open palm.

"Take good care of her," Henry said.

"Yes, sir. I will."

Henry pressed Samuel's hand once, then stepped back and took the empty seat beside Leora, who was already wiping her eyes with a handkerchief she'd had ready since morning.

Eliza's hand was warm in his. Her fingers curled around his, and she looked up at him with a smile.

"Dearly beloved," Webb said, "we are gathered here in the sight of God and in the presence of this company to join Samuel Ezra Porter and Eliza Constance Miller in holy matrimony."

Webb proceeded and read from the book of Ruth, and the words filled the dining room the way they'd filled rooms for thousands of years, old words spoken over new beginnings. "Where you go, I will go; where you stay, I will stay. Your people will be my people, and your God my God."

Samuel watched Eliza's face while Webb read.

"Samuel," Webb said. "Do you take this woman to be your wife, to have and to hold from this day forward, for better, for worse, for richer, for poorer, in sickness and in health, to love and to cherish, until death do you part?"

"I do," Samuel said.

"Eliza. Do you take this man to be your husband, to have and to hold from this day forward, for better, for worse, for richer, for poorer, in sickness and in health, to love and to cherish, until death do you part?"

"I do," Eliza said.

"Then by the power vested in me, in the presence of God and these witnesses, I pronounce you husband and wife." Webb closed his Bible and looked at Samuel. "You may kiss your bride."

He kissed her. Brief and warm, her mouth soft against his, her hand tightening around his fingers. Margaret sobbed. Eunice said something that was probably congratulatory and possibly a directive about the cake. Paul, against the wall near the kitchen door, smiled. Timothy asked if there was pie.

Samuel pulled back and looked at his wife. Eliza Porter, standing in a room full of people they'd helped save, in a boardinghouse dining room that had been a church and a meeting hall and a sick ward and was now, on this September afternoon with the cottonwoods beginning to turn along the creek and the Absarokas holding their ridgelines against a sky so clean it looked as if it had been washed, a place where vows had been spoken and meant.

He'd arrived in Providence Ridge four months ago carrying a medical bag, a cracked faith, and a lie he'd told himself so many times it had started to feel like the truth. The truth was simpler. He was a man who'd been afraid that caring meant losing, and God had sent him to a town where caring was the only option and losing was the risk, and the morning came anyway, every single time, with mercy in it.

Eliza's hand was in his. The room was full of people he loved and cherished.

Outside, past the porch and the boardwalk and the packed-earth road that led south toward the property where he intended to build a house with enough rooms for the future he'd finally stopped being afraid to want, the Absarokas held their ground the way they'd held it for thousands of years, and the September light fell across the valley floor in long, slanting bands that turned the cured grass to copper and made even the old volcanic stone of the mountains look new.

Leave A Review

If you enjoyed this book, please consider leaving an honest review on Amazon

Visit Our Website:

www.vivianbelle.com

Visit Our Amazon Author Page HERE

Find Us On Social Media:

Facebook

Instagram

Scan the QR code above to sign up for our newsletter!

Afterword

Writing historical fiction invites us into a world shaped by different customs, language, and ways of life than our own. In striving to portray these stories with authenticity, I have sought to remain faithful to the speech patterns, expressions, and cultural realities of the time in which the story is set. At times, this may include phrasing or perspectives that feel unfamiliar by today's standards, yet they are included with care to preserve the integrity of the historical setting and the voices of the characters who inhabit it.

It is never my intention to offend, but rather to tell stories that feel honest, immersive, and true to their time. More importantly, it is my prayer that every page reflects something far greater than history alone—the unchanging truth of God's love.

Scripture reminds us in Genesis 1:27 that "we are all created in the image of God" and in Acts 17:26 that "He has made every nation of mankind." These truths anchor every story I write. No matter the era, the heartbeat of each novel is the same: grace extended, redemption offered, and love that endures.

Thank you for stepping into this story with me.

With gratitude,

Vivian Belle